THE EVOLUTION WARS

THE AWAKENING

H.W. WALKER

First Edition

PAGE PUBLISHING, INC.
Conneaut Lake, PA

First originally published by Page Publishing 2021

ISBN 978-1-6624-2625-4 (pbk)
ISBN 978-1-6624-2626-1 (digital)

Printed in the United States of America

CONTENTS

CHAPTER 1

The Event

THEY WERE A normal middle-class family living in Las Vegas, Nevada. The year is 2020. The family unit had broken down in the United States of America over the last forty-five years. This is the story of one special family from that time. William H. Waters (sixty-one) and his wife Maria Waters (fifty-six). They had two girls, Joy D. Waters (thirty-four) and Sadie Waters (twenty). Joy had two boys, Jake (eighteen) and Lance (fourteen). Jake has a girlfriend, Lucy (twenty-one). They have a son, Easton. He was just about to have his first birthday. Lance lived with his father most of the time, the rest with his mother. Sadie was still single. This is my family, and what follows is the story of the awakening, as my great-grandfather told it to me before I was awake. My name is Easton.

It was the year 2017 when things started happening. Some things were getting better while others were still trying to get out of the hole from the economic collapse of 2009. We were better off than most. I had work, and we could eat and sleep in comfort. I was worried about almost everything, from my family and the world in general. It seemed that both were falling apart. Life was getting better from 2017 up to the event.

CHAPTER 2

The Event

Life was as it had been for the last five years in the city. It was a beautiful place to live. The two mountain ranges that enclose the city putts on a light show twice daily. No two shows are the same, every sunrise and sunset. There were deep blues, crisp skies, bright reds, and oranges each morning and night. There were the dark mountains at sunset. A lot of back and forth in the last five years. The trend was mostly good and was creative, a feeling that things would keep getting better. Terrorism was still a growing problem in many parts of the world. No place or group was fully safe. That all changed the day of the event.

It was a mild March day in Las Vegas. The air temperature was mid-seventies, and it was just after 10:30 a.m. Day one, as it was called now, March 17, 2020. The first day of the apocalypses. It was not a war or an attack in the normal sense as we understood at the time. It was just a large power outage. It would be days before the total effects of the event was known. This power failure was worldwide. All electric power sources failed. Only those with generators for backup had any power after the event.

* * *

The first to die started almost at once. All planes in the air lost power wherever they were. They started falling out of the sky. The engines would not restart. Most died on impact with the ground. The few that survived passed slowly as there was no rescuers to come to their aid. Very few where saved as their crashes happened in view of people living in a city or town and help came. This meant that on the day of the event, approximately 8,765,000 died from planes falling out of the sky. The people who saw the planes falling out of the sky were the first to know a small part of the true event. Many more died slowly on cruise ships that lost power out in the ocean, too far from shore. This number was approximately 20,335 per week. Many would die at sea on doomed ships. Many more would face trials of survival as the cars, buses, and trains just stopped. never to run again. A rough guess would be well over forty million people dead on the first day. The world had gone dark, and very little news was getting out of a few places. With no way of getting news, people at first just stayed where they were or, if close enough, went home. They were all waiting for help that was never coming.

CHAPTER 3

Escape from the City

It was a regular day for everyone, doing the same routine to start a workday. William awoke earlier than his normal 8:00 a.m. owing to strange bad dreams. The last time he had dreams of this type was just before the attacks on September 11. Just days before he was to take his plan trip to Texas, he had a dream of three jet aircrafts sitting on a runway. In the dream, the runway broke up, and all three planes fell into darkness. Just days later while in Texas, the three planes hit the World Trade Center and the Pentagon, killing over two thousand souls. This dream was very similar but much stronger and had a clearer view of an event that needed to be taken as a deadly threat to his family.

All his life, William had kept making plans in his head for what to do in case of worst events coming to pass—earthquakes, floods, nuclear bombs, or whatever came up. This morning, the dream was so intense that he had to tell Maria about it. In the dream, he saw the earth as if from space, like from a space station or ship. He was viewing the terminator line, marking day from night. He could see all the lights shining in the night side of the line. Then in a flash, almost all the lights went out. As he looked on as the as the line kept moving across the earth, darkness came, and no light came on at all. The world was going dark as the sun went down on the last day.

He was very upset by the dream. Maria listened and told him it was just a bad dream. He told her then of the last time he had this kind of a dream. Maria made them a quick meal, and they ate. It was just 6:45 a.m., and still he could not get the feeling of dread out of his head. He needed to do something. While sitting and looking out the window at the spring mountains in the morning sun, showing off the many colors from the bright reds to sandy browns and the dark green trees in the higher peaks, he knew that something had to be done to save his family and others if he could. His old habit of what to do kicked in, and in just a few minutes, he had an outline of a plan to get his family safely out of danger. He texted Joy to see how she was and to inform her of his crazy feeling and the dream. He asked her to call him as soon as she could. It was important! Next, he called his sisters living in the south. Getting no answer, he sent them a similar text to call as soon as they could.

The uneasy feeling kept getting stronger, and nothing could ease his mind. At 7:55 a.m., Joy returned his call, worried at the strange time and nature of his call and text. He did not know how to tell her and make her aware of the very real danger that was coming. He just told her that he had a feeling that something very bad was about to happen. He asked her to make sure that she had a full tank of gas and to buy extra if she could. Then before letting her go, he told her if something did happen to get all her kids and family members and come to the house or call him. At 8:15 a.m., Vivian and Jennet called back. By this time, the feeling he was having had grown to an alarming level. Maria stayed by his side, worried for his health. He told the girls that something was about to happen and to start getting ready for it. He asked them to go right now and fill their cars with gas and to get as much extra as they could. Then to gather the family members as best they could and come west. From the plan that had started forming earlier that morning, he knew he would be heading to the mountains for food and safety, so he gave them the name of the town where he planned to go into the mountains. The plan was forming in his head ever since he finished eating. He told them to head to Lone Pine on US 395 in California. It was 9:25 a.m. when he hung up the phone, telling them to go right now and get gas. Maria was trying to get him to lay down. She was sure he was having a spell or other issue. He did get her to call her brother, who was living in the Philippines, and to tell him to be on watch as William had heard something was going to happen over there. Little did they know they had less than an hour before the event would happen. And over forty million people were about to die.

Joy called back to check on her dad at 10:28 a.m. She told him she had called and texted the ones that didn't answer her call and passed the information on. Then she asked if he was okay. As she was asking for the third time what he was worried about happing, *it happened.*

The call went dead, and William tries to call back. The call would not go through. He tried texting her. To his surprise, this seemed to get to her. "Did your power go out as well?" Before he could get her answer, he heard very loud noises coming from outside. Maria heard as well and followed him outside. What they saw they would carry for the rest of their lives. They lived at the west end of the approach and takeoff lanes for the airport. As Las Vegas had the seventh busiest airport in the country, there were always many planes coming and going. What they saw were at least four jets that had just took off all falling out of the sky, some spinning and others on steep glide paths in the next minutes. They saw all of them crash and burst into large balls of red and orange flames with deep blue flames at the base of each of them.

Looking at his phone, Joy had texted that her power was out too. And she couldn't get the phone to call, only text. He responded, "I know. Same here. This was the event I am talking about. Text everyone and get what you can and meet us at the Big 5 Sporting Goods store on Warm Springs and Durango by 6:00 p.m."

"Dad, it's just a power outage."

"No, it's not. Look up. Can you see any jets from where you are? Can you hear any strange noises? Me and Maria just watched four jets crash and burn, and still there are no emergency services anywhere in sight."

It took a little time before she responded and said, "We could not hear any noises at all."

"Yes, the world just went dark. This is what I saw in my dream. We must be out of the city before dark tonight. Trust me, do what I've asked. Our family's lives depend on us getting out." He then turned to Maria and told her to text Sadie to come home as fast as she could. He had to grab Maria and give her a shake to get her to move as she was going into shock. "Maria, text her now. We got to get our act together." He then texted his sisters, "Did your power just go out? Can't call now. Just text. Seems to be working here. Please answer if you can and get to Lone Pine if you can." He never got an answer to his text.

He was looking around before going inside. Groups of people were forming to discuss the things they saw this morning. Portable radios were coming out, and they all just had white noise on all stations. Maria came over to be close to him and ask, "How did you know?"

"I told you, I had a dream, and it's not like a normal dream. And this is only going to get worse, and very fast. Did you get an answer from Sadie?"

"Yes. She wants to know if Donny can come."

"Yes, and his family, but only family. How much power do you have in your phone?"

"It's low less than thirty percent."

"Mine is low as well. Let's get them charged in the car if it works." William was hiding how worried he was as he wondered if the car would even run. He knew that whatever happened was not a power outage. It was an attack on the planet. That much was clear. He had Maria start packing bags for them, just clothes for all seasons. They would get more to be sure, but not for a while. He told her get things for camping. He took her phone and cord as well as his and went out to the car. In just seconds, he felt a great wave of relief. The car started, and the phones started to charge. Turning the car off, he went to help Maria. His phone started pinging with texts from different family members.

Sadie was first asking if he really meant it when he said Donny could come. He just sent back, “Yes, I did. The old world is dead and gone. All the problems of that world need to go as well. We will need help and people we can trust if we are to survive this.” He gave quick answers to all texts. They said, “Be at Big 5 by 6PM and all questions will be answered. Remember, family only!”

Then he got a text from Ben, Lance’s farther. “William, what’s up? I am at work, trying to close the place.”

William took time to send a quick message, followed by a larger one. The second message was this: “Great, in case you’re not sure, our world ended at 10:30 this morning. Need you to get as many hand tools for building cabins, log cabins, and nails and anything you think will be of use in the woods, then get Valerie and the kids and meet us at Warm Springs and Durango before dark. Oh, and don’t worry. You lost your job when the power went out.” (He had to send a second text to get it all in there.) “All we can do now is get out of the city and hope to survive. See you at 6PM.”

He and Maria had a lot to do. He had her packing very specific clothing and shoes. He got the things they would be needing for the bad times ahead. First, he gathered them all in the house to keep others from seeing what they had and were doing. William knew that until they were safe in the mountains, all would be against them for what they had. He mostly got what most would think as strange items. Books, his guns, all their phones and computers as they would be needed later. He also started cooking all the meat left in the refrigerator to take with them. It was past noon, and the air was getting bad from the fires still burring all around the valley. Every now and then, they could hear cars going by, always one or two. Only a few others had learned that only cars and probably other things that were not running during the event would still work. He got all the camping and fishing gear and all the full water bottles they had. Once he had it all stacked, he sat down to make his list for upcoming shopping trip he had planned in his head. He was just about to start on his list when Maria came out of the bedroom with tears still in her eyes.

"Come here, baby girl." He walked to her, giving her a very strong hug. He whispered in her ear, "It's been a very hard day, and the ones ahead are going to get worse for a while. I can't say how long or how bad. I can say that God willing, we will make it and see a whole new world that we get to mold as we wish. I have seen it at the end of my dream, a home and kids and family. It was not clear, but it was us, and we were happy with our family around us." He kissed her face and head till her tears receded. Waiting a few minutes, just holding her, he said, "I wish you could see my dream."

She looked at his face and said, "I wish I could too." With a gasp from each of them, a light flared in their eyes, and the entire dream passed before them, and she saw it all as well. "How did you do that?" she said.

William looked at her. "I think we did it. Something has changed in me today with that dream. I see everything differently than yesterday. I wanted you to see my dream so you'll stop worrying about it and me. When you said you wanted it as well, I think I was able to share it with you. It's ESP or something like it. I think we need to learn what we can do together. Will you help me make our shopping list?" He just thought the last, not speaking at all. She answered in her normal voice. He asked her to just think her next answer and not to speak.

Do you want the food or clothing list first?

I've been doing clothes for an hour between crying spells. Food, please. She was looking at him to see if he knew what she had thought.

He said, "You have a beautiful mind, my love. Food it is! We will always talk aloud when other are around, but alone, we can talk with our minds." With the newfound link they shared, the list was done very quickly.

Food and Medical Supplies

"Dry goods, rice, beans, flour, sugar, salt, pepper, corn meal, oatmeal, assorted spices, as much as we can get. Tea and coffee in large cans, and boxes as we can get. Also, as much powder milk as we can get.

"Next, canned goods. Take some of everything, as much as we can carry. Starting with fruits, at least two cases of every kind they have. Then move to the vegetables, corn, peas, green beans, same as fruits, at least two cases of each. Next, soups. Just a few types—chicken, beef, and, vegetable. As many cases as we can fit. And all the jerky we can manage. Do not to take perishables and candy and sodas. Kool-Aid, as much as we can find for drinks later. Powdered eggs if we can find it."

After the food, they would move to the store pharmacy to get all the meds members would need and take all the first aid supplies they could find. It might be a long time before they'd see a real doctor again. This list was to be finished later as he did not know what they were going to need outside of their personal meds.

They moved on to the last list—weapons and survival gear:

six rifles, bolt action (hunting), 30-30 or bigger
ten shotguns, 20-gauge or bigger
twenty pistols, .9mm or bigger
ammunitions (he wanted a thousand rounds per weapon)
all of the bows and crossbows in the store
all the arrows and crossbow bolts they had as well (practice and hunting)
as many canteens and camelbacks as they could find
all the dehydrated foods they had
thirty hunting knives, camp shovels (five to ten), five wood axes, ten hatchets

Then they turned to the camping and hunting (camo) clothing and boots (two pairs for all).

Last, all the fishing gear, ponchos, and reloading supplies they had.

It took much longer to write it all down, but that was soon done, and they started to load the car. William pulled the large SUV in the garage to load without being seen. It was almost 5:00 p.m. when they finished packing the car and started to the meeting place. He had Maria send a group text to everyone that they were on the way to the meeting place—the large parking lot, east end of the shopping center at Warm Springs and Durango on the west side of town, close to the road to Death Valley.

CHAPTER 4

The Gathering

THE LAST THING William did was load both of his guns, the 357 and the twenty-gauge shotgun, keeping the extra shells close at hand. Maria worried and asked if this was necessary. Looking at her, he thought, *I hope not.* Then he told her that very soon, more people would realize just what had happened. *When that time comes, they all could be dangerous to the family. We will all need to keep watch!*

From the event in the morning to the time they left for the meeting place, almost eight hours had passed. More people were becoming aware that this was not a simple power outage. Word spread out from the city that there was no help coming, and they had no idea when or if help was coming. So until then, they were on their own.

Sadie and Donny showed up just about thirty minutes before they finished loading the car and rode over with them. His parents would be meeting them there. After getting to the parking lot east of the shopping center, William gave everyone a quick lesson on the guns and how to load and use then. He also told them not to give any information to anyone not part of the family or accepted into the group. They started asking a lot of questions that had no place in the new world. William just let the kids talk. Maria had seen and now was fully in line with William. After no response to any of their questions, he explained what he believed happened and the new rules to living in the new world. He told them that in just a few days, the city would be out of food and become a warzone. There would be needless killings over food. And in less than a month, the food would be gone, and water would already be in short supply. Those still in the city would become cannibals as soon as all the dogs and cats have been eaten!

It was about 5:18 p.m. when the others started to arrive at the lot. Jake and Lucy with Easton were first to arrive. As was going to be the rule of the day, they just started asking questions William waited for them to stop talking and told Jake, "I will answer all questions once everyone is here." He gave Jake the job of telling them they would all be told at the same time what was going on and what William had planned. And they started asking him. He said, "I must wait as well."

When all five groups had arrived before 6:00 p.m. and there was still a bit of light left, William started sorting everyone out. He first checked on his own Joy and the boys. Then right down the line, he checked on Ben and his group—Valerie and Gracey and Larry. Next was Lucy's family. He had only met a few of them at parties over the years. Five of them came. They were all in their twenties or thirties. There were three men—Steve (thirty-one), Michael (twenty-eight), and Peter (twenty-two). There were two females—Shara (twenty-six) and Malinda (twenty-nine). This was the first place where things could have gone terribly wrong. Peter was not a blood relative to Lucy or any of them. When William asked each one if they were part of the family, Peter said no. This brought an outburst from the group. He asked if he was a blood relation. They all said no. He then asked why he was thought of as family.

Peter had been taken in by the family eighteen years ago when his parents abandoned him. They never got legal rights, but they kept and raised him as one of the family ever since.

"Peter, are these people your family? Yes or no."

"Yes, they are the only family I've ever known."

"Peter, your family has just grown. Welcome home."

He moved on to the last group, the family of Sadie's boyfriend. It was not right. William had a word with Ben about getting the shotgun and guarding his back. He did so and took up a place with a clear line of sight but not seen by the others. He had already checked his pistol and had it in his back when he went over to talk to them. Donny (nineteen) was with his parents with another couple with them, Missy (forty-one) and Daniel (forty-eight). The others were Alfred (thirty-eight) and Winnie (thirty) Brown.

"So, Donny, who is everyone? And how are they family?"

"This is my mother, Missy, and my father, Daniel."

"Okay, and the other two?"

Daniel spoke up at this point. "They are our friends that live next door of over ten years. We asked them if they would like to join us."

"Daniel, who gave you the right to do this? Were you not told family only?"

"Yes, but I trust them like family, so I brought them."

"This is my family here. Only my family. If you are coming with me, it will be on my terms, and you will accept them or stay behind. You think on that, Daniel. Mr. Brown, I am sorry, but you will need to leave. Take what you brought with you. I would get out of town if you can!"

"Who do you think you are, asshole? Telling us when and where to go.! I will decide what *we do, not you*!"

"Mr. Brown, you will leave here now. You are not part of this family! If Daniel wants to go with you, he can on his own." He turned to look over the rest of the family. He checked on Ben and then turned back to face Mr. Brown. He found he had a gun pointed at him.

"Now, *Mr. Family*, this is how this is going to go. We are taking over this group, and all the supplies are mine as well. No self-made messiah is telling me when and where to go!"

Once more, he turned back to his family members. During that look, he had his second vision of the day. This one was while he was awake. He saw the next three minutes before they happened. He shared it with Maria at once. *This is what happens!* Turning back to face Mr. Brown, he said, "This is the reason for family only, so we do not come to this point. We have no bond of any kind and no bases for trust, so as I said before, family only!" He faced Mr. Brown again, his hand behind his back, holding a cocked .357 revolver! He looked at Mr. Brown. "Mr. Brown, you have until the count of three to lower your gun and leave."

"You can't tell us what to do." Mr. Brown started to laugh and wave his gun around. At that very moment, William took a shooting stance and fired twice, hitting Mr. Brown in the head with both shots. He fell to the ground, dead before he reached it.

"Now, Daniel, do you still think you have the right to say who can come with us?"

Daniel was looking at the growing pool of blood growing around the body by his feet.

"Mrs. Brown, I am sorry for your loss. It's best if you leave now, and do not come back here. Daniel, I need you to answer now. We do not have time to waste here."

It was at this point the shotgun went off. Mrs. Brown had picked up the gun and was about to shoot William. Ben had done his job keeping William safe. Ben and William had a bond from that day on as they both had kill to keep the family safe. It was their first time and far from the last.

Without a pause, William asked Daniel, "For the last time, what are you going to do?"

"William, I see now that you are what you say, family-driven. We wish to come with you."

"Thank you. We are glad to have you join our family. However, there are a few conditions that all of you need to agree to. Everyone except Maria and myself will need to take the oath of parole to continue with us from this point. Also, there is one thing you should all know before you take it. I am not sure how, but I can tell when anyone is lying to me."

Oath of Parole

1. To keep all family members safe

2. To never reveal family or security
3. To follow the leader's orders without question
4. To never leave the family without permission
5. To only ask questions at open council meeting
6. To never lead outsiders to the family homes

I (say your name) swear on my honor and
love of my family to keep the parole given me.

"Now before anyone takes the oath, know this. After you take it, you are no longer free to leave or change your minds. Now at this time, if anyone wishes to leave, they are free to do so. After taking the oath you just saw, the penalty for breaking the oath. Take a minute, and when you're ready, you will be able to take the oath. It will always be given one at a time only."

All of them took the oath, and they became a true family by choice.

* * *

Shopping Spree

"Okay, here's our play. We are going to Big 5 just after dark. Three people will be outside as guards while the rest of us go in and load up on the supplies on the list. Once we have that store in hand, some of us will go to the market and start filling that shopping list. At each store, I have a promissory note to leave if the world returns to normal. It has my name and driver's license number on it. Once we are done there, if needed, we will go to the pharmacy to stock up on needed supplies as well. If you have special needs, see Maria so she will know what to look for. Remember not to take anything that needs to be kept cold, as there is not going to be a place to keep it for a while. After we stock up on supplies, we start for the mountains. We will be going in from the east and crossing over to the west face. Okay, let's get this done. Get the kids large bags. Their job is to get all the dehydrated foods in the store. The ladies will be getting the clothes for everyone, winter and summer. The rest of us will be taking weapons and ammo. Everyone look at the list that's being passed around. Do not add anything. We will be taking bows and crossbows and all the arrows. If you see maps, take all you see. Leave none for the next group that thinks of this. We are first but not the only ones that will try this. My hope is for us to disappear in the mountains and increase our chances of surviving the next year. Any questions?" There was a pause. "Okay, let's go shopping."

Big 5

The first order of business was to move the cars to the back of the store and assign jobs to everyone. The oldest teenager, June, was put in charge of the children to help. Next, Ben, Jake, and Daniel had outside guard duties. They were to take hidden places and cover the doors. They were in a place with clear field of fire and good cover. He made Donny the backdoor guard.

He sent Sadie to check and see if the store was open. During the time, everyone was taking the oath. Maria and Sadie made smaller lists for the different groups to use in the stores. The kids' list was easy. They would go and get backpacks and tote bags found in the store and take all the dehydrated food they could find. They would put them in the packs and bags, take it to the cars, and go back for more. The women, knowing the sizes of their family members. would be gathering clothes while the remaining men would be gathering weapons and ammo and the other supplies on the list. The plan was to take as much as they could fit in the cars.

Sadie came back. The store was locked with two employees inside. William gave Michael and the other men the task of getting in the back while he tried to get in the front. With Maria by his side, they knocked on the glass door. Two people came to the door. *Sam* and *Kati*e were on their name tags.

"Hi, Sam, Katie. I really need your help. We are going camping and need some propane tanks for our stove. I can pay cash. Could you please help us out? It may be tomorrow if we must wait till the power is back on."

"Sorry, sir, we can't even ring up cash without power."

"Tell me, Sam, how long have you been here today?"

"All day. We're the managers. We are waiting for the home office to call its procedure. We sent the crew home hours ago." There was a loud noise in the back of the store.

"Sam, listen to me. That noise is my people coming in. Please do not move. Look at me!" William had the .357 out in plain sight. "Sam, we are coming in. We are not going to hurt you. We don't want money. Your company policy is to not resist and give the robbers what they want, right?"

"Yes, but we have very little cash."

"That's okay. We do not want the cash. Sam, open the door, please."

He opened the door and they went in. Everyone got to work.

Sam was in a kind of shock. Katie was watching with wide eyes.

"Sam, come with me. You have the keys to the arms locker, don't you?"

"Yes."

"Good. Saves us time. Please open everything for us. Katie, help open all the locks."

With the doors all open, they made really good time getting the list filled. They did not have enough of a few things in the store, but it was enough to get them to the mountains. William found a holster that went at the small of his back for the .357. While they were loading the cars, William had a talk with Sam and Katie.

"Have either of you tried to call home?" Both said yes. "Didn't get through, did you?" When the power failed, so did a lot of other things. They said *no*. "After we leave, try to text. It seems to work at times.

"At 10:30 a.m., when the power failed, so did a lot of other things. The smoke you see all over the valley is from jet planes that crashed. Nothing is working that was turned on at that time. Cars can't be jump-started. They are dead. However, if your cars where off at the time, they should start. You need to find your families and get out of the city while you can. That's what we are doing. We believe this is not going to be fixed soon if ever."

The list was almost done, down to the last packs or totes being filled and loaded into the car.

Ben called, “William, a police car has pulled up to the door of Big 5 in the back. They are taking up positions behind the car!”

“Okay, get to the others. Tell them not to fire unless they are in danger. Then take up positions behind them.” Next, they heard the police call from the speakers to come out with their hands up.

“Hello out there! Who am I talking to? I want to send out the store employees that were so helpful with our shopping.”

“I’m Officer Tomkins.”

“Well, Officer Tomkins, we have two store employees we want to release. We don’t want to harm anyone.”

Okay, why don’t you come out with your hands where we can see them?”

“Sorry, that won’t work for us today.” Ben called on the walkie-talkies so they could have secure communications. They also found a scanner as well. It was running in their car. They overheard Officer Tomkins’s request for backup as well as the reply that it would take over two and a haft hours to reach them. Then Ben addressed the two officers from behind them.

“Officer Tomkins, I think that you and your partner are going to lay down you weapons and take three steps backward with hands high, please.”

“Why would we do that?”

“Well, first, the backup you wanted is over one hour away, and I have five guns behind you with clear targets.”

You don’t except us to believe that, do you?”

“No, I do not. However, it is true. I am going to prove it to you! One shot will be fired at your spotlight. Please do not return fire. We do not mean to harm you. Ben, the driver side spotlight, if you please.” One shot rang out, and the door to the store was dark again.

“Mr. Tomkins, do you believe now?”

“Well, I know one man is there. You know we cannot let you go.”

“Officer, you keep working like things are normal. When was the last time a power outage caused planes to fall out of the sky? I do not claim to know or understand what happened this morning. Whatever it was, it has changed the world forever. If you're smart, after we leave, you will go home, get your family, and get to a safe place."

"You think we are going to let you leave?"

"Officer Tomkins, it's not your choice. We have more guns and more people than you! Now please back up three steps and put your guns away."

"Stop, William! Trouble coming fast! Look east on Warm Springs. Five cars moving fast."

"Are they police?"

"No, strange cars. SUV or pickup trucks. I can see many people with rifles at the ready for trouble."

"How much time do we have?"

"Just a few minutes. What do we do?"

"You all go to cover and get in back of them, same as we did with our new friends from metro if they stop here. Officer Tomkins, you both have to decide where you stand. You need to take cover on this side of your car. We will cover you. If trouble starts, make a break for the store."

The five vehicles pulled all around the back doors. They jumped out, shooting at the back of the store and the cruiser. They all returned fire, including the two officers with their shotguns. As soon as the first pause came, they ran to the back of the store to welcome dark solid walls. William split them up, keeping Tomkins with him and leaving the other with Michael. They put out an amazing amount of fire. They kept up steady fire due to Maria's keeping the kids and women reloading weapons. It was almost three minutes before they realized that they were taking fire from behind as well. They quickly made a shield of two of their trucks and put men on it to guard their backs. It was a bloody fight on their side as they had good cover in the store. William sent Michael and Peter with the other officer to watch the front of the store because they were sure to crash the front windows to get at them.

Ever since William shared his dream with Maria, they could link and talk even when doing other things or talking to others. This was a great help in many ways and would become more as days went by.

After blocking them from breaching the rear door, the attackers sent about eight men around to the front. William sent Maria to tell Michael to push over all the sales racks to block and slow them down and to arm everyone over the age of thirteen and get ready. The rest just had to keep loading the empty guns. Michael was wondering if three of them would be enough. He heard his thoughts and answered him for the first time, touching his mind. *You have eight, all the kids and the women. They just need to shoot, is all.*

They kept the constant fire out the back door. Just about ninety seconds later, they all heard the shattering glass in front, followed by a great deal of gunfire. It was never even close at the front. Lucy killed two before they cleared the window, and Michael got three as they tried to get over the debris from the sales racks they had crashed all about the store. The rest crawled out on their bellies back to the rear door. Four more had been shot at the rear during this time. And an unknown number had been shot by Ben and his group. The firefight lasted about fifteen minutes before the attackers asked for quarter. William ordered a ceasefire and for the remaining men to walk into the light at the back of the store, where they were to lay down their guns and take three steps back. Then he told them all to sit on their hands. Ben and the two men with him came up from behind and took their weapons and checked them for hidden weapons.

While this was being done, William had Daniel stay with him as he talked to the two officers. "Well, Officer Tomkins, here is where we part company. You need to get people you can trust and form a protection group."

"Well, I guess you're right. I can't stop you, and now we owe you our lives as well."

"If you stay in the city, you'll find life will be short. If I give you a place I can check for you and your family, will you keep it to yourself? Don't even tell Officer Baskin. I still have bad feelings from him."

"Yes, I will. I feel you may be the only one that has a hold on what's going on."

"Okay, just you and family. Make your way to Lone Pine. Move to the trails going up to the mountains. Check around for the words *Ho Dog* carved in a tree. When you find this trail, move off the trail and make camp. Be ready to camp for at least one week. If we don't make contact, do what you think is best. Good luck."

After leaving the officers, William went to question the others. "So who's in charge of this group now?"

"I guess I am. Alfred Brown was our leader. He was supposed to meet us here."

"He's here. Look at the cars on the north side of the lot. You can just make out the bodies of him and his wife. Did he have *a boss* to answer to?"

"No, man. He was the boss!"

Using the link, William asked Maria, *Did you hear that?*

Yes, he lied. They both answer to another.

"So what is your name?"

"Call me Bloodbath, as that's what I do, kill people in the bloodiest ways I can."

"Yeah, okay, Mr. Bath. I just want to know who's your boss now." His thoughts went to a Mr. Black then to the lie he told that now he was the boss.

"You should know, Lee"—he used his true name—"that you cannot lie to me. Now what was your plan?"

He did not understand what was going on and lied to them again. "We heard that the police had all gone and there was no one to stop us, so we came to do what you did. Rob the place."

On the link, Maria spoke, *They were coming for us, and you are the reason. What are we going to do? We need a plan!*

We have a plan, and we are keeping to it! The problem now is what to do with these men!

William, can you see anything in their minds?

I've not tried. Let's look together. Closing his eyes, he tried to see Lee's thoughts. It took what seemed like an hour when a very dark shadow came over their minds. Maria started to talk. He shut her down, and they both just looked at the thought in Lee's mind and memory. It was the bloodthirsty killing of people at the orders of one Mr. Black.

They pulled out, both feeling sick at the things they saw.

Maria said what he could not, did not, want to accept. *These men all have to die!*

Yes, they do, and we need to get the rest of the shopping done and get on the road. You go get them started and I will have some of them come help me.

Maria went to get them all going again, loading the final things in the cars. The battle had now taken over two hours of their time.

Michael, can you still hear me?

Yes! But how?

Not now. Get Lucy and Ben and about eight others, and get over here. Bring guns, all loaded. Hurry. We have work to do.

Michael got the other and followed William's orders. He came up from behind the prisoners, taking the places as they had been told. William was asking questions when he saw the others taking their positions, and he now asked the one question he really wanted an answer to.

"Why did you all want to kill us?"

"Just you, man. Just you!"

He sent to Michael and Maria that he was surprised, as were Lucy and Ben as they heard him as well now.

"One honest answer out of all the lies! *Now*!"

It sounded like a single shot as all the men hit the ground dead.

"Did all of you hear that?"

Michael and Lucy both spoke at the same time. "Yes, one shot!"

And twelve men dropped dead.

"We must make that a part of who we are about to become! *One shot*. Are we ready to finish shopping now? We are running late."

They drove to the pharmacy just down the street and stocked up on medical supplies. This took about forty-five minutes. It was now close to 9:45 p.m. With all the cars loaded and ready to go, William had something he wanted to do.

"At this point, we are a group of strangers, and we need to bond and get to know each other as quickly as we can. To this end, I am going to mix the cars all around. Drivers stay the same. Everyone is to move to different cars, get to know each other, and learn to trust each other as you already saw our very lives depend on it. Our next task is to cross Death Valley tonight. I really want to get past death tonight."

CHAPTER 5

Death Valley

William also gave driving instructions to each driver for the trip across the valley at night. They would all drive in line behind his SUV. His lights would be on, and the ones behind would only use their parking lights, except the last one, which would drive with no lights at all. Due to unknown conditions, they would drive at 45mph, keeping a close but safe distance between them. In this way, they were hoping to hide the number of cars in the line as well as to be lost from sight from behind as the last car was running dark.

William was worried about the people they would find in Death Valley. An unknown number of people with no real idea of what's going on. He thought the numbers would be small. In a few a few places, there could be large number if any buses were in the valley. Also, the first step would be to stop at the last gas station on Blue Diamond way before going over the hump.

"We will pull in, circling the fill pipes in the station. All the cars fuel doors need to be on the inside of the circle so we can hide what we are doing. We will also fill the jerricans as well. Two will go in each car. Also, we hope to find running water so we can fill the water cans as well. The plan is to drive most of the way to 395 tonight and sleep and get an early start in the morning. No more than four hours of sleep when we stop. Three of us will be on guard for two hours while the rest sleep. The guards will get to sleep on the drive in the morning. Everyone, remember it's better to wake someone than to get caught trying to get some sleep while on guard. While on guard, if a stranger or possibly someone you know approaches our camp, shoot a warning shot and tell them to stop! This should stop them and wake the rest of us. If they do not stop, shoot them. Never try to scare or just wound. Shoot to kill. The next forty-eight hours will be the most dangerous for us! No one will be our friends. They will all want what we have! Now is the time for questions. Anyone? Okay, the time to go has come. Let's go!"

Getting over the Hump

So they left town at last. The six-car convoy started south down Fort Apache Blvd, the two or three miles to Blue Diamond Highway. Now each car had a walkie-talkie so they could keep in touch with each car. They did not know where the next problem would come from, but they all knew it was coming!

It was a surreal drive right out of the worst zombie movie. Just no zombies. Everywhere they looked, fires were burning out of control. They were the only lights they had other than one set of headlights. In a very short time, they began to see bodies, making a point of driving around them. And it was a giant maze as there were hundreds of dead cars all over the roads. They had to be maneuver around them. The driving time just kept getting longer. They had at least seven major crash sites to get around. William sent the message back to keep the kids from being able to look out at the human carnage all around them.

The drive was much worse as they drove south to the Blue Diamond Road. There was no straight line to drive on. There were people all over now, coming to the sound of the earlier gunfire, hoping to find help and answers. Added to the people was the road. The road was full of dead cars from the event. They had to weave in and around the cars like snakes. The only time they got to drive straight was when they had to go off the road to get around impassable groups of cars. They drove around fires and plane crashes in many places as planes were landing from the west, so there were many more planes in the area than when taking off. They all made turns to their destinations. What should have been a five- to ten-minute drive took much longer, giving them all a look at the new world they had to deal with. Once they cleared most of the crashes, they could use the night vision devices they found in Big 5. This made driving better, and they would soon be used by the scout teams on their walks to the station. They stopped one and a half miles from the station and loaded up the scout teams. They took two crossbows, and each carried a rifle and sidearms.

Ben and Jake each picked a second to go with them. Ben took Michael as they had formed a strong bond based on how well he performed at the Big 5 store. Jake took Peter as he had proven to be an excellent shot with a rifle. Jake took the right side of the road which would take them to the far side of the station. Ben and Michael would move up the left side. It was a shorter walk but with less cover. They all met with William to discuss the job ahead. The simple instructions were to reach the station at the same time, scout the area, and report on the conditions they found there. They were to only fire to protect themselves and use the bows as first choice. They were given a thirty to forty-minute walk. They all moved off the road about ten yards, close enough to see the road and stay on course as it was very dark. They had little light just from the fires now behind them, no moon, and the sky full of smoke with no wind at all.

Ben and Michael were a good match. They had learned a lot at the Big 5 and made little noise and moved forward at a good pace. Other than coming across a few of the big black tarantulas and one rattlesnake, they had nothing to report to William. They were waiting to hear from Jake before starting the sweep of the gas station. It was just a hundred feet ahead of them.

Jake and Peter moved only five to eight yards off the road as they had the far side. The dark was deeper here due to two jet crash sites and six homes that had or were still burning. The smoke was very thick, hanging all over the cooler ground with no wind. With the smoke, it was hard to see, and breathing was difficult as well.

They had to stay very close together so as not to get separated. After walking for about twenty minutes, Jake stopped and let Peter come up next to him.

Jake spoke first. "It managed to land on this little road. Can you believe that!"

A 737 jet was just sitting on a frontage road leading to a group of homes a little way to the north about a mile or two from the road. Peter readied the crossbow, and they approached the jet. They found all the escape slides deployed. Jake called in their find to William and told him they were going to check the jet before moving on. Peter had just about made his way to the top of the slide by this time.

"Peter, check that it's safe, and take a look around. I will keep watch from here. Yell if you need me." Peter reached the top and disappeared inside. In about two minutes, he gave the all clear to Jake.

"It's safe. We should have someone come out to check it for anything we can use. There is no sign of anyone at all staying here. What do you think?"

"I think you're right, and I believe we will find them all at the gas station, waiting for help to arrive to save them." He checked back with William, updating him on the conditions they found and the belief that the passengers and crew went to the gas station.

"Good work. We are sending a group to check it out. So get going. Ben is waiting for you to start the sweep. He's aware of your find."

They got back on the shoulder of the road, approaching the station from the far side. They went past the station and were coming back to the station from the east. From their position, they could see the front of the station while Ben and Michael were on the back side. Jake and Peter had a clear view of the station. It was a zoo. "Looks like everyone from the plane." He contacted William and Ben. They started their sweep of the station.

Jake and Peter took their position on the far side and took a first look. Using the night vision scope, Jake checked the area. He reported large numbers of people at the station. It was the jet's crew and passengers, and there seemed to be a fair number of cars there as well. With this information, Ben and Jack started their sweeps.

There were groups of people on both sides of the station. Most were in some state shock. There was a better organized group that looked to be from the jetliner from across the road. They had made it to the gas station and joined the others already there. They all had nowhere to go.

Jake and Peter walked slowly up the front, keeping their weapons low but near their hand. A few of the people looked at them but made no effort to approach them. Most of the people were talking over the day's events. Jake was in the front with Peter just a few steps behind him. It was Peter who saw them first.

Catching Jake and tugging on his sleeve, he whispered in his ear, "Jake, there are a few men with guns and seem to be holding certain people in the store area."

Jake passed the information along to Ben and William, and they moved on toward the filling pipes. Once at the fill pipes they waited for Ben and Michael to reach them.

Ben informed Michael of the large amount of people, and they now started up the east side of the station. Ben had one of the night vision scopes as well. They were about two thirds of the way to the front when Ben heard two beeps on the radio. They had a problem! As they were slowly moving up the far edge of the station, moving from cover to cover, they saw a large group of armed men. They tried to get a count on the total number of men they faced and type of weapons they had. Ben counted eight in the group, all with automatic weapons, just twenty feet short of the front where the refueling operation was about to begin. Ben and Michael had set up one move. One covered then covered for the other. Ben was leading with the aid of night vision. Michael was moving to Ben's last cover point. Just then, one of the armed men turned and saw the movement behind them. He turned and started walking right to Michael's position. Ben used hand signals for Michael to use the crossbow if needed, not the guns. He indicated he would wait for the man to pass his position. He leaned back into the darker shadows. The man still walked right at Michael. The space between them was less than six feet. Both he and Ben were in danger of being found. They both held their breaths as the man passed Ben's position. Now he had a clear shot at the man.

In just three more steps, he would be on top of Michael. Ben clicked the radio four times to tell everyone he was shooting now. With just a soft twang, the bolt from the crossbow entered the upper left side of the man's back, piercing his heart. As he started to fall forward from the killing blow, Michael stepped out and grabbed him before he could hit the ground. As he grabbed him, he covered his mouth to keep any sounds form getting out. At that very second, a second man on a patrol came around the corner behind them from the same direction they had used minutes before. Seeing what had just happened, he started shooting. Gunfire ripped the air. Pandemonium broke out all over the station. Ben saw the man just as he was raising the barrel of the gun at Michael and fired his crossbow at the man, making his second and third shots go high. Michael fell, still holding the first man.

At this point, the others in the front turned and ran, guns blazing at Ben and Michael's positions. Ben called for help and started firing at the men running toward them. They all took cover and stared returning fire. This was an organized group!

As soon as William got the news about how many people were likely to be at the station, he adjusted his plan. All the kids under thirteen were left with Britany, and he armed them with handguns. Her orders were to start walking to the station as soon as the cars pulled in. She was to stop if she saw or heard anything that did not look safe wait to be call in.

He checked the rest to be sure they were ready for whatever was waiting for them. With weapons and ammo, they were ready for whatever might be waiting for them. The drive to the station took a bit over five minutes, and when they pulled in, they saw Jake at the fill pipes. They pulled around them. In effect, they circled the wagons. They had received the message that Ben and Michael had a problem. William set up the perimeter and set a guard. At this time, Jake and Peter started to the back side to give support to Ben and Michael. When the six cars pulled into the station, they circled the fill pipes in the ground, keeping the fill doors on the cars all inside of the circle. This was done to keep unwanted eyes from seeing what they would be doing. They got the guards up and out, keeping the people nearby back. They didn't see the pumps and how they used them.

Joy, Donny, and Daniel were running the pumping operation. It took a very short time to rig the bilge pumps rigged to pump the gas back out of the ground tanks. Each of them took one pipe and started pumping gas into the cars first, and when all the cars were full, they started on the jerricans they had taken at the Big 5 store.

After William got things started at the pipes and as soon as that was set, he made a rapid response team out of the extra members not needed to get the gas. As in all groups, someone thought the restrictions in place did not apply to them. So it was going to be here as well. The pumping was going slow but was working. They were getting gas. Another problem that was solved and tested and working from William's master plan. He had no idea if this was going to work before this moment. So he told everyone that this was SOP for all gas stops. The cars with lowest fuel levels would be filled first. All cars would be filled before filling jerricans. The reason being they might need to leave in a hurry, so that was the order to gas stops.

They had just started to fill the fourth car in the circle when a man started to approach Maria. He stopped, but not before she threatened to shoot him. William heard her voice over all the noise. It was later that he realized that he didn't really hear her voice but her thoughts just before she said the words aloud. Their link kept getting stronger the more they used it. He went to check on the problem. They had just gotten a handle on the large numbers of people at the station, and now they were returning behind this lone man.

Moving over to Maria's side, he had Lucy as his backup. Her orders were to shoot anyone that became a threat to them. Then he addressed the man Maria had her gun pointed at.

"Excuse me, sir, what's your name?"

"Oliver."

"Well, Oliver, what gives you the feeling we should allow you to do as you please? To the best of our knowledge, you do not have a gun on you at least and are in no position to even approach us as the restrictions we gave out to stay back applies to all."

"Well, I'll tell you. I am a GS-18 NSA officer. I've come out here to check on some strange occurrences at the testing grounds."

"You mean Area 51? Something strange happened there? Did it have anything to do with the event of this morning?"

"That's a good question. I don't know, and no one is answering the calls, and that has never happened. Someone is always on duty for taking calls!"

"How do you call?"

"Always on secure satellite phone."

"Do you have a charged phone and way to recharge it?"

"Yes. What do you have in mind?"

"Checking if the system still works. I want you to get your phone and call this number: 702-560-0875."

Oliver punched in the number and hit send. It took eight to ten seconds for William's phone to ring.

"Your phone is working! No one here has a working phone."

"Thank you."

"Oliver, there are a lot of things still working. Don't thank me yet."

"Why?"

"Because you need to listen and ask no questions until I am done, please."

"Okay."

"I am going to take your phone and give you my second phone for your use."

"Your taking all—"

"*Stop* talking and listen, you will also get a working charger with the phone. As well as a full tank of gas and all the extra fuel you can carry. Now if you wish to have a choice in this, here it is. We are taking your phone, and if you do not agree to the deal, I will shoot you and take it anyway! So do we have a deal?"

Just at that moment, shots rang out on the right side of the station. William sent the rapid response team at once. He then yelled at Oliver and all the others standing around to lay flat on the ground, hands on their heads! He told Lucy and Maria to shoot them if any of them tried to get up. Than he ran to the corner.

* * *

Ben relayed that information to William. As he was doing that, Michael shot at two of them as they tried to advance down the side of the building. Jake was starting to engage them from the left flank. The response team had formed a line from the front using the different cars for cover. The attackers quickly became the targets from many different places and had become the ones on the defensive. They were being trapped by fire from four different directions! By agreement, the family had decided to never offer surrender to anyone they engaged in battle with. In a fight, they did always accept unconditional surrender when the other asked for it. As the firing slow, for a second a voice called out, "We want terms to a quick withdrawal!"

William moved forward and responded in a very firm voice, "I'm not sure how many of you are still left. However, our terms are this. Hold your weapons over your heads and walk into the light. Stop when we tell you. Then one at a time, put your weapons on the ground in front of you and take one step back!"

"What assurances are you giving us?"

"None. Do it and take your chances or start firing again. Your choice. You asked, and this is the best you're getting!"

After a few minutes of heated talk, they responded and yelled they were coming out. Ben called. Michael needed medical help ASAP. Maria sent Veronica with the med kit. She oversaw first aid for the family. She grabbed the kit, and with Steven at her side, she rushed to Ben and Michael's position. The few people that had been hanging around the family since they arrived had cleared out when the shooting started. They started walking toward what was left of Las Vegas and what William saw as their deaths in the city. As soon as he had control of the station, he started to get things back on track. He had a chore for Jake.

"Jake, I want you to go find the pilots from the plane and bring them to me. Ask nicely, but make sure they come, okay?"

"Sure, I can do that. Where will you be?"

"Back at the refueling operation. Get going."

William than ran to Michael's side. The looks on Ben's and Veronica's faces told the story. Michael was dying from the amount of blood everywhere. He knew the cause.

"Michael, it's William. Is there anything I can do for you?"

Michael was able to open his eyes but was unable to speak. This, at first, hurt William, as he could see Michael needed to say something. Wishing he could find a way, William opened his wall to keep the emotions of the others out.

During the first gun battle, he was almost overwhelmed by the flood of feeling from everyone involved in the fight. It was a new ability to deal with later. Now without knowing how, he opened Michael's mind, and they both could talk. Well, it was not talking, really. But in nanoseconds, they had a final talk. It would be many months before he told any of the family but Maria what passed between them. All he said was "Michael asked that I keep the family safe! I intend to honor his wish!"

During this time, Oliver had time to go over all that had happened since he started the drive to Las Vegas. He had stayed the night in a small roadside inn. He got in late and woke up late as the power was off. They had no idea this was anything other than a simple power outage. Oliver was worried that it was in some way connected to his trip out to the base. A fast trip with special instructions, no air travel allowed until further notice. This was the reason he had been sent as the only NSA member in the area traveling by car. He had several things he was trying to figure out by this time. One, what was going on? This was no simple blackout. Why was DC so unsettled, and how would he be able to report without his phone? His problems kept growing, and now he was being held at gunpoint while a battle raged just a few hundred feet away. He was having a hard time keeping the events straight in his mind while trying to put things in order. William startled him, breaking his train of thought.

"Oliver, get up! Well, now you know that killing is not a threat. Do we have a deal?"

Without a moment's hesitation, a very clear and loud yes came from Oliver's mouth. William had Steven take Oliver to find extra gas cans and get his car over to the fueling operation.

During this time, the refueling team had filled all the cars and the jerricans, getting them loaded back into the cars. While they worked on filling the car and extra gas cans, they found some in the station for Oliver. William asked him to join them.

Oliver and William talked for a few minutes, asking questions back and forth. First Oliver asked where William was going.

"Sorry, I can't tell you that unless you're coming with us and take the oath."

"I understand that. You seem to know something. Can you tell me anything?"

"Yes, but I think you already know some of it. Whatever it was that happened today was an attack on us! No power outage ever dropped planes from the sky. Cars do not fail because the power goes out! I've found that anything that was running during the event is dead. Things that were not running are still working. Soon more people will figure this out, and it will be a madhouse. Now do you have any information on who or what is behind this?"

"No, I wish I did. I am going to Nellis on a top-secret mission to investigate a threat warning."

"Oliver, I am not sure what's up with me, but I know you're not telling me the whole truth. I just seem to know if anyone is lying to me about anything. I will not press you as it's your job to keep secrets. I believe yours is a fool's mission, as this was a well-planned attack on us."

"I agree with you. Wish I had and could share with you information on this event. Until I arrived here, I didn't know how bad this was. Yes it must be an attack of some kind. Who and what are not easy to see. We are getting no information from anywhere."

"Oliver, I believe you're on a fool's mission and will find that the government you work for is no longer working. If you survive your trip and find no place, go head to Lone Pine. Check the trailheads and look for these words *Ho Dog* carved into a tree or sign. When you find it, move off the trail and be ready to wait up to a week, and someone will find you. If you are not met, we didn't make it and you're on your own. Do not give this out to anyone. Just you. And any that come with you will be welcome if they take the oath."

At just that moment, Jake and Peter came up with a small group of people. It was the flight crew from the jet he found earlier.

Families Growing

"Hello, my name is William. Sorry for the rudeness of my invitation. I could not risk your saying no. I would like to put you at ease after I tell you why I asked you over. If you don't agree, you will be free to go your own way. First let's get more comfortable. Come in the circle and relax a bit. Ben, please see that everything is ready to go in half an hour, please. Lucy, will you see about some food and water for our guests? The lady next to me is my wife, Maria. Now if we can get your names please."

"Albert P. Anderson, command pilot." (Age forty-eight.)

"Berry T. Smith, copilot." (Age thirty-nine.)

"Julie Ackerson, head flight attendant." (Age twenty-nine.)

"Sherry Swenson, flight attendant." (Twenty-four.)

"Jennet King, flight attendant." (Twenty-five.)

"Hello, everyone. Joy's back with our food. Please eat. I want to start by asking a few questions, if you don't mind." The group was quite hungry, being out there all day with little food and water and waiting for help that was never coming. They set about the food and water with a passion. William wanted to start his questions.

Albert asked a question first. "Excuse me, why are you not giving food and water to the others here?"

"Albert or Al, which do you prefer?"

"Al is okay."

"Well, Al, as I see it, my family are the only living people here. All these others are dead already. Before you judge me, answer my questions and then listen to my offer please." Not giving Al a chance to decline, he went right into his questions. "What do you know about what happen to your jet?"

"Not too much. We were lucky. Berry was doing some in-flight training on dead stick landings and approaches. We had just turned off the hydraulics when the power loss hit us. We started an emergency restart. The hydraulics were the only system to come back on. It allowed us to set down on the road where you found the plane. After clearing the plane, we walked to the gas station, and here we are. We were very lucky not to flip or run off the road as we had no breaks of any kind."

"Al, are you aware that all engines of any kind all stopped working at the same time?"

"No."

"Okay, do any of you know how many people are flying on any given day?"

Julie spoke up. "I have seen the numbers of people flying on a regular basis. It's between eight to ten million per day."

"Okay, so this morning, if I am right, ten million give or take were killed when the planes they were on fell out of the sky when the event happened. And do you still think someone's coming out here to get you? Do you think it's a power failure still?"

A load beeping coming from his radio interrupted the answer.

"William, it's Peter. We have movement to the east, coming fast at least five large trucks or Humvees."

"What do you think are they? Think are they hostile?"

"We can't see any marking on them. However, we can see that they are full of armed men!"

"Pete, how much time do we have?"

"Ten, maybe fifteen minutes if it slows down. Less if they don't."

"Okay, get back here on fueling detail. Secure the pumps. We leave in five minutes! Sorry, Al, we just ran out of time. Every one of you needs to make this decision. We want you to come with us!"

"I only caught the end of that speech, but I'm in if you will have me."

Jake spoke up. "I stopped and had him listen, so you could finish. This is the dead head pilot from the jet."

"My name is Sherman Walker, I'm ex-Air Force. I flew apaches and Blackhawks as well as jets. Also served as rotary instructor at flight school before leaving the service."

"Great. You're in. Find him a car to ride in. Well, what about the rest of you? Coming or staying?"

They all said yes except Al.

"Well, what is it, Al? You want to stay here?"

"I have a responsibility to the passengers on the plane."

"Okay, Al, if that's what you want to do. Your death will be a waste of a good man. I think your job ended when you got them here and out of that plane. If you want, go talk to them tell them that they are on their own or not. You have five minutes, and we leave.

"Steve, could you check on the kids and make sure they are all accounted for?"

Al walked back to the area he had left his passengers and started talking to them. The rest of the people started loading cars for the trip across Death Valley. Ben made sure all drivers had night vision for the drive across.

"We will leave with no lights. Jake, fill Sherman in on what he's missed on the ride to our next stop." William gave Oliver directions to the road where the jet had landed with orders to stay there. No lights in till after the station blows up then to head to the air base with no lights.

"Ben, get any of the extra small gas cans and anything you can put gas in. Fill them, and you take the last place in the line. We will rig the station to blow and use the extra gas as a fuse. Leave a trail so we can light it from the road or as close as you can get. Call me when you're out of gas." With no lights, the seven cars now started to leave the station. It had been almost two hours since they arrived at the gas station. As they were driving off, they saw a large number of people turning back to the station. William ordered for the cars to shoot over the heads when Ben lit the gas trail. As soon as they had all made the road, Ben called that he was out of gas. William gave the order, and the cars all started shooting. Ben shot a flare into the gas! It lit up the night, showing the approaching cars to be much closer as they were about to turn into the gas station. The people returning all now ran the other way. William had kept driving as the fuse was lit to get as far from the blast as they could!

"Ben, use your lights as needed to catch up, and stay as safe as you can. Jake, how are the others doing?"

"They are almost at the station. It will be close!"

William sent the order. "*Go, go, go*!"

They drove as fast as they could with no lights, the others following.

Peter had stay with Ben and gave the report. "They are pulling in right now. The gas is burning quickly toward the fill pipes. The fire has reached the tanks. We made a split at the tanks to make sure all of them go up. We did both ends so the middle should go as well. All the spilled gas from the refueling operation is also burning. I can see many men with guns getting out of the trucks. They don't seem to care about the fires!"

Before Peter could say more, the tanks went up in two separate blasts that were so close together they seemed like one blast to most of the people close to it. A huge fireball filled the night sky, with many smaller blasts as cars still in the station started to blow from the intense heat.

"Peter, are you all right?"

"Yes, we drove without lights so as not to be seen."

"Okay, we will stop just over the top at Mountain Springs. We will wait for you to catch up. You will check our back trail while I will send Jake ahead to scout ahead as well. Also, we have some family business to take care of. Peter, how does our back trail look now?"

"No, nothing left to follow us. It's just one big inferno consuming everything near it. If Oliver did not leave after those trucks pass, he may not make it! As the light died down, I will be checking with the night vision."

"Okay, meet us just over the top of the hill."

The drive over the hump was quick, almost normal. If they look, all the cars and trucks were just sitting where they rolled to a stop. There were even a few people wandering around the side of the road. William had to speed up when the people tried to approach and stop them. Each time William had to decide to not stop and offer aid to them. It took a heavy toll on him. He was still learning to be hard! It was quite apparent that he was right. There were far too many people to help. Many still didn't understand what had and still was happing to the world.

Some of them didn't know why he brought the six strangers from the station. William had sent Jake to see what was ahead of them and had Lucy set a guard while they waited. A short time later, Ben and Peter rejoined the family. They redistributed the load in the cars and riders.

"This meeting of the family is to give tribute to Michael for his sacrifice and protecting Ben and the family at the gas station. May we always remember him with joy and pride. He has set the standard high for service to family.

"We also have six people that I have invited to join as part of our family. They are all here, and you will meet them as they take the oath. Before they do, I need to finish giving them the details of being part of our family. If you take the oath, you are forever part of the family. You may choose not to join, in which case we will part here. We will give you three days of food and water and you're free to go. However, if you take the oath, you are bound to us until death takes you. We will all stand by you. Anything in your past is forgiven and forgotten. As new members, you will be on parole until we tell you otherwise. While on parole, you can ask any question in council meetings. The only penalty for breaking the oath is death. You will be judged on the facts by the full council. Who is the council? Everyone over the age of thirteen, including the other parolees at the time. Who wants to take the oath and stay?"

They all took the oath. Jake made it back about halfway through Lucy giving the oath to the flight crew. William had made her master at arms, so she was busy when he returned.

Jake informed the family that the road was clear to the Spring Valley cutoff. "There is some sort of a blockage with lights. We would have to scout the area to find out what it is and get around it."

So for the second time in three hours, William sent scouts ahead to secure the flanks and check for any threats to the family. Six family members were sent to check the road, two pairs of three each, to cover the road before the family passed that part. Ben and Jake led the teams again. Peter and Al went with Ben while Lucy and Sherman worked with Jake. It took over an hour before the two teams reported on the roadblock. They had each taken one side of the road and worked their way unseen to a place where they could cover the men manning the roadblock. They reported that there were four men in police uniforms at the roadblock, which was made up of two polices cruisers. The men behind it were armed with shotguns and sidearms.

Ben and his team moved to the left side again while Jake took the right. Ben and his team moved quickly with no major problems. They did have to deal with a large number of coyotes as they made their way down the road. In just over one and a half hours, Ben checked in. They were in place with a clear view of their targets.

Jake's travel was a bit longer. For some reason, he had a much larger group of coyotes and other animals to deal with. This forced them to move farther out into the bushes. As they moved over the wire fence and deeper into the raw desert, some of the coyotes snapped and bit at them. At one point, Jake had to stop and back away, not wanting to shoot them with the crossbows, afraid they made too much noise and give them away. They moved forward and then started back toward the road. They came upon two large coyotes blocking their way. In the dim light, they could see a large ditch, and they could see cars and bodies with a large group of coyotes eating the bodies. It was very clear to Jake that they needed to deal with this problem to move past and get in position at the roadblock. They backed out and planned to deal with this problem. Jake set his plan to take out the two animals.

Lucy and Sherman set up from a place behind them. As he and Sherman loaded the crossbows, Lucy was scanning the area. (She had the best eyes.) Ben was giving his report, and Jake listened to it. He knew he only had about fifteen minutes to get into position. Just as William sent his acknowledgment, Lucy called Jake over very softly. She was looking away from the roadblock and the two coyotes. Back and almost straight in front of their position, she pointed at a dark spot just off the road. She gestured for him to look. He could not see anything. She now gave him back the night vision scope and had him look again. Jake, looking again, was slowly scanning the road and then saw it—a sniper's nest with shooter set to cover the roadblock. Jake started to radio William with the information but stopped. Both he and Ben had received orders to take out any threats they came across. Signaling for them to come closer, he whispered orders. He wanted them to get to a position behind the coyotes and still have cover positions on the roadblock. He was going to go out and around behind the sniper to a spot where he could take him out as well. When they were all in position, they would all fire as one. For the sniper, he was going for a headshot, so no outcry (he hoped). As soon as they all agreed, Jake started to move to a firing position behind the sniper. Moving slowly so as not to be seen or heard, it took him about ten minutes to find the right place. Checking that Lucy could see him, he took a long careful aim and gave the signal to start the count. At one, they would fire. They practiced the count five times before they split up.

Jake was about to give the signal when the sniper rose up and flashed a signal to the officer. One of them responded. Then as he settled back into his firing position, Jake gave the sign. He held his fist up and then held up three fingers. When he dropped one finger, they all stared their counts.

Here was the moment of greatest risk. He would yell out or make other noise they might hear at the roadblock. If the officers heard it, the whole group would be at risk. At the count of one, they all fired within a fraction of a second, and the two coyotes dropped. Jake had fired as well. Once he let the bolt fly from the crossbow, it took the sniper in the middle of his head. The only sound was his head hitting the ground. Lucy and Sherman came up to taking firing positions on either side of Jake. From the sniper's nest, they all had great views of the officers guarding the road. Jake made his report to William.

"William, there is more just as we were passing the cars. We came across a large ditch. It's filled with cars and dead bodies. Men women and children all shot in the head. We kept going, being more careful now. The dead were still bleeding. After clearing the pit, we found a fifth man about twenty to thirty feet behind the roadblock. He has made a sniper blind that gave him a clear view of all incoming traffic to the roadblock."

Looking back up the road, Jake could see a dip that could hide the cars from all the police at the roadblock. Jake moved around to the back of the sniper's position where he shot him with the crossbow. They then moved the bodies to the back of the blind. Lucy and Sherman took up guard positions, waiting for the rest of them.

Now they moved up, staying in single file to hide their numbers. Having set their plans to cover whatever they might find, now was when they would find out if it worked. Both teams had orders to eliminate any threats they found along the way. William had a two scout teams and two snipers with him that were to take up firing positions at the cars' stopping point just far enough back to not be seem. So they drove up to the top of the hill Jake told them about. The other cars all pulled to the sides, out of sight below the crest of the hill. William started to drive over the top of the hill. He had Donny and Steve take two of the hunting rifles and started down the hill on different sides of the road. Each found a good place with a clear view of the roadblock and took up positions to cover William as he drove up.

He drove up the roadblock, stopping about thirty yards away. As he stopped, they hit him with spotlights. Maria, who rode with him, returned the favor, turning their two lights on them as well. William mirrored their moves like in a chess opening when playing a new opponent till he knew the way things would go. William made sure everyone knew what to do. He placed the .357 pistols in the holster at the small of his back and got out, walking into the light. He stopped at about twenty-five yards range. When he stopped, one of the police officers asked him to move closer. He took two more steps and stopped.

"This is good for me, sir. Why are you blocking the highway?"

"Town is closed until the power is back. That should be done by morning. Crews are working on it now."

"Excellent. Now make room so we can pass. I've been sent to restore order. The West Coast is under martial law. Now if you have means of communications, call and tell whoever's in charge to prepare for my arrival." William started to return to his car.

"Sir, stop right there. We have no knowledge of this. You cannot pass."

"Okay, that's it. I want your name and badge number! You need to make that call now, or is it that there is no one at headquarters to give orders? You're just out here taking whatever you can get from whoever happens to come by here."

"What are you talking about?"

"The eight to ten dead people and their cars pushed off in that ditch about fifty feet behind you."

Three of the officers didn't even flinch at the mention of the ditch. The officer he was talking to seemed to turn green and was about to get sick.

"Officer, what's your name?"

"Tomkins, sir."

"You did not know about this?"

"No, sir."

"Tomkins, shut up. I'll handle this."

In a whisper, William spoke to the officer. "Officer Tomkins, if things go bad, just drop to the ground and do not move until you're told to get up."

"You do not give orders here. We do!"

"Oh, but I do give orders to my people. As a matter of fact, they have already been given orders, and what happens next depends on your next actions."

William was waiting for confirmation that both scout teams were in place and ready to go.

While he was talking to the new officer, Ben and Jake gave the all clear signal that they were ready. Ben and Jake each had to deal with large numbers of coyotes on their way to the roadblock. Jake's was a bit harder as they were eating the dead bodies left in the ditch. Jake, confronted by two very large coyotes, moved his team out and around them, getting there a bit longer than Ben. It did make it easier to get past the sniper they took care of. All pieces were now in place.

"So what's it going to be? A shootout and you try to kill us and die trying, or you could give up and live a bit longer."

"For one man, you talk mighty big."

"Oh, I see. You're counting on your hidden sniper to kill me. Sorry, he's dead, and you have six of my snipers behind you now!"

Two of the officer looked back while the other started to take aim.

"Tomkins, drop now!"

William brought the .357 up and fired once at the man talking to him while dropping and rolling to his left. By the time he had recovered from the recoil, it was over. Only Tomkins was still alive and laying on the ground.

Ben's and Jake's groups came up from the back, checking to make sure the others were dead. After a quick check that none of the family was hurt, they collected all the weapons and ammo they could find. They also took all the SWAT gear they could get. William and Jake took Officer Tomkins to the ditch to see what had been going on earlier in the day. The ditch had only bodies now. The gunfire ran the animals off for a while. He was sick when he saw the ditch and lost his lunch. When he was able to speak again, he told them he was worried about his family. William gave him the one working patrol car and his personal weapons and one shotgun.

"Go try to find them. Try texting. It may still work. Then get out of town. Take only those you can trust!"

Officer Tomkins cleared the road, and the family started the trip across Death Valley at last! The drive was only about two hours in normal conditions. These were not going to be anything normal. In a few last words to Tomkins, William hid clues in his memory on how to find them if they made it out of town.

William got them back in single file. With only the front SUV lights on, they started across Death Valley. He planned on stopping at Rainbow Canyon for the night. There was a large vista point with restrooms and good cover from both directions. It was a good place to camp and eat and sleep. The drive was to be slow and very dangerous for the family!

With full tanks of gas, they had no reason to stop before reaching the vista point. They were able to drive forty-five and had no problems on the road until they came to Furnace Creek Campground.

The drive to the inn at the creek was full of people and light. Lit by oil lamps and candles were the sources of the light at the hotel. While just up the road at the campgrounds, there was a lot of activity. There were campfires and camp lights everywhere. Here the road was a mess. Many cars stopped on the road with no real clear path to drive past it. William passed the word to keep windows up and guns ready. He planned to drive right on without stopping if they could. There was nothing to be gained by stopping. People kept coming up to the cars, trying to get them to stop. As word spread that they had driven in, more and more people kept filling the road. They had just cleared the 180-degree turn, pointing them to the north side of Death Valley. A group of over 150 people blocked the road.

They were all asking for news and help and when it would come. William kept moving forward. However, his speed kept falling due to the many people moving on to the road till they had to stop. The cars were just short of the visitor's center. One man that seemed to be leading the group to block the road stepped up and demanded to know who they were and where they were going. He also asked when the power would be back on. The group made it clear that they could not go any farther. William had Maria take over the driving, and he took his revolver and got out of the SUV, walking to the front of the car.

"Please let us pass. We are a family group going to stay with family in the east."

"Who are you and what's happening? We had no news all day. The phones are all out, and our cars are not working. How is it yours are?"

"Sorry, we can't help you. We have nothing we can afford to spare. You need to move and let us pass. We want no trouble here!"

"Well, you have it. We need cars and food and water. We are taking what we need, and that's all there is to it."

"What gives you the right to say what we can do? Please move out of the way or we will drive over you!"

"You wouldn't do that."

"Yes, we would and have driven over many dead bodies already today."

At these words, the man talking pulled a shotgun from beside his body and fired it into the air above him. As soon a William saw it, he pulled his pistol and fired once.

The man fell dead on the spot! At that point, a CHP officer stepped up to the front. He had his gun out.

"Sir, I'm only going to ask you once. Drop the gun!"

"Officer, I didn't ask for this, but he pulled a gun on me first, and I fired in self-defense. If you wish to do anything about it, I suggest you look at the other cars behind me."

Every window was open, just enough to point a gun out of it.

"We had to fight our way here and will fight our way out if needed. We will drive over anyone in our way. So if you wish to save lives, clear this road. Oh, and my name is William Waters. When things return to normal, you can come for me then. What's it going to be, a massacre or a real death race? Choose now! Start moving. On the count of three, shoot anyone trying to stop us and run over any in the road."

William had his gun trained on the officer and never looked away from him and started counting. "One, two, thr—"

The officer put his gun in its holster and started yelling, "*Clear the road! Clear the road if you value your life! Clear the road!* We will meet again, and you will answer for this night!"

"That I already knew, Officer. What's your name?"

"Officer Rydell. Jerry Rydell."

"Well, Jerry, I think you need to get these people to safety after we go check all the cars and trucks. I believe you find some of them are still working, then get all the gas you can get and find a safe place to go to. Vegas is not safe anymore!"

The people moved off enough now that Maria had started to drive, and William jumped in the passenger side. They were off again. In just a few hundred yards, they were back on the long straight road across Death Valley. They were back in line again and traveling to Rainbow Canyon vista point. The trip took about two to three hours from the campgrounds. When they arrived, they found three families that were stuck there.

William and Jake went to talk with them. Joy asked to come with them as well. As they approached, the people kept moving back. At first, they wondered why they were acting this way. Joy was fast to figure it out. "Guys, we are still dressed for battle. We are scaring them."

"Joy, you take the lead. You're smaller and would pose less of a treat to them."

Joy moved forward, and William and Jake fell back a step or two. She was now talking to them as she walked, trying to put them at ease. Her words and the lack of any place to go soon got them to stop and wait for them. They told them that they would be free to leave or stay in the morning after they had gone. Joy also told them that if they would like, they could share their food and water for the night. They had already started the cook fires and were making food for everyone in the vista point parking lot.

It was a large thin teardrop lot with restrooms at the front by the road, only one way in or out, where William had the cars block and put up guards on rotating shifts till morning. Jake and Joy ate with them, explaining the way things were. They also told them they could all use the restrooms, but not to try to leave before the family had left in the morning.

After the meal, Lucy went around to the other parents in the family and explained about the children they had found and wanting to do something to help them. So at the end of a very long hard day, they had their first family council meeting. Everyone over the age of thirteen was allowed a voice at the meeting. The rest of the kids were given chores to do to keep them busy, and two excluded themselves to take over the guard duties.

The idea was to take the children of these three families with them and save them from the death almost certainly waiting for them after they left in the morning.

"Okay, Joy, I know what's on your mind. Please tell the others what you're proposing!"

Joy stood and told the family about the four kids they met at dinner with the three families. Her and the other parents could not stand the idea of leaving them behind to die in this place. Joy's plan was to take the kids from their parents and bring them along with them when they left in the morning.

William then spoke, and even he did not like the sound of his words.

"If we are to put ourselves above the parents in this matter or the kids for that matter, we would be no better than the man I shot not more than three hours ago. We cannot take them from their parents because we know that if we do not bring them, they will most likely die in two days. There will be no forced separation of these families."

After another ten minutes, they came to the agreement that they would tell them everything that has happened and what they believed the event to have been.

After hearing all of it, they would be offered the choice of the kids coming with the family or staying together. The kids had to agree, same as the parents. So after they explained what has happening that day, one of the parents asked, "Okay, so what is it you're offering to us?"

Lucy took the lead again. "We are offering to take your kids with our family as you see us now."

"What, you want our kids?"

"Yes and no. We want to keep them safe! We can't take the adults. We hate the thought of what might happen to the kids if they go with you back to the cities."

William now spoke up. "If you believe what you learned here tonight or not, yesterday was the first day of Armageddon on earth. We were attacked, and we do not know by who or what at this time. Anything that was running at the time of the attack died all over the world as best we can tell. And they will never run again. That was 10:30 a.m. yesterday. Now it's every man for himself. Anything that was running stopped and will never work again.

"Maria and I woke early, as I had a bad dream which made a nightmare seem like a good thing. I saw a dark and terrible attack on the planet. I only saw what was about to happen in Las Vegas. Planes were falling out of the sky and no power of any kind. Cars, trucks, trains everything with a motor just stopped where they were or fell. Maria talked to me for over thirty minutes, trying to get me past the dream. The problem was, I had a dream like this years before. I had the dream just about one week before the 9/11 attacks. I saw three jets all sitting in a circle on a runway. Then the pavement broke apart and fell into darkness, taking the three jets down as well. I woke in a cold sweat. Just one week later, three jets hit targets on the East Coast. I never forgot that dream. This one was stronger, and I knew it was going to happen. This one just showed everything going dark. Still not able to shake the fleeing, I called my oldest and told her to call all the family and warn them. I told her I would call back soon and hung up. Later, while checking on her, it happens the power went out. We lost the call; for some reason we could still text. I told her this was it. Everything was going dark. I told her to start getting ready to leave. We were all to meet at a small strip mall on the south side of town. Since that time, we have been in three gun battles with gang members and rogue police officers. We lost one of our own to this violence. Try to find a car that was not running at the time of the event. It should still run. We have a length of hose for you. When you find cars, check for gas in the tanks and use the hose to siphon the gas out of them. Beware of strangers. Do not trust them. This is how things stand at this point. We are going back to sleep. We will have an armed guard out all night so you can sleep in peace. Just do not come near our camp. Think over our offer. We will talk in the morning. You all need to sleep on this and talk with your children and decide what you all would like to do."

They all went to their beds. Most slept at once A few wondered at what had happened that day and what was to come after such a day.

CHAPTER 6

Oliver at Nellis Air Force Base

After receiving all the gas he could safely carry, he started for Nellis Air Force Base some forty-five miles away. He was told to sit on the far side of the jet and wait for the station to blow up then drive as far as he could without lights. He was soon to find there were no safe roads to his destination. His drive down Blue Diamond was soon at risk. Lucky for Oliver, he was on guard for trouble now. He was driving slow with only parking lights to guide him around the many obstacles in his way. He passed burning cars, crashed planes, and just wild sage brushfires. And in places, there was dense black smoke. The air was full of the worst smelling smoke and eye-burning air from the cooking bodies of all the dead everywhere. He was starting to understand some of things William talked about. The wild panic that should have taken days to start was well into every man for himself with widespread violence all over the city. He had made many trips to Las Vegas, and the lights were always the most beautiful of any city he had seen. Now what he saw convinced him this would be his last trip to Vegas, as it was now lit only by raging fires of a damned city!

He was almost to the freeway interchange, moving slowly when he saw lights heading his way. They were moving too fast to be anything good as they passed many people that were in need of assistance. Oliver quickly found a large truck that was still burning and took up a place behind it. Turning the car off and going dark, he waited for the cars to pass. He didn't have long to wait as the seven heavily armed trucks sped past at the fastest speeds they could go. With crash bars mounted front and back, they just rammed cars off the road. Some of these cars still had people in them! Soon they were all out of sight. He restarted his car and started off again. With the morning came the awareness that what had happened yesterday was no normal event. Fires still raged all over the valley, not just in the city. Nothing was working. Things that should work in such a situation did not. The emergency broadcasting system did not function. The police had some radio communications, but it was not reliable. Looting had started as dark fell. The gangs knew there would be no police response to calls if any could be made. That was what William had run into at the gas station, a gang trying to take over the station.

Oliver soon reached the I-15 freeway, only to find it packed with cars and many people! As he drove to the bottom of the ramp, he saw hundreds of people getting out of their cars and start toward him. Oliver heard William's words again: "You can't help them all. They will turn and take what you have." He put the car in reverse to back out. Sadly, the exit was filling with people almost as fast as the freeway was! He only had minutes to get away. He took the gun William had given him and pointed it out the window at the people behind him and fired it twice over their heads. At the same time, he was accelerating in reverse as fast as he dared. It was a terrible sight and sounds, and it would take Oliver a long time to find peace with his actions. There were the screams and sounds of bodies bouncing off the car that failed to get out of the way as it raced down the ramp. All of them were just desperate for any kind of hope or help after the long day just passed. He managed to get off the freeway and soon lost the people trying to follow him. He was still at least three miles from the end of the strip. He had a long day of driving. Without the freeway, it would be harder to find passable streets to get him to Nellis. He decided to stay out of the downtown area as well, keeping to side streets wherever he could.

Hearing a noise from behind him, he looked back to see the people were still trying to catch up with him. He drove off as fast as conditions allowed. It was the same all morning—long crash sites, dead cars, and nothing working. People were wandering all over the city as there was no place to go. Luckily, he did not have to kill anyone the rest of the day. It was just before noon when he caught sight of the air base! He could see large groups of people all around the base's main gate. When he got a bit closer, he could see armed guards manning barricades at the gates. He needed a plan to get past the gate safely. Remembering what William had said about the texts still working on many phones, he found General Custer's private number and sent him a text, telling him he was nearby. He had to wait nearly twenty minutes before he got a response, asking for proof of identity. Having come to these meeting many times, he had some personal knowledge of the general's life. His dog's name was Xenia, an eighty-pound German shepherd. The response was instant. "Where are you, and what do you need from us?"

He told them he had a car that was still working and was just outside the main gate. They directed him to a small side gate just down the road, and it would be open in five minutes. He asked if he could he make that. He said, "Yes, I'm on my way. The car is blue four-door. Don't shoot me please."

Nellis Air Force Base, day 2 of the event.

The commanding general was Patrick F. Custer, a four-star general of twenty-two years. He was first in his class at Air Force Academy. He had been the commanding general at Nellis for the last six years. He was on the fast track for the fifth star and the next joint chief of staff at the Pentagon.

The last day had shaken him and his command badly. The day started out as a heavy training day with over half of the base's aircraft in the air, running combat exercises over the training areas. In less than two minutes, he had lost half of his aircrafts in the air and another 25 percent that was on the tarmac, getting ready for takeoff or having just landed and taxiing to hangars.

On top of all that, the locals started coming to the base as soon as they realized something much bigger than a power outage was happening. Many thought the base caused the event. They manned the gates with armed guards. There had already been a few violent attacks at the gate. Nothing too bad yet, but it was coming soon, and the general knew it. He closed the base and sent armed escorts to get off duty and family members to the base. This was how Oliver found the base after gaining entrance at the side gate.

"Hello, Ollie. I am so relived you made it. We were worried that you may have some problems getting here. As you can see, we have quite a few of our own to deal with. Soon the barricades will not hold them. We may need to fire on them! Do you have any clue as to what happened yesterday?"

"Personally, no. However, I was helped by a man that I believe has the event, as he calls it, clear in his mind."

"Really? Where is he? I would like to talk to him."

"Sorry, General. He's taken his family out of Nevada. Someplace they can be safe from the very thing you have at your gate right now. Will you use force on the civilians you swore an oath to protect?"

"God, I hope it does not come to that."

"Well, his theory is that the event is the end of our world as we know it! He thinks of everyone staying in cities as already dead. He survived three gun battles that I know of yesterday alone. I am not sure where he is going. I do think he is one to make it if any of us do!"

"Well, did you get a name at least?"

"Oh, yes. He gave me all the information I asked for short of where he is going. William H. Waters, lived on the southwest side of town. Wherever he is going, it's in California. I did see a great deal of maps in the cars, which I can no longer see clearly other than California."

"Cars? How big was his party, and where did he get working cars?"

"He had six SUVs and eight to twelve adults and a number of kids in the group. They are well organized and led by William. Pat, before we go on, you need to do a few things. Get some people from motor pool and crew chiefs in here right now!"

"Okay, Sergeant. Get the people he asks for here ASAP. It's good to know that there are a few good groups that are getting out. He was right, you know. The people that stay and wait for the power to come back are probably all going to die and do not know it!"

"Really, you agree with him?"

"Yes."

At that moment, the sergeant returned with the personnel asked for.

"Sir, the personnel you asked for, sir."

"Thank you, Sergeant. Dismissed. Gentlemen, this is Oliver. He wants to give us some information to help us, I believe."

"Thank you, General. Guys, I made it here in my car, which I believe someone has already commandeered. I will need it back and right now. Send word please. No questions until I am done, please, as time is not our friend. What's working around here?"

Both answered, "Nothing, sir."

"That is not quite true. You're wondering why my car works, and a few others you see driving around the city, correct?"

"Yes, sir."

"Everything that was not running or on at the time of the event should still be in working order. Anything that was running is dead forever. Get teams out and check every car and truck and aircraft on the base. Find what's still good. You're going to need it all. Find a place that is secure and move all of the working cars and other items to a place you can keep them safe."

"What about gas? We can't pump anymore."

"William gave me something. It's in the car. When its returned, I will show you how it works."

The general gave orders, and the two men ran out of the office to get started. Oliver looked at the general and asked another question. "Why can't you help them?"

"It can only be attempted at the risk of my own people, and like him, I won't waste what little resources I have on dead people. Wish I could meet him someday."

"You may get a chance if you survive as well. Now I have to see the visitors please."

"Yes, we know they came to the conference room door and let themselves in and are waiting for you. Somehow. they got the doors to open after the event."

"Really?"

"Yes, they told us you would arrive today."

"That's somehow not a surprise, is it?"

"No, not really. I think that they could have left here at any time they wished to. What are your plans after the meeting?"

"I plan to drive back to Cheyenne Mountain with whatever information I can, where I hope they are working on plans to recover from this."

"Sounds good. Come back after you're done. I have a favor to ask of you."

"Okay. See you when I am done."

CHAPTER 7

The Visitors

For over fifty-three years, the United States has been holding three very special visitors. Two arrived in New Mexico. The other was found wandering around in the forest outside a US Air Force base in England. All were brought to a secret base now known as Area 51. The two from New Mexico were friendly and talked with them whenever they wanted. The other was hostile and was constantly fighting them, always trying to escape. When they asked the two about them keeping them against their will, they put the matter aside as if it was nothing. The other would not talk to them and was always trying to find ways to escape. The dark one would have made its escape many times if not for the other two. They called for a meeting and exposed the attempts to the general and his staff. They also asked for one thing since they had been there: a constant bright light in their holding area. They also told them to put lights on the dark one's area as well.

Other than these communications, they were only given two requests to meet with them. The last was received at the highest levels of the Pentagon two day ago. It was clear and simple: "Please send agent to meet. Do not use air travel. Come quickly." Oliver had been placed on the team a few years ago and had made at least eight trips to question them. This was only the second time they had asked for a meeting in the fifty-three years they had been in their custody. Oliver had been working a very important project and was told to drop it and drive to the base. Oliver's security level kept him off commercial airlines. He had to fly military or drive everywhere. He was already in the southwest and started the drive to Nellis.

Something he had been thinking about since getting to the base was that the request of no flying to the meeting. It probably saved his life!

The visitors were quite humanoid in appearance. They had hands and feet and smaller in bulk but taller and very thin. The dark visitor had six digits on hands and feet. The sixth was some kind of claw with a very sharp edge. They were harder than steel. This one stayed in the darkest places, avoiding the light wherever it could. It was almost impossible to see in shadows. When the visitor was first placed in the room, a number of soldiers were killed when because they could not see the visitor. So they sedated it and installed bright floodlights in his cell. They also put them in the other cell as well.

The other two were totally different. They had the same height and general appearance. They did not have the claw. They liked the light and were always willing to talk. The general told Oliver that after the event, they grew very agitated, as if they knew what had happened. The area of the base the visitors were being held had triple level security as well as power and manual locking systems. The first level was early 1900s, much the same as the type of locks used on Alcatraz. The visitors were under constant observation by remote video cameras as well as humans in overhead catwalks behind one-way glass. As soon as possible, the general had engineering working on getting into the holding area and secure the visitors, as well as make any adjustments necessary to maintain security until the power came back on. When the team reached the doors, they found the two visitors waiting for them in the conference room. The engineers told them they had to break the locks so they could get in the room. The visitors spoke to them, giving them a suggestion. They spoke strangely. Each would speak a part of any sentence they spoke.

"If you just input the code," said one.

"We could open the door from there," said the other.

Both at once said, "Side."

So they tried it, and as told, they just pushed the door open, went in, and waited for Oliver to arrive. They went to the place with the most light, which was the center of the room. In the early years, the lights would be turned off at night. This really bothered them, so they would escape the holding cells and go to the nearest light source and wait for morning. When found, they would go back to the cells. They never tried to leave; they just went to a light source. Soon the officials in charge left the lights on at all times, and they stayed in the cells.

So that was where Oliver found them, in the center under the brightest light in the room, waiting for him. He found the doors open as he was told. As he walked in, they turned and came to the table. They greeted him in their two-for-one style.

"Welcome, Oliver. It pleases us that you made it to our meeting."

Oliver was used to these talks to be slow with lots of long delays while they came to an agreement. Today there was no delays. They had things to say!

"I am glad I made it. Things are very bad out there."

"Yes, they are. Oliver, this will be our last meeting here! If we are to meet again, we cannot see it at this time. There is something different about you at this time."

"Yes, I had a very hard time yesterday. If not for one man, I may not have gotten here at all."

They both stood and looked at Oliver. They asked a single question: "Oliver, did you meet the one?"

"Excuse me, I do not understand."

"Oliver, there is no time now. However, if you can find him again, he will need your help in the months ahead."

"What do you mean? What help can I give him? He asked me to stay with him. I had to come here, so he helped me to get here."

"Sorry, we have no time to explain, and it would put you in great danger! We have three items for you. The attack was bigger than most people thought! They are on their way. We do not know when they will arrive. They have more dark agents here that will try to get the people of earth to destroy themselves."

"Who are you talking about?"

"They are the dark ones, like the one you had here yesterday. He will need to be found and dealt with if mankind is to have a chance. Also, there are more than the two here in the southwest. We are not sure how many there will be. We were going to form a link with you so we can talk from wherever we are. However, we now see the mark of the one is on you, and there is no need to form the link he has done so, and we hope to keep apart from him until the right time. We will send all needed information he needs to you, Oliver. Find him again. Oliver, we hope to see you again. Please tell the general we enjoyed our time here, and goodbye."

With their last word, they moved back inside the cell area and were gone from sight. That was the last time they were seen in Nevada.

Oliver got back to the general and gave his report. Just as he finished, a runner came with confirmation that all three of the visitors had left the base.

The general then told Oliver the favor he wished from him. After the information Oliver had given them, they had been busy and had cars and trucks working now, and sitting next to his car were two other cars. The general told him they were discharged airmen who wished to go east to their families and homes. The first was Master Sargent Bill Vargas and, Ellie, his wife. They had two children, Sally (sixteen) and Frank (thirteen). The next car held three airmen, all E-fives: West Brown (twenty-six), Trance Lee (twenty-four), and Zack Jones (twenty-three). All members of the ground crew all had no family at the base. They all wanted to go east to try to find their families. By this time, the general had given orders to move to the Indian Wells air base until such time as some order was restored.

Oliver took this time to inform the men coming with him what to except and what he had to do just to reach the base last night. He told them of everything that had happened since leaving the gas station. It seemed that some kind of madness had taken the people in the city. Oliver again heard the visitor's words about the dark one and how he would need to be stopped. The men had a few questions, and once they were answered, Oliver showed what the general had given them for the trip ahead.

Each car had one jerrican filled with gas, as much food and water as they could carry, and an assortment of guns and ammo for each. Oliver told them they would be going to Cheyenne Mountain, where the last members of the government were. The master sergeant (Bill) had another question.

"How do you plan on getting gas after the cans are empty?"

"Well, Bill, I met a man on the edge of town yesterday that saved my life and told me what I would have to endure just to reach the base. He had it all right. I'm sorry to say, he also gave me a spare bilge pump and showed me how to use it." The men all laughed at the same time until Oliver explained how it worked. They now knew that every gas station they passed was a fuel depo for them. The harder part would be getting food and water from that day on. Due to the size and type of trucks, they made Indian Wells in just over two hours. After a few last words with the general, they started off for Cheyenne Mountain. There were few people left out this far, and so Oliver's trip was much faster than he had hoped for.

CHAPTER 8

Leaving Death Valley

William set up two-hour watches with him and Sherman taking the last to be sure that they got an early start. The night passed without problems or surprises. He took the full two hours before starting to wake the rest. They needed the sleep as he believed today was going to be harder than the first. After one day of no help and no news of any kind, people would be start to panic, making them more dangerous than before. He did not think they would see as many people today. He did believe the ones they did encounter would be more of a danger to the family. As he started waking the family, he had them start making food for everyone, even the others as the family started to move about. The others also started moving about as well. William and Lucy went over to tell them that they could have food with them as soon as the food was ready.

And after that, they would be on their way.

Ben and Jake made sure all the cars had full gas tanks, topping off all of them. They even filled the one car of the others in the vista point. They also got them a length of hose to syphon gas from cars they found along their way. They would need to find some ways to carry the extra gas. After the meal was done and all were ready to leave, Lucy asked if they had made a decision about the kids. They were thankful for the offer and said that they could not just drive off and leave them with strangers. They would keep them and move on toward home. At this point, William stepped up and told them that if they found home was no longer safe and they could make, they should come back this way to California.

"You are the kind of people we want in our family."

He then gave them some strange advice and sent them on their way.

Soon after, William had the family on the road again. All were still a bit in shock over the events of the last thirty-six hours. With only a few exceptions other than Maria, himself, Ben, Peter, Lucy, and Jake, all seemed calm and at peace. Noting the difference, William took them aside to talk about their feelings. He just let them each talk about the day and how they felt. The stories were all very similar to his own, in that they hated the need for killing. None held guilt from the battles of yesterday or for not trying to help all the people they came in contact with on the way. All of them held similar views to Maria and him. So he asked them about their dreams as well as tell them of his sleeping and the waking dream and about how he knew what they needed to do to survive. They all had strong dreams last night, but none had waking dreams. He set a time after dinner for all of them to sit and talk.

The drive out of Death Valley was relatively clear with only a few places where they had to move cars off the road. In a few places, they had to slow and shoot out the windows to get the people to run for cover as they drove by. They should make highway junction in just over twenty minutes. Due to the ease of the drive, William widened the distance between the cars as they drove. This was done to ease a feeling that was growing as they neared the 395 Junction.

There was another roadblock, this one manned by military personnel. Sitting about a quarter of a mile from the junction was a large truck with a fifty-caliber machine gun mounted on it. Stopping the lead SUV with a distance of at least one half mile, William gave hand signals for the scouts to go take a look. Same as always, right and left, Ben and Jake plus two. Standing orders now, crossbows and rifles only if needed. For this stop, he got the two best shots to come up and give sniper cover for the scouts if needed and to cover him when he went down to the meeting after the scouts reported in.

He stopped the lead car just at the top of the hill when he saw the roadblock at the base of the small valley the two hills made in the road. He stopped in clear view of the troops below him. He and Sherman made a show of checking the car. They raised the hood, looked at it, then walked around it. They even made a show of adding water. They kept any watchful eyes on them while the scouting parties got up to the top of the hill and started the trip down the sides of the road. They needed to move farther out to find adequate cover. It was still midmorning with very clear blue skies and almost no wind of any kind. Even in desert camos, they would need to be extra careful. They had all learned at the gas station that the unexpected could kill. So both teams moved one hundred yards off the road before starting over the top of the hill. By the time they got into position, it was almost noon, and the sun was just moving to its zenith. This would keep their shadows very small and would be less of a problem to them. Meanwhile, on top of the hill, they kept walking around the car back and forth, trying to look as if they were doing something to the engine. The two snipers had taken fifteen minutes to set up their blinds at the top of the hill to both sides of the lead SUV. The rest of the family had moved all the kids to a single SUV, and the rest prepared for battle again. When they were ready, they all moved up close behind the lead SUV. Now they had the snipers tracking the soldiers they could see in their scoops.

It was a perfect early spring day with light winds, just after a heavy winter storm season. This brought larger sage brush due to the larger than normal water from heavy rains. This also set off an eleven-year bloom of wildflowers, mixing reds, blues, white, yellow, and orange wildflowers in the thousands all over the hills. All were giving the scout teams more cover to move with. So while the show around the car was going on, the teams kept moving toward the target.

Jake's team was first to report on their position and what they found! They made such good time to the target because of wide and deep dry wash. This gave him cover and a good viewpoint. As they drew near, they heard voices just up ahead near the road. Using hand signals, Jake had the team move behind the source of the noise, and with the other two giving him cover, he slowly moved up the far side of the wash. He found four men laying in sniper blinds all with clear views of the roadblock, giving cover to the soldiers there. Jake slowly pulled back, and then they moved away to talk over what to do here.

They had a problem. They had three against four, and if he was right, Ben was going to find another four on his side of the road as well. Jake asked if anyone had thoughts on how to take the four men without giving away their presence to the others at the truck.

Lucy and Steven wanted to wait until everyone was in place and use the guns to decrease the chance of one of them getting shot or worse. Jake had orders to keep things quiet at all cost. He called in the report to William, asking for guidance in this matter.

On the other side of the road, Ben had far less cover and had to move out even deeper in the bush twice. As he heard Jake's report, he passed the word on what to look for. They found the four men. They were farther off the road. Then he saw the men Jake had found. Without his warning, they would have walked right in front of them. They now stopped and took a careful look at this firing position and how the men were armed. They had full auto assault rifles, and each one had an RPG (rocket propelled grenade) loaded and ready. Ben found a good place behind and set Peter and Al in good firing positions. He then reported back to William as well.

William wanted them to take the two sniper nests out at the same time. He also did not want to use the walkie-talkies anymore. He had Sherman keep the car ruse going as he sat in the car and cleared his mind. He focused on Ben and Jake. When he could see them clearly, he just started talking to them in his head. It took about a minute before they heard him.

It's all right. Do you both hear me clearly? Do not speak. Just think your answers please.

They thought how this was happening, and he heard them.

I will take that as a yes. Okay, this is what we are going to talk about tonight, but as you know, we have need for fast communication now. We need to take out the snipers and make no noise at all. Do you have any idea how this can be done?

Both Jake and Ben, still a bit in shock, had known something was different about William since the event, and now it was clear he had abilities they did not.

Jake answered, *We wanted to use the guns when all of us were in position. The fourth man is a problem on each side of the road! To be silent, we need to use the crossbows, leaving us one shot short! How do we get the extra shot without them sounding the alarm?*

Ben spoke up, *While we had been watching them, we saw each of them get up and stretch then go back to their places in the blind. If we can wait for the next cycle of breaks, we can take them at that time. When the last one gets up, we take them first then the other three all at once.*

Sounds good. What do you think, Jake?

Sounds like our only chance to do this and not give our position away.

Okay, Ben, Jake, take up your positions, and I will keep the link open between us until this is over. Let me know when you're in place.

Both replied in the positive and moved to take up their places.

Ben and Jake explained as best they could about the plan. In just minutes, they were all in place, waiting for the opening to take the snipers out. As soon as they killed them, William planned to drive up to the roadblock and confront the soldiers there.

They planned to take the last one in the line to take his time off the line. After the others all went back in place in their line, Ben and Jake would take the man standing. Then as soon as they reload, they would take the remaining three at the same time.

They only had to wait three to four minutes, and they all started to rotate the line. Each had five minutes then return to the line.

By the time the last man got up, it had been almost two full hours since they started their walk down the hill.

William had them get ready, seeing everything they saw. He gave them the green light to move ahead on their own from this point on. Ben and Jake both reported they were ready.

As the third man got down in his place, they both took aim and waited for the man to move far enough away from the others. Jake's man walked straight toward him with his head down. He stopped about fifteen feet in front of Jake and looked up to see the bolt from the crossbow coming straight toward him. He hit the ground dead. Jake quickly reloaded, and he took aim at his second target. As soon as he indicated he was ready, Lucy and Steven nodded they were ready. Again, Jake held three fingers up and dropped one. They started their count, and when they reached one, all fired. The three never knew what happened. They died in the blinds with no noise to warn the soldiers at the blockade.

Ben's position was not as close and so he had an easier time for the shots and not have to worry about being seen. While the other man was getting back down, the last man walked to the back edge and relived himself against a large rock. He never finished this act. Ben's bolt took him right through the heart. He fell dead on the rock. He reloaded, and they took out the other team just minutes after Jake. William had Sherman start the car and drive him down the hill to a place they had agreed on. The two snipers on the hill were in place and ready to shoot if the need arose.

"Sir, the car's moving again, coming right to us."

"Okay, signal the cover teams to be ready when we give the sign."

Now the two men waited for the arrival of the SUV. As it got closer, the soldier took his place behind the big fifty-caliber machine gun mounted on the truck. He cocked it, ready to fire. He just made number one on the hit parade for the two shooters on the hill.

It took less than two minutes to reach the agreed upon stopping place, just a bit above the position of the truck so as to have a better view than being a bit lower and much closer if they drove the whole distance.

Sherman stopped the truck, leaving about fifty yards from the truck. They could see that the gunner on the fifty cal was ready to fire. William and Sherman got out of the car and walked a bit closer and in front of their SUV, giving their shooters a clear view of the truck.

William then addressed the two men. "Hello, who's in charge here? Your rank is all I need. Your name is not important to us at this time. You need to get on your radio or whatever you have working and call in to who's in charge. They need to know that the military governor is here!"

"You don't give orders here, asshole."

He shouted and ordered, and eight more men came out of the truck, taking up firing positions on them.

"Sir, you have to the count of three to make that call. Do you understand?"

All the time William was talking, his radio was open, so the rest of the family was ready if he called for them. Maria knew what he wanted from them.

"Okay, we will do this the hard way. On the count of three, we will kill all of you if you do not drop your weapons. *One, two, three.*"

All anyone heard was one shot, and every single soldier dropped dead. The look of surprise and shock on the officer's face was something William would not soon forget. The hole in the man's chest came from his .357 pistol.

At this time, a response came back to their call, and help was on the way. Another truck was on its way and should be there in fifteen minutes or less.

All the scouts came in. Peter was first to speak. "Well, what now?"

"Now we reverse the roadblock and set up for the next bunch. We have less than fifteen minutes before they get here. I need two fighters to go back over the hill with the children. The rest of us will set up here."

Joy and Donny took the children under twelve back over the hill and out of sight of the roadblock.

"Ben, you and Jake go up the road and take cover before they arrive. Call as soon as you see them. Get as much intel as you can without being seen. Peter, you stay with me please. You have my back, understood? Lucy, you're in charge of the rest. I want to have them in the box when we start talking, okay?"

Everyone replied and started the work. Lucy's first job was to get four teams to take the RPGs to new firing positions and make sure they knew how to fire them. Two on each side of the road and hopefully two in front and the other two at the rear. The teams were instructed to move if safe to get in the right positions.

"We will not know what we're facing until Ben and Jake, report back. Daniel, I want you to man the fifty cal I need a good steady hand on it. All of you, remember, we want the second truck and weapons. Remember as always, family safety first. If they fire or start any offensive action, open fire at once. Does everyone understand?"

With acknowledgments from all, they moved into their positions and seemed to disappear into the landscape.

They did not have long to wait. With the new link with Ben and Jake, William got the news. There was one truck and three officers in the front, one driving. The back was covered by a canvas top. Ben reported that the bed was full of troops but could not get a count. Should be at least thirty more soldiers inside.

"You should see them top the hill anytime now." William gave the order to trail them back at best speed they could make.

After topping the hill and seeing the new position of the truck, Captain Bryce gave the order to stop for just a minute. Then he started to drive down to the roadblock. He had his three snipers get out and start moving to find good firing positions to cover them. Without any further communication from his team for the last twenty-five minutes, they knew something was very wrong when they saw the truck pointed the wrong direction.

"Lieutenant Briggs, get the men ready for action. We will be retaking that truck and the fifty. Make your plan, and be ready when we get there. Then move as soon as we stop."

"Yes, sir."

Speaking through the rear cabin window, he gave orders to the men.

"Okay, you men listen up. Split up both sides. As soon as we stop, fall out in battle formation. Be ready for action against the fifty cal from the other truck. Everyone, lock and load. We have less than three minutes. Now move it."

The soldiers started getting ready for action. Back in the cab, the radio came to life. It was William making first contact. Things started to move a bit faster now as the distance was closing fast. As the truck came up the road, William wanted to be ahead of whatever planned action they had in mind.

"Hello, commander of the truck. Come in, over."

"Who is this, and where are my men?"

"My name is Commander William H. Waters. I have been assigned by the remaining government officials in Cheyenne Mountain CO. You are to drive up and stop twenty feet from the roadblock. If you have troops in the back, you need to keep them there. Any movement or aggregative action will be met with overwhelming force! Now give me your name and rank, sir."

"I am Captain Bryce, and I do not recognize your right to give me or my men orders. It is you, sir, and your men that will step out into the open and lay down your weapons."

"No, Captain, we will not! It is you who does not fully understand the situation you are in. You don't have the man power to make us. You did know what weapons they had up here, don't you? Just so we are sure, let me remind you. We have twelve RPG rockets with four launchers, one truck with a fifty cal mounted on the roof with what looks like five thousand rounds of ammo, eight M16s, along with six laws rockets. By the way, all four launchers are aimed at the truck as we speak. Now how many men do you have in the truck?"

"I do not believe you. You cannot just kill men in cold blood."

"Well, in the last thirty-six hours, we have been in three battles and have killed over twenty men. That's not counting the men you had manning this truck!"

At this point, the truck started slowing down.

"Okay, when the truck stops, if anyone tries to get out of the truck beside you three in the front, my men will fire the RPGs. Is that clear?"

"Yes. Briggs, tell the men to stand ready but not to get out until the shooting starts. Now we will get out and move to the front of the truck. We need to buy the snipers time to get in position. Understood?"

"Yes, sir" was given by both men.

"Sergeant, you heard the situation. When the snipers open fire, get the men out and in action ASAP. Understood?"

"Yes, sir, will do."

Lieutenant Briggs then fallowed the captain and Lieutenant Wilson to the front of the truck.

Peter stepped out in front of the other to better cover them.

"Stop right there. Make no fast move or reach for your weapons."

William then took over again. "Well now, Captain, I believe your plans are a mess. You should know by now things are not as you expect them to be. Nor are you sure who has the upper hand. Let me assure you, we do. Yes, you have more men. However, if you or any of them try anything, my men have orders to blow you all to hell with the RPGs. And if you have not seen him as of yet, I have a man on the fifty ready to fire as well."

"I still do not believe you."

William was aware that the captain was lying to him when he said it. His thoughts went to three men that were not in the truck.

"That's okay. Not sure I would either if I was in your place." He used the link to Ben and Jake and informed them to hunt the three men down. He had to keep them in the link so they knew what he knew. "Be that as it may, we are going to talk and ask questions. I will go first. I will tell the truth, and you will lie. You may want to think twice about that, as I will know when you do. First question. How many men do you have in the truck?"

"We have thirty in the back." It was a lie William knew. "We were just getting a look at the setup you have down here."

William had been able to tell lies from the truth ever since the dream before the event, and it just kept getting stronger. He had not seen the men leave the truck, but with the power of hearing, the lie was overwhelming, so he was going to force the next answer to see what information he could get.

"So now your question."

"Fine. How many men do you have in the field?"

"Nine, not counting me. All with orders in hand to kill all of you at the first sign of danger."

"That's a lie. If you have only nine, you can't have us cover the way you said."

"No, it's not. It's the truth. I have only nine men out there, and you are covered, as I said. But it's my question now, not yours. Did you know about the killing here?"

"No, of course not. We came in answer to the call for backup."

"I see. You're just here to help with the problem. Your next question please."

"Your story of being the military governor is a lie on your part?"

"Yes, it is. The sole purpose was to get you out here so we could talk and take care of our business with as little bloodshed as we could."

"I knew it. Okay, you're going to put your weapons down and all of your men will come out in the open!"

"Sorry, we can't do that yet. I have one more question for you. While you think about your answer, I wish to talk with Lieutenant Wilson, okay? Here's your question. How many more have to die before we can get going again? We need to be places by dark tonight. I will need your answer when I am done talking to Wilson." Then he turned to Wilson and asked him a question as well. "Mr. Wilson, are you going to carry out the captain's orders after he's dead, in light of all you heard? Think quickly as time is running. Okay, Captain, what's you answer?"

"That's easy. All of you, including the others you talked about. For us to survive, we feed off all the travelers that try to pass this way. Now my last question. Why do you think you're going to win this standoff?"

"Oh, Captain, it was won when you picked up the mike and we started talking and listened close. There are three things I need to clear up. When I ask you how many troops you had in the truck, you lied. You let three snippers out at the top of the hill. My people have found all of them. They are going to die with you now." *Bang.* Just one very loud shot was heard all over the valley. The captain dropped dead where he stood. He hit the ground dead, one shot in the heart. Lieutenant Wilson just stared at the body and was startled when William told him to get Briggs up here as well. He had been hanging back by the truck. Also to make sure the soldiers stayed in the truck. In a very short time, he joined them at the front of the trucks.

"Now, Lieutenant Wilson, you know the question I have put to you. I am going to repeat it for Briggs here. How many more men need to die before we can resolve this situation? While you work on your answer, I will talk to Mr. Briggs. As you can see, the captain did not get the right answer. And just so you both understand what your true position is, I have a few facts for you. Lieutenant Briggs, you sent three snippers out back at the top of the hill. They are all dead now, along with the captain when he got the wrong answer. Their names where Randel Jones and Wesler. Both men told the truth of the names. Mr. Briggs, I believe you have radio coms with your men. Please call them. Check what I am saying is true."

Briggs turned on the radio and called the team. He got a reply from a stranger.

"Yes, what can I do for you, Briggs?" a stranger's voice answered.

"How do you know my name?"

"I read it off your uniform as you exited the truck, and I have this fine scope to read it with now. If it helps you, your team picked excellent firing positions from here. I have you in my scope even now."

William spoke up again. "So, Mr. Wilson, have you come up with an answer for me?"

"Can I have a minute to speak with Lieutenant Briggs please?"

"Yes, you can have three."

"Thank you."

Stepping back, they spoke for about one and a half minutes.

"All right, William, your answer is zero!"

"Very good. So here's what happens next. You will give your troops the order to stand down. They are to exit the truck only after stripping naked, leaving all weapons behind. You will both take your weapons off now as well." In a very short time, they had dealt with the troops.

During this time, the rest of the family came up and began loading the trucks with their excess gear from the cars, making everyone more at ease in the mode of travel. All the kids wanted to ride in the trucks, so they were allowed to do so. They left only five assault guns and ten handguns with the troopers and were soon on their way again. With a truck in front and the other in back, each with fifty cals and over five thousand rounds each, they were about to start for US 395 just a short distance away now. William had a feeling they would have to deal with the people he was leaving behind again.

CHAPTER 9

Lone Pine, California

Now with the larger army trucks, William wanted to go shopping again to get the extra things they would need in the coming year! Up to this point, William was only working on one year at a time. They would need the first year to stabilize the family in their new home, as well as living conditions from two hundred years in their past mixed with whatever they could save. They were going to have to learn to be farmers and cattleman to survive. They all would have to learn to be better warriors if they were to survive as well. Each of the members of the family would need to relearn a lot of old trade skills, like shoemaking, sewing, grinding grains to make bread, building stone ovens, cooking with wood, etc.

So with Maria driving, he got out the three shopping lists and started going over them for things. They had done well in Vegas, but they needed a lot of other things that were not available in the Big 5 or the Smiths store. List one was food, two was defense and hunting, and last was home and wardrobe for everyone in all seasons.

The list would be worked on in the order they found warehouses with the right inventories in them. They needed some local help, willing or otherwise.

In their dreams, Maria and William had seen many battles to come. The only thing they had in common was they were always outnumbered three to one or bigger. Their stories told of their escape from Las Vegas by the store clerks, the two policemen and the families at rainbow cyn were growing with each retelling.

William got on the walkie-talkie to all cars, telling them that they would be shopping again for things they still needed to get by this winter. When they found the places to shop, they would only take large bulk quantities of each. With the trucks, they could carry a lot more. The same rules applied—nothing perishable. They were going to Lone Pine now. Like always, they did not know what they were going to find there. They should be aware and ready at all times.

"We are a small group now. However, we will grow in time." With these needs in mind, William was looking for warehouses that would have the items they needed in bulk sizes. They would all need to learn and master two or more skills according to their abilities. Farming and hunting would be the most important to the family's long-term survival. As all learned on the trip to California, self-defense was something they all needed to learn. They drove up the 395 to a large stand of trees where they could pull off the road. They stopped for the meal break. As the meal was being made, William told them they would be holding a family council after the meal was done and put away.

Here at last he would tell everyone what his plan was and what their parts would be as soon as they got the cars in order and filled the gas tanks with fuel. This was done at every stop. All the adults took part in this or would be working on helping to prepare meals for the rest of the family. All the children under thirteen years old were under the supervision of one of the older kids. And they would all be involved in these jobs. This was soon to be their normal daily routine. Soon as the meal was ready, they all sat down to eat. After the meal was done and the cleanup was complete, William called them to a small clearing in the shade of the trees at the far side of the clearing.

Family Council, Day Two

"Is everyone here? Please get comfortable as I have a lot to tell you all, and I'm not sure how long it will take. Please, no questions until I am done, or this will take forever, and time is not our friend! I have one question for all of you. Do any of you who think the power will be back on and planes will be flying in to help the people?"

One small voice in the back said, "*I hope so.*"

"Until that day comes, we all have to pull together to make a home for us all. We have already seen that we all are learning new skills, and we will need to learn more if we wish to survive the next year. We are just outside the town of Lone Pine. This has been my destination since leaving Las Vegas. Here we will fill the rest of our three shopping lists. We will be looking for warehouses, not the local supermarket as before. I do not know how or where yet. That's what the yellow pages are for. From this this point on, no one leaves the group alone. We should be three or more at all times. For the members that have been in the battles, they are to have a sidearm at all times, loaded and ready to use. We will all have to take turns as guards. As soon as we get everyone qualified, they will start to carry weapons at all times. Like on Blue Diamond Road, first we find a gas station and fill the cars and jerricans. When that's done, we will find the warehouses and get the rest of the items we need.

"We will then drive to a nearby trailhead where we will hide the cars. Then after packing the supplies, we will begin the hike over the mountains to the west side where we will find a suitable location and make our base camp. Once that is done, we will send a party back to bring the rest of the supplies to the camp. The ones not making the trip for the supplies will be working on the camp, getting firewood, making firepits, digging outhouses. In short, making our new home. Ben will be in charge of building shelters for us.

"Everyone thirteen and older will be given jobs to do. Work and you eat. No work for any reason other than illness or injury and you won't eat that day. We will hide our camp and put guards out in hidden places on all the approaches to the camp.

"Each day, all adults will start to learn how to shoot bows and crossbows as well as pistols and rifles. Everyone will learn all the jobs. As our numbers grow, it will still be important that anyone can do any job as needed. We will keep putting in security measures to protect us from the people chasing us as we tried to leave Vegas. They will find us up here, as will others. We will need to be ready at all times. I am sure that there are already people looking for us. Some may be friends. Other will be out to take what's ours. There are people in Vegas that tried to stop us from leaving. I do not know why, but they are still looking for us. Of that I am sure. So now who has questions or suggestions for the plan?"

It was dead silent for over a full minute when one of the young kids under thirteen asked when they would be able to go home. The question sent a wave of emotion through William and every other person who understood that there was no going back home.

"We will be to our new home in a day or two. As much as I hate it, our old homes are gone. We are now on our way to build a new home like the Swiss family Robinson. We will explain what's happening at the next family meeting in a few days. I wish to thank you all for your trust and support over the last two days. I am not sure what the next week will bring. I am sure there are even harder days ahead, and the horror we saw and what is yet to come will change us forever.

"Starting tomorrow, we will start one hour of meditation. Everyone of adult age will be required to attend one session morning or night."

Missy had a question at this time. "William, how is it you were ready to leave town so fast? Also, can you explain how you know so much about the event, as you call it?"

"Well, I'm not sure I'm ready to answer that question. Not because I do not want to but because I am still trying to understand it as well. Two days ago, I woke up early from what seemed to be a bad dream. I saw in my dream the destruction of the event. And after I woke up, I could not shake it as just a dream. I had a dream of this type just once before. One week later, the dream I had made sense. It was the three jets from 911! I saw them sitting on a tarmac, and it fell away into darkness. This dream was far stronger than that one, so after I convinced Maria to at least go along with me, we started to get the family members ready to go. After the event, I knew what we need to do."

"How did you know what to do?"

"It's something I have always done. I think about the worst thing that could hurt me and my family and make plans in my head on how to deal with them. I have had in my head for years the plan to move into the mountains if a major collapse of government happened.

"However, there is something that a few have become aware of as of yesterday. I can tell when anyone is lying to me, and I have had visions of things about to happen. Just before the gang attacked us at Big 5, I saw them come and shoot us. The rest you know. The part you don't know is that these mental powers are getting stronger. And others are also starting to show signs of them as well.

"That is why we are starting one-hour mediations, either one hour in the morning or in the evening. It's time the rest of mankind woke up. I woke up to a new reality, and each day I see it more clearly. To you I say *wake up*. Join me make the earth a joy to live on! Okay, here's our next move. We go to Lone Pine and fill our shopping list as best we can and move into the mountains and make a small village for us all. Okay, let's go!"

CHAPTER 10

Lone Pine

It was just after 1:00 p.m. when they entered Lone Pine. The town was a typical small highway town. The US 395 ran straight through Main Street. It's the heart of the town lined with stores and restaurants and motels with a few businesses just a block off the main street. Looking down the side street, you could see peaceful tree-lined streets where you could see bikes and toys in the yards. There were a few cars moving around in town. They found a phone book at the abandoned gas station about ten miles outside of town where they filled the all the vehicles tanks and then topped off the jerricans, as was their normal routine. Once that was done, they returned to the road into the town. After traveling about one mile into the town, they came to the police car with the officers sitting on the side of the road. The family already went over how they would deal with their greeting. All were armed and ready for anything.

William gave Peter orders to man the fifty cal but to take no action unless ordered to do so. The half day in Lone Pine would be hard on all of them as it was still an intact town at the moment. Having the two army trucks now, William had taken all the officers' uniforms and most of the enlisted men as well. They now looked like an army unit coming into town. He hoped it would make things easier.

The officers signaled for them to stop, which they did. Both officers were carrying shotguns on the front truck. The family cleared for weapons. They now all saw strangers as trouble!

"Pull to the side and exit your SUV! Keep your hands where we can see them. The chief told you to stay out of town."

"I'm sorry, Officer, could you repeat that? This is my first time in town. However, I would like to meet the chief of police. He could help me with my business here."

"Well, sir, it's our orders to bring you to him at city hall. Chief Loggins is there. You will need to leave your guns and come with us. Your men are to stay here. The sergeant will take you to the chief."

"Well, Officer Timmons, is it? I will see him, just not alone and not in your car. So please lead the way. We are all coming. Well, not all of us. You will stay here with my security detail, telling them who's okay and keeping all strangers out until I say otherwise."

The sergeant had problems with the orders William had just given.

"Sir, the chief said just you."

"Yes, I am sure he did, Sergeant. However, he didn't really mean it about me."

Sergeant McGregor walked over to talk with Officer Timmons. William took this time to have the scouts exit the rear truck and fan out and set a cover for the rest of them. Now as the sergeant came back, the scouts were on their way to cover city hall. The chief had called for men to come as part of their security forces. They were all spread out and coming as fast as they could to city hall. They all had guns, mostly shotguns and hunting guns and pistols. One of the scouts with Jake saw some of them and got word to Jake about them and where they were going. Jake opened to William and passed the information along. William sent back not to engage them, just follow along and set the circle as planned. Passing the information on to William had given him an even bigger advantage than he already held.

Walking into the city offices with the sergeant were William, Lucy, and Daniel, all fully armed with sidearms and assault rifles. William only had the .357 on his hip.

Chief of Police Loggins looked up and yelled at the sergeant, "Who in the hell is this? And why are they carrying weapons here? Did you leave Captain Bryce? Start a check of the city. Find where the captain is!"

"Chief, this was the only captain in the group and was in charge."

"Well, he's out their planning something while we waste time with this guy. Sergeant, get two men and go find him. Don't approach them. Just get word to me on their whereabouts."

"Chief Loggins, that will not be necessary. I can assure you that Bryce is no longer your problem."

"Are you my new problem?"

"No, I hope to be of great help to you. Bryce is dead. He was killed earlier today at a roadblock he was using to hold up survivors coming across Death Valley."

"Oh, really? Why should I believe you?"

"Because I killed him. We took all the weapons they had with them as well as their uniforms. We left them with the water they had and a few handguns and left them walking back to their base. They had a number of cars that still worked, so I believe the officers have gotten back to base by now."

"Still, that's not a good reason to believe you. I don't know anything about you!"

"Fair question, Chief. First let's get a few things straight. I don't want to know your name as I may need to kill you later."

This got the chief to think of his name, Benjamin J. Loggins, so now William knew it as well.

"You know a few things. *First*, me and my people came to meet you on our own, not by force, because I wanted to meet you. Also because I wanted to get your help, as I told the sergeant. Second, I know you have eight to twelve townsmen coming to back you up. They are arriving now, and my men are disarming them, and they are waiting outside. Third my people have this building surrounded.

I have six RPGs, the fifty cal, and over thirty military assault rifles handy and ready to use. Fourth, I wish to trade with you. I give you invaluable information and other items we can agree on if you choose to deal. Fifth, Ben, you need the help I can give you more than I need your help at this time."

Just as he finished giving Ben the reasons, a new officer came in and whispered to the chief. As he kept listening, a look of defiance came over his face. When they were done, the chief sent the officer away and turned to William. "Well, what is it you want from us?"

"Ben, first let us see what I can give you. First is respect for your time and your home guard. They have the spirit, but they take too long to assemble. So they would be of no real help!"

"Say, you have called me by my name twice now! I did not tell you my name!"

"Yes, you did, when I told you I did not want to know it. The first thing you did was think of your full name. Benjamin J. Loggins Yes?"

"How is that posable?"

"It is my new gift that I woke up with yesterday morning, and it keeps getting stronger. It is also why I know you have that. I do not trust your look since talking to the officer. However, this should change your mind. Of the building, up your defenses. Let's see what I can give you first." He sent the signal to bring the guns in. Jake and Steven pushed the cart into the lobby. William walked into the lobby as well.

"Your weapons are not up to the task of keeping you safe. Do you agree?"

"Yes, we are sorely outgunned by the soldiers that are coming back. I can feel it!"

"I agree. So first things first, we are not here to take without giving back in fare trade. So if you will all give me your word not to try to shoot my family, you can take your weapons back. And then make a line on the far side of the pushcart."

They looked to the chief, who was still unsure but told them to do as they were told. As soon as they were all lined up, Jake pulled the cover off the cart. Inside where half the weapons taken from

Captain Bryce and his men. In total, they received fifteen M16s and six sidearms, and they were resting on cases of ammo for them with another three cases of clips for each type they received. Everyone's jaws dropped, and they could not speak. Jake and Steven started handing the weapons and ammo out. While they were getting the weapons, William talked to Ben about the way they came to his call.

"The time it took your guard to respond to the call was far too long. They would show up just in time to die against the soldiers you're trying to defend against. The whole town needs to consolidate into a safer part of town. The place you pick should have limited access and be easy to defend. Get all your extra supplies and water to this place so you can stay at least seven days. Everyone will need to move to this location as there is safety in numbers."

"You're just giving all of this to us?"

"No, of course not. This is just the first part of the trade. We have to trade for what we need from your town."

"So, William, what do you need from us that's worth giving us these guns?"

"We need planting seed for as many crops as you can get us. We could also use an experienced farmer to tell us what we need to know to grow our own food. One that may be willing to join us and become one of the family. Also, any books that can be found and spared. Next, we need some bulk supplies we hope to find in the warehouses we located in the yellow pages."

"I think we all need to talk about this. The thing that officer came here for was to—"

"Tell you I was just a diversion while troops were moving toward the city hall!"

"How do you do that?"

"Can we have the room, just you and me please?"

"Everyone out now!"

In just a few seconds, they were alone.

"Ben, what I am going to tell you must remain a secret until I tell you it's not! Will you keep my secret?"

"I am not sure what's happening today. However, I do believe you're trying to help us! *Yes*, I will."

"Thank you. Ever since I woke up from that dream, I have been changing. I am not sure how to explain it. I am more awake today than ever before. It started yesterday, and it has spread to others, my wife, Jake, and Lucy. Ben and Peter, they are not equal to me and Maria, but they are growing as well."

"I see. What's so secret about it? And why do you need my promise? No one would believe me if I told them."

"Ben, I have checked your mind, and you will start to change as well. We will talk in our dreams and also from mind to mind like we've been doing ever since they all left. How long have we been talking now?"

"I think it's been ten to fifteen minutes."

"You're wrong. Look at my face and you will see that we are not talking like you think." Ben's mouth fell open a second time. "How can you do this?"

"You will learn, but you're already doing it. We've only been talking for about twenty seconds. The abilities to talk from mind to mind is the one thing that will give us the edge to win over the ones coming after me. We were attacked, and not by another country. That is the secret they cannot know that we know. Who is listening? Give us your names, please."

Maria, Jake, Lucy, Peter, and Ben had all been listening.

How long have you been able to hear me? The answer was a few hours to sometime yesterday.

Ben asked him how he could trust him so fast. *There was no lie in your promise or even a thought of telling anyone.*

You can always reach me in your dreams, and the talk will really take place. Soon you will start having dreams when you do reach out to me and we will talk about it.

Then really speaking, William told the others to return.

"You will all go to face the soldiers, but with your old weapons. We don't want to tip our hand just yet. We will be all around them. There are only six of them. Talk if you can. If they have other ideas, when you hear us yell, hit the ground. Anyone standing will be shot dead. Under stood?"

All answered yes and left to meet the soldiers.

William and the rest of the family moved out the back to take up positions behind the soldiers coming down the street, driving very slowly. They reached the city hall building and got out of the car. They walked right up to Ben and started asking questions.

"Hey, Chief, we want to know if you had any visitors today."

"Who the fuck are you to drive into our town and demand information? I don't even know who you are!"

"Captain Mears here on orders of Major Briggs to find a man by the name of William Waters."

"What happened to Captain Bryce?"

"He was shot from behind by this Waters at a road check."

"You know I was not born yesterday. You do not go from a lieutenant to major in less than a week. And even a blind and deaf man could hear the lies you're telling. You need to turn around and get out of town. And tell Briggs he's not welcome here anymore."

The man started to turn, and he gave a signal, and his men all started to pull their guns.

William yelled both mentally and out loud, "Hit the ground!"

The city men all fell to the ground, and they all heard a single shot.

"Okay, you can all get up now. It's over." As the men stood, Ben was amazed that all six men lay dead where they had been standing.

"William, how did you do that? I only heard one shot, but I see six dead men."

"We call it one shot. If you had kept your mind open, you would know we link and all shoot at the same time to make it seem like one. People will fear us because we can kill many people with one shot."

"I am glad you wanted to be friends. Now while they clean up this mess, what are the other things you were about to give us? But we are even now. What you did, we could not have done."

"It's okay. We are still going to give you the rest for two reasons. We need you to be our strong back door. Others will be coming, and they won't be nice."

"Why are they coming for you?"

"I'm not sure, but I think my new awareness is part of it. Peter, do you have it?"

"Yes, it's right here, if Ben will get a few men to come with me I will get them started."

"What's this for?"

"It's your gas ticket. Until you drain every tank in town, you have gas. It is a limited supply, so only use it when you have to."

Ben got four men to go with Peter, and they went to the nearest gas station to learn to pump gas.

"You should start by getting all the gas from the stations on the outside of town. Find a good storage tank and move all you can there. Also, get everyone in the same place and only go out to work. You will only survive as one large group. Find a place that can be defended and make it better. And when you have more problems that you can handle, let us know. We will send help. Later you will repay the favor by coming to our aid when we need it. Now if you can stay with us while we gather our supplies, it will help with the townspeople if you're there with us."

They all got in the trucks, and Ben led them to the places they needed to go. They did see a few people about. Ben and his men talked to them and sent them to gather at city hall and to tell everyone they saw to do the same. Soon they were loading the trucks. They had gotten almost everything on the list now and were loading the trucks. William took Ben aside for another talk.

"We will be leaving inside of an hour. I hope that the time we bought you today is enough to keep you safe. We will not be able to help you in the days to come. We will be fighting for our own place and unable to help you for some time. That's why you got all the things I could give you now. I am sure my plan will save us and make us strong! There may come a time when you will face a threat that you will not be able to stand up to. When that time comes, we will be here to help you!"

"William, why put your family at risk for us?"

"Easy. The ones coming will be looking for us! Our trail is ending here, so all the different groups will find their way here. Some will be coming at my request at meetings we had on my way here.

Others will be chasing a story of us that is even now growing back in the city. And the last group will be people wanting to take what we have and kill us. They will also want to take all you have as well.

"So from our first talk, you've been linked and can reach out to any of us you heard in our link. You call, and we will send what you need to survive And the last and most important reason, as of now, you and all in town are part of our family now. You just need to take the oath, and we will be bigger and stronger than before. We will leave this phrase at locations, and people who know it are our invited guess. It is *Ho Dog*. And anyone wanting to find us needs to find the words at trailheads and wait for us to come for them. It could take a week. Oh, and this was all in our heads, so never say it out loud."

CHAPTER 11

Into the Mountains

After leaving the chief, they drove north for almost twenty minutes until they came to a small road leading to the mountains in the west. It led to a small trailhead. They would take it to the west side of the Sierra Nevada. They would be taking this trail in a day or two. They needed to rest and get ready to move their supplies over the trail.

William's plan called for the family to live in the mountains. They were tired and looking for a good night's sleep before starting their journey. Everyone was still on alert, and as the last truck made the turn on the road, they reported a single car behind them. Lucy quickly put a plan in motion to stop the car and deal with who was behind them. Her plans was simple: the scouts would pull off the road after a turn and let the rest pass. After the car chasing them passed, the scouts would then pull out behind the car and without light come up from behind to give the rest of the convoy cover. Once they were all in place, they would all turn off their lights and stop around a curve. Lucy sent that ready and time now. William found a curve and gave the order to stop. All of this took a bit over ten miles to get in place, but they had now stopped and were waiting for the car.

* * *

Aaron Sutton was still trying to catch up to the cars, having gotten to the last warehouse just after the family pulled out. Going north, he was given gas so he could catch up with them. There was little obstruction on the 395, so he was able to make good time. The family was still driving with no lights here. Even the lead car was dark. They wanted no one to see their turnoff. Aaron was about two miles back of the rear truck when they started to make the turnoff of three-ninety-five as they all used their breaks. He could see the lights as they all turned off. He saw them and sped up so he wouldn't lose them. When he made the turn, all was dark again. Even with his high beam lights on, he got no reflection from the lights on the trucks. He sped up as fast as the road would allow. When he made the next turn, he saw the brake lights on the truck again. It was making the turn to the right. Now with his goal in sight, he pushed the pedal down, closing the distance in just a minute or so. When he had passed the large clump of three to his right, he failed to see Daniel and Steven in the scout car pull in behind him.

Daniel relayed the information that it was a lone male in the car. They were behind him, awaiting orders. William now started looking for a suitable place to stop the rear truck and find out who was behind them. In a few thousand yards, they came to a tight left turn. As William made the turn, he told Peter to stop the last truck as soon as they made the turn blocking the road. They had Daniel close the gap between the car in front of them.

Aaron was very close as the truck moved out of sight around a left turn in the road. He was very close now and was in a hurry to catch them. As he reached the turn, he was surprised that the truck had stopped. Slamming on his breaks, the car just missed, hitting the back of the truck. Just as he stopped, his car was hit from behind by the scout car. Before he could tell what had happened, four men were all around the car with guns drawn. The car behind had its high beam light blinding him. Daniel took the lead.

"*In the car, move very slowly. Turn your lights off and kill the motor!* Now place your hands against the windshield and do not move!"

Aaron started to speak. "I was just—"

"Quiet! Do not talk. Follow our orders. Lights, motor, and hands *now*."

Aaron complied, remembering Chief Loggins's warning that these were a hard bunch not to mess around with. So he did as he was told. In less than a minute, they had him out of the car, and he was being questioned. William came back to speak to him.

"Why are you following us? Please do not try to lie to me."

"My name is Aaron, and I have been trying to reach you since you were in town. The word got to me late as I was on the far south end of town. You wanted a farmer that would join your group?"

"So you're a farmer for how long?"

"I grew up there in Lone Pine. I returned three years ago from Texas A&M, where I received my master's in agriculture management."

William knew every word was true. Still, there was a problem if he did not agree to take the oath or terms of being on parole. He knew too much about where they were headed.

"Lucy, come here. Take Aaron over the oath after I finish talking with him. Jake, scout around for a camp site please. Now, Aaron, do you have any weapons in the car?"

"Yes, a nine-millimeter automatic and a 30-30 hunting rifle."

"Yes, we found them. I am going to let Lucy give you the details of the choice you just made. After hearing what it is, if you change your mind, let her know ASAP, please."

"Okay, Aaron. my name is Lucy. I am the head of security for the family. Here's the deal. We do not know you, and joining us is a lifetime commitment. Everyone thirteen or older is an adult in our family. Work every day or do not eat. Only illness or grave injury are exceptions to this rule. As a new member to the family and strange to us, you will be on parole until we are sure you are loyal to the family. You are not the only new member, and like the rest, you will have the same rights as any member of the family. Are you willing to make this commitment to us?"

"Yes. Something about the need for a farmer tells me this is the chance of a lifetime!"

"Okay, come with me. We'll get you in a car and a copy of the oath. After we make camp, we will give you the oath."

"Thank you. I am glad to be out of Lone Pine. I am afraid of what may happen there."

"Well, Aaron, I think the town will fare better since we gave them the arms they need to hold the town. As well as access to all the gas they have left in the gas stations in and around town." Lucy placed him with Daniel and went back to her other duties.

They had a final word at the turnoff to the trailhead they were going to use.

It would be midnight soon, so Ben got his team of workers that had set up their camp, and they started looking for a good place, roomy but with cover if needed and hidden from casual view. They would be here two to three days before starting the trek over the mountain.

William had Lucy and Jake come with him as he looked for the riding stables that should be a mile or two down the road. William was wondering if there was more to the strange and diverse people they kept meeting on this strange road trip. The good mixed with the bad. Was some other force at work? Of all the road trips he had taken in his other life, this one was the first that had no true destination. Or for that matter, it did not seem to have an end that anyone could see. The thought crossed his mind: Careful what you ask for. You just may get it. He had always wanted to be able to get in his car and just drive without ever having to worry about going back home. Well, now that was what he was doing, it gave him a small smile to know he was free from so many restraints that would never return, with no destination, and the true end was more a state of well-being. His smile returned and stayed. They were now at the end of only the second day of what William was sure was a whole new world, and the rules had changed Why did he know so much, and why were only a few of the others aware of the new insights they were getting?

He knew that the daily meditations was the key to unlocking them quickly, and the dreams were the start. He planned to have all the others along with him start asking the rest if they had slept well and if they had dreams.

They were just about to the stables when Daniel asked for William.

Daniel, you're waking up too?

William, what's this? How can I hear you?

Ah, your first contact, and it's me. That's good. Were you just thinking you'd like to talk to me?

Well, yes, I was. I've been talking to Aaron about our trip over the mountains, and he insists our plan is going to fail. We need to have pack animals, horses and mules, to get everything we will need to survive the first winter.

I see. What do you feel about him and what he tells you?

I can't say why, but I believe every word he said.

Laughing, William told Daniel, *Welcome to the club. That is just the first of the new senses and knowledge you're about to unlock. Will the rest of you tell Daniel who you are and how long you've been awake?*

Daniel was amazed and a bit shaken by the knowledge that he was now getting from the others.

William, this is a bit overwhelming. I cannot think. There's too much in my head.

Just think that you want quiet, and you will have it.

Daniel, do you hear me now?

Yes, I do.

We'll talk more later. Now what's the message from Aaron?

He said you need to find Bull to get what we need if he will help us.

Who is Bull? And where in the hell do we find him?

William, I think you're the luckiest man in the world. Bull is the foreman at the ranch you're heading for.

Daniel, get to a car and bring Aaron as fast as you can. Use the lights and let Aaron drive as I think he has driven this road a lot. He does know him?

Daniel laughed. *Yes and yes. We will be right up.*

Already on our way. Aaron thinks we can get a great deal of livestock if Bull will help us.

Okay, when you get here, I want Aaron to stay quiet and stay out of sight. I will call for him when needed. I will do all the talking.

It was a short drive to the ranch. Around the next turn, they saw the sign saying Mountain View Ranch Trail Rides Closed Monday & Tuesday. William stopped Jake's scouts along with Jake. They got out and started to circle the ranch house and the stables. It was William's hope to get a horse or two to pack the heavier items over the mountain. He drove up the drive close to the house. He and Lucy got out, leaving their weapons in the car and trying to look as peaceful and friendly as they could. They went to the door and got no response. They then moved to the stables and went in. Much to their surprise, there was a large number of horses and five mules inside. This was far better than they hoped for. With these animals, they could make only two, maybe three, trips to get their supplies to the other side of the mountain. Here again they found no one, and so William started to take inventory of what he believed they would need. The barn was a long stable barn with a large tack room at the far end. He and Lucy walked the full length and found no one. William checked with the scouts they had radioed for keeping Jake informed. William could talk to Jake as he was also awake now, and so radios were of no need for them. As each scout reported in, they had seen no one. Steve, the fourth scout, responded with a beep. No words. He had contact with someone! Was it Bull or a stranger? William was telling Jake to take control and keep him informed. He set to working on what they needed to take for the trip? He had Lucy count and categorize the livestock in the barn. She called to him about a henhouse just outside the back door full of laying chickens.

He had just found the pack saddles for the mules when Jake told him that Bull had just entered the barn and was coming up behind him. Then Steve called to him, "We have three guns on him. What do you want done?"

"Thanks, Steve. Just keep him covered for now. We are the thieves here, not him. I know you're there and have a gun on me. My name is William. Please don't shoot."

"Just what do you think you're doing?"

"*Well,* Jim, we are getting needed supplies for living in the mountains for the next year or two. We need horses and the mules to pack our supplies in for us. Our truck won't make it this way, and it's too dangerous to drive around."

"It looks like you're taking everything!"

"Yes, sorry about that. I'm not sure what to take or even how to use it."

"I should just shoot you where you stand, stealing horses and all the gear. I will have the chief up here in ten to twenty minutes."

"Jim, or can I call you Bull? I want to clear up a few things between us, okay?"

Slowly, he turned around to face Bull with his empty hands raised over his head.

"Who are you keeping the ranch for?"

"Well, the owners, Kevin and Missy Turner, should have been back yesterday. They must have been delayed by the power outage."

"Is all the power out here, Bull?"

"Hey, how do you know my name?"

"I will tell you in a minute. How were the Turners traveling home?"

"They chartered a privet jet to fly them to Pocatello and back. They should have landed in Ontario Airport about eleven a.m. Wednesday."

"It's as I suspected. They were in the air when the event happened. Bull, when the power went out, so did every other motor running at the time all over the world. Two days ago at ten thirty a.m., the world you knew ended, and a lot of people died. You're waiting for the dead.

"Aaron, will you come out now please? I know your name because Ben gave it to me. He wants you to come into town as soon as you can."

Aaron walked in from behind Bull and spoke to him.

"Hi, Bull, good to see you're alive and okay."

"All right with you here, Aaron. We can get these people back to town and let the chief deal with them!"

"No, Bull, I can't. I am a part of this group now. I do have a letter the chief sent with me knowing they were coming here. The chief asked me to give it to you if I saw you. William is telling the truth. Somehow, I don't think he can lie if you ask him a question."

> Bull, I hope this letter finds you alive and well. A lot has happened since you left town last Tuesday night. We have managed to get one of the ham radios working, and the few responders we get are all asking the same question! *Where is the government*? *What's going on?* And *When will the power come back?* Everyone is looking for some relief. Since he came to town, he's been very helpful with some big problems we had here. William seems to know things, and the biggest is that the event on Wednesday changed our world, and the old one is gone along with a great number of the population as well. If you meet him, believe him. I do. And help him if you can.
>
> B. Loggins

"So what happened to them if you know so much?"

"Me and my wife watched as over six planes taking off over our home all just lost power and fell out of the sky, bursting into flames. I have some people with me that tell me at any one time, there are millions in the air on any given day. They all died a terrible death. Have you seen or heard any motors, jets, or cars other than ours in the last two days?"

"Well, no, but I've not been looking."

"Fair enough. Now the answer to your question. Your friend Aaron just told me your name and told me you're the man I need to get my family safely over the mountain."

William thought for a minute then asked Bull to take a seat. He sat as well.

"Bull, close your eyes and think of someplace or time that made you happy. Do not think of anything but that memory."

Bull did as he was asked. William closed his eyes and relaxed, and the memory bloomed in his mind.

"It's your favorite memory. The first time you rode a racehorse and you won!"

Bulls eyes popped open. "How did you know that?"

"Honestly, I'm not sure how I just can A few more of us are starting to see things as I do. It started the night before or maybe that morning. I saw it all happen in a dream, and that woke me up. And it seems to have woken me up in more ways than just not being asleep. My mind woke up and has been changing every day. I seem to have stronger and new abilities. Others in the family are having similar changes as well. So time is short, and we can't afford to waste any. I want you to join the family as well. I have a job for you. Let's call it herd master. You come with us, take over the move over the mountain. Just ask for whatever you need and we will get it for you. *What do you say?*"

Bull looked at Aaron and the letter and gave William a long look.

"Yes, this feels like the right thing to do. Okay, who do I see about getting help?"

"See Lucy, the young lady that was with me at the barn. She's our master-at-arms. Tell her you're taking the oath after dinner with Aaron. Also ask her to get you the people you need to get us ready to go. We leave in three days at first light."

"Okay, boss. I sure hope you're right about all of this, or I just lost the best job I ever had!"

As soon as he took over the process of gathering the needed gear for the horses and mules, it went much faster. Lucy found eight people who wanted to help with the horses. She gave orders for the rest of the family to come to the ranch as they would be staying there till they start up the mountain. Bull was complete. He got a large supply of horseshoes and all the needed tools to do the farrier work. He made a list of things they would need to make a blacksmith shop on the mountain.

They made themselves at home at the ranch, filling all the rooms with a larger outside BBQ. The cooking was easy. Sarah and

Missy had taken over the cooking operation for the family. Everyone pitched in for the cleanup after each meal. The girls made a great meal, and they were getting ready to have their council meeting and give the oath to the two new members.

The girls asked if they could take the BBQ to the camp for cooking. So they hit it big at the ranch. They stayed two more nights, giving Bull time to teach everyone the basics of trail riding. Bull and Aaron, along with William and Jake, planned the trail they would take. Bull's lessons were easy. Mostly he just made sure they could get on and off and ride at a canter. Lucy and Bull got the packing going. She started putting the loads together, and Bull started to load the mules with the heavier packs as they were better suited for them.

They counted over thirty members now and had acquired a lot of stuff. The horses and mules would carry the load. Bull had been checking on the numbers and asked to see William.

"Yes, Bull, what can I do for you?"

"I was thinking of what I could do for us. If I can have one person to help me, I can change the conditions."

"Okay, take Jake. That way, we can keep in touch if needed. What is this for?"

"It's a surprise. We'll be right back. It should not take too long."

He and Jake left on horseback. They came back a little over two hours. The people working on the packing operation heard them about three to four minutes before they could be seen. Coming from the east, they could all see a dust cloud and heard the livestock moving down the trail. They road into the corral with eight cows and one real bull. Each had a lead rope with a string of six horses, all with saddles. They now had twelve more mounts. Added to the eighteen they found in the barn, they had thirty horses and brought up the rear where three more mules. Later that night, William asked Bull if he saw any problem going forward the next day.

"We are in good condition for a nice slow ride over the mountain. It should take two days with the load we have to move."

They had an early night and a cold dinner as the BBQ was taken down after breakfast so it could be cleaned and packed. The ladies cooked a lot of ribs and chicken they had found in a freezer, so it was cold chicken and ribs that night. They were to die for. After the meditation hour, a family meeting was called. William opened with how proud he was with the way everyone pulled together.

"Now as I have been looking into other things, Lucy and Jake have been getting things ready for the next stage and will now give us an update on what's next and how we stand."

Jake went first. "The scouts have been busy with a map provided by Bull and Aaron. They started up the trail the first day and returned just after dark last night. The trail is open and should be an easy ride. There is still some snow, but nothing that will give us any problems.

"We also have thirty horses and eight mules to carry the heavy items. We will be ready to leave in the morning. We had six scouts on patrol keeping us safe from any strangers seeing what we did here and where we are going. We had no contact with anyone since Aaron tried to find us. Lucy, are you ready?"

"Yes, thank you, my love. Good evening. I hope you all had enough to eat. We will be getting up early and have a long day ahead of us." Lucy opened the link they shared. She gave a second report to them per William's order. *If you can hear me, you are to stay behind after my report as we need to compare our skill levels. Some of us may have questions as you may just be hearing this for the first time. You stay behind as well.*

"We will have a light cold breakfast and then load the animals for the first trip over the mountain. We hope to make the trip in two days and then one to find and secure a safe base camp. Once that is done, we will send a smaller party back for the reminder of out supplies. The rest will stay with Ben and Jake to start building and secure the area. Now the evening meditation is about to start. Then everyone needs to get a good night's rest. William?"

"I have a few people coming to discuss a few things. Then anyone not on watch should get to bed. The next ten days are sure to be busy.

CHAPTER 12

Who's Awake?

In reflecting back on the last four days, the whole family got some much-needed time to stop and think about what had happened. It helped them understand why they were here.

Since the second day, William had been having meditation sessions at the end of the day. Now they had one morning and night. The family had a great time over the last four days, even with the ten-hour workdays getting everything ready for the trek over the mountain. It was after breakfast and after dinner. It was mandatory for each family member to attend one each day. These had a great calming effect on the family with only three exceptions. The first was Joy. She stood out the most. Next was Berry and Malinda. On the evening of the second night at the ranch, William made arrangements for each of them to receive some direction from family members that had already awoken. William was going to talk with Joy on a walk after the evening meditation period. She was a bit on edge in one-on-one situations. This one was no different. Malinda was asked to see Ben after dinner. They also walked out of the main area. This left Berry for Maria to talk with. All of them were resisting the meditation sessions and needed some help to learn to gain a true calm center. When they mastered this, they should be ready for what William had been calling the awakening or waking up. All the members of the family who had woken up were asking the others, *Are you awake?* Anyone confused was still not awake. Others had different answers: *I am not sure* or *I think so*. They were watched and guided to become more awake. Dreams were the real sign of being awake, when they had dreams that were true dreams.

William took Joy to a place that had the best view of the sunset. They were going to the log he and Maria had been going to when they had the chance. He asked Joy to take a seat. As they sat, he started to ask her questions.

"Tell me, Joy, why do you fight the meditation sessions?"

"Dad, they are a waste of my time. Things are bad, and I've been shot at and I have shot and killed men. We run for our lives, left friends, and gave up on family just three hours away."

"And how do you feel about all of this?"

"What, really? I am pissed off and scared to death at the same time. I am so mad at times I want to yell at some of the stupid people with us and the ones we meet."

"And why didn't you tell them how you felt?"

"I got so angry that I could not even speak. By the time I could, the moment had passed."

"Well, Joy, that's not quite how it happened. Ever since the event, I have been changed. Remember the dream? It was the second time I had one like that. And now after each crisis we pass, my awareness is increased. In simple terms, I know things before they happen, giving us the upper hand. In each of our battles, I knew what was going to happen! Unbelievable? *Yes*!"

"Yes, it is does. Maria knows your delusion?"

"Yes, she knows," he said, laughing. "Today when Bull was telling you how to check the saddle on your horse, you were about to make a smartass remark. Do you remember? Let me remind you. It was something like this, I believe. About how you're not going to let a broken-down cowboy show you anything! Remember?"

"Yes, I was, but I restrained myself. Hey, wait a minute. How do you know about something I didn't say? Or do?"

"I will tell you in a minute. First I want you to think of Allen. Please, not a sexual thought. Ahh, okay, that was perfect. Do not say a word. Allen does not like his middle name, which is Patty. Allen Patty O'Gill."

"How do you know?"

"Let's do the clearing exercise and I will tell you how and why I know."

For William, he could clear his mind with just a thought now. The four days at the ranch had been amazing. He went to all the meditation sessions each day. The effect of the peace and quiet seemed to double his strength each new day. He could feel it. The same was true for Maria, and the others reported the same as well. If he wanted, he could see into the thoughts of anyone nearby or anyone he knew well, close or far. The dreams became more. Some were still just dreams, but others were far more than idle thoughts. They were previews of things to come. So as he opened his mind to Joy, she was still in turmoil and now a bit scared. He found the right time and pushed happy and soothing images into her mind. She soon found herself moving to a happy peaceful train of thought.

"Look at me, Joy."

She turned to look at him.

He told her that he could send his thoughts to her without speaking.

She made a smartass remark about ESP.

So he next told her about a secret idea she had been keeping in the back of her mind. When she heard it, she turned away in anger, and he had to make her turn back to him. Reaching for her, he gently turned her back to face him, sending to her, *Please look at my mouth.*

As she turned and looked at him, he sent this thought to her: *Are my lips moving?*

Her eyes flew wide open!

"You have not said a word since we sat down, have you?"

That's right, daughter. I talk all the time but with close members of my family and others that are awake. I do not need to talk.

"How is this posable?"

"I am more awake each day since the day I called you before the event. You would be waking up as well if you can put your fear and anger aside. It will always hold you back. You should be right behind myself and Maria. Start going to the meditation morning and night. Find peace of mind and let yourself be happy. If you do, you will start to hear people talking to each other and have dreams that you will know are true. I can send messages and receive them as well in my dreams. Everyone but three people in the family are moving toward being like me and Maria. The ones that are not getting stronger will keep getting weaker as the strain of this trip will make them sick, and they are going to die soon. You are one of them, and in the worst condition. Tell me, you feel weaker each day than you did last week, don't you?"

"Yes, but I am just tired from all the work. That's why I just go to bed."

"You have to leave the old world behind. It's dead. And many of our friends and family are too. Some are not. Listen, I called back to my sister and warned them just like I told you to call your mom and family in California. I know that most of the family back east are still alive. Not sure how they are doing, but I still have dreams of them. They are trying to come west.

"If you will open yourself to the peaceful thoughts, you will soon know what's happening around you. Let the old world die. Awaken and come forward with the family. For the next two weeks, you will attend meditation, and your workload will be reduced. Any questions?"

"Will I be able to do what you're doing now?"

"The others are not where I am, but they are all getting stronger each day, same what Maria and I had done. So I would say yes, you will. The only problem I see is you want it for the wrong reasons. As long as that is the same, I fear you will never wake up. Go think on what you learn here tonight. Sleep and dream, Joy." They walked back to the camp.

The kids in the family spent most of the first two days of the trip to the ranch hiding in the floor of whatever SUV they were in. Most of the time they were afraid and crying. When they stopped to eat, they took the food and drinks and stayed very quiet and near their parents. In the four days at the ranch, with play and a lot of work, they started to come alive again. The younger ones—Gracie (six), Larry (four), Easton (two)—were only slightly affected at this young age. The other older ones, Seth (seven) and Lisa (twelve), had a bit of a harder time getting on with life. The days at the ranch worked wonders for all of them, and the children were all coming around by day 2. All were looking forward. To them, it was some summer camping trip. They were all looking forward to a horseback riding trip. It was good for all family to hear them running and playing at the ranch.

Their energy and stamina were back. A few of the group were having some minor stomach problems. Just the ones taking daily meds for different reasons—high blood pressure, bad heart, COPD, that type of thing. William was the worst case. He started to track the effects they all had. He soon realized that the problems went away as the day wore on and came back right after they all took their meds. It was affecting between ten to fifteen members. The only one not having the problem was Joy. William called all the affected people to him before breakfast of the last day at the ranch. He told them his idea, that it was their med making them sick. All of them were awake to some degree. The more advanced they were, the stronger the effect the pills had on them. So for the next week, they would not receive them. If anyone had a problem, they went to Veronica to get their meds.

Every day, everyone had to practice at the gun range and the archery field that was set up behind the barn. Here they could practice with live ammo with no worries about the noise it made. Even the kids loved it. For the ones that did not like it, William had them learn how to load them so they could be of help when needed. This was added to the daily riding lessons. Lucy had been keeping tabs on the family, looking for ones with talent for one thing over another. When found, they got more time on the best skill. The family learning curve was much higher than anything William had seen before.

They all helped with the general care of the livestock. By the end of the third day, it was looking like a cattle drive out of the 1870s old West. With help from Bull, they had acquired quite a bit more than William hoped to find. The count was now thirty-five horses, eight mules, one ram), and about fifteen laying hens and two rosters. And maybe the most important ones were Bull and nine cows.

As the days drew to an end, the cars and trucks were all moved and disabled to appear as nonworking. They would be there if needed. Next, they got all the weapons loaded so they would be easy to reach. All the thirteen and up were carrying guns every day, so now it seemed more normal than before. Everyone knew they would need them again at some point. They all needed to sleep as they had an early day. Many of them had dreams that night.

CHAPTER 13

The Others—Friend or Foe

Oliver had made it to Interstate70 with his group and one bilge pump. They were making good time toward Cheyenne Mountain, home of the missile defense command and SAC headquarters. On the third day, they reached the main gate of the mountain. The gates were wide open with no one on duty. They had not seen another living soul for over thirty-six hours. The last group they saw was about fifteen to twenty people. They tried to take the car and their food supplies. They had to kill about half of them before they gave up. When they left, they took their dead with them. Oliver did not want to know why. He was able to get a text through to the people inside the mountain. They were trying to find a way to open any access to the outside. When he tried to give his report, they told him to take it where he knew it would do some good. To anyone that could make use of it to save the people!

"We can only make a few more days, and then the air will start going bad. Go. If we get out, we will call you. Good luck, Oliver." This was partly what he wanted, but not at the cost of the people he worked with the last ten years. All they found on this trip was more death. Oliver kept thinking of William's advice to not try to help any of them as they were already dead. It was a waste of resources that were needed by the living.

"Do any of you have a place to go? I mean really go to with family and friends waiting for you?"

There was silence and lost looks over the last three days. They all tried to text their families, and everyone got no reply. That was when he really told them about the family and what they had done. When he was finished, he told them that he was going to find them. They could go their own way or come with him to find William. They all chose to go find William.

He wished to stay with him that day, but he had a mission to completer at the air base. Now he and the others were going to find him. They asked him where. It was a place called Lone Pine. So they started back. Oliver started to think about William just before going to sleep at night.

On the first night at the ranch, while Oliver was hundreds of miles away, he was thinking of William. He came into William's dream. William sent a memory to him.

They were now returning the way they came. They were low on gas and food. They knew of three gas stations along their route; however, food was getting harder to find. When they stopped for the night, Oliver slept, and in his dream, he relived the talk with William about how to find food and other needed supplies after the easy sources were used up: "Look for hidden treasure in abandoned trucks and trains if you come across them. If you find the right one, they will feed you for a long time."

The next morning, Oliver told the other what to look for as they started their drive back to California.

* * *

Things in the Hawaiian Islands were both better and worse at the same time. Their food supply was much smaller than any other part of the US, being a state made up of eight major islands and many smaller ones, about 109 altogether. After the event, like with the rest of the world, nothing seemed to work that was running at the time. That that meant many ships and planes and all kinds of small watercraft were adrift at sea. In the first days, the people all pulled together to save the ones at sea in dead boats and ships that they could see.

On the big island (Hawaii), the ranking army general declared martial law and made himself military governor. His first order was to take control of all the food supplies and set a curfew at dusk. No one would be out after dark without permission. On about the third day, the fighting started for food on all the islands. The general had anticipated this and put down the food riots very quickly, saving the islands and people. They in turn gave him their trust. The fighting on the other islands continued for months until each island had only one group in charge. Once this was over, the different groups started to think of taking over the other islands. General Burk had control of three of the islands as he had managed to make contacts with the other bases and so had better luck on those islands. Something was wrong in the islands as well. There had been many killings for no apparent reason. Many people on all the islands seemed to just lose hope and just stopped everything. They did not even try to eat. Many died from starving themselves to death. A great number committed suicide! This was the work of one of the dark visitors.

Overall, the islands came through the early days much better than the rest of the world. There was not as much devastation as most of the planes fell into the sea, sinking with all aboard as doors would not work. Some managed to get out and died in the water, waiting for help that was never coming.

On the islands, it was much more like a bizarre power outage and took longer for the people to come to the conclusion that something more had happened. In the first week, General Burk had the big island under martial law and in good order. With control of the food supplies and a rationing plan, everyone would be able to eat one good meal at least once a day. Water was not a problem as the islands all had large amounts of fresh water. He also gained control of two other islands due to the bases there. Working together, they held about 45 percent of the population. At other bases, the civilian population—forced by needs for food and, in some cases, water—

attracted some of the smaller bases. Now there was fighting on all the other islands. When it could be done, the forces under General Burk made safe zones and fed the people.

On the island of Kaho'olawe (the target isle), a second group was getting stronger and had taken a few national guard bases and now had the second biggest force on the islands. Only General Burk's forces were better armed and trained. They avoided any contact with them.

The general soon learned that this group was led by a native girl claiming to be a direct descendant of Victoria Kamāmalu. Living in the islands in the old ways, she had true natives following her rule. They made a caste system much like the old Spanish rule set by how pure their blood was. Pure Hawaiian then half, followed by the rest one quarter and last one-eight. She soon had the warrior chiefs doing her bidding. They soon had control of three islands and moved on to Kaho'olawe to build their base camp and village.

The general and Queen Leilani Kamāmalu would meet face-to-face in just a few months and form an alliance by marriage to unite the islands, ending the fighting. The eight islands became the first new government of the new world. In just weeks after the weed-ing, the others still fighting gave up and joined or were completely destroyed. It was a good start and might have been a haven if not for the work of the dark one that was on the island. They worked on the fears the two had. The general was the easy one to move, and he seemed to get the queen to follow as well. Their plan was to push the war on the West Coast, starting in South America in the drug-torn fields. The cartels came through stronger than the government and soon had rule over all they could hold. Tiny wars were raging everywhere in the continent with no rulers in site. So the islanders, as they came to be called, invaded the south. Stories started moving up, reaching William and others.

* * *

Far to the south in South America, a SEAL team was just about to execute a strike on a drug cartel cooking plantation. They had just finished rappelling from the choppers a few minutes before the event. They lost coms and heard and saw the smoke from the chopper crash sites. With no coms, they had to abort the mission and then start walking out of the jungle. They avoided the crash site as they were sure to have people checking on them.

They had no idea what had happened. They only knew that they were deep behind the enemy lines with no help and no way to call for any! They only had enemy troops all around them. So being SEALs, they did the only thing they could do. They started walking home.

SEAL team 18 was one of the best teams working for the last three years.

They were a six-man team led by Captain O'Brian and his five team members—Master Sergeant Jeff Steadman (thirty-eight), Gunnery Sergeant Juan Martinez (twenty-three), Corporal Victor "Vic" Stevens (twenty), Corporal Angel Ramirez (twenty-one), and Corporal Len McGriff (twenty-one). Everyone was a part of the team since BUDS training. This would have been their seventh mission. It took them two days to make the coast. Once there, they started to think that something far worse had happen and they were totally alone. They did the only thing that made any sense. They found a sailboat and loaded it with what supplies they could and left for the California coast.

William had a dream about them, as well as Oliver. In his dream, he told them to head to Sierra Nevada west side Central Coast of California.

CHAPTER 14

The Mountains

It was Tuesday, one week after the event. The family started keep track. It was day 7 of the new world. The morning came clear and a bit crisp. The dew was hanging on the leaves and grass. The family did morning meditations while waiting for the food to be prepared. After the morning work was complete, Bull and his team of new wranglers got the mules and horses ready for the trek over the east side passes to the mountains. Having moved and disabled all cars the night before, they had a clean start up the horse trail to the first summit. The family was going to disappear into the mountains and build a home and base camp.

The kids were happy to be going for the first long ride. The trail started up into the trees. The ash and the dogwoods mixed with the pines. The trail was covered in pine needles and large pinecones. The lower part of the trail was a long switchback, making a gentle climb up the face of the hill. At just about every curve, the riders were given a vast panorama of the valley below. The houses and ranches of Lone Pine grew smaller as they rose up the side of the mountain. The only noises they heard where the clip-clop of the horsehoofs mixed with the birdsong. As it was still early, they saw a great many deer and a few bears with cubs just waking up from their winter sleep. The long switchbacks brought them to the first crest just after noon. Stopping for a light lunch, they loosened the cinches on the saddles, giving the horses a rest as well. Bull had every rider take care of their own mount. The wranglers saw to the mules and their own mounts. They were careful to not ride side by side so as to not give away how many were in the group. This, like many other things, they started today would become normal for them from this day on.

For the ride, up all adults were armed with sidearms. The scouts and rapid response team had rifles. The rest carried bows and crossbows if they passed the training test back at the ranch. The rule was that guns were to be the last resort, only to save lives! About halfway up the next ridgeline, they moved into the remaining snow. They would be traveling over a great deal of it before they reached their destination. Later that day, after they crossed the second summit, William had Bull take them down below the snow to find a place they could make camp in for the night. They would make stopping a regular affair. They would find a site and stop about three hours before dark, giving the family time to make camp and find greater need supplies like water and wood, first on the list at each stop. Just like when William was a child, the kids did this work while the adults started the cooking and making the beds. As soon as the kids got back with the wood, the fire and dinner were started. While all of this was being done, the wranglers and any extra members helped with the livestock before the evening meal. Except for the three guards and the cooks, they all settled into their evening meditation before the dinner was served. William was glad to see that all three seemed to be doing better since the talks. After dinner, before the fire was put out, all the day's trash was burned. This first day set many new daily practices to be learned and perfected over the next few weeks or months as needed. All in the name of safety of the family. It was also one of the best trips many of them had ever experienced.

It was not all just fun and games. Everyone got instructions on how to place landmarks so they could find their way home if they needed to. It would be very important to many of them, so they would not be lost in the woods. It was a sure thing that word of their escape would spread and people, good and bad, would come looking for them. No one knew how long they would need to stay hidden, maybe months or years. So each day was a great adventure and good days as none were marked by any gun battles like the first two days of the escape from the city. As they rode, the air became cleaner and a bit cooler in the early spring days. On the noon break of the third day, Bull stopped at the tree line near a large rock dome. It was like sitting on top of the world. If they looked back, they could see Death Valley. For many of them, that name had deeper meaning. Not too many looked back. Those that did could still see pillars of smoke in many different places. The same or new, they could not tell. Most of them looked to the west while eating the cold lunch they made that morning with the breakfast meal. Looking to the west from this spot, they could see the coastal range as well as large parts of the Central Valley. They would start down the mountain after lunch and start looking for the place in which they would build their new homes.

Before leaving, William had a talk with Ben about building a watch cabin at this place as the view was so good. They could see east and west, which would give them an early warning on any unwanted visitors. So plans were made to build a watchtower on this rock. They could also see a great many fires burning as well to the west, but it was not as bad as the east. They could see the golden-brown rolling hills and the many different crops and orchards in the valley. Many of them now understood why they came to this side of the mountains. Food could be grown here. They could live and eat here if they could survive and find a place to build a shelter for everyone. Besides the many foods grown there, they also had a large cotton industry in the valley and nuts, fruits, and corn to name the big ones that would allow them to live. It was to be their supermarket while they became self-sustaining in their own truck patch on the mountain. They took a bit longer than normal for lunch, looking at the valley they would be living off for the next year or so.

They started down the west side, still learning landmarks and looking for a place suitable for their needs. It would have to have good cover with a protected lower entrance. In the back, it would need many exits out the back if they had to leave in a hurry. They would need to be close to the growing fields yet far enough up the mountain to give them an advantage in a fight when needed. Their choice would have to cancel out an enemy's greater numbers in any fight. So they started down with everyone wondering what they would find.

There were still other things to learn about their new mountain home. After two days on the trail, the forest seemed to accept them, and the normal sounds came back for them to hear and learn from. At night, William and Ben would ask what animals and birds had been seen or heard on that day's ride. They all needed to know what type of animals came into or around their camp. Each morning, a different group would check the tracks around the camp, identifying the different types of tracks and how many there had been that night. The kids made a game on who found the most tracks and what they were. They all learned that when the forest went quiet, there was something strange passing close by. Most of the time, it was them. However, every once in a while, it was a bear or mountain lion passing by. They never shot any of the animals they saw unless they were hunting, as they were getting needed food and never took more than that. The rest they let pass. Like the Indians before them, they only took what was needed and wasted nothing.

It had been a long day, and Bull found a nice group of sequoias to make camp in that night. It was the first they had seen since coming over the summit. The next day, they saw young trees and more larger groups. William knew them from his childhood trips to the mountains. He was looking for a high pass outside of the Lodgepole Campgrounds at JO Pass. It was about four miles up on the mountain from the campground. There was water and good cover in the pass and two ways down the mountain. He knew this area well. They came here many times as kids. And he knew it would be great. It was close to the valley and far enough up the mountain to be safe. So by moving down the mountain north by northwest, they should find the right area of the mountain. The sequoia trees were a good sign they were getting close as long as they did not pass it.

As routine demanded, they stopped three hours before dark to make camp. This night they made camp in a large grass meadow with a good stand of the giant trees on the north end. It was the second day on the west side, and they needed to find their position and a way to JO Pass. This was what Bull, Jake, and Peter were trying to find as they studied the maps they acquired at the Big 5 store. It was a high mountain pass with exits on two sides, giving the family many escapes routes if needed.

* * *

After the evening meditation, William made the rounds, asking how everyone was doing, if they were getting enough sleep, and if they were having dreams. It was here that he found the ones about to wake up! Mostly they were just dreams. A few, however, were much more. These he shared with the others already waking up. After all the routine work was done, everyone would have an hour or so of personal time. The dreamers took this time to go over the dreams from the last night and to practice their new skills. They were not sure if *mind reading* was the right term. All the ones showing signs of being awake had the ability to enter other minds. William and Maria were the strongest. One thing they all shared was they knew when anyone was not telling the truth. William could influence some people as he did with Joy. All of them had dreams that involved others not in the family. Maria and Peter shared part of the dream of Oliver trying to find them while Ben shared the part about the SEAL team and O'Brian and a sailboat. They all talked about the dreams together at night just before going to sleep. It was nice to have these meetings mind to mind so they could be anywhere in camp. William gave them insights on what to think about so the right messages got to them. So when the next dream came, they would all be ready. William took some private time with Maria, and they took stock of the members that were now awake. Jake and Lucy, like them, William believed one pushed the other awake, then Ben, Peter, and Steven all were awake as well. Another four to five were about to start having real dreams and hearing their thoughts.

William looked at Maria. "You know this is our true power and the thing that will save us if we are to survive."

"Yes, it is truly a gift that you have given us all. I still can't believe it at times, but the serenity and peace is a true gift."

"It is far beyond anything I ever dreamed of. And why me? Well, that will come in its own time. Do you know what I want from you?"

"Yes, and I would love to do it as it's a mom's job to teach her children, and all of them are our children."

"That's why I love you!"

They then spent personal time, blocking out all the outside world. Then they slept without dreams, waking up refreshed.

CHAPTER 15

SEAL Team 18

O'Brian and his team found getting to the coast easier than expected. There was no government presence, and everywhere they expected to find aircraft, they only found crash sites. The villages they passed were normal enough with the one outstanding fact there was no TV or radio working in them. Record players and live music was all they heard. A few cars were working. In a short time, they had acquired a small van and collected food and water for the trip home. O'Brian called for them to keep heading north along the coast, looking for a sailboat, at least a two-mast schooner or bigger, hopefully with a working diesel motor so they could sail north and be safer than land travel. They had to avoid five different cartel wars, and they still had a long way to go.

It became clear that what had happened was not directed at them but at everyone. The only other groups that came through it were the drug lords, who had their own small armies and so were taking control of the area they worked from. They had seen the scene of some of the battles after the fact. The strong were killing the weaker ones. They just wanted to get out as fast as they could.

They approached a small port city on the coast road named Port of Ponce de Leon. They found the village had a guarded gate blocking the road a little over one mile ahead. Looking at it, they saw it had armed guards, all with automatic weapons. They changed guards every four hours. They needed to get past or through it. They had hoped to find a boat there. O'Brian gave orders.

"Martinez, Stevens, get flaking positions on the right and left signal when you're in position on the gate." It was just over fifteen minutes when the two SEALs signaled. They had good cover positions. In just a few more minutes, they both had reports of how many troops they could see. They flashed the light again, and when O'Brian had eyes on it, he gave the return signal. Then by hand signals, they described the type and number of forces manning the gate. There were at least forty men at the gate. Then Stevens signaled again. His next report was there were two roving patrols walking the village, four men each. He had seen them meet and reverse directions twice. They were told to stay and watch.

"Angel, front and center."

"Yeah, boss. What you need?"

"We need to find a way around the gate and if there is even a reason to go in there. I want you to go native. Take only your sidearm and find a way to the docks. See if you can find us a ride home among the boats you find there. You up for it?"

"Sure am. I want to get home."

"Okay, it will be dark soon. Get changed and take off. You have until this time tomorrow. Got it?"

"Aye, aye, sir."

While Angel got ready, they informed the two on guard what was going on and that they would be relieved at midnight. They went on infrared lights at full dark so they could see just fine. Jeff had a better view into the village and kept looking for items of interest to them. They had almost all their ammo left as they used very little of it getting this far. It was now the fourth day since the event. They were hoping to get past without any shooting. Like the rest of the world, everyone was trying to hold it together until the power came back on and order could be restored. This small village like many others had come under the control of the strongest group left in the area. This village was under the control of the Cordova drug cartel.

It was soon apparent to the master sergeant that to pass the gate, you would need to give up at least half of your food and all your weapons to pass the gate. At this point, O'Brian was looking at finding some way to overrun the gate and get to a boat and out to sea. They would be getting ready to take the gate after Angel reported back.

Jeff reported that they had the two large roving patrols. He estimated there were over four hundred men in the village. There was no way to survive the run to the harbor. O'Brian told him to report as soon as he was relieved.

"Angel should be back soon," he hoped.

* * *

Angel started down the back side of the hill they were on, working to the seaward side and looking for a way over or around the fence. A place that would allow quiet passage for the team. With only his sidearm and three extra clips and his boot knife, Angel had just over twenty-four hours to get in and back out with his report. He was wearing local garb as they all had been since coming out of the jungle. It only took Angel twenty minutes to find a drainage culvert that would allow easy access to the village due to a large washout from a heavy rain in the last few days.

He was now in the village and moving to the marina, keeping watch for the roving patrols and any other cause of trouble. He moved slow and silent and avoided well-lit seconds of the village. It had been a thriving coastal town serving small pleasure craft and fishing boats. A cruise ship would stop from time to time. After getting past the fence, it was only a bit over a mile and a half to the docks and marina area. They had five mooring docks, all only partly full and about ten to twelve sailboats more at buoys in the bay. He saw three at the buoys that might fit their needs. He took ten minutes to fix their positions and then took a closer look at them all. This would make them easier to find later. Just as he was about to turn back into the village, the lights came on in the second biggest boat of the three on his short list. The boat's name was *Dream Wind.* He took his night vision out to take a closer look at the boat.

There was a man and woman on board the boat. After watching, he could see they were getting ready to eat and then sleep. Angel looked around and found a small dingy nearby and rowed out close enough to hear them talking. He just drifted close by, listening to them.

"Yes, I agree. It's not safe here. However, our host is not showing any move to harm us."

"Wayne, how long do you think that is going to last?"

"I do not know. Not long if things are as bad as we think. We need to come up with a plan to get out of here. They keep delaying us on the fuel and food. We need to leave. They do not say we can't leave, but they won't give us what we need to go."

Angel had heard enough. He rowed back to the pier and returned the dingy where he found it. This was the boat they needed, and it came with crew that wanted to leave as well. It had a diesel motor that was working but needed fuel. It was a schooner. They would all fit easily on it, and they seemed like US citizens wanting to go home as much as they did.

He stared back with the news. He had only been gone three hours. Going back should be a bit faster. Moving as before, he kept to the shadows and did not go back the same way he came. This was in case he was seen going in. They might set up on a good place to catch him on the way back. He could hear men coming, so he took cover at the side of an adobe house with light in the front and none on the side or back. It gave him cover and a view of the men as they went by. The patrol passed by on the far side of the road. They were moving slowly. It took them almost five minutes to clear the road, and he could leave his cover.

While hiding there, he could hear voices in the building, a girl and a man. She was crying while he had a cruel laugh. In just a short time, Angel knew the man was one of the cartel men taking his pleasure from the girl against her wishes. Angel wanted to go in and kill the man; however, that would put the team at risk. He bit his tongue and waited it out. The patrol moved on, and he was about to move when the man came out the front door. As he was leaving, he told the girl to get cleaned up and make some food. He would be back in three hours, and they would spend the night together. She cried even more! Angel so wanted to do something, but the team's safety came first. So he waited on the side of the building for the man to leave. All he wanted was to get back to the team and then get the hell out of this village and back home.

The door opened, and light spilled out on the street. The man came out. It was easy to see he drank too much and was not quite steady on his feet. He stopped and looked after the patrol and then turned and walked right at Angel's position.

Angel, seeing his change of direction, pulled his knife and waited for him to pass. The man walked right up to the place he was hiding, stopped, and turned to yell back to the house. He stepped in a hole and fell right on Angel. He started to yell. Angel jumped up, covered his mouth, and stabled him through his lower jaw, straight into his brain, killing him at once with no noise at all. He pulled the body into the darker area behind another house not being used.

He started back as fast as he safely could. He was thinking of the team's safety. Soon that man would be missed and found in the daylight. He was also thinking of the girl as she would be a target because she was his comfort woman, and someone would know it. He would talk to O'Brian about her.

He made it back to the fence in just twenty minutes and another ten to get back behind the hill out of the sight of the guards. The SEALs saw him, so of course O'Brian knew he was coming, having gotten the reports from them. He gave his report on what he had seen and done, starting with the dead man and the girl and moving on to the boat and how they could get in at the rain culvert. He had devised a plan to get the boat out with the man and woman as well.

O'Brian was just starting to make plans for getting the boat when Jeff returned to the group. He called him over and brought him up to speed on Angel's report. They had too much equipment to try and carry it to the boat. And they could not afford to leave it behind. The three of them had to make plans for getting the boat and all their equipment home.

Between Jeff's and Angel's reports, they now knew there were over two hundred men in the village and no way to get everything to the boat. They would need to enlist the couple on the boat, and Angel was right. The girl would die due to his actions. After pushing a lot of ideas around, they all agreed they could not drive in or fight their way to the boat. And going in the way Angel said would take too many trips to get all their gear in. All of these ended with the team getting caught or killed. They needed the boat and could not get to it. O'Brian told them to take a break. They would start again in thirty minutes. He told Jeff and Angel to check on the supplies and get something to eat while they waited on John.

* * *

John went for a walk down the short hill to the beach. Then he walked down to the surf. He knew they needed a new way to look at this problem. After a short stroll down the sand, he turned and walked to the top of a small hill looking south and out to sea, just looking at the swells as they rolled by. Just a little farther down, there was a lone grass hut sitting near the high tide marks with a dirt track leading down the road. It was a very peaceful place.

This was O'Brian's awakening. Here was the very dream he had the last four nights, and here it was in reality, just as he saw it in his mind. It was the very place where they left to sail home. He went back, getting the team together to lay out the plan for getting the boat and sailing to the Central Coast of California. That's where he needed to go.

"Okay, guys, here's what we are going to do. Angel will go back, taking Jeff and Len with him. They will secure the boat and take care of the other item. Angel will fill you in on the way. Time is short. The rest of us will get everything down on the beach by the hut over there in the small bay. Once we have them ready to load, we will rig a bomb in the van, and Vic will drive back to the top of the hill and wait. If needed, he will blow the gate with the van and make his way to the shore and swim out where we will pick him up. After loading the boat, we will then sail out to sea, only turning north after we are out of sight of the coast. This is not normal for us, so please take no unnecessary chances. We need all of you in one peace. Questions?"

Angel asked the only one. "When do we go?"

"As soon as your team is ready go. We have about two and a half or three hours of dark left. We need to be far out to sea when the sun comes up."

Angel led them back to the drainage ditch and then slipped back into the village less than two hours after getting back out. As before, the guard's watch was poor, and they passed without notice. They started for the marina and the *Dream Wind*, the schooner they planned to take for their trip home. The roving patrols were moving east to west and were no problem to avoid.

The first sign of trouble literally walked right into them. As they approached a corner building, four semi-drunk men burst out of the double doors and ran right into them. They were all armed and yelled and went for their guns. The SEALs fired four shots, killing them all. The silencers made quiet work of them. However, their yells brought answers from inside and out. They could hear others coming. They quickly hid the bodies behind a large wooden crate and ran toward the marina. Very quickly, the sounds of alarm fell behind them. They slowed and went into silent mode, making no noise at all. About one block from the marina, he stopped. He needed to get the woman. Back on the hill, O'Brian and the others were busy getting everything out of the van at the beach hut and making the bomb.

Angel approached the door. It had only been about three hours since he left the body just down the street. He had Jeff check to see if it had been found. It was still dark; however, that was going to change fast if they weren't out of the harbor before that. There would be big trouble. Casually, he knocked on the door and spoke in Spanish.

"Hola, my name is Angel. We need to talk please."

"No, go away. Hector will be back soon, and if you're here, he will kill us both!"

"So Hector was his name. No, he is not coming back ever again. However, you are no longer safe here!"

"*No*, Hector will be here soon. He is late already, senor. You should leave."

There was a strange noise in the house as he spoke again.

"What's your name?"

"Carlita. Hector has made me his woman."

"Yes, I know. I was hiding from the patrol as it passed by. I was on the side of your home. I heard the two of you in the house. I am a soldier. We are leaving the village now. The action I had to take when Hector left has put you in great danger!"

"How can that be?"

"I was hiding outside here, waiting for the patrol to pass for close to ten minutes. Just as I was getting ready to move on, Hector came out, giving you orders to shower and cook for him. He came around the side of the house and took a misstep and fell right into me. He started to yell, and I killed him. I hid the body down a few houses in the dark. He is not coming back."

Angel heard a second voice. It was very low. "That's him. Open the door."

"When they find him, they will come looking for you! Come with me now. We will get you to safety."

"Oh my god, is that bastard truly dead?"

"Yes."

"Oh, thank you. Can I bring my sister? She is only ten, and I can't leave her in this place. And those men."

"Is that the other voice I heard just now? We have a time problem. We need to leave right now."

"See, I told you we will leave tonight."

"Okay, we can leave quickly. What do we need?"

"Just get clothes for a change of weather and personal needs. I will be right here after I check with the sergeant."

Angel went to check with the sergeant and told him of the slight change in plans and asked about the body. It was still there, so no extra effort was looking for them. They needed to get going. The two girls came out in just minutes with a very few things. The sergeant instructed them to ask no questions and make no noise. It was just three and a half blocks to where Angel had left the dingy. He and Jeff rowed out the boat. By now, they should be asleep!

They boarded the craft without making noise. Jeff went to the cabin door and spoke softly.

"Wayne, we are Navy SEALs. Please do not yell. Wayne, wake up!"

They were both out cold. Maybe too much wine at dinner, or they might have taken something to help them sleep. Wayne started to come around after Jeff moved next to him and gave him some gentle shaking. Veronica woke first with a start, which might have been what woke Wayne up.

"Please stay calm. We are Navy SEALs. We are here to help."

Jeff, getting up and sitting at the galley table, told them what they needed to know and nothing more. If they believed that they had come to save them, all the better. They were glad they would be taking the boat but did not understand why. Jeff had them getting the boat ready to sail. They were going to sail out of the marina as quiet as a mouse. Angel row back to the pier to get the others. Soon they were all onboard with the dingy tied to the stern of the boat. They were lucky to have a light but steady wind of about 2 mph. He had Wayne head out to open water. Angel broke radio silence with one word: "Underway." This let O'Brian know they had started out of the marina. On board the *Dream Wind*, they hoped that the shootout with the men would have a large search going and allow them to slip out to sea. Wayne had been given the course to the beach. Running without lights, he was working his way out. The wind was perfect for him.

* * *

Back on the hill, Vic waited in the van, loaded now with only the bomb. He was seeing a lot of new activity as people were looking for something. He did not need to guess what they were looking for. All the supplies were down on the beach with O'Brian, waiting for the boat to arrive. They would be loading the boat as soon as it arrived. Vic had gotten the job of driving the van to ram the gate if needed. It was to give them time to load the boat and get out to sea safely. The attack on the gate would bring everyone that way away from the marina, giving them the time needed to slip out into the dark waters even before they knew it was missing. Vic signaled he was in position and was waiting. As soon as they neared the open water, Jeff had the motor going, and he had Wayne turn to the south.

"Sergeant, why are we going south?"

"Two reasons. If we are being watched, they will report we went south, and we have friends waiting for us on the beach. We are going to get them now. We have the dingy, but it's small and will take a few trips to get all our gear on board. Do you have a small boat?"

"Yes, a zodiac with a small outboard to power it."

"Great. Speed is our best hope of not being seen leaving. Get it ready. Len, take the helm. Let me know when you can see the beach."

As soon as Len saw the beach, he called for Jeff. When Jeff could see the shack, he used his red light to signal O'Brian that they were coming ashore. Soon they were dropping the anchor and lowering the second boat into the water. Angel stayed on the boat while Jeff and Len went ashore.

They had just finished the first loads for the two small boats when Vic called in over the coms systems still working.

"John, there is a lot of activity in town, and men are leaving the gate and moving toward the marina. They are searching slowly, and I guess about six blocks away from the marina."

"Okay, you know what to do! Hurry. The faster you get back, the shorter your swim will be."

The men looking for the cause of the yelling earlier had found Hector's body, and another group had found the four dead men as well. Lights and torches stared moving all over the village now with loud cries that could be heard all over. After finding Hector's body, they all headed to Carlita's house.

Vic, having been given the go order, set the van up so it would keep going straight to the gate. He started it up. He came roaring over the top of the hill. As soon as he could see the gate, he started firing his AK-47 out of the window and at the men on the gate. They picked this weapon on the way so they could use it and leave no clue they were US soldiers. He set the course control and checked the steering wheel. When the clip was empty, he turned the lights on high beam and jumped out of the van. He rolled to the side of the road, waiting for the blast to cover his run to the beach. It seemed like the longest twenty seconds of Vic's life. Then the van hit the gate, and the bomb went off. The extra gas they had left in the van created a giant fireball. Hitting it just at center, it blew a hole in the gate and the ground over fifteen feet wide and up to eight to ten feet deep. At the sound of the blast, all the troops turned and moved to the gate. They had reports that over half the guards died in the blast and they were under attack. Everything worked fine, and with no other surprise, they got the boat loaded. O'Brian was last to board the *Dream Wind*. The deck was a mess with the gear they had loaded as well as food and fuel for the motor. Even before it was stored, he had Len give the helm back to Wayne and started to store the supplies below decks.

"Wayne, take us straight out to sea due west until all light from the shore is gone, please."

"Okay. Can you now tell me why? And also, who you are?"

"Sorry, Wayne. My name is Captain John O'Brian, US Navy leader of SEAL team 18. I have a lot to tell you all, but first we must be safe. Please help get us far out of sight of land, then turn us north to home. We will store the gear and supplies. Then we will talk later."

In just over an hour, they had made the turn to the north and had stored all the supplies. Veronica and Carlita made a late meal. O'Brian called a meeting of all hands in the galley. The tiller was tied down to hold course, and the sea was light and clear.

"My name is Captain John J. O'Brian. First thing is, we do not know what's happened to our world. We know almost nothing yet and are hoping to learn more when we get home.

"As to our situation here, I have set three watches that me and my men will stand. Someone will be awake at all times. Anyone who can sail will stand a tiller watch. Age is not a factor. All common duties will be shared by all. We have enough food and water for a week. In normal conditions, we would be home in nine days. I think it will take a bit longer, seeing as how nothing in the world is working anymore. We hope to find food along the way. Water will be no problem. If we don't find food, I hope we all like fish. We will make sleeping arrangements and assign work as needed. Okay, first let's get to know one another.

"Our ship's captain is Wayne Young, and his first mate is Veronica Young. The two young ladies are Carlita and Sonador Mendez, sisters we put in danger. And this is the rest of my team. Jeff Steadmen, second-in-command. Juan Martinez, Vic Stevens, Len McGriff, and you all know Angel Ramirez. As I said before, I'm not sure how long it will take to get to the Central Coast of California, but we will get there. Any questions?"

There were none.

"Okay, let's all help get this boat sorted out for sleeping arrangements."

Sonador walked up to O'Brian, stopping him. "I have a question for you that I don't want to share even with my sister. Can we talk please? It's about how well you know the wizard you're taking us to."

O'Brian stopped dead in his tracks and knelt down next to her before talking at all.

"The wizard? I don't know of any wizard."

"Sure you do. I've seen you in his dreams a lot the last few days, always followed by the dream of Angel coming to get us. Every time."

"Sonador, what dreams are you talking about?"

"I share the wizard's dreams, and you have been in them the last few weeks. When his dreams end, I dream of Angel coming to rescue me and my sister. Today that dream came true, like many of my dreams do. I have tried to talk to the wizard, but I am not able to. I see in his dreams that if you wished, you could talk to him, but you don't."

"So you're seeing my dreams?"

"No, they are his and yours. He enters the dream, and I come with him. Tonight, you will dream of him. Talk to him and when I wake, I will repeat your words back to you and his answer if any."

"You're a strange one, and we will talk again tomorrow and put your mind at ease as there will be no dream."

"Yes, John, we will."

In short order, the *Dream Wind* made fourteen knots heading north. They were just west of Quito, Ecuador. Normal sail time would be nine days to cover the 3,033 miles. John figured it would take three times that under the new world they were traveling into.

CHAPTER 16

Red Sky in the Morning, Sailor Take Warning

As O'Brian turned north for the California coast, others were trying to find a way to get through as well. There was the army under General Burk and the islanders led by Leilani, living in the old ways since before the event or even the tall ships that came to change their peaceful lives forever. In a very short time, the two groups had taken control of the islands and were set to fight for total control. By some chance, Queen Leilani fell into the general's hands.

Leilani and Burk quickly came to the conclusion that if they joined forces, they would be much stronger and would fully control the islands in mere days. The queen and the general were poised to become the strongest force in the western part of the world. They set about building a very strong base with a working system to care for the people and feed them all.

This was also the most violent times in the islands' entire history. Over half of the people were murdered in some strange darkens that overtook them. There was some other force at work on the island during the early days of the post event.

Someone in the army had discovered that only things that had not been running at the time of the event would still start and run, and many of the things they had might still be of great use. They wasted no time in finding and putting this knowledge to work. Starting at the military bases, they found and serviced all the equipment they could. In less than three months, the islands were back up and running in an almost normal fashion. A few cars and more buses were back on the roads. They had a small air force limited by the number of pilots not working planes. And their biggest source of power was the seventeen working navy ships they found. Finding crews was underway at the base, and plans for invading the South American continent had just about been completed. Soon they would move on to the west. It would be months, not years, and they could very well take complete control of the North and South American countries in less than a year. There was a feeling between the queen and the general that they were the strongest force left on earth, and they were on the move! They moved to South America first, where there would be less resistance. They would look like saviors to people living under cartels!

* * *

On Highway 395, Oliver and company made it back to California with little trouble. This was mostly due to the abandoned trailers they found along the way. They had been far more help than he could hope for. On the third night of the return trip, after the evening meal, Oliver stood the first watch as he always did before finding his bed. Oliver was asleep almost as soon as his head touched the small travel pillows they had. He was in a deep sleep very quickly. He had a number of strange dreams. The dreams came every night. Most were just images that faded as fast as they came. A few, however, were very different. Like the ones he had been getting from William. These he knew were messages to him. He was not sure if it was William or his own mind putting William in his dreams. Tonight was very different. This dream was like reliving his last day in the old world at the air base. He was in the conference room with the visitors.

"Hello, Oliver. Sorry to bring you back here. This is the place you know us best. We have a gift for you."

"What gift? I don't understand. This is a dream, right?"

"Yes, Oliver, it is, and so much more. You will be awake soon. The one has seen to your awakening. However, you need this gift to get you safely to your destination."

"Okay, what is the gift, and how does a dream gift help me?"

"Our gift is already given to you. Remember, you will always be able to hear the one when he is thinking of you. Believe in your dreams when you wake, Oliver."

Oliver awoke with a start. He remembered all the dreams, even the fast and strange ones from this sleep. He knew they were just random dreams, except for the visitors. That one was different. Still a dream, but it also felt very real, like he was at the air base just two weeks ago, talking to them. Something had changed, and it felt scary but good as well.

In about thirty minutes, Oliver was asleep again. As soon as he reached REM sleep, William felt Oliver and reached out to him in his sleep to touch his mind. William had been able to keep tabs on him and leave hints for Oliver in his dreams. Tonight, something was different from when he looked into Oliver's mind at the gas station. Not bad, just different. He could tell Oliver was close to waking up. William reached out and was surprised to find Oliver's mind open to him already.

"Oliver, can you hear me?"

With a bit of a start, he replied, "Yes."

"Oliver, you are close to waking up. I know you can hear me. I still do not know how this all works. I just know it works. Can you see me?"

"I do not know how to do this. No, I can't see you."

"Okay, in your dream, just see yourself opening your eyes."

Oliver did so, and there was William right in front of him.

"Oh my, there you are, just as if we are in the same room. This is just a dream, is it not?"

"Yes and no. We are both sleeping in our own beds. Our bodies are resting, but our minds are here. Please do not ask where here is, as I am still new to this as well. This is real, and from now on you will know the difference as most of your dreams are just dreams. A few will be like this, and you will remember them."

"So this is the gift they gave me, but they said it came from you as well. Do you know what they meant?"

"Whose gift, Oliver?"

"The visitors' gift is all they said to tell you. Until I see you in person. They also said I would always be able to hear you. Do you know what that means?"

"Yes, I do. You are waking up, is what it means. I have looked and found no darkness to this. It is safe. And when I say waking up, I do not mean from sleep. I know you're on the way back to find me. Go south on US 395 to Lone Pine, California. When you get there, ask to see Police Chief Loggins. He will take you to a place where you are to wait for us to come for you. Be safe, and just bring the ones from the air base with you. Be safe. I have others to talk to tonight. I will see you soon, Oliver, and we will talk.

CHAPTER 17

Homes in the Tall Trees

After finding their way to the JO Pass above Lodgepole Campground in Sequoia National Park, they moved up the mountain to a large meadow that few people ever found. William found it many years ago as a teenager hiking in the forest. The back was a large rock face wall going straight up at least one thousand feet. With a meadow of some fifteen acres of grass with a good mix of the redwoods and tall pine in a tight mix all the way around to the wall on each side. Many years ago, his mind saw this as a place to escape to if needed. You could live here. There was food and water and everything one needed to survive for long periods. Ring of trees were deep and tight. If you walked by and the people were silent, you would never know it. It had taken them eight days to reach this place. They had marked many places they could use as lookout positions. The mountain was beautiful and very peaceful.

Now was the start of real work. They set up their normal night camp at the back edge. Once that was done, William called a family meeting for all, kids included. So after dinner, he called them all together before the evening chores had been done.

"Everyone, please gather round. First, before I start, I want everyone to take a good look around. This place is about to become our new home. Many of the kids still ask when we are going home. Well, this is home. We are home. It's full of trees and wild animals. We will have four seasons—mild summers, very cold winters, and colder springs and falls. That's not why I want you all here right now. Everyone look around and remember how it looks right now because after one full day, we will transform the meadow to our fort and shelter from all harm that may come for us.

"In case you missed it, only normal chores tomorrow, like food and firewood. The work starts the next day. And no more days off until we have built what we need for the first winter. Shelter and food first. So, everyone, eat well and have a *great day*!"

Like the trip up the mountain, after work, if anyone wanted to go for a walk, two others had to go along. Always in threes, never alone, and never out of sight of the others.

The next day, everyone did their own thing. Some slept, and others wandered the meadow, getting a look at their new home. Everyone helped with the needed chores, like getting wood and cleaning up after meals. The cooking was light. Tomorrow was the first workday at the new home site.

After the first meal, William put Ben in charge of laying out the compound and started getting the right people for the building crews. Others were put in charge of cutting trees for building material as all the buildings would be log cabins. The kids knew their jobs now. After the meal, they had to get firewood for the kitchen staff. They had new instructions to not go more than four trees into the woods around the meadow. And three of the older kids had watch duty with bows or crossbows if they passed the qualifications test.

They kept the same hours as they did when coming over the mountain. Three hours before dark, all work stopped, and everyone was at the camp meeting area. This was to be their routine for the next two and a half months, getting ready for winter.

Aaron was given two teams of men and horses as he looked around for a place to plant the crops as time was running short for this year. Thanks to Bull, they had three plowheads with harnesses for them. Aaron had been looking for places big enough and with water nearby for planting food crops so they would have food in the winter months. He took six men, and they rode out at first light, looking for good planting meadows.

Lucy, Jake, and Peter went looking for access points for watch-towers and were working on ways to keep the camp safe. They checked on all the known ways into the meadow and found choke points along the trails leading to the campsite. They needed guard posts all around the camp and fast means of moving from one post to another.

And the last item was picking the team to go back to Lone Pine for the rest of their supplies hidden in their SUVs near the trailhead. William had Bull decide to go or pick the team to go. He had work to organize with Ben on the best place to place the barn and stables. It needed to be downwind of the living and cooking area as much as posable.

So their new lives started to take shape, and the spring slowly moved in too summer.

Each day was a new adventure. They had good people in the jobs they did best. The people were happy, and each day the feeling of truly being a family grew stronger. It took the local wildlife about five days to get used to their being in the meadow and started coming back to the edges and at time to camp as well. They had to keep tight control over our food. No food was allowed to leave the cooking tent unless it was for one of the work parties, as the bears would come and take it if they did not take proper care of the cooking and cleaning of the kitchen. The large BBQ brought from the ranch was great, and soon it was in place on the side of the dining hall. It was big enough to seat a hundred people at a time. They had three outhouses built on the edges of the living spaces. In the back against the wall, there was a small but constant waterfall, and Ben was able to make a bathhouse with tubs and firepits for hot baths. There were five shower stalls, but cold only at this time. They rigged running water sinks with mirrors, and the last was a large bunkhouse. It could sleep three hundred if needed. At one of the councils meetings, someone asked William why it was so big.

"It is this big because we are going to grow, and it will start soon. We will all have private cabins in time, and when new people come, they will stay here while on parole and only move out once their parole time is over."

Down by the barn and stables, the deer and elk would come and jump the rails and eat with the horses. They would follow the groups when they needed more meat. The hunters would follow them and take the older animals, and like the Indians of old, they used the whole animals. The skins were made into clothing or boots for the ones who would need them first based on their work. They never took more than they could use or needed. They took bears only when they got old and would go rogue and had to be taken down. Same as the others. Bear skins made the best winter coats and blankets.

The amazing thing was how the younger kids learned the ways of the forest, and in the first two and a half months, none have ever gotten lost. They found many of the best features of the meadow, like the ice caves just to the north side of the cliff wall outside of the ring of trees. They learned all the birds and their calls.

They were high enough to have a very small risk of snakes of any kind. One would be found from time to time. They were moving lower down the mountain.

William asked three different times if anyone wanted to change the base camp's location. All three times, they all voted to stay, even the kids. They had made their home and were going to stay.

All the work projects had great starts. The majority of the family worked on logging at first to get the shelters built before winter started. William and Lucy walked the ring wood as they had started to call the trees around the meadow. They would only take a few trees from here and only to give them better sight of anyone moving toward the camp. The rest of the trees came from groves around them. They never took too many. Just one in five was the limit they set. So by the second workday, the logs stared to arrive from the forest, pulled by the large Clydesdale they found running wild on the mountain on the second full day of work.

Everyone was working and happy for the most part. There were still a few that could not make the change. Mellissa was the worst case. She made sick calls almost every morning and then went to her work assignment every day, but her health was falling fast, and she was becoming mean and nasty to the people around her.

William called a family meeting to talk about the health of the family.

"I have called this meeting to discuss the health of the family and the benefits of the daily meditations. Many of you are waking up, and others are having a hard time. For those involved, we will not use names at any time. If you know one of these, please give positive support whenever you can, and please keep a watch on them if you can. We are all one family now, and we are about to start growing. The story of our escape from Las Vegas is growing all over the west, and people are looking for us. Some good and the others wish us harm. For us to survive, we need to be strong with all of us working together.

"Another thing that is going to affect our health is getting fighters up and down the mountain when needed. If anyone has any ideas on how we can get down the mountain, please tell us. No matter how silly it may sound, we will listen. Now at the end of the meeting, for all people that are listed on the pharmacy list, we need to check the need and inventory of your meds. Please stay behind. Oh, and one last item. A small group of us will be leaving today to go to Lone Pine. We could use a few more if anyone wants to go and your job is not a priority. You're welcome to come along.

The trip back to Lone Pine started early the next morning after all the people were selected. William had Daniel come with him and the two security teams. Lucy had sent four men each, and they needed four more to lead the extra mounts for the new members of the family. Altogether they had a total of thirty-two mounts, including the mules. The trip to Lone Pine was much easier now as every adult had made the trip at least twice now. This trip was important as two groups would be waiting for them by the time they reach the ranch house. One of the extra riders asked William why there were so many mounts.

"Are you awake?"

"What? Of course I am. You woke me not more than an hour ago."

"Ahh, okay. The reason we need the mounts is because in my dream, I saw us coming back with fifteen new family members and the three pack mules."

On the trip down to Lone Pine, they trained and were armed and fully supplied. Ben (Sheriff Loggins) would have supplies ready for them to come back up the mountain. The horses and men could and have taken the trail many times now, so the trip was only four to five days, not the ten it took the first time. The days went quickly and without any problems.

On the third day, just after the noon break, William heard a call.

"Aaron, I hear you!"

Aaron jumped when he heard William speak!

"William, is that you? Where are you. I can hear you, but you can't be here. I thought you're on the way to Lone Pine."

"Aaron, are you awake?"

A bit put off by the question, he stopped to think about it. "I think I am. So that's the open secret you all share. Are we all waking up like this?"

"Yes, all at different times, and some are not showing any signs at all. It does seem that all of us can wake up, as we call it."

"So why did you call me?"

"I did not call you. I answered your call to me. We are about one and a half days out of Lone Pine right now. I was the first to wake up, and Maria followed closely behind me. There are many others in the family that are awake. We will talk later about that and many other things. So what was it that caused you to want to talk with me?"

"It's the zip line., Steven tells me that once they are done, we can get to the new farms we are staring in as little as thirty minutes. The problem is how we get back to camp after zipping down. Ben is going to be building small corrals and stables. Wwe just need to increase the size to hold extra horses for getting back up the hill faster. If we zip down and then need to leave in a hurry, horses would be a great help. Better than a man on foot."

"That's a great idea. Tonight in the meeting, ask Ben about it."

"What nightly meeting? I was never told about it."

"That's because you are now awake and can hear us." Opening fully, William asked, "Who is awake?"

Many of Aaron's friends answered and greeted him into the ranks.

William went back to his ride and spent a private moment with Maria just before they stop for the night. They stopped early so they could be up and ride the last six or seven miles in the dark, arriving just after sunup. A big day was coming up.

* * *

Lucy had Jake and Peter head the two security teams that would go with them. Maria would be in charge at the camp and work areas. Aaron had found two good fields large enough for his needs and very close to the mountain so they could get the crops back up the hill when needed. It also made it better if they needed to defend it. The day after the meeting, Malinda's youngest son, Seth, came to Joy with an idea for getting down the mountain as fast as possible.

"Lucy, I have an idea for getting down the mountain. Do you still need them?"

"Hi, Seth. Yes, we do. Well, I was walking with my friends collecting wood, and we were talking about things we miss, and one of the older boys talk about how much fun he had riding zip lines. Why can't we make some zip lines? They could be used for playing as well as getting down the mountain. I think it would be fun to do if you will let us ride as well."

"Seth, you're a genius. Are you awake, Seth?"

"Of course, mom woke me up before sunrise to start the cook fire like always."

"Seth, if we can make your idea work, we will build a few zip lines in the meadow's edge for you and your friend to play on when you have free time."

She kissed him on the head and rushed off to find Ben. She opened to a special group that included William, Maria, Ben, Aaron, Bull, and Jake.

"I think Seth has solved part of the problem of getting down the mountain quickly."

As one, they all asked "*How*?"

"Zip lines from the top of the trees, as high as we can safely go. If we keep them in the foliage, we can travel without being seen and travel very fast compared to walking or riding horses down to the farms we are building there."

"Maria, how many workers can we make available to start looking into this?"

"According to my count, we have about ten. We can move from their current work and not put their projects behind schedule."

"Ben, I can feel you're thinking hard already." There were mental laughs from the group. "What's your thought on this? Can we do this?"

"Seth is a genius. Is he awake? I will have him come work with me as we start this. He will keep me clear and simple, and zipping in the trees will hide us and gives us the advantage in battle in many ways. I say that because Lucy's thoughts are also amazing to me. I will need a day or two to work out the details, but yes, this will work."

Jake spoke up. "Still long-winded when he excited about something." There was more laughing. "The only thing is they have to stop at least two hundred yards behind the tree line, and they must remain a secret from all outsiders coming to the mountain."

"Okay, everyone, if you have ideas, get them to Ben. And, Ben, this is now number one job. Make it work, and fast! For as you all know, we are going to need it before full winter comes."

Maria was in charge of getting the camp set up. She worked closely with Lucy, making sure the camp was safe. The building jobs kept everyone busy for six full weeks. At the end of that time, the common house was almost done. The bathhouse was complete and had running water. Winter might be a different story. Time would answer that question. Maria had given Lucy orders to have guard posts all around the camp. Lucy had ten hunting blinds set high up in the giant trees, giving the guards a far better view than anyone on the ground would have. They were all armed with bows or crossbows depending on their skill level. The also had rifles and sidearms and a combat knife. They all took duty on watch on a rotating schedule. The zip line gave her more as the last station would be a guard stand as well. Seth's idea was truly brilliant, and it covered all three of the trails into the pass, giving them at least one-hour notice from there. So security was coming along quite well.

From day 1, William asked Maria to get the grass cleared to fifteen hundred yards from the buildings. Maria had seen a good use for all of the cut grass and had the kids clear the area back by the cliff wall where it could dry out. As soon as the required area was cleared, she had the kids dig a big hole by the wall as well. Then she asked them to get water and some of the dirt they had dug up out of the hole. They started to make a wet muddy paste mixed with the grass.

"Ben, can I see you, please?"

"Yes, is it important? I am staring to lay the logs."

"I think it is, and timely as well. Bring one worker and a wheelbarrow with you, please."

"Okay. On my way."

In just a few minutes, Ben and Donny came to the wall where they were waiting.

"We noted the other day that the bathhouse and toilets are drafty. That may be good in those buildings. Have you found a way to make the logs fit airtight so the common house and other buildings will not be so drafty?"

"The truth is, we have been so busy just trying to get them up before the winter gets here. We haven't even thought about it. Why do you ask?"

"Come with me please."

She led him to the pit where the kids all strode around, looking at them as they came to the pit. Ben and Donny walked past the kids and saw a large amount of the mud and grass.

"I see you have had ideas on the cold weather to come. Kids, did you do all of this yourselves?"

There was a loud yell of "Yes, all of it. Maria told us what and how to do it, and we did."

"Ben, this is great. Now we don't have to try and fill after the logs are in place. Only problem I see is that we have no available workers."

"That is how I see it too."

The kids all yelled, "We want to finish our work!" The young ones would keep making the mud, and the older one would apply it as they told them."

"I think they will be of great help, and I will assign one adult to be their guard as well as safety man for the work. Will that work for you?"

"Yes, I will be in much better shape now than I was. This was so easy to fix, yet we need you and the kids to get it done right. Thank you."

The camp had its regular routines, like food at the same time every day and box lunches for the workers out in the fields. There was weapons training every day—guns, bows, and crossbows. Once they passed the test for each weapon, they only had to go once a month and shoot a passing score. The alarm system Peter devised was being set up. It was simple and also went along the zip line and the guard towers as well. They were heavy lines attached to tin cans filled with small rocks. When pulled, they made a hell of a noise in camp. The family was getting better at all the skills they had been training on. In all, the camp was now looking like a ranch right out of the old west with a few modern touches. This was how William left it to go get their new friends at Lone Pine. He was always connected to Maria and knew of all the changes that were getting done. The big surprise was the kids. They were always ready to get in and help when asked. Earlier, Aaron had a manpower problem as he had more truck farms laid out but had no hands for the planting. He went to Maria, and the kids were always around her. She was grandma for all of them.

"Maria, I need at least twelve to sixteen people for planting seeds. We have a three- to four-day window this high up. Can you get me that many people?"

Maria was wondering the same thing as she started going over the work party that was already out working.

"We are here and ready to go. We are bored, and no grass is needed for a week or so."

It was Lance that spoke for them all!

Aaron and Maria looked at them, and they all nodded. "We want to help."

"Well, they are yours if you think it will work."

"You kids will be the reason we eat well this winter. You're all great. Only question I have is, when do you want to start?"

All of them yelled, "Right now!"

Maria, laughing, said, "That's one problem solved. Was there another?"

"Just one. After it's planted, we will need to put fertilizer down to get the growth we need."

"Okay, we can work on that at the meeting tonight."

Later that night at the meeting of the minds in the real since Bull told Aaron he had been saving all the cow and horse manure and mixed it with straw and should be ready in a week or so. If needed, they could use their own as well like they did in Japan.

"They did that in ancient Japan, didn't they?"

"Yes, William, very good. And with our mix, we will do very well. We will work out the details and let you know what we need later today."

"Maria will see too all of your needs. If there is nothing more, I have a busy day and I'm going to sleep now. Good work, everyone. Tell the kids great job for me please."

The next morning before dawn, they started down to the ranch house to see Chief Loggins and the two groups waiting for them. Both groups had made arduous journeys to get here. Ben had kept the two groups apart at different sides of the trailhead that was about one mile south of the ranch. This was the last safety measure to keep the camp's location a secret from prying eyes and minds. Chief Loggins was sitting his house as they rode out of the trees onto the road.

"Ben, it's good to really see you. You're looking good."

"Thank you, William. You're looking a bit different than my mental image. You look a bit younger than when we first met."

"Laughing at my looks, are you? Not to worry. It will start for you soon. You have grown faster than many as well. I believe it comes from the leading nature we both have taken in our lives. What do you think of the others that found their way here?"

"I believe you invited them. The one leading them claims to be a Las Vegas police officer you met the day of the event."

"Officer Tomkins Kevin. I was hoping he would make it. I didn't have much hope, but I am glad I can see him again. Have you talked to him much?"

"Just enough to know he is not a threat to us or you."

"Great. And how is Oliver doing? He had a very long road to go, and such a short distance."

"They are great. And Oliver is awake or about to be, am I right?"

"Yes, there's something special about Oliver, and we will know soon what it is. Let's go see them and get started as we need to leave first thing day after tomorrow. Things are going to get busy on my side of the mountain."

"Is it the people that keep showing up at the lower farms?"

"Yes, we both have interesting times ahead. When you need us, help will be there for you. I keep watch on you as often as I can. Now take me to Oliver."

"Just Peter is coming with us. The others are going to keep an eye on the people that came with Kevin. Something seems wrong with the group. Can you feel it?"

"No, they all seem fine to me. What is it I should be seeing or feeling?"

"That's the problem with this stuff. I am still learning as well. What I see and feel is a darkness in and around someone in that group. Sorry, that's the best I can do. Did you see it?"

"Yes, and it's going to be hard to separate from the group."

With that, they moved to Oliver's camp.

CHAPTER 18

Oliver and Friends

William with Ben and Jake turned and rode to the trailhead where the two groups waited to see William. It was near 8:00 a.m. when they rode into Oliver's camp. The day had great promise to be clear and warm. Oliver's camp was at the tree line at the mouth of the trail they had been camped at, this being the east side of the mountains. The camp was still in shadows, waiting for the sun to clear the top and spill sunlight on them. It was a good place to camp if you wanted to sleep in as the sun would warm you up fast in a tent. However, they were all awake, and the remains of a meal was visible around the table by the firepit.

"Good morning, Oliver. It so very good to see you again!"

"Well, William, truth be told, I never thought I would see you again. That group that was speeding to the station was after you. They passed everything to get there before you could leave. I learned a lot that night, and I did not like any of it."

"As did we all. I still don't know who or why someone would be after me except maybe the law. We broke a lot of them that night. Most in self-defense. Others out of necessity."

"Yes, you did, and it was a good for a lot of people that you did! It took me a day and half to reach the air base. After the meeting with the visitors, I spent another two days getting ready for my trip back to Cheyenne Mountain. After sharing some of the knowledge you gave me, the general and I got the remaining airmen to move everything of military value to Indian Wells Air Base. The commanding officer there had been killed, and a major was in command. They had problems, but the general knew that base was better to defend than his, so we moved his whole command up there. I saw them move into the base as we started on the way to Wyoming with my new friends that think I'm a bit crazy."

"How does he know about me?"

"Ahh, well, that is why I went to the base to meet with the visitors. They told the general about you even before I reached the base. They told him that you were getting people out of the city and harm's way, then when—"

"Stop. This is to loud. Open your mind to me. Listen with your eyes closed, please!"

Oliver closed his eyes and listened for William.

Okay, can you hear me clearly?

Yes.

Okay, now do not speak and remember everything you can about the visitors.

Oliver started to go back to his first meeting with the visitors six years ago and found it blocked. His mind jumped to the warning they gave him ("Don't tell him too much about us or he will be in more danger than he already is!") Then the part about how he already met the *one* and how he would help him with knowledge of them and the dark ones. When it was time, they would come to him and tell him about the dark ones!

Well, Oliver, open your eyes. It seems the visitors want to stay away from me and have blocked you from telling me all you know!

Oliver was looking at him and heard all his words, but he was not talking.

You can read my thoughts and send me yours.

Yes, and they can, too, *yes*?

Yes, and when I was sent here, it was at their request. They wanted to warn us about the attack about to happen and that you were coming, and that was all they would tell me. Oh, they said the gift they gave me was that I would always be able to hear you. They also said that you had already given me the gift as well.

Oliver, you are awake and a special case, I think. I want you to open your mind and think as loud as you can. Who can hear me?

Oliver did so, and his face went pale as he was flooded with responses from the town and the mountain.

Hello, Oliver, we've been waiting for you ever since the gas station on the first night! Glad you made it. See you at the meeting tonight.

Looking at William he spoke. *You are the one!*

What one?

The visitors. They have a prophecy of the one that will come and halt the advance of the dark ones and bring peace to the galaxy for a thousand years. It said the one would be able to hear and see without his ears and eyes. You meet the conditions.

Great, well, let me ask you a question. Have you heard of the wizard's mountain?

Why, yes, we met a number of people who asked us if we knew where to find it. Having no knowledge of it, I sent them to find you with a few clues I found in my head. They needed to find the signs—Ho Dog—and follow them to trails leading into the mountains and you. I told them that you could help them. Hope that was not a bad thing.

He laughed. *Remember your dream when I said just bring the ones with you? That's what I wanted you to do, give clues to find us on their own. You did great. I understand about the visitors. You done well, and all I can say is welcome home, Oliver.*

They left Jake with the others and went back to the ranch. They would be ready to leave on the second morning for the mountain.

As William was leaving, Oliver asked him a last question: "What do you call this mountain home we're going to?"

William laughed again. "That should be clear to you. Look, what do you see as the name?"

"*Wizard Mountain!*"

* * *

William and Ben went to the other side of the trailhead where the other group had set up their camp. This one's leader had learned to keep people like William out of his mind. William had no idea who this could be, and there was a sense of danger in the group as well. He felt nothing as he got no read at all. He had the two security teams slowly encircle the group. They used some of Ben's people to get full circle around them before William entered the camp. All this was done while they were talking to Oliver.

Now he rode his horse into the camp, yelling, "Who's in charge here!"

A man with long well-kept hair and beard came out of the big tent at the back of the camp by the trees.

"I am William. Is my invitation no longer good?"

"Officer Tomkins. How good to see you. You have grown some since our last meeting. Ben, this is the police officer who tried to arrest me at the Big 5 in Las Vegas on the day of the event."

"Ahh, I knew I liked you for a reason. A fellow officer with good instincts."

"Thank you, Ben. You're a good man. Sorry I did not tell you more sooner."

"No, Kevin, you did it right. So who do you have with you?"

"Just as you told me to. I went home and got all my family and a few others I could trust, and we at first waited for normal to return. After just two days of things getting worse and having to kill a few crazy people in our block, they all came around to leaving as I had been pushing for. It was clear that if we stayed, we would die in our homes! Something dark had taken over the city, and killings were everywhere."

"Kevin, you learned to keep some things out. Did you know this?"

"I'm not sure what you mean."

"Ahh, a natural talent. I think I may have been the cause that night at the Big 5. I was able to read you, and I put the destination for you to follow if you could. I also put a block on giving out that information as well. Kevin, will you let me in please?"

"In where?"

"Your mind. I want to see your thoughts and memories please."

"I don't understand. You want to read my mind?"

"Well, yes and no. You will see my thoughts as well. We can talk without speaking out loud. Just believe and say you agree and let me in."

"You saved my ass at the Big 5, and your advice saved my family by giving me a place to come to. I trust you more than another man alive. I would be proud to share my thoughts with you."

"Thank you, Kevin. You have a very strong block. It has been pushed by someone back in the city. Oh, and you do not need to talk, please. Just remember the events that brought you to Lone Pine."

"*Wow*, I saw what you wanted me to see, and I understand. It went as you thought it would be."

The horrors of the last few days in the city, of the raiders going around the city looting and killing and the rape gangs taking all the women they found. They showed them getting set to leave for the mountain and the people that came with them.

"Kevin, we have a problem. The number of people you remember bringing is different from the number you have here in your camp. Okay, Kevin, we are going to have our men come into the camp now. We need to have all your people be interview and sent to see Jake to get a copy of the oath and the meaning of parole to become part of the family. I need you to point out the extra person in your party so we can separate him or her from the rest."

"What's the problem with this person?"

"He or she is hiding a darkness and is here to try and kill me. That is their only purpose for being here. All your people who pass will become part of my family and go back to the mountain with us. The one and any he has corrupted will not."

"Okay, let's get this done and move forward."

Kevin called his group to come forward and meet William and the others from the mountain. He told them they would be interviewed and have the conditions of joining explained to them. After that, they would have time to make their decisions to join or not. During this time, Kevin was looking for the one that did not belong with them. It was hard to count as there was so much movement among the group. Then about a third of the way through explaining the process, he saw him. He was a stranger and had not come to town with them. They assumed he was Loggins's man.

"William, the tall thin man moving to the back of the campsite."

"Chief, is he one of yours?"

Linked as they were, Ben confirmed that he was not from the town.

"How do you want to do this?"

"Peter, are you ready?"

"Yes, we are all around him."

"Peter, who's with you at the back of the camp?"

"Steven and Donny are with me."

"Great. As soon as he's out of sight of the others, take him. Did you check how Kevin had been blocking his mind?"

"Yes, I think we all did very impressive."

"Good. Have that block ready as he is holding some kind of power he planned to kill me with. At this time, we don't know how bad it could be. Be careful please."

The stranger kept watching the front slowly slipping backward. He never looked to see what was waiting for him! Just as he was out of view, he turned to find four men waiting for him.

The stranger opened his mind and started to reach for some kind of blast. It was all Peter could tell at the time.

He slammed him with a blinding light that he used for meditation. This was also done at the same time by Steven and Donny. "Bring him to his knees." Once down, they knocked him out. They tied him and put a white bag over his head. They took him back to the ranch, where he awoke in the basement in a room filled with the brightest lights they could find and three guards. One was awake and keeping a mental hold on him all the time.

"Okay, we will soon see about this man and his reason for being here."

Oliver, the one is in grave danger. Do not let him go to the dark one's agent. He is not ready to face the trap they have planned for him! Go now. Stop him!

Oliver left at a dead run. It was just across the road. He could see them turning their mounts to go farther up the road. Oliver wished he could open like William so he could hear him right now.

Oliver, no need to yell. I hear you your very strong, and you are now officially awake wow!

I just had a message from them. You are not to go near the man you just caught.

How do you know that?

They told me. Somehow they can keep track of you but still want me to be your link to them.

We will talk again. Seems I need to know a bit more. Thank them. I will let others take this risk."

Well, Ben, call all the townspeople that are awake to join us please.

Ben opened and called the members of the town that have awoken since the event. William opened to them and answered all the questions they had to the best of his ability. When they finished, he asked them just two question: *How many of you are having dreams, and are any of you taking medications for some illness?*

Only two besides Ben had dreams that they knew were different from the rest. These people were given contacts at the mountain to share their dreams with.

All but one was taking meds for some illness.

How many of you are still taking the pills?

All but one still took the pills.

I want all of you to stop. You will feel better by tomorrow night. Now that you're awake, your body will heal itself. The meds are making you feel worse as you no longer need them. Only people taking meds on the mountain are still not awake.

* * *

The man woke to a bright light in his eyes. Even with the bag still over his head, he had to shut his eyes to stop the pain. He was tied down to a chair with his head tied so it could not move and was pointed up to the ceiling, looking right at the light in the center of the room. Once he was awake again, the guards sent for Peter. Peter came back to the basement room where the man was being held. Steven and Donny came with him. They were going to try and find the one that sent him. Second, they were going to try to discover what type of weapon he had. It was a mind attack of some kind. They came into the room, and the first thing they did was put a block on his powers to open. This was something they had learned in practice on the mountain. You could block someone if you were strong enough. And they soon learned they could link others in as well. The more people, the stronger the block.

"What's your name?"

"Fuck off."

"Okay, this is what's going to happen here. You're going to tell me everything you know. You will lie, but we will still hear the truth, Sid!"

"How did you learn my name, asshole?"

All three of them pushed an image of pure white light into his mind, which brought a scream of great pain from him.

"Sid Hutcherson, we ask the questions. Do not speak again unless you're answering our questions. Is that understood?"

"Yes."

"Where did you come from?"

"Barstow, Las Vegas."

"Where did you join Kevin's camp?"

"Who's Kevin?"

Once again, they gave him a blast of pure light, longer this time. The screams lasted a good twenty to thirty seconds after they had stopped.

"Do I have to explain the rules to you again?"

"No, please, no more. I'll tell you what you want to know."

In the link they were holding, the others asked what just happened. Something was different about him. Peter responded, "I'm not sure. Let's ask a few more questions."

"Sid, why did you come here?"

"I was selected by the leader for the task. He said my mind was pliable and I could slip into the camp. Once in, I was to wait the coming of the one. And then with the weapon he put in my mind, I was to kill him."

"Okay, Sid, listen. I want you to lie when you answer the next question. Do you understand?"

"Yes."

"Okay, Sid, who did you vote for in the last elections?"

"I voted for Dan Meaney for senator." He did not vote at all.

"Sid, something is different now. Can you tell us what it is?"

"Well, when you put that light in my eyes this last time, it got so bad, he left. I can't feel him anymore. For the last time, I'm not sure how long. Six weeks or so. He's been there all the time. Most of the time I can do what I want. When he wants something, I can't stop him from taking over, and I am just along for the ride. He did something to make me blend in, or better, like I was just not there. I eat and slept with them, but they just didn't seem to notice me at all."

"How did he get in your mind? Do you know?"

"I was in a group that was doing work for food, and this man came up to us, asking for men willing to do special work. We were offered better food and housing if we agreed. I was doing so badly that I jumped at the chance and agreed to anything he asked."

"Okay, just one last question. We want you to go back and remember him from the first time you saw him to the last time please."

Sid did as ask, and Peter, Steven, and Donny all got their first look at the dark visitor that had chased them from Las Vegas. Luckily, they had been linked as the pure dark hatred would have overcome them had they been alone when the memories hit them. After a few minutes, they recovered and made plans for Sid's further stay and away from William as they deemed him a great danger. Getting the chief to come over, they showed him the interview and gave him the recommendations for keeping him safe in town. They also told him of the danger of the dark one getting control of him again, so he would have to be kept with one of the towns men that was awake and strong. They then went to inform William of the interview.

"You are aware they will have blocked some of the memory from you."

"Yes, but with the agent we found in the other group, I need to look anyway."

"What agent? When? How?"

"Slow down. You will see my reasons, and then so will the visitors. We have questions for them. And we intend to let you be the go-between until they come out in the open."

"Okay. When do we want to start? Who are we waiting for?"

"Just you. They are already with me. So we can see your memory of that meeting?"

"Yes."

So William entered Oliver's mind a second time that day. With him were Maria, Ben, Peter, Daniel, and Lucy. It took less than a minute for all the events of the morning and all of Oliver's meeting to pass to everyone. They all could see the visitors were friendly and that the dark one should have been killed when first taken as the other had explained. They had view of both visitors.

"I am sorry for the pain you had to endure to get here. We will all be leaving before first light after tomorrow. I now need to speak with Ben and his men. Thank you, Oliver!"

"It's good to be here. And just so you know, they agree on your means of contact with them."

"I thought so. At this time, my abilities are still growing and getting stronger. I know we need time to be ready for the dark one. That's why he's trying so hard to find me now."

* * *

William went to town with Jake and his team as escorts. They rode to the police station where Ben had gone to get his defense force. All were there unless on guard duty.

"Hello, men. Sorry to break up your off time. Ben is aware of what I am about to tell you. I have just met with the two groups waiting for me here. All of them will be coming with me. There was one that followed the Vegas group. He was an agent of what we now know as the dark one. He is a visitor from space. He is the driving force against us. He gave knowledge to the men in the black cars that pursued me out of Las Vegas and is now controlling Lieutenant Briggs and his soldiers. Now they are getting ready to come to Lone Pine together. I don't know when or how many, but soon. It will be before winter. Some of you are awake, and if you have dreams, Let Ben or me know ASAP. Okay, questions?"

"If you're going to help, how will you be able to get here in time?"

"As you all know, we have scouts, and there is always two on this side of the mountain. They will let me know when to come back. Now we will not come into your camp. We will wait for them to find and attack you at the compound. And just when they think they are winning, we will attack them. We will always send help even if we are under attack as well."

"We need more guns and ammo. We can't fight with what we have."

"Yes, you can. Ben and I worked on the strategy you will use. He will start your training the day we leave, two mornings from now.

"You have not all been going to the daily meditations. You all need to go. The benefits are what will get you through the days to come. Things are going to get worse for the next year at least. Together we will survive. There will be a price to pay. If you choose not to pay it, all will die or wish they had!"

"When you came before, you offered a chance to join you and move to the mountains. Can we still do that?"

"You can still take the oath. However, you still need to stay here now. We on the mountain already think of you as part of us. You as a group need to find that to be true as well. They are calling our home Wizard Mountain and I am the wizard they are looking for. We have to get back as we have less time than you. A large group is looking for us and will reach the mountain base in less than ten days. We will turn them back, and a few will escape to spread the tale on how the wizard beat them. As time passes, more will come. One day, we will call for your aid in saving us like we will be doing for you soon. We are already one group, and in time you will all understand. Just go do meditations please."

"Okay, that's enough for William. He has other work to do now. Oh, and thank him for as you saw, he came with three loaded mules and a few of the horses as well. All loaded with guns and ammo for us. Tomorrow we will be issuing them and start training with them. Only those attending the mediations will be given the new weapons. We are going to make traps in front of the compound starting tomorrow, and everyone over the age of thirteen will start training with weapons. The kids ten to twelve will learn to load and clear jams so the others can keep fighting. Now go enjoy the rest of your day. We start early in the morning."

* * *

It was a nice day of rest for them after the fast trip over the mountain, and they and the horses needed it. They started from the camps of the two groups which merged into one. All of them had taken the oath after dinner the first night. It was spent getting to know each other. After dinner, William had all of the people in town come and join the nightly meeting if they were awake. This would be their early warning system and much faster than a rider or dream messages. There were about eight more than normal as Ben had not brought any in that had not found it on their own by hearing it and asking. So on the morning they left, they had become stronger again, and Lone Pine now knew how important they were to them. They were one. After their talk, about forty of the townspeople came to the camp and also took the oath. William had Maria's link as always, and she had Lucy joined as well.

So they left up the road to the true trailhead that led over the right mountain and home. The trip back was like the first, only they knew the way now. The others were led by one of the members that came with them. Their job was to teach landmarks to the new members. It took them an extra day to get back as everything took a bit longer with this many people.

One of the airmen asked William a question as they neared the end of the first day.

"Excuse me, sir. I hear talk about coming back to help them when that force from Las Vegas comes for them and us. Just how do you plan on being their when we are needed?"

"Bill, right? Have you noticed that a lot of things just seem to get done without anyone saying anything? Well, the same methods will be used to get us to Lone Pine on time." He laughed. "Wizards are never late!"

"That's not very reassuring to an old solider."

"I would think not. Just so you know, I was in the Coast Guard and understand your concerns. It's done the same way I sent Oliver messages to help you get here safely. Does that help?"

"So you were the source of his trick of finding what we needed just at the right time."

"Are you happy now on us being on time?"

"So you're like an officer, never quite telling everything right, Admiral?"

"Yes. So you're the first, Master Sargent. We are going to be good friends. So tell me, how will you be the most help to me while you wait to take control over my ground crews?"

"You plan on having aircraft? Yes, we will go and find them later, and you will get them running and take care of them for us."

"Yes, I am and happy to be here."

Oliver and Kevin both came to William as they reached the trees just outside of the camp. They had become good friends. They stopped by William as he was looking forward.

Oliver spoke first. "Did you get lost? You seem to be looking for something."

"Both of you look straight ahead. What do you see?"

"A small grove of trees leading up to a thousand-foot cliff at its back."

"Kevin, what do you see?"

"Well, I see the trees and the cliff. I am not sure how deep the trees are, but that's all. What should we see?"

"That is what I want strangers to see. What it is really your new home." He called out at the top of his voice. "Come on, everyone. They are ready for us now. We are home!"

The next four days went by all too slow, and when they entered camp in the late afternoon hours, they were surprised to see how much work had been done while they were away. Maria and Lucy were there to meet them. After introductions, Lucy took the new members to the common house and got them settled for the night. They had one day to rest and learn their way around the camp. They were told not to pass the tree line without a family member. The next day, they would have jobs assigned to them.

CHAPTER 19

Discovering a New Life

WITH THE NEW additions, life soon got back to the normal daily routines with everyone doing their part. The kids under thirteen just kept coming up with some great ideas and always willing to help wherever they could. Just like normal kids, they all had different things they liked to do. Bull could hope for taking care of and collecting eggs, and they even liked to muck out the stalls. Aaron had more than enough pickers or planters as needed. The military men that had skills in weapons took over our training program. They started getting better results with the one-shot practice. They started spending time in Lone Pine to train them as well so that when they came together, they all understood what the tactics would be, and the orders were the same.

With all this going so well, the biggest gain was in the people! Over half of the original group over eighteen were awake, and the rest showed signs that they soon would be. This gave them their biggest advantage over our adversaries. They had to use radios if they had them at all. Or hand signals. They could speak instantly to any member of the family that was awake. So every work or hunting party had at least two members that were awake. An added bonus to this was they could feel the animal's thoughts and knew if it was young or old. They only took older animals and never any with young to raise.

Waking up meant something had changed. They could hear the thoughts of others in the family, awake or otherwise. Some had dreams. All of the ones waking up learned how to send messages in their dreams to people they knew. Some came to awareness by thinking of a family member that was awake. When this happened, that person would hear you as if you called their name. They would open to you and answer you call. When it happened this way, that person became their guide into their new life. They had over eighteen people in camp that were awake now, and most were not far behind. The one that was not and was getting weaker under the workload of the camp life was Malinda. Even with going to morning and evening meditations, she was showing no sign of getting better. She was starting to miss work due to illness. Maria had taken over dealing with her, trying to find out what was holding her back. Talking with Shara, the one who knew her best and before the event, she had learned that Malinda lost her fiancé and his two young sons to the event. And she could not move on.

All the others would be paired with one of the awake members when they showed signs of waking up. That was why they asked daily of the ones not yet awake, "Are you awake?" This is your first step into a whole new life.

They all had telepathic abilities when they first woke up. These were a great help to them in a number of ways. The first was that no one could lie to them. When a person was going to tell them a lie, the first thing they thought about was the thing they were about to try and keep from them. Somehow, they could see this as if they had said it to them. So when they then told a lie, they already knew the truth. This was a secret we told people they wanted to question. They then asked questions as they did with Sid in Lone Pine and saw the truth and lies as they asked questions. Unlike his case, they just asked and recorded the truth and let them think they believed them. As a result, they learned everything they wanted. Next and sometimes first for a dreamer was being able to send and receive messages in dreams. The dreams were few. They could send and receive dreams from others. Most of them could not do this. They could all be reach in their dreams. And if they wished to speak with someone who was awake and a dreamer, they just needed to think about them before they went to sleep, and they would come to them. The other great benefit was that as time passed, they got stronger and better. You could contact any of the others that were awake, and so far they have not found a great distance to be any problem. William and Ben in Lone Pine talked all the time, keeping up on how well things were going and if there was any danger coming their way. The last gift that William gained was the ability to sense other minds and know if they were close or far.

The major benefit to all of these new powers was health. The mind, once awake, turned on the body's full healing powers. This was the reason those taking meds, for one reason or another, had to stop as the body started to cure or heal them from the ills we each carried. In the first month, they had three broken bones. Two of them happened to members who were awake. The other to one of the boys not yet old enough to be awake. In each case, regular treatment was to put the bone back in alignment, make a cast, and wait six to eight weeks. The two that were awake started to complain after just five days. And when they took the cast off, their bones were healed completely. The young boy took the whole six weeks and then had to rebuild the strength in his arm. The rest of them started to get sick if they had daily meds. They kept doing what they learned, that as soon as they felt worse and taking medication, they had to stop for a day. If they felt better after not taking pills, they would stop taking them. Once someone woke up, even old injuries started to get better. Unknown to them at the time, Albert, at forty-eight, was fighting cancer and had been given one to two years to live. He had not told anyone. He just kept taking the meds they had for him. He was special, and he would have woken up much sooner than he did. Or he woke up sooner than they knew, and his illness took all his strength to get him cured of the cancer before the rest of the gifts could start to work.

The other thing they gave credit to was the whole foods diet. They lived on no processed foods as they ate fresh meat and grew their own foods and got plenty of outdoor work every day. Over the next three months, they had a very peaceful time, not counting the large group of men that came looking for them just after they returned from Lone Pine.

* * *

The scouts had been looking for them for the last five days. Now all the dreamers had seen them coming. They had guns and a bad light around them. Not like Sid, just a shade of gray, they called it. By the time they found them, they had the zip lines all done, and Lucy had a plan to use them. They would find them, track them, and once they passed the far zip line, they would start to move in behind them.

They were coming right up the road straight to Lodgepole Campgrounds. It was there they planned to stop them. So after they passed the General Sherman tree, they started to infiltrate behind them using the zip lines. Jake's team was followed by Peter's team. Next, once they reached the tree, they started up the mountain behind them. Lucy and the main group then took the lines that stopped above the campgrounds. William went with her team. Every time they did these things, Maria kept watch so they could see it all and do better the next time.

They were in the tree blind at Lucy's request. She and the others took up positions to wait for them to reach this part of the camp. To make it easy, they started a fire in the nearest fire ring and had two volunteers wait by it. They were all linked, so they knew that Jake and Peter's teams had made visual contact and were following them. They had all seen the fire and were trying to circle it. Lucy had the two teams each take a side while giving the two men orders to move to the safe areas that they had made just in case. They just made it to their safe fallback positions when the men came into the campsite.

The leader, calling himself the Revenger, had the men start to circle the campsite with the fire. They spread out in a tight organized formation. They had training and discipline. They moved quickly and quietly. When they had the site encircled, they moved in. They found two men, well-armed and waiting for them. As soon as he could, Revenger sent word back by radio for the rabbit to take the news back. They had found the wizard.

"You men, lay down your weapons and stand up so we can see you better."

"No, I'm afraid we cannot do that. Tell you what. You lower your weapons and we won't have to shoot you. What do you say to that? What's your name, so we get it right who we kill!"

"My name is Revenger, and that's what I came to do, ravage your whole group."

"You will be dead in minutes if you try."

"What make you think so?"

At this moment, Lucy had her force charge with their weapons from the uphill side of the camp, all from cover, and then she called to him.

"I think your men heard us. We are ready to fire just as you are. You thought you have my men trapped. All you got is armed and dangerous bait. Now, Revenger, you've been looking for the wizard. You found him. All who find him that were not invited die."

"Your force is much smaller than mine, and we do not fear the wizard."

Peter and Jake reported they had closed the gap and taken two back guards as well as the rabbit.

Not knowing how much danger he was in, the order was given to open fire. For the next five minutes, shots rang out all over the mountain. It could be heard clearly back at base camp. Once he heard the shots, William went to the zip lines and was on his way to the campground.

With his first shot, the security force all took one shot and dropped seven of the attackers. On the other side, they just started spraying the woods, hopping to hit something. They hit three of the family. Maria reported that all three were dead. William had everyone take cover and gave orders to only shoot to protect themselves or another family member. The zip lines made the trip just over ten minutes! It was a twenty-minute drive and about two hours on horseback. William was surprised at how well they worked. He arrived at the last landing just after the shooting stopped. He opened to all in the family who could hear him.

"I want status on all targets at this moment."

"We have six kills at this time."

"Okay. I want the leader alive. On my signal, take the others."

Then there was yelling. "Revenger, this is the wizard speaking. As that is not my name, it's safe for you to use. You have killed three of my family and will soon pay the bill! However, do you wish for all your men to die? You killed three of mine at a cost of seven of yours. A bad exchange rate, don't you think?"

"What are you talking about? I have the upper hand here, and soon I will have your head in a sack."

"Good plan, if you can make it work. Check on how many men you have left. We know you have radios of some kind. Check? Oh, and you should know that we caught your rabbit and the two men you left on back guard. We have two skilled teams of men behind you, and you're surrounded. You have already lost and do not seem to know it."

"Show yourself and I can end this with one shot."

"Did you mean like the one shot we used to kill your seven?"

"No, like the single bullet I will put in your brain!"

"If you check, you'll find that the seven are dead. And if you do not surrender, I will kill—" *How many now?*

Eight, sir.

"Eight more with just one shot. Do you understand?"

"That's impossible."

"I am waiting for your answer."

They could all hear the radios and reports of the dead. None of them could tell how many of either side had been firing, but they did have seven dead.

"We cannot tell how many of your men fired at us, so I believe you're bluffing!"

"Well, you don't know me very well, or you would not think I'm bluffing." *When I say hand, shoot the eight.* "I used to teach poker in Las Vegas, and all my students knew my definition of bluffing. And that was last to act with the best hand."

As he said the word, one clear loud shot rang out over the campground.

"Now I think you need to check. I think you just lost another eight men, and I only heard one shot. How about you?"

"What, you fired a gun and you want me to believe you killed eight more of my men?"

"Yes."

"Get me a count. Did we lose anyone to that shot?"

There was a lot of talking on and off the radio, and it took about two minutes for the count of dead from the one shot to come back—eight dead, one badly wounded by a through and through shot.

"The question was, do you surrender? It's okay. I will add a second question. I want you to give me a number. How many more have to die here today? Beware, there is only one right answer to that question. Now before we get to that, who is your second in charge?"

"You don't need to know who's second." Butcher popped in his mind clear as day. "You deal with me."

"Butcher, please step forward. Did you hear my questions? Now you see you cannot lie or evade my questions, so surrender or answer my question please."

Butcher moved forward, somewhat against his will, but he came to stand by Revenger.

Revenger looked up toward the source of the voice, and there was a man all dressed in white with a glow all around him.

"It's a simple answer. All of you."

"Ahh, sorry, that's the wrong answer." A pistol was in his hand, smoke still rolling out of the barrel. "So, Butcher, who is your second-in-command?"

"Harold, get up here now. And now what? You shoot me as well?"

"That depends on how you answer the question I ask him. Don't answer now. I have to talk to Harold first."

"Begging your pardon. I don't think you do."

"Why?"

"The answer is zero."

"Well, Harold, seems like you're not getting a promotion today. Now how many men do you have left? Have them all come in the campsite. Sling or holster, any weapons they have. If they reach for any of them, they will be shot dead on the spot. Is that understood?"

"Yes. There should be about twenty-five left. What are you going to do to us now?"

"Lucky for you, we don't kill everyone and leave them lying in the sun. Some of you will be allowed to stay here. The others can leave and go wherever they please. They just have to give their word that they will never come back to this place unless invited by us."

"Really? That's it? Nothing more?"

"Most of the people remaining do not realize that we have been attacked by an alien force and that they are coming to take our world and make it theirs. Any of us who are left will be slaves if they have their way. I am building the foundation of our defense and army to fight them. Tell all your men they have till tomorrow morning to make up their minds on what they want. Anyone who wants to leave and gives their word to never reveal our location will be given three days' food and water to take with them."

"How can you know they won't tell if you let them leave? We are not living in the best of times, and we have done many terrible things in the last few weeks."

"That is all true, but have you forgotten what you've just been a part of here?"

"Well, no, but people lie about these things all the time or later change their minds. How can you trust any of us?"

"I am the wizard, and I will know! Go make your beds here in this site after you bury all your dead. Talk it over as a group, and all have to make up their minds. Lucy will take care of the details for me."

* * *

On the islands to the west and in and around all the major cities and towns, people were banning together. They were making new associations and forming armed groups to protect and some for raiding parties. They had good and bad, and fighting was ongoing, mostly over food and water. The drug cartels in the south had become the power in the areas they held as their organizations did not fall apart like governments did. Next were rogue army units fighting. Here was some of the worse. The one group they all talked about was the islanders. They had started to take control in South American, and no one seemed to be able to stop them. The only other story that seemed to be traveling was of a small group that fought its way out of Las Vegas the day of the event and disappeared in the mountains. Many of the groups in the area were looking for them. As time passed, the stories of their escape grew with each retelling, with just enough facts to lead them to the east side of the mountain and Lone Pine.

CHAPTER 20

The Islander and Other Visitors

THEY NOW CALLED themselves the queen and king of the Pacific. The two had set about building up the largest armed force in the western hemisphere. It might have been the biggest in the whole world. In the last three months, they had gained four working navy ships and, through the general's rank, as much military equipment and a total of approximately thirty thousand soldiers and sailors. They sailed to all the nearby island groups and taken over or just moved in as the local population had left or were dead by one means or another. In many places, they found less than 20 percent of the people alive. At these places, they gave aid, food, water, and a reason to hope. Some of these islands held up to thirty to fourty thousand people on them.

By the end of the third month, their military force was awesome. They had four ships of the line (a ship of the line was a warship), three destroyers, and one aircraft carrier. They also had one oiler to fuel them. None of the nuclear ships were working as they always had to have pumps running. These all stopped the day of the event. They had an odd assortment of working aircrafts. Their problem was, they only had six pilots to fly them. They used the carrier as a troopship. It only had small guns and made a great floating base for them. They left for the west coast of South America, leaving ten thousand men behind to maintain order. By now, the islands were the most normal place on earth. They took twenty thousand plus to deal with anyone who had any kind of soldiers to deal with on the mainland.

Their forces spread fear and panic before them. The few pockets of resistance were brutally crushed, their bodies left on the field of battle. They took only young women and girls alive. For most of them were just a small force pulling up to a compound, and the groups inside gave up and joined the islanders. Those who resisted were given the full measure of the military might they brought with them. After the battle was engaged, no quarter was ever given. They killed them all. Word would spread, and they would run or join them.

They had simple tactics: use the missile destroyers to break any shore defenses and then land the eight tanks supported by overwhelming numbers of troops. They killed any fighter they found once on land.

The first effect was that all the peoples, in the way of the islanders, started to move north, pushing the people there to fight or move themselves. It was not long after this started that William, Maria, Lucy, Ben, and Peter started having dreams, showing them what the islanders were doing and which direction they traveled! At first it was a dream here or there. As time passed, it became once a week. William did not want the others to know until they had time to plan for them. So all talk of the islanders was done is silent mode only.

* * *

The place they chose for their home was picked for a number of reasons. It was not easy to get to, and they hid off the main trails. They always knew they would be found and had been training and working on defensive plans since they got there. They would have to fight on both sides of the mountain in Lone Pine and in the valley below. They started out with only seventeen adults and some twelve kids. They learned to fight on their way out of town in those first two days. Since then, they added many new members to the family—the crew from the one lucky jet that landed just off Blue Diamond,

Aaron, and Bull. All of Lone Pine was under their protection as well. It seemed they were linked from here on out. They needed each other. They already helped them with the troops from the desert base.

The most recent additions from Oliver and Officer Tomkins were numbers to forty-two. Add to that the nine who asked to stay with them after their failed attack. Adults counted in at fifty-one. The reserve was all the kids that passed qualifying tests with weapons. There were about fifteen now. They would be runners, keeping the fighters supplied during any fighting. They all carried weapons if qualified. And all over the age of thirteen fought if needed. So they now had one of the best trained groups of fighters at about sixty-one.

They were going to need a lot more people or some other means of keeping the mass of people moving up from the south. All were being pushed by the islanders. Up to this time, the stories about Wizard Mountain had been keeping them away. With a greater threat moving up from the south, they had become the lesser of two evils.

Now with the islanders coming, they were going to come for them to take or to join. They saw it in their dreams. They needed to get more soldiers and new ways of fighting. They were going to be outnumbered in all the battles. It had been a bit over six months, and they had good crops to get in so they could eat. Now people would come for their food and them. They had all seen three different battles, and they had to survive and get stronger as they did it.

William called for a family meeting with only awake guards on duty so they could be there as well. Unlike other meetings, this one was mandatory for all, including children!

The evening meal was over, and the cleanup was done. Everyone gathered for the meeting. With the whole family coming, the common room was not going to be big enough. William ordered the large firepit to be lit and as many seats as could be arranged. In short order, they all arrived on time and took seats, waiting for William. Almost no one knew why the meeting had been called. The last meeting all had to attend was at the ranch in Lone Pine. For most of them, life had returned to normal with daily routines. They all had jobs that they were good at and liked to do. For most of them, they knew there had been a fight as they had been on alert but never called. Lucy, as always, took care of the problems that came their way. Maria stepped up to the front and started to address them.

"Good evening, everyone. We are here tonight to talk about our family and its safety in the months ahead. As many of you know, we are all waking up. Some faster than others. Tonight we are going to talk about that and other things. First, however, we need to tell you that we lost a family member today. Malinda has slowly been getting weaker, and she passed in her sleep last night. We believe she died of sadness, unable to move past the day of the event. The services will be held according to her wishes. She wants to be buried on a hill facing the sunrise. We will see you there. Now here's, William."

"First, I would like to say we will miss Malinda. She was a great cook and a lovely lady. I will miss her greatly. Now we have a lot to cover, and we will stay till we are all done. How many of you know why we ask if you're awake? Please, just by show of hands." About 25 percent of the hands went up. "Okay, well, if you're right and know what I'm about to talk about, you will soon be awake. It started for me the day of the event. I woke early from a bad dream. It was such a strong dream. I woke my wife with the violent nature of my waking. I know now that the manner of my waking was to make sure I acted on what I learned in my dream.

"I have mental powers and have been using them to guide us here and keep us safe from all harm. Now first things first, we believe that you will all be awake, but with what we are going to face over the next six months to a year, you will all need to know what we can do. Things started. I am a dreamer. That was my first gift. It allowed me to see what was about to happen. Just hours after I woke up, everything running at the time stopped working, no matter what or where it was. Just as I had seen in my dream. The original family knew this, but not right away. This knowledge gave me time to get them all to this mountain. The second gift I got was that no one could lie to me or anyone who was awake. For most, it the first thing you notice when you wake up. The third is I can enter most people's minds and see their intentions. I can also make people look straight at me and only see what I want them to see. The man leading the group against me was shot by me with a gun I had in my hand the whole time, and none of them saw it. I had seen in his mind that he planned to kill me the first chance he got. Had he tried to keep me out, I could not have made him see what I wanted him to see. Keeping this secret is very important to our safety. Because the weakest person here with no powers at all can keep me out forever. I want everyone to practice keeping us out the next few days. All you have to do is say to yourself, 'I want quiet please!' Those of us awake will acknowledge that you are blocked. After the first time, you can stop and go back to normal. But always remember that you can block us. Okay, some of you have just tried, and it worked. We lost you. Practice tomorrow please. Once you're awake, you can send messages in your dreams to others, awake or not. They do have to be asleep to receive them. Do not get confused. Being awake is different from waking up from sleep. Those of us that are awake can talk to each other at great distances. We have not found a limit on how far we can send messages. I can do a few things others are still working on. We learned that waking on your own is best. However, things have changed. Now I am going to ask a question, and we want you to allow us to hear your thoughts and just think the answer in your head. Have any of you heard of the islanders?"

All the awake members heard almost all of them. Maria and Lucy took note of the ones that failed.

"Excellent. You are not awake yet, but with very few exceptions, you can all hear us. This will be our greatest advantage in the months ahead. We dreamers have all seen three battles coming our way, and we need to get ready for them. And if we survive all of them, there is a bigger challenge after that. They are called the islanders. They were over thirty thousand strong when they left the islands five weeks ago. They sailed on five navy ships and have been taking over South America city by city and are moving north. They are coming here. How long we have is unknown at this time. Starting tomorrow, all weapons and combat training is doubled. Our free time here is over, and we need to be ready when the shit hits the fan."

That night, Oliver had his first dream of his own. Peter and William both shared it as well. Each saw the same dream, but each saw it a bit different, like one was the first and some of the middle while the other saw more at the end the other did not. After the dream, they all woke up, unable to sleep. Oliver and Peter both reached out to William. William, already awake from the same dream, had them meet him at the common room, and they talked about it.

"In your dreams, you both saw the six men making their way to us?"

Peter spoke first with Oliver right behind him. "*Yes*."

"It's that group from the south I saw coming up the coast when I sent you the way to find us, Oliver. I do not know if they are friend or foe. It is clear they are dangerous. Something is going to happen with them very soon. Peter, go wake the rapid response team on duty today please. We need to be ready for anything. Well, Oliver, you no longer need to listen to the silent council. With my help, you are awake and a dreamer as well."

"Yes, I have much more input than before yesterday. It's a bit overwhelming."

"Yes, take it slow. Make sure to keep up the meditations as they will help. We need to inform the family that company is coming and their intentions unknown."

Peter returned with the team, and they were given orders to find and follow the six men without being seen if they could. They would be becoming from the west, and they would be looking for them.

"I am not sure how, but I think they know where we are. Take rations for two weeks. I am not sure how soon they may arrive. You need to find them and let us know."

* * *

It had been a long and dangerous voyage up the coast to Moral Bay. They managed to slip out of the harbor and got everything loaded from the beach and made it safely out to sea. With eight good sailors on board, they kept moving, running three shifts so they could make the best time to the California coast.

On the second day, they had to deal with pirates trying to take the boat. The SEALs had all changed to civilian clothes to look like harmless and normal people caught on a sailboat at the end of the world. They tried to outrun the boat. At last the wind fell off, and they did not want to use the motor unless as a last resort as that would make the prize worth much more.

So the plan was to have the Youngs on deck and in full view and run as fast and as far as they could, hoping they could get a way. Below deck, the SEALs and the girls hid from sight. The SEALs were armed, and if they had to fight, the pirates would have a nasty surprise waiting for them.

The Youngs would sail as long as they could and then take cover below decks. Under full sail in a poor wind, the boat was only making four knots, running with the wind. At that speed, they would be overtaken in five minutes or so. It was less, and the Youngs ran to the cabin below decks and took up arms. In less than two minutes, they felt the boats bump and the men come on board the *Dream Wind.* The plan was for the SEALs to shoot them when they tried to come below decks. The pirates all started yelling in Spanish and English when they came aboard. They were waiting for a response from the Youngs. No one below responded. The SEALs had all found their targets and signaled for the Youngs to answer they would not come up on deck. His wife made the response. They were more likely to rush a woman than a man. As hoped, they started to rush into the cabin. As soon as the door opened and cleared, the SEALs all took their shots, killing the men on the boat. The two men that remained on the patrol boat started to move away. O'Brian was waiting for that move. He quickly rushed to the deck and jumped on the other boat, killing the last two men onboard. They quickly took anything of use onto the *Dream Wind* and then set fire to the craft and set it adrift by starting the fire below decks. They hoped to be out of sight before anyone could get there to see them sailing north. They started the motor and ran as fast as they could until the fire on the horizon was all they could see. O'Brian had them run without light at all times and no light after dark.

Checking their course with Wayne, they planned at least a nine-day voyage up the coast to the central California coast. After the run-in with the pirates' craft, they decided to go out west deeper into the pacific. For the next two days, they sailed northwest to give the coast an even bigger gap. Like the soldiers they were, they monitored all the radio traffic they could, including short wave. They only listened when they heard something. They never replied. As they moved farther out, they started to hear regular chatter from a number of different boats to the same call sign: island one. It seemed to be a command center for a group out of the Hawaiian Islands. They were scout ships looking for and taking any and all boats found. They were pressing them into service and becoming part of their navy. It was clear they did not wish to be found by this group. They turned to a northeast course, heading back to the Mexico coastline. They were just north of Mexico's southern border.

The night watch was targeted. The boat was under sail, doing a nice eight knots. Juan had the tiller on autopilot and was making his rounds, and staying alert was his habit when on wheel duty. He walked around the boat, stopping at all four quarters and taking time to look around for anything not normal. He would spend from five to ten minutes at each point. Tonight was just more of the same until his third walk. When he reached the bow's starboard quarter, he had been using the night vision as it was so dark that night. He was just about to move on when he saw it coming right at them. It was an armed navy vessel, ninety-five-footer with twin fifty-cal machine guns on the forward mounts and two more singles on each side. It was flying an unknown flag. Juan could see at least six men on deck. Judging by the bow spray, it was doing fifteen to twenty knots. His first action was to start the motor and drop the sails. At the same time, he called for O'Brian to get up on deck. They were hoping that if the other boat had radar, it had not seen the sails yet. They dropped them and changed course, seeing if they changed as well. The radical actions had the rest of them up as well and on deck. They got organized and pulled the sails down and got the boat to full speed, which on the motor was fourteen knots in a calm sea. They turned to the south and made a run to the south. They were trying to lose the other boat in the dark. The course changed. Soon the other boat out of sight. They cut the motor and returned to sails for the quiet of no motor.

As soon as they could, they changed back to the northeast course. As soon as they settled on the new course, they heard the boat call for a second craft help to cut them off. They had surface radar, which picked up the sails. Dropping the sails, they turned back to the south. Going back to the motor, they turned out to sea and headed due west for the next fifteen minutes. They had the radios, listening to their every move. It was a game of hide-and-seek as they did not know where the other boat was coming from. Had the SEALs not kept all the radios, they would have been in the bag already. They got just enough information to stay a step ahead of them. That would all change at dawn. They all put their heads together to find a way out of this mess. First, what did they know? Two patrol boats were trying to intercept them. One was known to be behind them. The other assumed to be in front or on one side or the other. The second ship was of unknown type and armaments and ability at this time. The first boat had at least five machine guns mounted and six or more crew on board. The current course was south and west, away from the shore at full speed against the wind. The plus side for them was the boats chasing them had no idea how many people were on board or how well they were armed. The second ship was of unknown type. Their armaments and abilities were also unknown at this time.

Their first decision was to change course and hoist full sails and increase their speed. The new course was north by northeast. They kept this course until they reached a mile from the shoreline. Now the shore gave them large blind spots from the radar and lots of room to run. So the chase began. The two boats kept updating speed and location over the radios. They were trying to arrive at their target at approximately the same time with the *Dream Wind*. Upon hearing this, O'Brian lay out his plan.

"First, we want to mess up their timing. So using the radio traffic, we can pick place of our choosing, not theirs. Cut the motor and fill the tank so when we need it, it's ready to go."

They managed to make the chase last eighteen hours due to a heavy fog for about five hours that first morning. After cutting the motor, they had a light wind and hid in the coastal clutter. They hid from them many times as the boats passed by without seeing them.

O'Brian got the timing he wanted, and it would be just minutes before they would be spotted. He had the Youngs on deck and had Wayne start the motor and ran straight at the nearest boat. It was a thirty-five-footer and had a fifty cal mounted in the front and a crew of four. They saw the sailboat they called the second start toward the *Dream Wind.* The response was they were six minutes out. They gave the order to stop and detain the boat. At this time, the master and gunny were getting into their scuba gear the Youngs had on board. They slipped into the water fore and aft, waiting for the boats to come in sight of the *Dream Wind.* They only had a five-minute wait for the first boat to come into view at the rear of the boat. As soon as he saw the bow, the master sergeant started to swim to the boat, keeping a steady pace and moving to the stern of the boat. Shortly after that, the second boat came into view slightly to the west at about a forty-five-degree angle on the bow of the *Dream Wind.* As soon as he saw it, the gunny started his swim to his target as well. He had to fight the current, which kept trying to push him ashore. This was going to make the timing harder for him. Luckily, the boat was still moving, helping him reach his target. Now that both targets were in sight, Wayne and Veronica started working the sails like they were not even aware of the two boats converging on them. The four SEALs still on board were below with the two girls hiding on the floor out of the way. They had the guns loaded and ready if needed. However, if his plan worked, they would be free with no other boats chasing them.

At the first order from the boats, Veronica would go below. On the second order, Wayne would come below. Then they would wait on the sergeants to start the party with the mines. Both swimmers had light to signal each other when they arrived and then when they had placed the mines to the boats ready to blow. The first call to the boat came about three minutes after the gunny started his swim. The distance was still closing as each chase boat moved to within one hundred feet of the *Dream Wind.* When they reached it, they both stopped, and by this time, they were both pulling a SEAL with them. This was better for the swimmers and harder for the ones on board! Because now the divers lost sight of each other and had to relay signals to the boat when they were both ready to start their timers. As soon as the two had sent the ready signal, the boat sent the go sign.

By now, the first boat was yelling orders for Wayne and Veronica to come out on deck with their hands up, saying they would not be harmed.

O'Brian answered, "We are not armed and just want to sail home. What do you want?" He yelled all of this. It was done in perfect Spanish to lend a bit more confusion, stalling for time for the swimmers to reach the boat.

As the sailor on the first boat started yelling back, the two swimmers knocked on the hull. A quick look on the time showed they had less than a minute before the big bang! When that happened, the four SEALs still on the *Dream Wind* would fire at their targets. At the same time, Wayne would start the motor and start their run up the coast to California and safety they hoped. Just as the crewman started to speak, the boats both leaped up out of the water by the bows. A large boom from the underwater blast came with a huge wall of water trying to fly up. The SEAL fired at the same time and then kept shooting as the *Dream Wind* started its run to the north. When the spray all came back down and the air cleared, they could see at least six men in the water. The gunfire had stopped, and the men in the water tried to swim away from the sinking wrecks before they went down. The run the *Dream Wind* made had taken them out about two more miles from the shore. As it was coming on sunset, if the men in the water didn't make a start soon, they would have to spend the night at sea. Vic had been listening on the radio and reported that one of the boats got a radio call just after the mines went off. The reply was "send us your position." They never answered. Veronica and Carlita helped the swimmers back on board, and the *Dream Wind* was running in a strong winds to the north with a following sea, making a full eighteen knots now on a northeast track. In the after-action reports on boat status, they determined that the chase had cost them too much of the fuel, and if they could, they needed to stop and get more. They also learned the islanders were the ones sending the boats.

O'Brian decided to take a chance and send a response back for the last call from the sunken boats. The message was "We've been hit. One boat sunk. We are taking water. Need assistance. Our position is about five miles north of the Mexican border, approximately seven miles offshore. We need medical aid as well. I repeat, we are—" They left the message like that. The position was a good thirty miles behind them. The plan was to get all boats rushing to help the sunken boats behind. They had lost at least a week, and as they would need to stop for fuel, they decided to get more food and water if they could as well. They ran in sight of the coast now. As far as they could tell, the islanders had not reached this far north as of yet. For the next three days, they worked the coast, looking for a place where they might find what they needed. They were checking the many small places on the Mexican riviera, looking for food and fuel. They found a small marina just a little north of Manzanillo Resort. There was a fair amount of small sailboats coming and going in the two days they lay up on the edge of the horizon, watching the place. Their water was getting low and nearing the critical level, so they sailed in on the third morning, not using the motor and keeping that secret at all times. O'Brian and three other SEALs went ashore. Angel and Vic stayed on board with the others.

O'Brian and the others went looking for the supplies they needed to get on with their trip. They needed food and water and fuel if they could find any available. As it turned out, the port had limited power and lived off the grid, only having internet access for a few hours at a time. Their power supply was still working as it was a generator system and only ran for four hours in the evening, giving lights and hot water. If they had phones, this was the only time they could charge them. The power was on every night from 6:00 p.m. to 10:00 p.m. So the event had little effect on this small port.

In a very short time after docking, they had found and made a deal for water. The food was a different story. Seafood was all they had. No use paying for what they can get free as they went. As it worked out, they traded a good deal of the fish they had caught while watching the port.

O'Brian also wanted to get some current information on the islanders and any other news they could find here. So after the deal was made for the water, they went to the local cantina for drinks and information. There was only one in the village, and it was busy as the marina was bigger than it looked from the outside. They were surprised to find their beer warm but very good. They just drank and listened to what they could hear. There was a lot of talk about what had happened! Was it a war? Who was behind it? The place was busy, and there seemed to be a lot of misplaced people wondering the same things. Asking around, they learned it had been the same talk for a week or so. They were now the talk of the village, replacing the islanders that came in five days ago. O'Brian had been talking to the bartender and an old sailor at the bar. He asked the sailor to join them at the table for another drink if he liked. At the table, the old sailor was a bit more open. Jesus had a bad feeling about them.

"Senor O'Brian, you need to avoid these men. We heard stories about what they do when they come. If the people resist, they kill all the men and take only the women and young girls, never to be seen again."

"Are these stories you heard or information that we can check on?"

"There are two young boys that made it here in a small sailboat about two weeks ago. We have them hidden and hope that we can find a way to avoid them showing up here!"

Hearing this, a group of seven men turned and said, "We are here already."

O'Brian's hair stood up on the back of his neck. This was trouble, plain as day. As the locals started talking to them, O'Brian and the others started to take their measure of them all. They all carried guns in the open, and two of them were very large Samoans standing over six feet two or better. One was at least 280 pounds. The other was an easy 325 pounds. The rest looked like regular navy personnel. O'Brian decided it was time to leave, and he and the others got up and started for the door.

One of the islanders and two others had come in and asked the bartender where the people from the sailboat were now.

"There they are. Why don't you ask them?"

"Hey, you there. Stop where you are!"

"Keep walking," whispered John.

Just as they reached the door, two men stepped in front of it as another reached for O'Brian's shoulder. The only word John said was "*Go.*"

In the next three seconds, the two men in front of the doors were laying on the floor and trying to get up. The other one was gasping for air as John had him by the neck against the wall, a .9 mm pistol stuck in his mouth!

"Now listen as I tell you once. Never touch me again or I will kill you! Do you understand?"

"Yes," he said with a short gasp for air.

"Good. I am going to let go of you. If you say or do anything, I will shoot you! Do you understand?"

Again, a one-word answer. "Yes."

"Good. Did you two get their guns?"

"Yes, boss, we got them."

"Okay, let them up and join the others. As for you four, if any of you reach for your guns, we will shoot all of you."

One of the locals spoke up. "What do you think you're doing? You heard them. The islanders are coming!"

"How long have they been hanging around?"

"Just about four days now."

"And no one asked them where they came from or what their business was for being here? These are strange days, and with the little news you get here, you should be a bit more cautious about who's coming ashore. Well, here's a news flash. These guys are taking over! I do not know if it will be for good or bad. I do know it will be their way!"

One of the four men spoke at that point. "You don't know."

"Shut up or die. Do you understand? Just nod."

After a second, the man did as he was told.

"Good." He was now talking to the man at his feet. He asked, "Why are you here?"

"Fuck off. I'm not telling you anything."

"Hmm, so you're tough guys, right?"

"What do you mean?"

"Well, you run around in a pack, bullying people to get what you want. You like having power over the people wherever you go. Hey, guys, let's see if we can out bully them. What do you say?"

"Okay, boss, sounds like fun. I think after the last week, I'd feel better if we beat the shit out of someone. Might as well be them."

"Okay, stupid, you're the boss, right?"

"Yes."

"The four of us are going to kick the shit out of you and your men. When it's over, you're going to tell me what I want to know. If by some miracle you win, we will answer your questions. Deal?"

"Hey, asshole, you lose. We have seven men. There are only four of you!"

"Good, you can count. I know it's not really fair, but you just have to do your best. Now here's how it works. I have a gun on you already, so you pick four men to take on my friends. And they kick their asses all over the place. One of them will hold the gun on you, and I will fight the next two by myself. At that time, it will be four to two in our favor. Or you can just tell me what I want to know. Talk or pick three men."

O'Brian knew he would pick the two Samoans in the first three, with one other guy. As soon as he pointed him out, the three attacked the last guy he pointed to. He was out in just one punch. Now it was three on two, and at first it looked like the Samoans were going to take the SEALs. They were fast, but the SEALs were faster still. If not for the extra man, they might have lost. O'Brian was way ahead of the dummy that was leading this group. They went after the smaller one first, and no matter which way he turned, he was hit in the mid-section or chest. They did not ever hit his face. They did kick the right knee from behind each time he turned. He was building into a huge rage, then all at once he yelled and rushed them head down. This was what they had been waiting for. The back of his neck would be the weakest part of his head. They lined up for him, so he rushed a straight line at them. They both pivoted and landed a doublehanded blow to his neck. He stopped and turned for a second. All his limbs turned to rubber, and he fell face first to the ground.

Juan was getting tired, and as soon as the other two stepped up, he backed out to breathe again. They started all over again, and in less than a minute, Juan was back and fell into the rhythm with them. This time, it took much less time as Juan was no easy target, and the Samoan was already getting tired. Once he reached his rage stage, it was over as well in the same fashion as before.

"So now you see how this is going, and it gets worse from here. Now do I have to kick these guys' ass or do you want to talk now?"

"Fuck you, asshole."

With that response, O'Brian turned to the men nearest to him, and in just two punches each, they were out on the floor next to the others.

"Now we will fight. The guys want to play with your last man a bit. Oh, and it's too late now. You made us do this, so you get to be part of it."

The last man was out in just three blows, one from each of the SEALs. The boss did not have it so good. O'Brian was the one who could have taken the Samoans one at a time if necessary. He was going to make him pay. He beat him so fast the guy never sung more than once. Just as he was about to fall, O'Brian held him up and let him recover. As soon as he could stand, they started again. At this point, the locals stopped everything to watch the world-class beating the seven took.

"Your men are all down, and you can't even stand up. You may never pee standing up again, so do we do more, or do you want to talk now? Or do we need to go another round?"

"Who the hell are you, man? I can't talk to you. If I do, I'm a dead man as soon as they get here."

"I see your problem. I think I can make it an easier question. Do you want to die right here and now or take your chances later with the islanders?"

"*Who in the hell are you guys?*"

"If it will make a difference, I will tell you, but it would be better if you don't know. Are you sure you want to know?"

"Yes, I need to know please."

"Okay, we are SEAL team 18 on our way home. Happy now?"

"Oh my god, we really never did have a chance, did we!"

"No, you did not. Are you here on one of their patrol boats or some other class?"

"We are advance scouts moving far ahead of the main fleet. Our job is to keep the stories of us spreading too fast and try to filter what is allowed out."

"So you're still here looking for the boys, right?"

"Yes, and these people were just about to give them up as we started killing their kids if they did not."

"All of you locals, leave three people here and go start getting ready to leave. Bartender, you stay please. Juan, have them take you to the boys. They are coming with us as well. Go. We leave as soon as we take care of that boat. Last question. Where is the boat, and how many men are on it?"

They got the location of the boat. They went back to their boat, got the rest of their gear, and went after the boat. It had a crew of twelve men and three more of the group they had just dealt with. The locals, seeing what was coming, decided to go north as well as soon as they could. While they went after the boat, the old sailor made sure they got the fuel for the *Dream Wind* and saw that they had cover if needed. Another five of the fishermen took the seven to the local freezer and locked them in.

* * *

Len was back in three minutes with an older man in tow.

"This is Martine. He is the alcalde of this burg."

"Martine, do you speak and understand English?"

"Si, senor."

"Great. I asked for you because you need to hear what this man is going to tell me. However, if he lies to me, I will punish him violently. Do you understand?"

"Si, I do. We talk about the men seeing they are big trouble."

"Well, this seven will not bother you again. Are there more of them?"

"On the boat. They have four or five more men."

"I see. Can you get me someone to show my man where they are?"

"Si. Carlos, show them the boat."

"Len, recon only and report."

"Okay, boss."

The two men left quickly. Now turning back to the islander leader, O'Brian explained what was next. Having taken all the guns from him and his men, O'Brian had everything he needed for the Q&A session about to start.

"Here's how it works. I ask questions, you answer. If you tell the truth, nothing happens. At the first lie, I will impale your hand on the table with this knife. For each lie after that, I take off half of a finger. So you have twenty lies. After that, no fingers! Do you understand?"

"Yes."

"Okay. Just so you know, I will be able to know a lie when I hear it. Answer the three questions for me. Lie one time only please. One, how many men are still on your boat?"

"Five!"

"Two. Is your boat an armed patrol boat?"

"No!"

"Three. What is your age?"

"Twenty-seven."

"Thank you. Now you think you're smart, but you're not. You did not tell the truth once, so the free part is over. Put your hand on the table!"

He did not move at all. His skin got about five shades whiter. O'Brian picked up one of the pistols, cocked it, placed it against the man's knee, and repeated the command.

"Place your hand on the table now!"

Slowly, he put his hand on the table.

"Okay, so let's try again. No more lies. What's your age?"

"Thirty-seven."

"And is your boat an armed patrol boat?"

"Yes."

"Very good. And how many men are still on board?"

"Eight or ten. I'm not sure."

In a bright flash, the steel knife impaled the hand to the table. It was followed by a long and loud scream! When the man regained control of himself, O'Brian said, "The number is fifteen men in your head, was it not?"

"Yes, it was fifteen men on the boat when I left it."

"What is your reason for coming here?"

"We came for the two boys, and two days ago we received orders to look for a sailboat that escaped from two of our patrol boats south of here."

"Why? What did they do?"

"I don't know. They are wanted for stealing a boat."

"Where are they now?"

"I don't know that either. They were last reported seventy miles south of here going south. We were coming here for the boys and told to stay and keep watch that they didn't turn back north."

"How many other boats are in this area?"

"I am not sure. I believe mine is the farthest north."

"My last question is two parts. Part one, how often do you check in? And what plans do you have for this village?"

"The boat checks in twice a day if needed or not. In the morning before eight and in the evening before seven. Although island one is always listening if anyone calls! Based on my previous operations, we will cleanse the village and then move our people in."

"For the alcalde, describe a cleansing."

"We surround the village, and with three to four times the population, we would start at the outer edges and push all of them to the beach right down to the water's edge. Then we sort out the young women and girls. Then we kill whoever is left at the beach."

"How long before they get this far?"

"Two weeks or less. Depends on when they find that boat!"

"Well, Martine, he is all yours, and the others as well. I am going to see to the men on the boat. They will not bother you at all.

I do, however, recommend that you all leave this place as soon as you can. We will be leaving just after seven tonight."

During the time they talked, both Martine and John had been in a heat-filled rage over how calm he talked about it. O'Brian, seeing the look in Martine's eyes, knew that when the islanders did arrive, all they would find would be the wasted crew from the boat.

"I see you know what to do after that. Make your way up the coast to a place near Monterey, California. You should find friends there. I must go now. I have some work to do."

The leader spoke up as he started to leave. "You said if I told the truth, you would not hurt us!"

"That's true, but the mayor did not."

"Why would you do this? Wait, you are the ones the queen wants. It's your boat we are looking for!"

"No, it's not. We stole it and kidnapped the owners, asshole. Oh, and have a great day!"

The man with the mayor left and came back with others, and they took the islanders away.

* * *

O'Brian found his men outside, all armed, and they started for the islanders' boat. Just out of sight from the boat, they all stopped. Here three of them made ready the gas cans and the rest of their mines. The other three set up a rear guard for any threat that might show up. The three had changed to their swimming gears and lowered themselves into the water. They swam to the boat and quietly started letting the gas out all around the boat as Jeff (master sergeant) planted the last two mines on the center line of the keel fore and aft. In just five minutes, they made it back to the second pier from the boat. They left the puncher gas can float around the boat. They now took up position to cover the pier the boat was tied to. They would shoot anyone who made it that far.

All they were waiting for now was the nightly report, and then they would have an eleven-hour start before they missed their morning call. Checking with Wayne, they waited for his call after they sent their nightly report to islander one. The radio was busy tonight, a lot of possible sightings of the *Dream Wind* all over the southern coast. At last they made their report: "Still looking for the boys. Believe they are here, and no sign of the missing boat. Any new orders for us?"

"*No*. Find the boys and return to base for resupply and fuel for trip to central Mexico coast. Over and out."

As soon as the radio switched off, they hit the button, and the mines went off. The twin explosions lifted the boat ten feet out of the water. They took their positions to make sure no one survived the blast. They just made it to their places when the blast wave hit, causing havoc on all the boats and building splashing fire all over the place. They held their places until the fire was low enough to see. The boat was just small pieces of wood and body parts in bloodred water.

"It's time to go. Good work, guys."

* * *

They stared back to the *Dream Wind*. As soon as they boarded, they had the Youngs set sail at once. O'Brian quickly explained that they had approximately eleven hours lead time before the islanders started to ask questions and sent another boat to check on the missing men. After that was done, he asked Carlita and Sonador to tell him about the two boys.

"They do not talk much. They are very afraid of everyone except Sonador. Her they speak with a little. I think in time we will get their trust."

"I see. Not to surprising. I was told they hid and saw their family die and they ran. I was told they sailed in a skiff from the far south. So what do we know about them?"

Sonador spoke now. "Their names are Matias and Diego. They are best friends and fish together almost every day. They are both ten years old, soon to be eleven. Other than that, they only ask for food or water. We know they can sail, so we will give them work. My sister believes it will help them recover."

"I believe that you, my young friend, have a new job on board, and that is to take care of these two and help them. If you need anything, come to me and we will take care of it, okay?"

"Yes, that's good for me. I like them, and now I am not the youngest anymore!"

While talking to the girls, the Youngs had gotten them out to sea and going north. They now had clear sailing to the north. It only took them ten more days to arrive off the California coast. They started looking for a friendly harbor. After the ten days on the boat, the two boys recovered and talked to everyone about fishing and sailing.

They still did not open up about anything they witnessed. So things on board were good, if a bit crowded, due to the number of bodies they had.

O'Brian decided on Avila Beach as it was in a secluded bay and not as well-known as some nearby. It had a small fishing pier and held a few fishing boats. For safety, they decided to stay on the boat and to always have a guard on duty. They pulled in and dropped anchor about five hundred yards offshore. There were no people in the area when they pulled in. After the long voyage, they all just slept on the boat that first night.

The second night, three of the SEALs had the same dream but just off a little from the others. They all did have one thing in common—two generals and tall red trees. The generals were Sherman and Grant. When they woke up, they were eating when Sonador came up and asked what type of trees they were.

Everyone looked at her and she said, "The wizard showed you trees. What kind, and where are they?"

"They are giant sequoias east of here in the mountains."

CHAPTER 21

Migrations

SUMMER WAS IN all its glory in the high mountains. All the trees were a deep green, with only small patches of snow left in the sheltered places in the high valleys. Only the tops carried snow all year. The camp was now a compound and almost complete. All the required buildings—the common/dining hall, the showers, the privies, the barn, and the stables—were completed. There were still a lot of tents. Ben also managed to build two larger barracks, one for women and the other for the men. The tents were for the married or families. Five cabins were completed with four more in progress for the families. They would all be done by first snow, according to Ben. The crews had gotten quite good at putting cabins up.

The children had been much more help than anyone would have guessed, from the zip line to cutting grass and clearing the dead wood from the fields. They were also good at setting the lines for new zip lines in the tall trees. The family had grown. And as more new members slowly found their way to them, they had close to fourteen new members looking for them. And once they found us than ask for parole. There were close to fifty adults and kids around twenty or so. Maria and Lucy kept track of them. They built well, and anyone that just happened to find their way up to the valley would only see the ring of trees. And there was no one path in. They kept going in and out at different points so as not to make a trail into the compound.

The number of the original members to have awakened was at about 80 percent now. With the knowledge of something special about William and some of the others, they started to look for things they did. And the meditations brought many more closer to awakening. It was clear that William and more of the original members could speak to one another over great distances. They kept in touch with the sheriff in Lone Pine. Some of the kids had heard them discussing their dreams. As the stories grew, more people were watching them. It had been a while since William explained what had happened to him the day of the event. The one thing that was whispered about was the silent council. Even Ben in Lone Pine was included. In fact, it was not a secret. If you could hear the mind speech, you could and were welcome to join in. Just like the regular family meetings, all had a voice. The topics were a bit more intense and unsettling to most. It was full of dark images and people coming to take what they built and food they grew by force. No, this fine summer day, they were dealing with a problem in Lone Pine.

"Today we need to make plans to send help to Lone Pine as the chief has seen Lieutenant Briggs is getting ready to march on Lone Pine with a force of sixty trained troops. His mission is to find where we have gone to."

Since he first started having his dreams, he kept getting them more often and in greater detail. He passed the information to William, who also started getting the dreams. And everyone in the silent council had seen the dream as well.

"We need to keep one of the R&R teams here, so Jake's or Peter's team will go with you. Kevin and some of his people would like to go as well, and ten others from the general population. Five of them are awake. Counting you makes six. So you have a platoon-sized force."

"That will be great. We are going to come in from behind and only shoot when they are to find our positions. We will be leaving tonight as soon as everything is ready! Did you get all that, Ben?"

"Yes, so we will be on our own for the first day. On the second, we will need help."

"We will be there. You have more time than you think. Briggs will want to talk and try to get information about me. You just need to keep him talking. You and the others will know when we are in place, and then you piss Briggs off and he will forget discipline and try a bull rush. And then we have him."

"Great. So I see you want to keep this from the others so they react as if we are alone."

"Yes. Just make sure you have the ones awake in every part of the ranch so you have instant communications. See you soon. Go get ready and just tell the group we are coming."

"Bull, there are seventeen of us leaving as soon as we can. Will you get your wrangler to ready three mounts a piece and as many horses as needed to carry light supplies? We will not be stopping until we arrive in Lone Pine."

"Okay. I will send three wranglers with you, and they are all weapons qualified. They will keep the mounts while you take care of business."

"Okay. You get going. We will be leaving soon."

"Okay, so Briggs is leaving tonight or tomorrow. We need to make sure he is never a threat to us or our friends again! We will ride day and night to make sure we get there just before or close behind him."

* * *

Lieutenant Briggs had taken time to secure his hold on the troops still left back in Death Valley. He started by instilling more discipline into them. Before he set out for Lone Pine, he had sixty well-trained men, all with the best weapons. In the time since William had left them on the road, he had used almost all his fuel reserves. As a result, they would only be able to drive a little less than halfway, leaving a one- or two-day march, just over thirty miles to Lone Pine. The chief had been watching Briggs in his dreams, so they had warning and were well ahead of his arrival.

Lt. Briggs had poor intelligent on the state of Lone Pine, thinking it would be as bad off as all the other people they had come across. He had the superior force and weapons and planned on having an easy time subduing the townspeople. His first order of business would be killing the sheriff. He knew the town would fight. He was overconfident of his victory.

It took them almost a full two days to reach the large rest area just south of the city. They camped there and rested and got ready for the fight to come. If nothing, he did have good training, and a rested force would make less mistakes than one worn out from the long hot march from the valley.

As they reached the edge of town and started moving to the city center, everything they saw looked like normal activity. As soon as the townspeople saw them, they yelled out and started running toward the center of town as well. So far, everything was going just how he wanted. Briggs could see men and women drop what they were doing and started running to the west side, going to the center of town. It was soon clear they had an escape plan and were trying to get a way. He was ready for this and ordered a chase at the best possible speed to keep them from getting away! In the chase, they paid little attention to the surroundings. They soon started getting random shots fired at them. They slowed at once and started clearing the path with a point man and moving once the way had been cleared.

Ben's plan for drawing them to town was working well by pulling his people to the best possible defensive ranch right on the edge of town. They started to get it ready after the first dream. Briggs and his men, seeing the last few people rushing in as the gate closed, charged the gate. As soon as they cleared the cover of the houses and trees, they were fired on by single-shot weapons It was a lot, but it was still not going to help them in the long run. He ordered a recall and set up a command center in a house just up the street that had a view of the gate. He sent his best scout to check the back and sides for threats or a second way in. It would not be easy to get in. This did not bother him as they could not get out.

He was working on a plan of attack to check the defense abilities of the townspeople and their choice of taking a stand. It was a good three hours before he had a plan ready to launch. His scout came back with the news that a small force guarded the back wall.

It was higher and had only one small door. It could be used for a breach, but not in any stealthy way. They did not have the needed manpower to carry it off. So it was the front gate and walls they would have to break.

Setting his plan in motion, he had one-third of his men make three teams. They made advances on the gate and two points just north and south of the gate to draw fire from the gate defenses. It was just past noon with the sun starting to shine right in the faces of anyone standing on the wall. Briggs had the remainder of his force open fire on the wall from a large line to keep the men over there, keeping their heads down. With the start of the shooting, the three teams ran forward, shooting at the wall or the gate. This drew a lot more gunfire from the ranch. There were a lot more weapons, all single shot or semiautomatic and, as the teams got closer, shotguns. As soon as they believed they had a full response, he sounded recall and started to get the counts from his team. He was surprised that there was not more semiauto guns in town and that there were more people in their but not enough. The worst case was to siege and starve them out. So he decided to lay siege and wait them out. He set up a regular routine of firing on the ranch just to keep them from getting any rest. He ordered all the men not on a post to return to the house down the street and set up camp at that house.

It was a little after 4:00 p.m. when Briggs started thinking of ways to breach the walls. They brought a few satchel charges and hand grenades. They were not ready for a long siege. So he was planning an action just after dark to breach the wall and charge the compound. The plan was simple, with the greater firepower and larger numbers to just overrun the standing defensive positions. His scouts found two cars that had fuel and still worked. They moved these into positions just out of sight of the walls. His pieces all in place. He waited for the sun to pass below the tops of the mountains. He had his men check and load all of their weapons, eat and sleep if they could so they would be fresh for the battle to come.

CHAPTER 22

First Battle of Lone Pine

Just as the sun passed below the tops of the mountains, Briggs launched his assault on the ranch house. It had three different points like the testing one, but this time all his men attacked, except the reserve squad. One to each side of the gate and the gate itself. On the southeast end, they tossed the two satchel charges at the base of the wall. All the rest fired at any point of the wall where they saw mussel flashes. It seemed like the longest thirty seconds to Briggs. With a loud booming noise, that section of wall disappeared in a large wall of smoke rolling out and up slowly in the cool mountain air. Briggs, keeping watch, saw the large breach they had made and sent the order for the cars to ram the breach at both sides to make it much bigger. Except for the placed guns firing on the wall positions, all his troops started to move toward the breach.

All of them could feel the letdown behind the wall. They could feel the end was near. They all started firing into the breach to keep it clear. Everything was going just as planned. Briggs was waiting for the cars to come out of the tree line. The fighting intensified around the breach as townspeople were giving a better defense than they had planned for. They rolled a wagon in front of the breach and tipped it on its side, blocking the hole. At least ten shooters took up places behind the wagon. They opened up, and a large amount of return fire cut the soldiers down that were too close to the breach. At least half of them had full auto machine guns. As this fact was pressing into Briggs's brain, as in most battles, it was time gets very strange. It could seem very slow, and the next second you could not keep up.

Briggs waited on his surprise car rams. They were to be his big advantage in this battle. He started to yell, "*Where are my two cars*?"

* * *

"William, where are you? They have entered town. We have started the fade back to the ranch house with our decoys. Only use our fastest runners. As expected, they have fifty plus men. We will all be safely inside by noon! Will you be in time?"

"Yes, Ben, we are here. I will let you know when we are in place. You need to hold the first wave off on your own!"

"We can do that. Preparations have been made for everything we could think of."

"Okay. If anything goes wrong, we will engage them from behind. Otherwise, we are going ahead with our plan."

* * *

While Briggs was probing the compound, William, Ben, and Peter were moving their teams into positions behind the soldiers. They reached the town less than an hour before Briggs started to move into the main street. As soon as they started chasing the townspeople to the ranch house, they all moved past the teams already in place. As hoped, this would put them behind them for the plan to work. Then when he sent his probing attack, they moved up to right and left flanking positions, and William had the center so he could move in whichever way he needed as the battle moved forward.

"Okay, if we are all in place, hold if you have any problems. Use the bows only. Just hold and wait! Peter, take one man and sit on the back door so those men don't happen upon us when they return."

Turning back, they could see that Briggs had his troops pull back out of range and stopped right out in the open where they could be seen from the house. William opened his mind and asked who could hear him. The chief was first to respond.

Well, what's he waiting for?

Well, Ben, he is setting something up. He sent some men back into town, and we are waiting to see what he's trying to do. No matter. All we can do now is wait. When he starts his next move, we will be ready to counter his moves. At the first shot, you must fire back. Tell your people we are at his back, ready to engage them from the rear.

Peter called that they were on the way back and to take cover. They brought two large cars moving to each side of the gate in the tree line. Peter was watching as they worked on the front of the cars. It was clear they were to be used as battering rams on the fence. All that could now heard anything on the link. So the chief saw what was going to happen with the cars. He sent Sergeant McGregor to find something to put in any breaches that were made in the wall.

William, seeing how hard the cars would make defending the wall, gave the job to Daniel to deal with.

"Daniel, take who you need, and you and Peter take care of the cars for me please."

"Ok, boss. Consider it done."

Soon the forest started to darken as the sun was slipping behind the mountain, making red and orange streaks across the sky. It would be a sunset to watch if not for the battle about to start. As soon as the light was only going up, Briggs launched his attack on three places, the two sides a bit closer to the gate but not close enough for them to aid the defender there. All of his troops not rushing the wall were laying down, covering fire at the five positions near the front gate. Soon Ben could see the places and had one man from every position redeploy to one of the five points under fire.

Briggs had seen the response and set his second phase in action. He had his men launch smoke grenades at all three points. The charges were going to the left side of the gate, so his men stared displacing to the left so the largest amount of men they could afford would rush the breach.

"Satchels charges now while the smoke is at its thickest."

The four men running the charges reached the smoke screen and passed through. They were only eight to ten feet from the wall. Pulling the cords, they tossed them close together and right at the base of the wall. Turning, they tried to get back in the smoke. Only one made it as William had shown the men on the wall where they were coming out of the smoke. Then the blast went off, and all of his attack force started to rush the wall.

"When it's clear, ram the breach on both sides with the cars. Troops, as soon as you can see a hole in the wall, run for it."

As the smoke cleared, they could see a good-sized breach, and the men started running for it.

"Cars! Where are the cars? Someone go check on the cars. Hurry!"

Two men took off back into the trees. William saw them and sent word that company was coming uninvited. "Also take out the cars with bows only if possible!"

"Okay, we got this," said Daniel and Peter as one.

The charges had opened a three- to four-foot hole in the wall, and it was wider than they hoped. The troops started running for the wall, firing as they came. Sergeant McGregor had a wagon ready, and him and five others pushed it even with the breach once it was in line. They tipped it over on its side and took up firing positions behind it. They were joined by one of the rapid response team, all with full auto weapons. The rate of fire jump was way up. Again, Briggs called for the cars. Another four men ran to get the cars. They were badly needed as the wagon was putting out a great deal of firepower, and they stopped the advance. Briggs's men had to take cover at the wall and could not move too far in any direction without help.

At one of the cars, Peter and Steven had taken out the men. They were waiting on Daniel to do the same before blowing them up. As Peter and Steven moved to the center, they came around a large outbuilding right into the path of the four men sent back to help with the cars. Peter saw the first man and fired his crossbow at about two feet. The bolt struck the man dead center of his chest, lifting him off his feet. The bolt stuck out front and back as he laid dead on the grass. The next man a few steps behind started shooting at Peter. Steven yelled, "Drop!" He came around the corner with his rifle and fired two quick bursts and killed two of the men. Peter, having dropped and rolled, came to a stop with his pistol in hand, shooting the last man twice in the chest. With all four of them dead, they both got up and found that Daniel had taken out the other car's detail. They quickly set the explosive and set the timers and cleared the area. The shots from the rear brought shouts and the sound of more men rushing to the site. Six men came into view just as the cars went up in two large orange balls of flame. Glass and metal shrapnel flew in all directions, killing or wounding the men chasing them.

Briggs was just beginning to see that something was very wrong. First the townspeople had more and better guns as well as a strong fortified position. The cars had not been driven to the breach. He was about to send more men to report of the situation when the double blast went off. He heard and felt the heat and wind. He knew that this was the cars. He called for a retreat to the command post, firing more smoke to cover his troops' retreat from the breach. The thing that bothered him most was how the townspeople got behind him. As the smoke rounds hit just inside the fence line, the troops ran for the safety of the trees some fifty yards away.

William, seeing this, gave the order to fire on the retreating troops. They had set up a fifty cal back in the tree line. Many of them fell dead or wounded in the grass. In the opening round, Briggs was at the tree line and was running back to the house when he was shot down by the fifty caliber, leaving the men without a leader on the field. The order to fall back was given to all. William could see that the actions of the rapid response teams had broken them. At first only a few of the troops started dropping their guns and putting their hands up! As soon as William saw this, he spoke to everyone in the ranch and his teams using his mind only.

Stop! Cease fire.

For the troops, it was clearly more than they were ready for! Now in a normal voice, yelling as loud as he could, he gave orders to the retreating soldiers.

"Drop your weapons and turn and face the wall! Take two steps forward and strip naked and sit on your clothes with hands on your heads. Anyone not complying will be shot!"

The sound of gunfire was now a shot here or there, all back in the houses as a few tried to escape the town. The people in the ranch led by Ben started coming out and taking the weapons from the troops. A few of the people started to beat the prisoners.

Ben and William put a stop to this at once. He called for Peter and Steven to come with him.

"Dear, there's something wrong. Steven needs help! Go quickly before it's too late."

Back at the tree line, Peter turned to check on Steven. He saw that Steven stopped back about ten feet, leaning against a large tree. His face was a very pale white. Peter ran to him, calling for a medic. Steven had been shot at some point and closed himself and did not call for help as it would give their position away. It was just a few minutes before William and Ben arrived to find Peter holding Steven, and just steps behind them was the medical team. Steven was gone before they got there. Peter had taken the memory from Steven, showing what had happened and sharing it with all the others that were awake.

Leaving Peter to care for Steven, William and Ben went to deal with the soldiers.

Both Ben and William, standing on the wall, now spoke to the soldiers standing in the field.

"Okay, everyone, listen. I will only say this once! If you have not already done so, drop all weapons on the ground in front of you. Next, take one large step backward! Now strip naked and sit on your clothing. Place your hands on your heads!"

"Who the hell is this fuck that I—"

Bang. The man dropped dead before he could complete his thought.

"Now does anyone else have a question? You all gave up. If you want to start up again, reach for your guns!"

They all did as they were told after the shooting. Chief Loggins and Daniel supervised the collection of the weapons. After that, they were allowed to get dressed again. Maria told William that other than Steven, they lost twelve souls from Lone Pine, and another was in critical condition. Overall, she thought they had been lucky. Steven had saved most of the R&R teams by his last action. They went over the names of the lost and wounded.

Now that everyone settled down, William spoke to them again.

"Now you all have three choices. We will give you your choice. The first is we give you three days of food and water and you return to your base. The second is you can take parole and become a member of the family. Last, you can choose to do neither. In which case, we will kill you here and now!"

He turned to Peter and asked him to take care of the rest for him. In mind speech, he told him to ask for anyone that was thinking of the third choice to speak up so that they could get served first. *If anyone does, just shoot them dead.*

"You will all have five minutes to make up your mind."

"Hello, everyone. You all did great. We know that you lost twelve souls. We lost one as well. We have information from the perimeter guard that one got out and with a guard left outside of town, escaped back toward Death Valley. I do not know what will come of this. However, I don't think we heard the last of them.

"We have spilled blood together twice now. You are going to need our help again, and we are going to need yours. The chief has told me most of you have seen the oath and were told about joining our family. Is this true?"

He saw that almost all the heads nodded yes. A few looked confused.

"For those of you that have not seen it, the chief will get you copies. Give a yell when you've all seen it, and we will finish our talk." In just a short time, they all read the oath. During that time, William was seeing to the wounded. The dead would wait. The living always came first.

The dead were Steven and twelve from town. For the wounded, William had four, and town had fifteen. Three of them were serious. The soldiers had twenty-six men left out of the sixty they started with, and nine of them were wounded. William insisted on the wounded being treated by need of their wounds. The side they fought on was of no matter.

"Now back to the prisoners," William addressed them again.

"Peter has taken care of your choices. As none of you are dead, it was go back with three days of food and water or take the oath. As I understand, all but six wish to stay with us. I am very glad to hear it. The others will be allowed to go back if that is their wish. Those of you staying will take the oath tonight after the evening meal is served. After you take the oath, you are a new person to us. All your past actions are forgotten. However, we have only a few laws: never talk to strangers about the family. Do as you are told. And only ask question about how you do your job. At family meetings, you can ask any questions. Unless told to do so, never leave the areas you're assigned to. We have only one plenty for these. *Death*. As you may have guessed, we do things fast. The person who catches you will kill you on the spot.

"Now dinner is almost ready. Does anyone have a question now?"

Slowly, a man raised his hand.

"Yes, you can speak."

"You've been giving a lot of information to the townspeople. What can you tell us?"

"At this time, nothing, as you have not taken the oath. After you have taken the oath, we will talk again. Any other questions?"

There were none. William now took the six aside to talk with them. Peter sent one of the team to get their supplies ready for their walk home.

"Now you six wish to return to the base. Is that right?"

They all answered that they did.

"Okay. Are any of you being forced to return against your will? Please all answer one at a time."

They all looked at each other. No one was sure who should go first. At last, they all said no. William was looking for a lie but found none, so he moved forward.

"Okay, I am going to talk to you each alone, and then we will send you on your way. You, come over here please." The man he pointed to walked over slowly. "Just tell me why you wish to return."

"I don't want to. I have to return. My family is being held to force me to serve. I need to get my family and keep them safe!"

"I see." William opened to see into this man's mind. He was a good man and had a wife and three kids. He put the idea in his mind to come to Lone Pine. It he could safely get them out. "You have true and good reason to return. I wish you luck." Some just thought they would be safer there. Others minds were open, and a darkness was there. He worked in their minds, wiping away the memory of where and what had happened here. He set the block to take effect if anyone asked question about what happened here. Two of them had no good reason to go back. After a short talk, they changed their minds, and only four left to return.

Taking the two men back with him, William found a slightly different discussion of the oath and parole going on.

"But how do we have an equal voice in these family meetings when we are here and you are all safe on the mountain?"

William, walking into the center, spoke. "May I answer that for you, please?"

All of them turned to see William as he entered the group. The speaker, Joe Danvers, was happy to hear the answer from William.

"First, you all have been hearing rumors about me and my family. I will start there." Looking at Joe, he asked. "May I have your help with this?"

Joe nodded a yes.

"Fine. Please try to clear your mind and think happy thoughts, or a memory is best."

Giving him time to settle his mind, William opened his with his focus on Joe's thoughts. Joe was a father, and the birth of his first child, Jenny Danvers, four, was his happiest memory. William spoke first only to Joe. "That is a perfect thought. You will wake soon, I think."

Joe was looking right at William the whole time, hearing every word, but his mouth was closed, and never did his lips move! Then it opened and out came this.

"Your name is Joe Danvers. You're twenty-eight years old, father of Jenny, age four! Is that correct?"

"Why, yes, it is. How can I hear you when you don't speak?"

"That is our secret. I and a good many of the family can see and hear other people's thoughts. We cannot force our way in. That was why I asked for your help, which you willingly gave, so I was able to see and hear your thoughts as you did mine. This is how we won the battle today. Now do you all trust Chief Loggins?"

They all said yes in some fashion.

"Good, because he is also awakened and has the same abilities as I have. So far, no one I know is as strong as I am yet. That being said, everyone who has awakened keeps getting stronger. I have been talking with Ben ever since we left Lone Pine last march. There are at least five others in town that are awake as well. Joe here will be awake very soon as well. This is how you will all be heard in meetings. You will be allowed to attend the meeting, and by linking with the ones here, everyone will be able to hear and, in some cases, see us on the mountain. That is how you have the same input as the rest of us. We always arrange the time so many family members can attend all meetings. So those of you who wish to join and also want to stay here can do so. We need you here, and you will soon learn you need us on the mountain. Just so you know, the link works the same for us. We will see and hear you as if you're in the same room. This is our greatest advantage over the larger forces that will be coming for us. Only together can we hope to win."

"What if we disagree with what you wish us to do? I worry about this a lot."

"The unity of the link shows all of us the best way to move forward, and there has not been any dissention after the decision is made. Some of them take days to get sorted out so that all agree on a course of action. You all know about parole. While on parole, you are not allowed to ask questions that do not pertain to your work. However, when you're in council meetings, you're allowed to ask any questions equal to me or any other family members. Even the soldiers that will take parole today that fought against us just hours ago will have the same rights. One other thing. You have the right to know before you take the oath. The chief has seen this dream as have all of us that are awake. We are all in danger from a rogue force coming from the Hawaiian Islands. At this time, they are engaged in taking over the West Coast, starting in South America. They are moving north, and we will be in their way. So please decide what you want. Only together can we survive. We leave to go back to our camp in two days."

"One more question. will you tell us where the camp is?"

"No, we won't. If you take the oath and need to know how to find the camp, you will know how to find it." With that, most went on their way. A few turned to the chief with many more questions. William simply asked for quiet in is mind, and the room went silent for him. He started back to the room made for him. Just as he reached the door, Ben said they all said yes. William opened to all on the mountain and said that the family has grown and was healthy, numbering over four hundred, many of them awake or about to be. A very tired William slept a dreamless sleep for the first time in weeks.

The next morning, as William was crossing the yard, he saw Joe and asked him, "Are you awake?"

Joe, with a huge smile, said, "Yes."

William stopped and reached out to Joe, and he could see he had woken up.

"It looks like I am to be your guide. You will have questions about your new abilities. All you need to do is think of me and ask your question, and I will hear you no matter the distance between us. So what do you think of it?"

"Thank you. It's like a totally new world and so amazing, and yet it's been here all the time. we just never saw it!"

On the second morning, William and all the soldiers able to travel started back. Oliver sent to William that he had the dream of the six military men coming from the south. The number had gone up to twelve now in the group. Maria, Lucy, and Peter had it as well. They were coming closer daily now.

CHAPTER 23

Defending the West

THEY GOT THE news and confirmed that a team of trained soldiers was coming toward them, moving fast with no delays. Add to that the much greater movement of people in the Central Valley. The family needed to upgrade and move more people down to keep watch on the truck farms they had established at the base of the mountain. As the winter was coming on, they had many more mouths to feed, and the trend was to grow more and at a faster rate. Even with the growth in numbers, they were still going to be the smaller force in every encounter they had foreseen so far. These farms were the life of the family this coming winter. They also started to keep livestock down the mountain, splitting them up. They had acquired a large amount of livestock. They currently had fifteen milk cows, one bull, seventeen breeding cows, twelve pigs, and about forty chickens. Due to a ban on eating chicken, they had all the eggs they wanted. The remainder of the stock was mostly horses and other pack animals numbering just over 140 altogether.

The zip lines had been extended to all the perches of the lower farms with horses kept just out of sight. People working the farms had a quick getaway depending on number of people working at any given time. None of them were in sight of any roads Whenever the farms were being worked, Lucy had four scouts as security, keeping watch.

Bull had made simple stables for the horses, and with Allen's help, they got twenty people to come down and help with all the late planting in so they would have food for the coming winter. All this activity brought a lot of attention to the farm areas. The family needed to work hard to keep the farms a secret. William had a number of tactics to help conceal their numbers and locations.

First was the way they did their hunting. It was all done with bows or crossbows. The gun they carried were always a last resort and only for their safety. Only bears when needed were allowed. Even then, they had to use one shot, and only if someone in the hunting party was in mortal danger. At times, they would be hunting for more than one animal like deer. If they wanted to practice one shot to kill all the animals they wanted at the same time. William saw it as one of their major physiological weapons in the battles to come. The goal was to shoot as many of the opposing forces with what seemed to be one shot. This would be done by linking with as many of the family and everyone picking a target and shooting at the same time. The effect was to make all the shots sound as one very loud shot! They crossed over to the east side of the mountain in groups that were able to link and practice the timing. After months, they had a very good team of shooters able to do one shot while hunting. They could take down three to five deer, and it sounded like one shot. If there were any strangers on the mountain, they could not track them from only one shot. If used in hunting, if a second shot was needed, they'd use bows.

Some of them with the ability to enter the dreams of others have started rumors of the wizards on the mountain to scare them and keep them away. More and more people were coming in the valley together with food in the fruit and nut farms all across the valley floor. They avoided being seen as much as they can. Still they were not always successful, and some people needed to be dealt with. Others followed the clues that they left behind on their way out of the valley. And stories of the wizards on the mountain have spread and grown, bringing many others to the foot of the mountain. They have taken in quite a few new members. Most stayed in the valley until they completed parole. Others they tried to scare off. The stories of the wizards and the few people that took them back kept most away.

Shortly after returning from Lone Pine, they had alerts from the scouts about a family working its way up the valley to the newest and largest truck farm. Peter and Aaron were nearby and went to check on them. When they arrived, they found a group of five people. All were picking food from the trees and fields. Peter and Aaron split up so as to have them in a crossfire. Once they were in position, they opened to William so he could see what was going on.

Peter had the lead as he was a scout and had been awake much longer than Aaron was.

"You in the fields, stop where you are!"

The people all jumped at the sound of Peter's voice.

"Drop what you've taken and don't move, or you will be shot!"

The five were a ragged looking group. Their clothes were torn and dirty, and they smelled of sweat and other unspeakable things. These people have not been doing too well. Two women looked to be skin and bones. The one adult was just slightly bigger than the women. The last two were just teens or preteens, a boy and a girl.

"What are you doing in our garden?"

"We are starving and running from a rape gang that's after my wife and daughter."

William and Peter both knew he was speaking the truth. Then the man started to bargain with Peter. "I want to pay for food and protection. How much do you want? I can pay cash or trade for goods with precious stones."

Peter moved closer to the field, moving away from the zip line so they could not see them. William told Peter to move so they would not see him arrive on the zip line.

"I am coming to talk with them myself. Feed them and give them all the water they want."

"Okay, boss."

By the time they gave them the food and let them eat, William was walking into the farm from out of the woods.

By use of the zip lines, they could reach all the outlaying posts in fifteen minutes or less. It took William just over fifteen minutes. Getting back up the mountain took a great deal longer. Bull had placed stables with horses and tact rooms so they could ride back up the hill. Walking up to the table, William spoke to them using their names. These people were so worn down, they were easy to read.

"Good day, Winston. I am told you want to buy your way into our group?"

"Yes. As I told that man, we can pay."

"Yes, I know what you said. So how much was that meal worth?"

Winston was thinking, trying to put a price on the best meal he had since the event.

"I would say at least one thousand per person."

"Okay, Winston. Here's the first rule. You cannot lie to a wizard. We always know the truth. The price you thought was two million a plate. Can you not afford that?"

"Well, no, not right now. Later after things settle down, I can get the money I will need."

"Although that's not a lie, it is also not true. Your mind holds no secrets from me. The stones you carry may have a value, but not as you think of it. Winston, does the world look anything like it did in February?"

"No, but I still have access to millions. We just want to be able to eat and sleep in safety. We will pay any price you name."

"Well, we don't need any of your wealth here on Wizard Mountain. You're trying to live in the old world. It's dead now, Winston, and never coming back! Are you truly willing to pay any price for the things you say you want?"

"Yes, we are."

William brought Peter into the link so they could talk about the five people they had to make a decision about. *Keep them here for at least two weeks. Give them the information on the oath only if we see improvement. Treat them all as singles as they may break up, some staying and others going onto some other place. If they earn the right, move them to the tents behind the cabin after two weeks.*

The whole time, Winston kept talking about the cost and that they would pay it. He just wanted to know what it would be.

"That is all I can get. Please tell us what you require for us to stay here."

"Okay, this is the only work you're qualified for, and it's workers we need. So this is how you will pay. You will move into the farmhouse. Aaron will give you work assignments for each week that you will be required to complete. He is the farm master grower for the family. In exchange for your pay, the work you do, everyone will eat three meals a day as much as you want. You can leave at any time you want. Be careful. If you choose to leave, you will no longer be trusted. Steven is one of our best security officers. Take food and he will know it. If you are caught, the council will decide your fate. You are all over thirteen, so all must work a ten-hour day. If one of you fails to work, you will not be fed that day!"

"What other way can we pay? None of us are farmers."

"That's true, but Aaron is the farm master. Do as you're told and you will learn like the rest of us did. So do you want the food and security, or do you wish to leave now? You can take what you pick already, and we will give you water. This will be your only chance. What's it going to be?"

"Can we talk about it first?"

"Yes, but don't take too long. It's getting late."

They talked a short time and then agreed to the terms.

"Okay, great. If you work out, you will be given the right to take the oath and become one of us. Here is Aaron now. He will tell you what is needed and give you lessons as needed as well as keep an eye on all of you. There are others besides him, and they will all be keeping a mind's eye on you as well." Aaron then talked to them as William left the room.

"Okay, you all had a long hard trip to get here, so take the rest off today. Get cleaned up and rest the remainder of the day. We will start at sunup for the first day of work."

That night, they were the topic of the silent council. They represented the danger they all knew was coming wave after wave of it. The council identified three major groups that would soon be coming for them. One was from Las Vegas. It was part of the same group that came after them at the gas station. Some of them survived and were building a force to come looking for the family. The other two groups were coming from Los Angeles. All these groups had close to a thousand troops or more. When they came, the family would face three to one or greater in every battle. The group that had the Stanlys running to the valley was being pushed by an even bigger group pushing them. At night, all the dreamers had been getting bits and pieces about their leaders. Each night, the silent council would map the progress of each of these groups they had links into.

On the third workday for Winston and his family, they had a breach as everyone in the family was thinking about William! At once, William was aware of this breach at the farm. This allowed William to see the plans of the first group from the LA area. He could see into their leader's head and all his plans. He now knew when and where they would come from, as well as how many men they would face as well.

How on earth did Jesse, the leader of the LA group, come to know of William? He referred to him as the wizard and could only have gotten that information from Winston's family.

"Start checking on them now. I am on my way to the farm now. We need to learn how they are passing the information to each other! Men are coming with me. Start setting up a defensive position that will lead them away from the campsite. Looks like we could face one hundred forty to five hundred men."

"William, how much time do you think we have?"

"They can show up as early as tonight, no later than day after tomorrow! Peter, send your best scout to find them and report their strength and speed. Make sure the scout is awake. I am linking with Chief Loggins to see if they know anything. You handle this. I will be linked."

So Peter went to talk with Winston to determine how he sent a message to see if they could make a deal to allow them to travel and work with them as spies.

"How did you get the information to them?"

Winston's mind flashed on the bird they had kept. Peter pulled the image of the bird up in his memory and then checked with the link. They found that the bird was a homing pigeon. No mental powers at work, so no warning as it happened.

The RR teams had arrived about thirty minutes ago at all the truck farms. Jake and Donny led at the other farms. William and four others arrived last. The family kept horses at all the truck farms to take people and needed items up the mountain. Bull brought twenty extra horses to carry everyone back up the mountain. After conferring with Chief Loggins, he put Lucy in charge of camp and organized escape plans if needed. Everyone who passed qualifying weapons training was issued a weapon now. All others were on loading detail. The days of peace here and in Lone Pine were now over. Now they had to face their worst fears and survive if they could. The dark days were upon them all now.

William sent a call out to Jake, Donny, and Daniel. They were to be the back stops if needed for each new farm Aaron put together. They made zip lines to the closest edge of the forest to it. These were the places that would be feeding them in the winters ahead. From one line to four, they all ran as high as they could in the trees, keeping the riders unseen from anyone traveling on the trails below. From base camp to any of the farms, in no more than twenty minutes. At all the other farms, they were stripping them and hauling it all up the mountain. The RR teams would stay and take up defensive positions at the other farms, waiting for the coming attack. After the direction of the attack was known, the teams not under attack would wait for the battle to move beyond them and then move to the rear of the attacking forces, cutting off their escape routes.

Peter was waiting for William with two horses to take them wherever he wanted to go. Due to the greater numbers of the awakened, everyone knew what William had planned for the attackers. Not since the first day had William been so hard on the troops. William and Peter rode up to the cabin they gave the family to live in. It had two guards at the door.

William dismissed the guards, saying, "You have better things to do very soon!" Now he addressed Winston. "Well, what did you tell them about us with your pigeon?"

Winston's face just went pale white with shock as he heard the question.

"Tell who? Nothing. I've talked to no one."

"Did you forget we all know when you lie to us? What did Jesse promise you for the information on us? *When do you expect him to get here*?"

With each question, Winston went paler!

"So after three days of good food and shelter, you want to go back to being hungry and homeless. Was the whole family involved in the plot or just you?"

Still he did not speak at all.

"Okay, this is what I am going to do." He pulled the .357 from his back and pointed it at Winston. At this, all the blood drained from his face.

"I am going to ask you a question. If you refuse to answer, I will shoot you in the head. You will be dead before your body hits the floor! If you lie, I will shoot you where it hurts and will shoot you again each time you lie to me. So are we ready? What did the note say?"

He cocked the pistol and placed it against Winston's head. He started stammering as he tried to talk. Chocking on his own spit, he finally talked.

"I told him that things were good. That there were only four to six people here and lots of food."

"I see. Well, you know Jesse is never going to keep whatever deal you think you made. How long do you think it will take him to get here?"

"I don't know. He is always talking about some wired type of battle. Said it would have conquered the world had they not stopped using it."

"Who was using it?"

"I do not know. It was some kind of war that used light. It was used in World War II in Europe."

"It used light?"

"Yes, it was called Lightning War. He used another word for it. Sorry, I can't remember it. You will get a chance to ask him soon. You cannot stand against him. He needs the food you have and will not stop until you give up or are all dead!"

"We will see about that when he gets here. This type of war, would you remember the name if you heard it again?"

"I think so."

"If it's what I think, it had a few names. Lightning War was one. The other was Blitzkrieg."

"Yes, that was it. Blitzkrieg!"

"Does he have accesses to many cars and trucks?"

"Just a few."

"Then how does he move so fast?"

"He has over twenty motorcycles, and they ride double on the bikes."

"Damn! Well, Winston, if you and I meet again, we will decide your fate at that time. Peter, get everyone to gather now in the farm back by the tree line."

He talked to Bull somewhere on the mountain. "Bull, stop at the first place you can hide the horses. We are coming to you. Everyone, here's the new plan. Make sure everyone understands it. Everyone not awake or able to hear us will keep falling back to base camp as fast as they can. We are going to be collapsing our lines and falling back much faster than originally planned. We will stop and defend each position with one or two shots and then falling back, getting stronger at each position. We will make our first real stand when the numbers and the mountain are in our favor. They are coming on motorcycles, so they will be fast. These are your primary targets. Kill the riders, and try not to damage the bikes.

"All the ones we can fix will be a great help to us later. Find strong places with cover before you shoot and fall back until we reach our last stop. They can be here at any minute. Everyone get to your positions. Everyone who can, send positions and speed. After the second stand, I want two scouts to fade back and fall in behind the attackers. No guns. Just bows until we reach the final position. Only take the ones at the back. And do not let any of them get past you for any reason. Okay, everyone, go now. Stay at your post until this is over. Peter, you're in the key spot. You have the lead. I have a message for you to pass along, okay?"

CHAPTER 24

First Battle of Wizard Mountain

Peter went back to the farmhouse and first made sure everyone knew the plan and started them up the hill to the first positions. He went back to the farmhouse where the two guards waited.

"You guys get your things one at a time, and be ready to leave in five minutes."

Opening the cabin door, Peter went in to give Winston William's message.

"Well, Winston, we only have one thing to ask of you. We are leaving, and when Jesse gets here, we would like you to give him a message for us."

"You're leaving just like that? Giving him the food?"

"Shut up and listen for once. Tell him that if he leaves and does not take or damage our crops, we will not come after him. That he is never to return with troops or bear arms. That will be seen as an act of war against us, and we will act accordingly. Any attempt to follow us will also be considered an act of war against us."

"You're truly nuts if you think he's not coming for you!"

"We know, and still we try the peaceful course if we can."

Peter then handed him an envelope with Jesse's name on it.

"What's this?"

"It's the message I just gave you."

"So why give me this?"

"Well, Winston, we think you stand a fifty-fifty chance of being killed when he gets here. So this is our backup to make sure he gets the message. Good luck." Peter turned and left the cabin, taking the two guards and a few stragglers walking into the woods. They moved up the trail. As Winston watched, they just seemed to melt into the trees.

They stopped at the first small clearing. They left five of the best shots there to wait for Jesse. The rest kept moving to the next two staging areas that fit the requirements of open space with good cover at the upper end for cover. At each place, Jesse and his men would have no choice but to cross open ground to get up the hill to them. They had found and were fortifying six different places up the trail. After the third stage, the bikes would lose their speed advantage. After the second stage, the scouts would start to filter back to get behind the rapidly advancing force as planned. William moved to the fourth stage to wait, making sure that the horses and everyone was ready to fall back in an orderly fashion. It had only been twenty-five minutes after leaving the farmhouse when they could hear the roar from the bikes entering the farm. They found only Winston and his family waiting for them.

* * *

Jesse came up to Winston and backhanded him so hard across the face that he fell to the ground.

"I have a message." He got up. "For you. They told me and gave me a written copy. The written one was in case you killed me."

"Let me have the message!" Jesse read the letter, his face getting redder with each word. "Which way did they go!"

"They moved up into the trees there." Winston pointed to the small game trail leading up to the rocks and trees. "The wizard said we should leave. What are you going to do?"

The question got him knocked to the ground again.

"Do not ever ask questions of me again. Stay here. Get the food ready to go. Quickly. These so-called wizards won't take long to catch and deal with!"

Jesse set the troops to moving up the trail as fast as they could go. With eighteen bikes equaling thirty-six soldiers, they reached the first clearing in just under six minutes. They were moving too fast. As soon as each family member had a clear shot, they fired as one and then all took a second shot. They killed four men and disabled one of the bikes, leaving them with six wounded men to care for. As soon as they fired the last shot, they all fell back. They ran to the waiting horse and galloped up the hill as fast as they could. Having ridden this trail many times, they made it to the next stage well before Jesse could get his men ready to clear the first stage.

They opened fire, but no one was sure where to fire at. Unknown to Jesse's men, the shooters were already waiting at the next stage for them. They heard the bikes stir up again, but they seemed to be going in circles, looking for them. Jesse had his men take a clearing walk and ride at the first stage. Finally, Jesse came into the clearing and talked to the leader of the attack.

"What happened here? How many of them did you kill? I don't see any bodies that are not ours!"

"Sir, we came in fast as we always do. As soon as the first half cleared the path, a single shot rang out, and five bikes went down. Almost as soon as we cleared the down bike, a second shot rang out, and we all opened fire at the trees, but everyone shot in different directions. As soon as I got them to cease fire, we found we had four dead and the six wounded. We lost one bike and do not have trained riders for the others that now need riders."

"Let me get this clear. You and your men fired hundreds of rounds and hit nothing. They shot twice and killed four and wounded six others with only two shots?"

"I believe so, sir. I can't explain it. They must have been shooting at the same time we fired and so did not hear or see them."

"You do not believe that, do you?"

"No, sir."

"Okay, let's go after them. At the next clearing you see, go in shooting, understood?"

"Yes, sir."

They had all just gotten settled into their positions when they heard the bikes start up the trail again. Peter was waiting with two other fast runners just a few feet from the back tree line again. The plan was to keep them thinking the men were running up the mountain, not riding horseback. It was only about two thousand yards to the next clearing. It took only a few minutes for the bikes to make the trip, and they came into the clearing, firing their weapons this time. As soon as they could be seen, Peter and the other two ran into the trees as if they had just arrived. They jumped into the foxholes that had been placed there for them and to make getting the bikes over harder.

Zane, the leader of the bikes, saw them and directed all fire at them at once. And this time, they started to circle the outside of the clearing, not a straight charge across as before.

Peter had ten guns here and linked to them all for shooting orders.

"How many targets do we have?"

"Only six at this time."

"Okay. When the count reaches eight, we shoot again, then take the second shot if the number is five or above. Keep your heads low. They will be spraying bullets everywhere."

That was already going on. They only stopped firing to reload.

"We have nine! Shoot!"

One shot and again nine bikes went down this time. Seven dead were and eleven wounded with two bikes burning.

They reached seven more targets and fired and started to fall back. As they moved, three of the men were hit. One was hit badly while the other two could still ride. As they fell back to the horses and started their next ride, the clearing came under much heavier fire. The ground troops arrived and started to clear the field quicker this time.

Peter called for medical help to be ready at the next stage. Maria linked in and told him it was already on its way. This ride was to be longer than the last. The men from the first stage were to keep riding all the way to the fourth stage and set up, giving their horses a better rest as each stage after this one was higher and harder, taking away the bike speed advantage but bringing larger firepower into each stage. The third stage was to be held as long as they could. This one had a single narrow entrance, and William had set up three different crossfires to allow cover as each of them were about to be overran. Once again, Peter and five men waited in the open just outside of the entrance to the next stage.

* * *

Jesse was talking to the new leader of the bike squad as Zane had taken a fatal wound on the second round.

"Sir, we came in shooting as ordered. And at first it seemed like it was working. Just as most of us were reloading, we heard a loud shot, and bikes fell all over the place. We started shooting into those areas. And then again, just as most of us were reloading, a second shot was heard, and more bikes went down. We have shifted into threes so at least two groups are firing at all times. We sent two parties around the tree line of eight men each, trying to find the wizards shooting at us."

"Okay, that's good. What is the damage on this run?"

"Still waiting on the count, sir."

Just about then, a man came over and gave them the count. Seven KIA and eleven WIA.

"Okay, so they have any dead yet?"

"We found some blood trails that stopped, but no bodies yet."

"This clearing is safe. It's time to move on. Do not enter the next one unless we are all ready to make an assault. We will all go in mass this time and circle as far as we can before entering."

"Okay, I am sending scouts. This will take longer."

June, at age sixteen, now had become one of the best scouts as he climbed trees and could hide in the tops and see everything. He was not awake. They thought it was an age thing, but he and

Peter or Jake could link and made him the perfect one to watch their movements.

"Peter, they changed. They are all coming together this time just as we wanted. The number is still about three hundred."

"Peter, this is what we needed. You need to hold as long as you can. What are your numbers?"

"We have a hundred and ten fighters and fifteen loaders here."

"Okay, make sure they leave at least fifteen minutes before you collapse the line. Are the traps all set?"

"Yes, and as each gun goes offline, they will leave at once to be reset at four."

"As much as I hate this part, you need to hurt them here badly. We need at least one hundred KIA and as many WIA as we can get. Remember not to stay too long. We need you."

"Okay, boss. I will keep a sharp eye on the timing. June, what does the time look like?"

"They are getting ready to leave as we speak. I'm not sure how fast they plan on traveling. It will be an all-out attack when it gets here."

"Okay, keep me updated on the timing please."

It took them thirty minutes to reach the next stage as before Peter and the others were running in the entrance just as they got there. They did not rush to chase them as before. They took up guard positions at the entrance and sent the two eight-man scout teams to circle around, looking for an advantage. They were gone about an hour in all.

When they got back, Jesse was waiting.

"So what did you find? You've been gone over an hour."

We came back faster than we went. The trees end at a vertical cliff wall over a thousand feet straight up, and if there's a way out, we can't see it."

"Okay, we had a few peaks in the front, and we can't see anything. They may not even be in there anymore. Jesse, what's your plan?"

"We send a scout team in and they see what they can find, and we go from there. I thought we'd be done by now. This is taking too long. Be careful and come right back."

One of the scout teams went in the entrance and slipped around the side of the clearing. It was much larger than the others, and it did seem to be a dead end at the cliff wall. There was no sign of the wizards they've been chasing all morning. They moved a few hundred feet and saw nothing, just a large trampled path right down the middle. They came back and reported what they saw and didn't see. Jesse then got all his leaders off to the side.

"Here is what we are going to do. We will make three groups, two of the foot soldiers and the bikes supported with foot soldiers. They will go up the middle after the sides and draw out there in placements. Is everyone sure of their responsibilities?"

"Yes."

June linked to Peter and told them they were coming.

Jesse set them loose, and they started up the two sides, checking every blind curve in the trail. There was little room for them. They had another eight feet to be under the first pair of machine guns.

William had three crossfire positions covering each other. They were about to walk into the first one. After nothing, they started to loosen up, and that's when they hit them. The two thirty cals opened up with the support of ten riflemen. They had the invaders locked down for over fifteen minutes. Finally, during a reload, they broke the chain by sending the bikes through the middle, getting behind the first guns. They had lost some twenty-plus men to this point. Just as the bikes started to fire on the first guns, the second opened up on them. These were fifty cals with a third shooting straight down the middle. They abandoned the bikes, taking cover where they could find it. About half of the bikes blew up and sprayed burring gas all over the place.

During this, the first guns had made their escape and were on the way to the next stage. By now, Jesse knew he was in for it and had only one way to go forward, so he ordered a full charge. This got them past the second set of guns and right into the third set, and they could now see the defensive wall in front of them. They turned and started for it when over a hundred guns opened up on them Two things happened then. Jesse sent for the reserves and pulled the men in the field back just out of firing range of the wall to wait for the rest of his men.

"William, June just told me the troops at the farm have started up the trail. What's the play now?"

"We now activate the rear guard. They are to form up and follow the reserves up the mountain. Jake and Daniel should be just outside the farm. Jake, Daniel, report."

In a link, they answered as one. "We are approaching as we speak. Gather most of the scouts that fade back as well. We brought all the workers from the other two farms as well. We number thirty, all armed and trained, awaiting orders."

"Great news. Get bows and crossbows and trail them up the mountain. Only take out stragglers with bows only. I would like more information if you can get it safely. Retake the farm and leave a few people to guard it. They will be having company soon, I hope. Chief, how far out are you now?"

"We are making great time. We just passed McFarland, and the road is filled with dead cars and trucks. Should be there in about ninety minutes."

"When you get there, link up with Jake and Daniel. They will bring you to the battle. How many of you came? We need both of the trucks you left and four large Penske trucks, altogether one hundred and twenty men and equipment. We are making good time. The road is full of cars and trucks but passable."

"Great. When you get there, you will link with Jake and Daniel and come up from behind the reserves. They are just now starting up the hill. They number one hundred. Did you hear the others?"

"Yes, we did. See you soon."

Everyone who was awake or linked all had questions at once. It was an overload. William never felt before.

"Quiet now. This information was withheld because we did not know when or if they could make it in time. They started this trip two days ago at great risk to themselves. As they are at least still three hours away, we have to survive until they arrive to save our asses. All questions will be answered later. Now focus on the battle at hand."

The reserves were making good time up the mountain. They would link up in about thirty minutes, and then Jesse would launch his final attack on the wall. He was planning on breaching the wall before him. They were making up large satchel charges and readying bikes to run them up to the wall. He still had close to two hundred men in fighting condition. He had them pull back and make a camp and cook a meal for the troops. They needed the rest.

His entire battle plan never got off the ground. Jesse was still working out what had happened. His Blitzkrieg had been foolproof in every other battle he ran. Small losses and fast results. He moved forward faster in this one but achieved less with greater losses than any other attack. Many of his men talked in wonder at the so-called wizards they were fighting. Soon they would see they were just men and bled like all the others. They found blood at different battles, but no bodies at all. Their losses had risen to thirty-five dead and over fifty wounded. Some would not make it. Jesse was going back to the lightning war as soon as the rest of his troops arrived. They would attack from four different points, all to meet at the center where the charges would be set off.

"Squad leaders, front and center now!"

It was less than two minutes, and all his remaining officers gathered around him as he laid out the final attack on this wall. They would order the rest of the troops as they arrived.

June had been high in the trees above the leader's tent since it went up. After hearing this, he called for Peter.

"Peter, look at my memory. Take all you need, then please help me. I have tied myself high in the tree and will not fall out. I need to sleep, but also wake alert when they start to move. Can you do something for me?"

Peter linked with William and then read the memory together. William showed Peter how to fulfill June's request, and the young boy was asleep until the troops started to deploy.

June was going to be a hero of the first battle, and as soon as he becomes awake, he would be an even greater leader in the family.

"Okay, we know what's coming. It's time to leave. I hate to ask this of you, but can you take as many troops as you need and put up a good defense and then run like hell back here to me? We are leaving you the best-rested mounts we have, and let them see you ride away this time!"

"I will go ask for volunteers for this. I think we need about twenty to make it work. I don't think he has a real clue how many we are."

Opening to all, William told everyone what was to happen next.

"We have two stages left after the next one if needed. If we are forced to move to five, Maria will start the evacuation to the high spot with the kids and others at the camp. We will hold each of the last three stages as long as we can and still get to the next with strength to fight. The longer we hold, the more time for Lone Pine to come and save us. Peter and his twenty are going to make them pay for the wall and give us more time to be ready here at four.

"Our adversary is going back to Blitzkrieg to finish us off. He finally saw what our plan was and now is going to fight his way. Now we hold him as long as we can at every stage until the chief comes to save us. For a while, it will look to him as if he's winning at last. This is what we want. When the time is right, I will ask for surrender terms. I believe his ego will make him agree to this. If he does, that's when we win the battle and the day. We have suffered a great many losses today. He has lost more. Everyone, keep your head about you and stay safe. Good luck to all!"

Jake and Daniel split up at the farm. Two men stayed with Daniel. The rest followed Jake up the hill to catch up to the reserve force marching to stage four. He was collecting the scouts and others that had faded back after each stage. They had bows and were very good shots. They told him they were about ten to fifteen minutes ahead of them. Jake found the fastest scout he had and sent him out on point to find the soldiers marching to the third stage.

"I want you all to look at this. Something is not right, and I cannot tell what it is. I can see it's wrong, but I don't know what it is. Can any of you see it?"

A large group was looking at his view of the marching troops, and at last Maria spoke.

"You are all seeing the rear guard that's keeping them safe from attack from the rear. Yes?"

"Yes, Mom, that's their job when you have trail duty."

"Well, what would you do if you found one of your men on rear guard never checked the back trail?"

At once, they all saw it. They were not protecting them. They were making sure they marched into battle if they wanted to or not.

"Of course. I have an idea, if you will allow it? We will take out the guards at the back and see what happens once they are gone."

"Great idea. Jake, keep us linked in and get going."

* * *

Jesse was waiting on the troops coming up the hill to arrive. His men were resting.

"Everyone count off one to three. And as soon as the count is done, all ones go eat and relieve yourselves. Come back as soon as you can. In this way, you all get the same chance before the final assault on the wall will start."

The relay for food and of relieving themselves was working great. Each man first went for ammo and whatever they had lost or used up in battle, then food or the latrine, whichever need was the greatest. Then they went back to their positions, and most took naps if they could. Jesse had a well-trained and skilled force of men. He still was trying to figure out how this group of farmers was holding them off for so long. Jesse believed this to be their last defensive position before reaching the main camp on the mountain. With the proper intelligence, this might have gone much different for both sides.

The forward edge of the troops was just leaving the second stage. Jake sent that the guards were not to leave. They must be down before they cleared the site. If any other were still in the clearing, they, too, had to be killed. Jake could not risk giving away their position behind the main group. As the last of the main group was passing out of sight, it left a total of ten men still in the clearing. Two or three would pass out of sight, and that's when they would shoot. A silent (they hoped) one shot with bows.

"Everyone link and wait for the go. And then move to the far edge and wait and see what happens be safe at all times." The three men at the front moved into the trees, and Jake gave the word. Seven bows all twinge as one all the remaining men fell to the ground. Each man ran to his target to made sure they would give no alarm to the rest. All the others moved to the tree line and moved forward slowly, not clearing the trees. The soldiers had heard nothing and were moving away. There were still quite a few hanging back. After a minute or two, they started to check behind them for the rear guard. Some stopped walking, waiting for them, Jake thought. By now, the main body was out of sight, and these men moved together and stared talking.

Jake linked as he was told. He was going to show himself and see what their reaction was. Just him, no others.

"Be careful, son. Your mother will blame me if you get hurt."

"Hahaha. I will, Gramps."

Than he stepped out of the trees and waved at them to walk to him. They all looked stunned at a man behind them and started walking toward him.

* * *

Chief Loggins was making much better time than he had planned for. It seemed that Jesse was helping him. Jesse had cleared a path for his trucks as he moved on the farm. So when the Lone Pine caravan reached this point, they picked up the pace from forty-five to sixty. They had gained almost thirty to forty-five minutes and would be at the farm in less than fifteen minutes as that road was all clear and held by the scouts. Ben linked and gave his position a quick strategy meeting, and it was decided if they had no problems and Peter could hold them at three for at least fifteen minutes, they could have them surrounded at four and end this.

"Daniel, start getting every means for transportation you can to get up the mountain as fast as possible. Run relays until it's not workable any longer. Check all the bikes you find. Use them if you can. You brought all the horses with you, I hope."

"Of course we did. You said plan for any contingency, and we did. I have eighteen horses here."

"Great. Who are you leaving at the farm? And how long do you think it will take to get them all the bottom of four?"

"I will get back to you on that after I see what we have to work with."

Daniel had Steve get the horses ready to go and found two working trucks and two trailers used for hauling crops from the fields and hitched them up to the trucks. Steve would stay with some of the Lone Pine troops to hold the farm and take care of the people they would be sending down to them as prisoners very soon. Taking the easy path, they might be able to get most of the small vehicles close to the stage two clearing in just over fifteen minutes from the time they started up the trail. Just as he reported this in the link, he saw the front truck rounding the last turn in the road leading to the farm from the main road.

"We will tell you as soon as we start up the mountain. Just have to get everything in line now and go."

With the plan sent to all the linked members in the group, it took little time to put the light small truck in the front and heavier one in the back as they would soon have to be left behind as the road became more of a path than a trail! It was just ten minutes, and they had started up the mountain.

At this time, Jake talked to the men at two and told them they had a choice to leave their guns and walk back to the farm where they would be held. Or if they wished to help, to hurry and go back to the troops and pass the word to any others who did not want to be here or do this, to slowly fall back and sit down when the fighting started, and they would not be harmed. They split down. The middle half stayed, and the others dropped their guns and eight men started walking down the hill.

"Sir, what if someone asks questions about the others?"

"Tell the truth. You don't know what happened to the guards, and the others started walking down the mountain. We will take care of any men they send back. You will be safe."

So the seven men took off to rejoin the rest and started passing the word to the men they knew were being forced to fight for Jesse. Soon an officer came up to one of them and asked why they took so long to get there. They told him just as Jake had said. As it was about time to launch the attack, they sent no one back as Jake had predicted.

Jake asked the man who asked the question if he would share freely any information Jake might need. The man said yes and spoke the truth. So in this way, Jake linked with his mind but did not make his presence known to him. He just kept an open link, seeking and hearing everything he saw when he wanted to. He kept the link private so as not to give it away. Separately, he passed the information onto William and Peter as they would need it first. They in turn sent it to the whole family. Jesse had lost all his advantages and had no clue. The last charge at three was starting just as Daniel and Ben were unloading all the troops at two and would be starting up the two trails in minutes. The battle at stage three would be over in an apparent victory for Jesse's forces. He would continue his lightning war against a foe that was running out of places to go.

* * *

"All right, we have it straight. We send two columns up the sides, and when the fire is at its heaviest, we send the remaining bikes up the middle to blow the wall."

It took about five minutes to bring the reserves up to speed, and then they were all set. They started slipping into the clearing.

* * *

Due to the longer time they needed to hold the wall, Peter had another ten troops arrange a wagon that had been brought down with extra supplies to be made ready to block the breach in the wall after they blew it. And they left two extra machine guns, the thirty cals. They barely had things set when a warning came about the crawlers moving in the clearing now. The lookout had spotted them shortly after and opened fire. That started the battle in full. With the loss of surprise, Jesse let them all go, only keeping the bikes back. As soon as they all started shooting at the defenders on the wall from both sides, their rate of fire started to decrease. Jesse, seeing this, gave the order to advance at once and not to let up on the rate of fire. In just minutes, there was a marked reduction of return fire. The order was given for the bikes to go.

The bikes came roaring out of the trees and ran straight up the middle. Just as they cleared the trees, the four smoke shells fired as they started. They landed just in front of the wall. A dense thick smoke filled the area and hung low on the ground. The bikes came under fire at once from the sides of the wall. Once they cleared the tree line, a heavy machine gun opened up right down the model. It only took forty-five seconds for them to come out the other side of the smoke. Four bikes made it to the wall. They all tossed the satchel charges near the center of the wall right at its base. The bikes turned and ran for the tree line. At fifteen seconds, they all went off. The shock wave knocked over anyone within two hundred feet of the blast. Jesse ordered a charge to the wall even as the smoke was still clearing. Some two hundred men came running at the wall, all weapons firing. The return fire was much lower probably due to the shockwave from the blast.

The troops reached the last of the smoke shells and passed through where they were shocked to find the complete section of the wall completely shattered and laying all over the place. The even bigger shock was the large wagon blocking the way in and the heavy fire coming from behind it. They had to take cover on the wall to each side of the breach. They were taking fire from the top of the wall and were pinned down if they moved too far from the wall by two fifty-caliber machine guns.

Jesse was now able to see the wall again. He sent the bikes back to toss the extra charges at the wagon. Once again, the bikes came under heavy fire. This time, the shooters took aim at the drivers with great accuracy, taking out six of the ten bikes they had left. They all pulled the cords and tossed the bags into the breach. All the troops hiding against the wall ran back into the field to get away from the blast. Fifteen seconds was not much time to run. Most were knocked down by the second blast wave. All fire stopped with the blast, and another large smoke cloud was spreading, showing in the cool mountain air. Jesse had the troops fall back and reform for the move into the breach!

* * *

"Peter, it's coming very soon now. Remember, tell your people not to shoot anyone that just sits down. Also only leave fast runners behind."

As soon as the battle started, Peter had a withdrawal plan. Everyone on the wall would fire three clips. After that, some would pull back and go to stage four and get in place for the next battle. After every two clips, another group would fall back in the same way. They kept this up, so it looked like they were losing men at a much greater rate than before. Soon it was just the rear guard left as the bikes came roaring into the field. The thirty cal was set to autofire down the center of the field. They had four snipers on the right and left side to take out as many bikes as they could. Peter pulled everyone from that part of the wall. So when the charges went off, there was no one on that part of the wall. Even before the shockwave cleared, the wagon team was rolling the wagon into place and turning it on its side as close to the hole as possible. When the next charge came, they would find it with the two fifty cals waiting for them. They hoped to hold for two waves of the soldiers to crash on the new wall. Everyone was off the wall from end to end. The only loss was the thirty cal.

The next wave was rushing the wall as Peter's troops scrambled back to their positions. As soon as they cleared the trees blocking the narrow trail, the two fifty cals opened up on them. As each member reached their position, they resumed firing as well.

The leader of the charge saw no opening as soon as they cleared the smoke. He had the men go to the wall for cover from the fifties.

This brought them under fire from the wall. Once they got this close, they noticed that it had a curve in it, so the side could fire at the outer fence. Here they were still getting fire, but not from the fifties.

Jesse was seeing this. He called for all the bikes left to take more charges and try for the wagon. He had the rest of his force move forward and fire on the wall positions. Just three minutes and they were on their way. Had it not been for June still in his tree, this attack might have hurt them a lot.

"Jake, we are pulling out. If we can't stop the bikes, make sure you pick up June. He saved us again."

Peter then told everyone about the bikes coming again. He had one of the fifties pull back and the last one he told to grab and run as soon as they tossed the charges if they got that close. With the manpower he had, Peter was able to hold eight minutes and then gave the order to fall back.

This time, they were going to run and be seen doing it. They had horses for everyone and made sure they saw them. They all mounted and ran for the tree line as Jesse thought they had done every time before. Maria directed people to pick up the dead and wounded in this battle. By the time Jesse's men returned to the breach, there was no one left at the wall.

"How do they do that in full retreat and still leave no one behind, alive or dead?"

"Sir, due to the blast, we had to pull back, and the resulting smoke screen hid all their movements from us. We did find one thing that explains a lot. We removed two machine guns that had been set to fire automatically with set positions to cover. We think they used a lot of this against us. I believe you're right. It is a very small force."

"Yes, I see. It makes for a good scare tactic, and I believe you're right. It is a very small force. We will have them soon. Let's get going!"

* * *

As soon as Jesse and his men cleared the third stage, Jake set up a collection point for anyone trying to escape when they learned that they had lost. Next, he and Daniel took the troops in two groups to encircle the remaining troops moving up the hill. They were only minutes behind them now. He got June out of the tree and sent him back to the farm to keep watch on the roads just in case they had more troops somewhere.

"Daniel, Ben, are you all ready?"

"Yes, let's get going. I want dinner. It's been a long day already."

"Everyone move out. Do not use your guns until they fire first. We must be a surprise if they choose to fight. Good luck."

CHAPTER 25

The Wizard's Offer

After a short march of just ten minutes, the point man stopped and called for the officer.

"Sir, there's an even bigger wall here."

The information was passed back to Jesse, who moved to the front just far enough to see the wall. They could see no one and knew that to move forward was going to be difficult. Jesse ordered more charges to be made up. As he was trying to make a plan to get past this last obstacle, William made his entrance!

From a safe place of concealment, William yelled out to Jesse, "We wish to talk about terms for surrender! Will you and your second-in-command come forward and meet with me?"

"And who are you?"

"I am the wizard you came to kill, and I'm not as crazy as you and Winston think. Will you come out and talk? Bring your weapons if you want. However, do not have them in your hands or we will shoot."

Jesse agreed at once. He had lost enough men, so if they wanted to give up, he was going to make it hard on them. William sent to everyone that if any of them looked like they were going to fire, use bows and shoot to kill. He had his revolver at his back as well. They made a smaller wall for him to stand on. It was just behind the first but far enough that it looked like he was floating on air from Jesse's point of view! Ben was just behind him with a fully automatic assault rifle.

William stepped on to the wall, making him visible to the men on the other side of the wall. As hoped, they all thought he was floating on air. He could see Jesse and another man walking forward.

"Stop where you are. Which one is Jesse?"

The one to William's left waved at him.

"You are not Jesse. Turn around and go back. Jesse, if you try to send another one in your place, we will all open fire. I see you still do not believe in the wizard. Okay, how is this? You are standing behind the sequoia tree on my right side. Come forward please!"

"Okay, since it's a surrender, I will come forward." And he did so. Soon the two men stood about twenty yards apart, and William let him start the talks.

"First thing is you and all your men will come out in the open and drop your weapons. Next, you will take us to your camp, giving us everything we need. And last, you will become part of our support staff. So now all of you who are left, step out and put down your weapons!"

"*Hahaha.*" The loud laughing from William made Jesse very mad.

"What's so funny?"

"You are. You thought we wanted to give up! You have lost all of your bikes. They are in our hands now. We found your base camp, and at this very moment, fifteen of my men are liberating it. You only have about one hundred and fifty men left here on the field. All of them are low on ammo. I can use one shot and kill you all right where you stand. That's what's so funny! *That brings me to my question for you! How many more have to die before you accept my terms?* Don't answer yet. While you think on it, I want to talk to all of your men."

By opening his mind, he made everyone in the clearing hear his words.

While Jesse was thinking about his answer, William told them, "I want to tell you all that some of you have already surrendered and have gone back down the mountain. Others stayed and helped us in the last battle. Some just sat down and dropped their weapons. They are already walking down the trail back to the farm where they are being fed and cared for if needed. Anyone here who wants to surrender on their own only has to place their weapons on the ground, take one step backward, strip naked, and place your hands on your head. Then wait for one of us to come over to take your guns. We have men behind you. There is no escape from this mountain anymore. Jesse is waiting for the men he sent back to arrive with more ammo and food. They are not coming."

Jesse reacted to this at once!

"Any man who tries this will be shot at once!"

"*No, you won't*! Because my men have everyone in the clearing covered, they can be killed with one shot now. So, Jesse, did you find an answer to my question? Wait, before you answer, you should know that a wrong answer will get you shot on the spot. Do you understand?"

"I understand. There will only be one surrender to me, and how many have to die depends on how long it takes for you to give up."

A lot of the men started yelling. Some for, some against. In all of that yelling, no one noticed the pistol that was in William's hand. As soon as Jesse finished his statement, one single shot rang out across the clearing. Everyone turned toward the sound to see Jesse drop to the ground. He was dead before he hit the ground!

William turned to face the man who had been standing next to him and asked, "Now out of all the soldiers here, who would be the second-in-command after you?"

It turned out to be the imposter from when they first came out to talk.

"Okay, while we wait, do you remember the question I asked Jesse?"

"Yes, I do."

"Do you plan on following this man's orders even if he's dead like Jesse? Do not answer now. Well, first, what's your name?"

"Israel."

"Okay, Israel, how many more men have to die before you surrender?"

Israel turned, looking around at the men behind him. About half of them had or were stripping off their clothes and sitting on them.

"I think the only answer is zero, sir!"

"Excellent choice. The other right answer was one. That one being you. Now tell them all to do as most already are doing please."

Israel gave the order and then turned to William and asked a question. "Sir, if you don't mind, would you answer a question for me?"

"Depends on the question, I guess."

"How did so few men beat us so badly?"

"Okay, fair question. How many of us do you think there are?"

"Our information was that you had maybe a total of fifty to sixty people in your group."

"Winston, I guess, yes? Don't answer. We already know."

He used the open mind again.

"Will everyone move into the open and help with the prisoners please? The fighting is over! Look, Israel here is my family now!"

From all around the clearing, over three hundred men, women, and young kids came out of the trees, all armed and scary looking to Israel!

"My god, we never had a chance, did we?"

"Yes, you did. You could have left when you got my note."

"What happens to us now?"

"Now we keep you here and see what you are and if you are a danger to us."

At this time, the last bit of this battle was taking place back in the valley where they found Jesse's base camp. Fifteen men from the farm moved to take the camp. There were few guards here, and like the rear guard, they were to keep the people in the camp there. Steven decided to take the guards out as Jake had done and wait to see how the rest reacted to the loss of the guards. They had clear shots on three of the eight guarded they could see and fired their bows, killing all three. The remaining guards all came to the site of the shooting while looking at the golden hills where Steven and his team lay in the grass. Without notice, the people in the camp came up behind them and attacked them, killing all of them in a quick one-sided fight as they all had guns and shot them many times over what was needed to kill them.

Standing up, Steven yelled to them, "Hello! We are friends and come in peace. Please do not shoot!"

He stood up and started walking forward, followed by his team. The battle of the valley was over. Steve brought the rest of the force into the farm and waited for orders. Only three of the guards survived as most where killed by the people they held against their will.

At this point, William had everyone fed and cared for by need, not side as equals. Having all of the troops brought back to the farm for the openness, he addressed them all.

"Welcome to all of you that are here. Jesse is dead, and you are all going to have choices to make in the morning. Some of you will have different choices than others. Some of you will be staying, and some will be leaving to go wherever you want. If you choose to leave and we agree, you will go with three days food and water, and we will wish you luck. Now here is the deal. We offer parole to anyone who asks for it. If we accept you, anything you did before taking the parole is in the past and forgiven and forgotten. It belongs to the dead world we all left behind. This is true for you and for the guards being held. They're on the other side of that fence. Everyone who takes it in good faith is welcome to join us as a person without a past.

"Parole comes with responsibility. Each person of thirteen years or more must work each day. This gets you food for the day and a safe place to sleep. It also means that you cannot leave. You will all have an equal voice in family meetings even while on parole. Your voice and opinion carries the same weight as mine. Each person's time on parole is based on their behavior, not a clock. Some of the family members are passing among you with copies of the oath you will need to take to join our family. Winston, this is also available for you and your family.

"Now the last thing for you all to think about. If you take the oath and fail to keep it, the only penalty is death! When you make a decision, let a family member know, and they will take care of you."

By the next morning, only six people chose to leave. The rest all stayed. William sent for two building kits and some trained family members to help and guide them. He also sent to all who could hear that the family had grown by some three hundred people, and they would be building down here and act as first line of defense on the valley floor. First thing in the morning, William went back up the mountain. Six new stories of the wizard started that night!

CHAPTER 26

SEALs Appear

The battle for the truck farm was costly. They lost thirty-eight family members, and Jesse lost 171, and another fifty-eight were wounded. All the wounded had taken the oath. Israel had taken the oath first and was making a great effort to help the family in any way he can. The others were following his lead. None of those keeping watch on them had any problems. They all were truly happier with them. The parolees' first duty was to gather all the dead and burn them.

It was just days later when the building kits arrived, and they started making log cabins near the farm where they would now work. They would still have the scouts who would help guard them and bring them meat.

Bull and Aaron had plans to build extra stables to move livestock and increase the crops here as there was a lot of land they could use and still keep it hidden from the main part of the valley. Now with the extra people in the farm, they could move up their plans. The farm was moving right along, and so they started a drive to bring cattle and other livestock down to the farm. Aaron had them prepare two new larger tracks to plant next spring. It would be needed now that the family was so large.

Aaron took some of them as extra hands to get the harvest in. Aaron was also given the task of getting and keeping Winston and his family in line. Even after the battle, they still had the thought they deserved special treatment. Allen saw that they received it in the form of all the dirty jobs he could find on a farm.

All in the family that was awake had few or no dreams for the next two weeks. A few kept tabs on groups they knew of. Oliver and William kept having dreams of the islanders and the small combat unit. For some reason, William could not get a lock on them. So he had set a watch for them. Better to be ready at all times. The islanders seemed to be going south for some reason. They were sending fast boats south, looking for someone or something. William didn't care as long as they were going south.

In the next few weeks, William was planning a large feast of thanksgiving, as it would have special meaning to everyone in the family. It seemed that crises situations always pushed more members of the family to wake up. By now, all the original members had woken up, and all the teens could be linked in as well. In total, almost all the adults and about half of the others that have been added as well were able to link into the silent councils. With each week, more of the family quit taking their medications for old illness that the awakened body would cure.

William, Maria, and Alex managed to keep the feast a secret all the way up to one week before the meal was to be served. In the week's council meeting linked with Lone Pine and the three farms, everyone was told of and invited to come to the feast. William had Maria make the announcement and the invitations to all who could make it. They planned it for the first distribution of the winter food supplies. Lone Pine would already be planning to come to the mountain, and the others would be getting ready to move down the mountain for winter. With just a few family members and parolees that pulled work and the guards, almost the entire family was going to make the feast, and food would be sent to all the members not able to make it. Bull went with two others, taking strings of horses to the closest farm and waiting for them to drive around the mountain as it would only take a few hours now. Since the battle, they cleared much of the roads so they could drive it as needed. They would ride up the mountain in a few hours. Everyone would be staying the night. This was the first party since the event. The family had grown and worked hard for the last five months. They all deserved a chance to let their hair down and relax.

The feast was just one day away, and the cooks had been at it all day since yesterday.

Thanksgiving Menu
Garden salad with choice of dressing
Soup—beef or vegetable
Corn, green beans, broccoli, carrots, potatoes
Meats—deer, bear, pork, chicken
Fish—trout, bass, catfish
Dessert—assorted cakes and pies and homemade ice cream

This feast would be the best meal any of them would eat in the last six months!

The Blessing

"Today we take a day to honor those we have lost, as well as giving thanks for what we now have. In both community and silent council, many are not really clear on our goals and the new rules. On this day, we are combining two old holidays: Thanksgiving and Memorial Day. The old world of elected government and money-driven government is gone. Many wonder what I use for a guide, how, and why I do what I do. I have kept two things as my guiding lights. The original bill of rights as it should have been used. Also the US Constitution. Both in the original forms. Where it said all men, it means all humanity is created equal. Race, color, and religion have no place, giving one more or less rights than the others. Sex is also missed by the word. Man, women, and all other sexual preferences are welcome here. We are the birth of the second or maybe the third cycle of human evolution. We are a family. We are stronger together.

"We have three farms, soon to be four, so Aaron tells me. Each will be enlarged by fifty percent next planting season. So next year, we will all eat better even with all the new additions to our family. So now that I've talked too long, let's all eat, drink, and be merry!"

With that, the food was served potluck style from three long tables, and it was first in line, first to serve yourself. The meal took almost two hours before the games, music, and dancing started. It was a great day for everyone!

* * *

Jack Stanly was the first in Winston's family to get off parole, and he had volunteered for the SW sector guard duty the day of the feast. He worked hard to become part of the family. This had, for a time, made it difficult at home with his family. Jake had befriended him and became a teacher to him. So he was the natural choice for him to reach out to when he discovered a problem in his area.

About one hour and fifteen minutes after the meal, Jake got a mental shout from Jack. He had found intruders far inside their guard post in the valley! Jake stepped aside, and in a private link with William and Peter and Chief Loggins, he had Jack calmly repeat his report in full.

"I am in the second ring about fifteen hundred yards up the trail from Lodgepole. There has been no warning from anyone from the outer sections. I took a break to relieve myself by climbing down from the blind I was using. As I started back to the blind, I was shocked to see six fully armed men slowly creeping up both sides of the trail to base camp. They had already passed my position, so I only saw their backs. They were wearing full combat gear and carried their weapons at the ready. I let them move on a bit before I started to follow and wished I could speak to Jake for help. Much to my surprise, as soon as I thought of him, he was there in my mind. Jake responded with instruction to keep them in sight without being seen myself."

Jake sent out feelers to the post that had missed the four men coming up the trail. He had them all move to back up Jack. He also sent word to the other scouts to converge in Jack's location as fast as they could. Three of them found Jack, and they kept following the four men up the trail.

William opened to everyone awake or not (something he could do at will now) and gave this warning.

"We are going to have company soon. I want you all to just continue with the party. It's only six men." He then closed down to private link to the RR teams and planned on them moving out and letting them pass so they could find out first if it was only four men. "We need our best scouts in the woods on both sides of the trail. We also need to find out how they got so far inside our security rings without being seen. He then called Oliver in as well. Oliver was thinking the same as William these were the soldiers who kept dropping in and out of their awareness as they kept looking for them. They had eyes on them and knew they'd be in the camp in ten minutes. They would be allowed to enter the camp safely if they made no overt move to hurt anyone. Just after that was determined, they found the other two men. They were on point, one on each side of the trail. By now there were twelve scouts and RR team members on their tails. They could be taken out at the first sign of trouble. William hated the idea of killing them if it was necessary. He would like a better solution to these types of problems. Then right on time, the four men started to enter the camp.

CHAPTER 27

Upgrades

After the long trip up the West Coast. O'Brian and his people reached Monterey Bay. Looking for a safe harbor to shelter in, they chose Avila Beach. It had a long fishing pier and was not a very busy area of the bay. There were groups of people nearby, and they came around looking at the boat. As soon as they saw how well armed the people were, they mostly left them alone. Others came with more people and guns, trying to take what O'Brian had. After very brief firefights, these groups moved on as well.

After the last group had been driven off, O'Brian got everyone together and had a talk with them.

"We came here to be safe and at home. Since we arrived here, we had to defend ourselves against a lot of roving gangs looking for food and other things. It's clear we can't stay here. If we do, we will become like them, looking for food and other needed things. That is not why we came home, is it?"

The team didn't say a word. The Youngs and the girls and boys all said no. They wanted to find a normal place.

"Okay, of late, I have been having a dream of large red trees and of two generals, Sherman and Grant, from the Civil War."

"I, too, had this dream, but the one was not a part of it."

After Sonador spoke, all the rest told of having the same dream, even the young boys.

"I am not explaining it too well, but I feel we need to find them!"

Wayne spoke up. "What kind of a tree did you dream of? Veronica and I have been dreaming of trees for the last few nights as well."

"They were larger than normal trees with a dark red bark. Did you not see this in your dream?"

"No, we saw mountains full of dark green trees as far as the eye could see. Dark red and larger than the others. How much larger?"

"I remember asking to stop on the coast that year so we could go and see them. The two oldest trees were called Sherman and Grant. They are east of here and not too far away at that."

"What's not too far? Veronica, do you know?"

"Yes, it's about a two- to three-hour drive due east of here if the roads are clear."

"So they are real and close by. We need to leave here as soon as we can. Jeff, take three men with you. Also some gas. Find us some transportation to get there. Take extra ammo as well. No telling what you find out there!"

"Well, O'Brian, now what do you plan for us?"

"My plans ended when we got here. Now it seems I need to go find trees. Me and the sergeant are going to start taking our gears off the boat and get ready to go find some trees. If you want to come, you're welcome. Or you can take the *Dream Wind* and go wherever you please. As for the others, they can go with you or with us. If they wish, they are free to go wherever they please."

Sonador spoke up. "My place is with you until we meet the one!" The boys had come to wanting to be left alone to becoming a SEAL. They voted to stay with the SEALs.

"Looks like I get to see the trees at last. We are staying with you as well."

"That sounds good. We would miss you both. Okay, if you're going with us, we need to make some changes in our plans. We need to take everything of value with us, leaving behind only what we can't carry. Next, we need to fill the boat with water and fuel supplies and then find a place we can hide it for some need we may have for it later. Do you have any ideas for this, Wayne?"

"Yes, I do. Did you notice the islands we passed coming in the other day?"

"Yes, what about them?"

The one on the far north end bay on the east side has a fresh water source. It's not well-known as there is nothing there. I can sail back and leave the *Dream Wind* there and come back to shore in the zodiac."

"Okay. You and the others get the boat squared away while Juan and I take care of the rest."

Everyone got to work. Diego was pulled to be a lookout. Due to their recent past, they made excellent lookouts. Juan and John made quick work of unloading their gear and sorting it so they could load it fast when the other got back. They took off as soon as everyone knew what was to happen.

Jeff, Vic, Angel, and Len got loaded up on weapons and extra ammo as well as two five-gallon gas cans. Jeff's team started walking up the hill and inland away from the beach. As they passed the pier, John told them they were on their own and to be silent and safe. They disappeared around the far corner and were on their way.

Wayne and the others started storing the boat's equipment and other items needed to sail the boat away, leaving nothing not needed on board. John and Juan took about two hours to get all the gear and other items sorted and loaded into eight big duffel bags. John sent the girls to get from the marina store rope and any food they might find. The girls found the bags and rope. They also got rain gear and shoes for the boys as they had none. After two hours, they were ready to send Wayne on his way.

"How long do you think it will take there and back?"

"About a four- to five-hour trip if the wind is good and we get a good line to sail. The fuel tank is quite low, and I am not putting the extra in the tank until we come back for it. I have a tact light and will signal when I am at the inlet."

Matias spoke up. "Senor Wayne should not go alone. He may need help. I would like to go with him."

"Well, Wayne, do you want a mate on this voyage?"

"Ah, Matias, come aboard. You'd be good company for the short voyage."

The two pulled out of the harbor with all lights on, making a big scene of leaving, hoping the few locals who saw it would tell others they had gone. It would give a safe wait for the rest of the team. John set a five-and-a-half-hour alarm on his watch. Next, they moved all their bags up to the boat warehouse at the top of the small hill. It still had secure fences and many good shooting positions if needed. All the SEALs had problems since getting back! They all joined up to protect the very people they were now having to kill to stay alive.

They left the three at the top, and they went back down to wait on whatever came next.

* * *

Jeff and the others had a three-mile hike to make to the first car lot they had seen. They were moving slow, trying to not be seen by any of the people still trying to live in the area. A coastal city was a great place to stay. If you could fish, you eat, and then you'd just need a water source. This city had a lot of fresh water, and the bay was teeming with fish of all kinds. It took almost six full hours to reach a car lot that had the right type of SUV and trucks they wanted and could use.

They found a lot that had the right type of SUV they wanted They were Jeeps fitted with snorkels for high water and large enough to carry a lot of gear in the back or on the roof racks. They also had tow packages. They could use it as long as they had not been running during the event. The only problem was, a small group of local people had moved in, and from the looks of things, they were living there full time. They had three guards out at all times. Angel and Vic were the two best shots in the group here. They worked on getting the best shots on two of the roving guards. When Jeff signaled for a hold using hand signals, he told them they had incoming at their six (behind them).

A large group of armed men passed by the four SEALs. They were walking in, and not in a hostile set. Two men walked out to meet them. Jeff was on point and could hear them as they talked. He became quite attentive when he heard the *Dream Wind* and them being talked about.

"Yes, they have better guns, and they have food other than fish. No, we are not sure how many came on the boat. With your men, we will have forty-five men. If you come with us, we can overpower them and take their food and weapons and the boat as well. We want to get there just at sunset so we will have the sun at our backs and in their eyes."

"How do we split up the goods after?"

"We don't. We stay together. Seems like there's another threat coming. Just as well we stay together. We are stronger that way. How long before you can be ready to go?"

"I need to leave just a few people to stand guard. The rest will be ready in ten minutes."

"Okay, let's get going. The sun will set soon!"

Jeff had heard every word as well. He stayed put, not moving, letting them all leave the lot. They has almost fifty armed men heading straight back to the pier and O'Brian and the others. Soon it was safe to pull back to the others. About fifteen minutes had passed. By the time he reached the others, his first action was to get the SAT phone on. He called Wayne's phone. While waiting for the phone to ring, he filled the others in on what he overheard. The phone took almost two minutes to start ringing.

* * *

"O'Brian here."

"Hey, boss. We found the vehicles we need and should be on our way back soon. We have only five people here to deal with. If the cars run, we'll be back long before the trouble gets there."

"What trouble?"

"About forty minutes ago, just as we were about to move in, a large group of heavily armed townsmen came up and moved into the lot. It was about thirty of them. In short, they came on a recruiting party, building a raiding party on us. They left here a bit over fifteen minutes ago. They walked out of here, so with a straight walk, they should make it in an hour or a bit more. If they have other means of travel, it could be sooner. You should take the boat out and meet us at another location!"

"Can't. Wayne and Matias left on the boat two hours after you started out. We have to stay here and wait. The idea was to hide it so we can get it later if we need it. He should be back in"—he looked at his watch—"about two hours, give or take. We have eight large duffel bags here, and we moved them all to the boat shed at the top of the small hill. Diego is our lookout."

"Okay, good. You better fort up just in case they find you. I'll call when we start back."

"Okay, we will be waiting."

O'Brian explained what was about to happen. "Our best-case senior is they come here and see the boat is gone and just leave. Second, they come to the pier where we tied up to see if we left anything. Third, they had people watching us and know we are still here. That is what we are going to get ready for."

For the next thirty minutes, they checked all the guns and loaded them with five extra clips for each. Then the two SEALs walked slowly back down the hill, checking for good fallback positions. There was one on each side of the road. They found good spots. They would leave a weapon and the extra clips. They each set up three fallback positions before ending at the boathouse. Each one was approximately twenty-five yards apart. They would be going back to the gate to wait on whoever was coming. While on the boat, everyone learned to fire weapons and load them. He gave them instructions and set them to be their back guard if they needed one. They then moved back down the road, taking up their watch post. They took water and food as they didn't know how long they would be there.

Back in town, at the same time they were walking the road, Jeff had his team ready to move on the car lot. The plan was simple. Anyone with a gun was hostile and shot first. Three of the men were armed, standing guard still. There were some women and kids still there as well. They all took up their targets with the silencers on. It was over in less than thirty seconds. Three men dropped dead, and no one heard a thing. They all moved on the office from different sides. They entered from the back at the same time Jeff went in the front door. With guns out, they quickly had the rest locked up in the sale meeting room. They found the keyboard locked. They busted the lock and found the numbers matching the SUV they liked. They were about to go when Jeff had an idea. They hid behind a large dully bright yellow pickup truck. He got the stock number and quickly found the keys for it as well. They were in luck all of them started. The pick-up had half a tank of gas, the SUVs needed fuel. The remaining people watched in wonder as the first SUV started up, and then the second and last the pickup. They were spellbound by what they saw. One had the courage to ask how they did that.

Jeff told them what they had learned in South America. If a motor was running at the time of the event, it was dead forever. However, if they were not running and had no other problems, they should still run as long as you could get gas.

"We are not your enemies. And we are not prey either. If any of your people make it back, show them what you have learned."

Now with the three vehicles, they loaded up and started back.

"We are on are way with two SUVs and one pickup, bright yellow be used as a truck if needed. What's your situation there?"

"We took the boathouse as a last stand and have set up three stages up the hill. Me and Juan are waiting and hiding at the bottom. We are going to fire first and ask questions later if they show up. We also have trap lines set as well. It's clear they've been watching us. It's just a matter of time till this starts."

"Okay, we will take up positions at the rear and lend support where needed."

"Great. We will work back to the boathouse and see how many of them we can take out. Than we attack them from behind and the front. We will have a few surprises for them as…wait one…"

It was two and a half minutes before he returned to the phone.

"Yes, they are here. Looks like fifty men moving to look at the pier. Glad we moved the boat and left there. Had we been caught there, this would already be over! You set up and don't fire until we reach the boathouse. They will be sure they have the two of us trapped by them. When the shooting starts, it will be the six of us, which should slow them a bit. You then take the rear and engage them from there. We will see if they have what it takes for a real fight."

Jeff put the two SUVs in the back of the closed shops and loaded the truck with all the guns he could. Vic and Angel took their rifles and sidearms only. They would be high cover for this engagement. They were the top two snipers in the Navy when they went to SEALs training. Victor broke records while at the school that had stood for twenty some years. He held seven school records when he graduated. Angel broke three of them eight months later and tied another one. Each took a side and went to find a high place to shoot from. Their needs were easy for this one clear view of the boat storage yard and sight of each other for cover if needed. They walked together until they found spots, and they split up to make their climbs. Both hide-outs would be about eight hundred yards out, an easy shooting range for them. Meanwhile, Jeff and Len were making some changes to the truck. They rigged a swivel mount on the roll bar. They mounted the B.A.R with the belts with extra clips close at hand. Jeff would be in the bed, and Len would drive the truck up the road when the time came. Using a light, they signaled to O'Brian they were ready.

The locals had made better time than Jeff estimated they would. He failed to take into account how they did not worry about being seen, and they had a downhill trip. He could see them just out of sight of the pier and the boat storage building.

CHAPTER 28

Battle of Avila Beach

WITH THEIR NUMBERS swelled by joining their two groups, they had a large enough force to just swarm the pier and the boat. They would kill everyone on it and take the boat and all it carried. They sent a scout to look it over and report back. He returned in just over twenty-eight minutes. He went to the pier and then walked past the boat storage yard. He reported that the *Dream Wind* was gone and there was no sign of them on the docks. He then told of his walk past the boat storage yard where he noticed that the gate was open, and there had been something pulled or pushed up the hill. He believed that they should check it out. Upon checking further, they found the gates to be open and had signs of people staying there. It might not be the people they were looking for, but it was worth checking it out. So after talking over, they decided to go to the boat storage yard and use the same plan to just find them and overrun them by sheer numbers. They made two groups and took up places on each side of the small road leading to the boatyard.

A few things had changed. The sun was no longer going to be at their backs. It would now be in their eyes, and it was much lower now and harder to block out. There was less than twenty minutes of sunlight for it fell behind the coastal hills just the other side of the 101 freeway. They moved with little care for cover now. They had only gone about one and a half blocks when O'Brian challenged them to stop.

They talked about this. At the moment he finished, they all started firing at location they believed the voice was coming from! They also started running right at him! O'Brian and Juan returned fire at the leading men. The first trap was a staged line of personnel charges, set in a stage line to catch them as they move to avoid the first charge right into the next one. It was hard to keep fire on the men as they ran back and forth on the first line. As soon as they hit the fourth charge, John fired his weapons and got up and ran to his next stop. Juan was giving cover fire for him. The result had been that their two groups became one, all taking cover on the right side of the road. In the deep shadows cast by the buildings, at almost the same time, an explosion came from the position O'Brian had just left. Just as the blast went off, Vic and Angel heard the pop of a mortar tube. Quickly looking around, they found three tubes being set up and about to fire. They both shifted to fire on the mortar teams. They opened fire as soon as they were set up. By now, they all fired once and were setting up for their next rounds. These rounds had forced the two SEALs to fall back to their second positions where they held their fire until they had clear shots on about ten to fifteen men. Once the townspeople started up the driveway, they set off the second string on O'Brian's side and the first on Juan's lines. They could not go to either side for cover, so they ran up the middle, right into the SEALs' line of fire. Using quick three-round bursts, they cut down about half of the men they could see. Still the numbers would overwhelm them very quickly. Same as last time, they fell back to the third positions and set up for the next round. They had both taken their last positions before the boathouse.

The mortar tubes only got off one round each as the men manning them lost three men and had to take cover from the sniper fire. They left the mortars, showing how they were untrained and lacked discipline. By use of hand signals, Angel kept watch over the mortars while Vic went back to the oversight of the boathouse.

The townspeople had regrouped and seemed to be waiting to advance again. They were waiting for the mortars to fire again. Finally, one of the men came to tell them the mortars had been found and taken out. They now started to look behind them as the mortars had good cover from the boat storage and could not be seen. After a short meeting, they all agreed that everyone needed to charge the boathouse at the top of the hill.

They were down to about half the number they started with. They all checked and reloaded their weapons, now making three different lines, and all with different places at the top of the hill. This would give them cover fire on the doors. They set a five-man team to lay down, covering fire as they started up the drive to the top of the hill. They shot wildly all over the top of the hill. They started running up the sides and straight up the middle as well as soon as the men in the front started firing. The five men took off and up the hill as well.

John and Juan knew they had to fall back to the warehouse or they would not make it. O'Brian called Jeff.

"Hit them now with everything you got. We need time to make the top of the hill."

"On our way, boss."

* * *

At the bottom of the hill, Jeff was driving with Len in the back with a BAR mounted on the roll bar. They came flying out of the dark behind the townspeople. Len opened up, laying down very accurate fire while Jeff had a fully automatic machine pistol firing from the driver's window. At this point, they had to put up a rear guard as the rest charged the hill. In the confusion caused by Jeff, they made the storage building. Veronica had made good defensive positions for them all, and everyone had a gun. When the next wave came, they would be facing six guns in front and four highly trained men at their backs. They decided to send a few men back to see if they could recover the mortars and put them back in action.

Five men started for the tubes. They went around the back of the building and safe from the sniper fire, they hoped. It only took them two minutes to get to the outside of the parking area at the back of the north end shops, and they could see the three tubes just sitting there. They knew they had been under fire but could see no one. They all took a job. One was to get the rounds, and the others to get to the closest mortar and set it and on to load it. The others were to give cover fire if the sniper was still there. Angel was dividing his attention between the tubes and the fight going up the hill. He missed the first man running to the ammo box so there was a round already on its way to the far tube from him. The two started toward good cover positions. This caught his eye, and he fired at the far one. He went down but kept moving slowly. He move to check the others, and just as he was lining up his shot, his rooftop came under heavy fire. Moving back and down to get a safer firing spot, he quickly moved up to the roof line again. As soon as he lined up another shot, he took fire again from two positions. The first round was going down range again with a second round already waiting to be fired as soon as the tube was ready. With no shot at the men at the tube, Angel decided to fire on the ammo box holding the mortar shells. Coming back up to the top, he peeked over the top just as they shot the second round off. They were at the edge of the building. There was the box with the man just starting back with the third shell. Taking careful aim, he fired a single round into the box. The resulting explosion was very large with a giant fireball rising at least two hundred feet into the night sky with bright reds and oranges mixed in the sky. After the heat died down, he came back to the top of the roof, which was on fire and starting to burn quite well. He looked at the men in the parking area. All were down. Some he could see were moving, but all looked to have many wounds and bleeding. Some would not make it. Angel left the roof and started back to rest of the team.

Back in the street, Jeff started his run up the alley in the pickup, the guns mounted on the roll bar being fired from side to side by Len as needed. The townspeople all scurried for cover as they went by. In front of him, the last two rounds from the mortars went off.

Just seconds later, there was a very large explosion from behind them. They knew Angel had stopped the shelling and kept on going. The townspeople started to return fire as they pushed through to O'Brian's position. There were still about twenty men able to keep fighting, coming up the ally to the boathouse. The large explosion stopped then for all of thirty seconds, and they started up the road again. Guns blazed as they ran to the turn at the top. From there, they could see the warehouse doors closed and many guns barrels sticking out of windows. They opened fired and ran for cover from the return fire. There were at least ten people there, and most were very good shots. They had five new wounded after the first exchange. They were reloading and yelling orders at each other, trying to get some kind of plan together.

At this point, O'Brian yelled out to them. It took about four tries before someone answered him.

"You outside, I want to talk to you. You have many wounded people. They need treatment now or they will die. If you keep up this attack, many more of you will die! It's your choice to make. Before you decide, you should know we are SEAL team 18 just back from South America. We brought two citizens and four refugees back with us. If you continue this action against us, we will only shoot to kill from this point on, and you will all die!"

They could hear them talking, and it kept getting louder as many of them wanted to stop the fighting and go help the others.

"If any of you want to stop, just leave, walk out. We will not harm you."

More loud voices, and then a single shot. After a few minutes, a voice called out. "My name is Benny. We just had a change in leadership here, so there is no more reason to fight. If you will let us leave, we will."

"My name is John, and I'm charge here. We wish to talk first. Lay your weapons down where they are and step out in the open."

"We will be at your mercy if we do that."

"You already are. We have men all around you as we speak. And you attacked us, so we are the ones that are taking a chance. If you want to leave here alive, that's how you do it!"

They all came out and laid their guns down and walked forward. O'Brian and the others came forward to meet them. In just a few minutes, they made arrangements to take two of the mortars and two-thirds of the remaining rounds. Jeff told them about the cars and what he told the people back at the lot as well. O'Brian told them of the islanders and their war of conquest in the south as well as how the others came to be with them. He also told them to start getting ready for them. They used the pickup to get their gear and then the wounded as well. They sent Angel back to the lot with them and their wounded. While there, Angel showed them how to get them running if they could. Then he started back to the harbor.

* * *

Back at the boat storage, they moved the SUV up and were loading them and scrounging for fuel and food that could be found. Sometime during the battle, Wayne's timer ran out about forty minutes ago. He gave Diego another watch to keep on the harbor for the zodiac's return. They finished loading them and started making dinner in a barbeque they found, complete with charcoal bricks. As it had gotten dark, they lit a large fire to help guide Wayne back to the harbor.

Soon the food was ready, and they all sat down to eat, careful to save some for Wayne and Matias when they got back. They talked about the locals and what they found since returning home. It was agreed that they would leave at first light to go find the two generals on the mountain. Finally, the phone rang.

"Hey, John, is everything all right? We heard what sounded like gunfire and saw large explosions earlier. Now we can see a large bonfire burning on the pier."

"Hey, glad you can make it back. We were starting to worry about you as well. Tell you everything when you get here. The fire is to light your way. You missed dinner, but we kept some for the two of you. How long will it take you to reach the pier?"

"We should be there in fifteen to twenty minutes."

"Okay, we will meet you at the pier to help with the gear and fill you in on our day while you eat!"

Soon they reached the docks, and they made quick work of the gear they had and fed them with tales of wonder and the last of the food. Soon everyone was sleeping. Three of them took guard duties. Carlita took the first watch with Veronica taking the second. As they planned on leaving early, John took the last watch so he could choose the time they would leave.

CHAPTER 29

Sequoias

THEY HAD THE pickup in lead. It carried the zodiac and the motor and still had the gun mount on top, ready to fire if needed. Their luck was holding as they skirted the outer ring of the town, looking for missed gas and food items and found both soon after getting off the main roads. They filled all the tanks and filled their two jerricans they took from the marina when they left. Now with the tanks filled and food for at least four days, they headed to Highway 41 east. There they would take State Road 198 to the entrance of Sequoia and Kings Canyon National Parks, where they would find their two generals.

Not wanting to spend another day in battle ravaged Alva Beach. they drove until they crossed the coastal mountain range. The drive was much longer than it should have been as there were cars and trucks everywhere. Where they found cars, they checked for gas but found none. All the trucks had been cleared as well. The drive was slow as they had to wind around so many cars and trucks. After reaching the Central Valley floor, they found a small side road to pull off on to eat a quick lunch. They ate a light fast meal and started off again. In the large golden hills of the valley, they had to deal with the heat as it was still summer and much hotter than the coast. They soon cleared the hills and were driving on the long straight roads, the heat and the bugs filling the air all around them. The roads ran as far as the eye could see. Large groves of fruit and nut trees lined the roads as well. Other crops were also still in the fields. Some of the fields had guards around them while others had been picked almost clean by bands of people that all looked worn down by exposure and hunger.

The California water systems still had water in it. They chose not to stop as the water was filled with dead men and fish and other farm animals as well. The valley looked normal and inviting; however, if one looked closer, all one would see was death. All around were bodies of men and beast decaying in the sun. They had to use the AC with the recycle feature on to help clear the smell as well as cool the air. They could also see signs of people living nearby. They saw no people alive on the drive, and they had just crossed the I-15 interstate highway. Soon they would turn up the 198 and go straight up to the park's entrance. The heat of the day was building as they kept driving east. In a short time, they crossed Highway 99. It was now very close to the mountains and tree-lined roads. There were many homes but no signs of the many people that once lived there. In a short time, they came across a small group walking west.

They were the few soldiers who refused to take the oath and were sent back to warn the others. Their warning was not to go to Wizard Mountain. This was about to be the first people they would see since being released a week ago. They had not chosen their path well and now had to scrounge for food and clean water. O'Brian ordered a stop. Lenny, the leader by default as William killed all the others above him, spoke first as the SEALs all came out of the cars, armed to the teeth.

"Hello, we don't want trouble. We are just trying to get home to Los Angeles."

"What happened to you?"

"We heard that a small group had been growing food in the hills around here. We needed it, so we came to take it. The wizards on the mountain were too much for us to handle. You see, we only brought fifty soldiers with us."

"This is all that's left? How many did you face?"

William had wiped their minds to keep these few that left from giving away any facts about the mountain and the people on it.

"I am not sure. We never saw more than six of them. They would fire one shot, and five or six of us fell dead on the spot."

"So they were good shots, and they all hit their targets."

"No, there was only one shot, not five or six. Just a single shot, and many fell dead. And we saw one or two fading into the trees on the far side of the clearing. We would follow them, and at the next clearing we came to, they shot once, and many of us died or fell wounded. At the seconded clearing, they gave us our first warning to turn back and leave Wizard Mountain. After a brief battle, we charged and saw twelve men ride out on horseback. We kept charging in, and now all we remember is how we lost, and they let us go. We are to warn people not to go to the mountain. That's all we remember now."

"So where are you going?"

"Back home to the San Fernando Valley. We are part of a large group of survivors there. Would you like to come and join us?"

O'Brian looked at them for a minute or so. Then he said, "No, I believe we have business with the wizards on the mountain. Tell me how to get to the farm you talk about. And how do we get there? If you tell me how to get to the farm, we will give you more food and water for your trip home."

"I am sorry. We have been trying to remember that all day, and none of us can agree on which way the farm is from here. We cannot help you."

So after talking to them for about an hour more, they gave them some food and water and moved on up the road toward the mountains.

None of them believed the tales of one shot killing five to six men at one time. Or their ability to move uphill as fast as they say had happened. They looked for the way to the farm but failed to find it. So they kept going up the road. It was getting late, so they found a place to set up camp, and everyone knew what to do for the night. They made a meal and made things ready to go the rest of the way in the morning. It was the night before the Thanksgiving feast, and they made camp in running springs and set guards out in two this night.

Early the next morning, they loaded up quickly and drove up the mountain and saw nothing but wildlife along the road. This road was much harder to drive as there was little room, and cars needed to be pushed out of the way in many places on the way to the higher regions where the many campgrounds were. This drive allowed them to get inside the third ring before being seen. The road was their blind spot, and they didn't even know it until O'Brian and the SEALs showed up that day. It took them almost four hours to reach the first tree, the General Sherman tree. IT was the oldest living tree in the world, well over 2,500 years old. They stopped there to look around, not as tourists do but as soldiers on recon. They found a few clues and information on the other tree. It was on the other side of the mountain. After looking all over the place, they all got together to see what they had found. There was no sign of people living here, even with solid cabins and hotels in the small village. On the mountain, O'Brian saw why the wizards came here. There was food and water, all a small group could use for many years. The question is, where were they hiding? They had shown great skills in staying out of sight so far. It would not be easy to find them on this mountain without some kind of help.

"I had a dream, six or maybe seven times going back about three weeks. It's strange, but there is nobody in it. Just words, two, and always the same. *Ho Dog*, and then the dream is over."

"Sonador, how is this helpful?"

"Well, John, as we looked around this place for some clue, I have found those words in three places around the outer fences here. I think it's what we are looking for!"

Everyone started talking at once, asking her questions until John yelled, "Quiet! Let's go see the places where the words are."

So she showed them where she found them. They were not in plain sight, and all had different slants to them. It was clear they had meaning and seemed like they pointed to something. Was it the wizards? The general direction was to the information station in the backwoods trails in the area. They all searched the board for something, anything that might help them. Diego found the key to the riddle They were in bold letters. It was the phrase "Let god be your guide."

"This is where you start, and you follow the phrase to the wizards on the mountain."

"Diego, they're not the same at all."

"Yes, they are. Look again. We are told to let God be our guide. Yet this was meant for friends who knew what to look for. They do not want just anyone finding them as you said, so a simple code and friends would find them. Just let God be your guide. *Ho Dog* is just *Oh God* spelled backward, so that's what we follow."

John and Sonador saw it at once, and soon they were looking all over for the direction that the words would lead them to. It took about two hours, but they found the words on a trail sign to the JO Pass out of Lodgepole Campgrounds. They loaded up and drove the six miles to the large campgrounds where they soon found the trailhead leading to the pass.

* * *

They set up a camp, and while a meal was fixed, the SEALs got their gear ready and packed supplies for three days. It was just after 4:00 p.m., and they would start up the trail after dark. They talked while they ate about what they planned to do.

"Okay, Wayne, you stay here for three days. If we are not back, load up and get out as fast as you can. We will leave just after full dark. It's only about two miles up the trail. We should make it in about three hours. After dinner, they made sure that the Youngs and the kids all had enough supplies for getting away if needed. They all could defend themselves now. The team had trained them on the proper way to shoot. As soon as the team started up the mountain, they set the guard routine, youngest first to oldest last. All would stand two-hour watches then wake their relief and get to sleep.

As the sun faded into the western sky, the team started up the trail to JO Pass, at first staying to the center as they left the camp. They switched to field craft now. They went up the trail as anyone would. As soon as they could no longer see any part of the campgrounds, they left the trail half to one side, the rest on the other. John took the upper half and Jeff the bottom. Vic always went with John, and Angel was with Jeff. The rest just filled out the two sides. They then moved off the trail so they could see each other and cover the trail.

As they moved into the bush, they faded from sight of most men that might be looking for intruders. In less than a minute, they found a well-covered guard station high in a tree. Had they been just walking the trail, they would have been seen. They were in infiltration mode and avoided all contact with the locals. At first sight of the high blind, John used hand signals to stop the other half and gave them the guard's location. It took them over ten minutes to move past the blind. Once on the uphill side, they moved quickly again.

About five hundred yards past the first guard, they found another blind, but it was unmanned, so they moved past it.

Jack peed on the back of a tree just out of Jeff's view, and both sides moved past him. Having climbed down and just started to relieve himself, he saw John's group first. He moved so as to be hidden by the tree and stopped peeing. When he saw Jeff's group moving close by him, he froze, hearing Bull in his head.

If they had not seen you, moving can only give you away.

He remembered what his responsibility was and the things Jake had told him. "You're never really alone when you're on guard duty." He really wanted to talk to Jake right now as he was scared and worried about how to get the alarm out. Jack started to follow from the very far back so as to not be seen by the men moving toward the main camp. He now kept Jake and the rest informed on what he was seeing. The first guard that they had made it past was sent back down the trail to check if there were more back at Lodgepole. He soon reported on the others back in the camp and the tree cars they had gotten up the mountain.

At first, a number of members started to worry until William told them all not to worry. He had pulled a lot of guards for the feast today, and they are all right.

As the SEALs moved closer to the pass, they started to see signs of a lot more people than they were led to think were on the mountain. He was sure the man told him the truth as he knew it. The fact that they had only seen the one guard had John starting to worry about their plan to just walk into the camp when he found it. He could see many horse and wagon tracks all over the place, going up and down. Other than the tracks, there was no sign of the people to the casual eye. They had just moved another few hundred yards when they heard voices.

"Well, these guys deserve the best and special order for their plates as they all volunteered for this duty."

"They did? Wow, I did not know that."

"Yeah, let's get to the horses and get back for the music and games."

The two men turned up the hill to a hidden stable where they mounted their horses and started up the trail. The SEALs fell in behind them and started up the hill as well. They quickly lost sight of them but could see their fresh tracks and still heard the men talking, not trying to hide at all. They felt safe here. They made it past the bulk of their security. John called the other team to join them. They followed the sound of their voices until the trail ended at a wall of trees. They had a change in deployment tactics. They would now walk right up the trail with Vic and Juan on oversight and cover. They started up the trail where it just ended in the middle, like they stopped to listen and then change direction to follow the music they heard. Jack reported this up the line.

"We are close now, and this is their last line of security before we enter their camp."

* * *

It was just a few minutes when they could hear what sounded like a party coming from behind a large tract of trees. There were load voices and laughter as well as smoke from many firepits, and the smell of the food had all their mouths watering. John picked a path and started into the camp! They started to encounter the people.

At the party, they seemed not to notice them or said good evening and just went about their business. Ahead of them, they saw a sequoia tree laying on its side. It was enormous, having fallen on its side and overcome by the elements. It had been made into a platform, and one man was standing on it, watching them walk in. The four of them walked right toward William.

* * *

Back at Lodgepole Campgrounds, the Youngs and the kids got a surprise about two hours after the team started up the trail. Jake and three other men sent by William were to find out how they had gotten so close to the camp. The SUV and pickup told them most of the story. Jake called out to them from behind a tree!

"Hello to the camp. You're on our mountain. We want to talk, not fight. Please do not reach for your weapons!"

They all took up their guns. Jake had expected this and had given orders not to take any action if they did.

"My name is Jake. We know you have men moving up the mountain, and they are being followed. We have been sent to bring you to the camp. We want to do it the easy way. How do you want to do it?"

"My name is Wayne. We don't know anything about any men."

"Funny, we heard them talking about you as we passed them on our way here. Listen, there are four of us here. We are all around you. We could have killed you all if that was what we wanted. We have food and shelter at our camp, and we have orders to invite you to join the celebration we are holding right now at our base camp. Will you join us please?"

"Why should we trust you?"

"You would do well not to trust anyone you do not know. In light of this, you can keep your guns. Please sling or holster them, and we will come out in the open."

After a brief talk among themselves, they all did what was asked. And as they did, Jake and the others all came into the camp slowly. They led ten horses, all saddled and ready to ride.

"Great welcome to Wizard Mountain. If you will get what you need, we will make some food for you. There's a lot more in the camp. If we hurry, we will reach camp just a little behind your friends."

"Excuse me. May I look at you please?"

"Sure, young lady. But I must warn you, I am already spoken for."

Sonador looked at Jake for a few seconds then yelled, "Yes! You're William's grandson."

"How did you know that, young lady?"

"I shared many of his dreams for the last year. I have seen you many times."

"Ahh, I see. And your name is?"

"Sonador. I am eleven years old."

Jake opened to William. "I have a surprise for you. See you soon. There are six of them, two US adults and four others, three just kids, one a young woman, two boys, and two girls."

In just a short time, they were on the trail headed up the mountain. Wayne, after a few minutes, started to ask questions, nothing of any real importance. Just the same, Jake spoke up so all could hear him.

"One of our most important rules is never answer questions from anyone who's not a member of the family. So please wait. We will make everything clear to you very soon." They rode up the trail, and in a short time, they reached the pass. It was another forty-minute ride to the camp. William sent orders to wait just outside the tree line when they arrived. Jake called for a rest stop to get down and walk a bit before going on.

* * *

William asked them to stop as they cleared the last few trees and were in the open. In their meeting, O'Brian gave orders for no one to make any aggressive moves or gestures and to follow his lead. So when asked to stop, the four of them did so. Everyone they passed showed no surprise at the four armed men walking into the camp.

"Good evening, sir. Sorry, we seem to have intruded on a celebration of some sort."

"Not at all. If we find you're good company, we would be happy to have you eat with us. You are a bit late. As it's our first Thanksgiving dinner, we have more than enough for all. We've been here six months, and we have managed to feed and shelter everyone in the family. Now my name is William and the head of the family. May I have your names, please?"

O'Brian gave him their names. When he stopped, William waited about thirty seconds then asked his question. "Captain O'Brian, may I call you John?"

"Yes, please."

"John, why don't you give me the names of the two snipers you have left in the woods?"

O'Brian was taken totally by surprise that William knew. That caused him to think of Victor and Angel, and their names flashed in his mind. Before he could make any answer, William spoke again.

"If you are here to do harm, you will fail and die. All of you on the first shot. So why don't you ask Victor and Angel to join you here in camp?"

Again, John was unable to speak. When he was settled, he tried to relax before he spoke up. "*Victor, Angel, please come join us.*" He then looked at William. "Are you the wizard here?"

William laughed. He told them to move closer. He then answered his questions with his mind. O'Brian asked a few simple questions.

"John, look at me right at my face. When was the last time you saw my mouth move?"

The others were looking at John strangely as well as he was the only one talking. His mouth fell open.

"You are the wizard!"

"No we are not! We are awake, and soon you will be too. Had any strange dreams lately?"

By now, Vic and Angel had made it into the camp. They were followed by eight guards. "Please sling your weapons and join us. Now, John, you can see you were never a threat to me or anyone here.

We've been waiting for you for weeks. However, there is still a matter of trust, so please tell the truth. How many are in your party?"

"Six in the team."

"John, you lied again. The number you gave me is still not right."

"It is. There are six of us on my team."

"Yes, we know that, but my question was how many in your party, not your team. You seem to think that you walked right into our camp undetected. And that you have some kind of advantage over us. This is not true. Let's go back to the walk. You were most impressive getting by the first guard. Remember the second blind you passed?"

"Yes, it was empty."

"Yes and no. Jack saw you and alerted us, and we had you covered ever since. Didn't you think it strange that no one took any notice of you as you came in? John, why are you hiding the truth from me?"

"I am a US Navy SEAL and under orders and can't answer your questions without clearance."

"Oliver, I need you. Can you come over here please? John, this is Oliver. To the best of my knowledge, he is the last official government agent. Oliver, this is John O'Brian, Navy SEAL."

"Hello, John. You're the leader of team 18, yes?"

"Yes. How do you know that?"

"Your last mission was to take out a group of drug lords. I talked about you with General Simmons at Cheyenne Mountain just before coming here."

"Did you know him?"

"Yes, he gave me all my assignments. His last orders were take the information I gained on my last assignment to the person that could make the best use of it. That's why I came here. I am a GS 35, and I give you permission to give this man any information he asks for. Understood?"

"Yes, sir."

"Okay, John, will you now tell me the truth and allow me to see all your thoughts? And now tell me about the others with you. First, how many, and who are they?"

"Yes, I will no longer hold anything back."

With those words, the wall fell in John's mind, and William saw the memories of the last six months and the voyage back home. These men were heroes.

"Thank you, John. That's a hell of a tale. We will talk about it in more detail later. Now let me answer your questions. You have come to find me. I am the wizard, and I am also the admiral as well. Our magic is in our minds. We also have dreams that tell the future."

"Hey, what the hell? How did you do that?"

"That is why they call this Wizard Mountain. Once you agreed to answer all my questions and meant it, I saw it all in your memories. And we need your help. Jake, bring them in please so we only have to do this once. Lucy, front and center please. John, this is Lucy. She is my head of security, and if you choose to stay, your first student and your teacher as well."

At that time, the others came into the camp riding on the horses. "Maria, can we get them all some food and drinks please?"

"William, we have a lot to talk about. I saw you and Oliver in my dreams a few months back. Then things got a bit busy, and they stopped."

"Yes, me and Oliver had you in our dreams, and you dropped out. We did not know if you were going to be a friend or foe! Glad to know you're on our side."

"How do you know that? We didn't really talk at all."

"Yes, we did, or I did when you agreed to let me have your thoughts, I read your memories back to the event, and I know about your intentions, and they are in line with ours."

"So you really are a wizard."

"I hope it doesn't bother you too much."

"Why, there's nothing I can do about it."

"That's true, but there is more to it than that. We are not sure yet how you blocked us out of your dreams. We will know soon, and it will be good for all of us."

With a bit of true fear in his voice, John asked how that might happened.

Laughing, William told him, "Why, you will tell us, of course. John, are you awake?"

"What? Of course I'm awake."

"Well, soon you're going to be more awake and will have the same abilities most of us have now. Just take a few days to get settled. We need you and your men to train all the members in warfare tactics and soon. I believe I can link you in tonight's silent council meeting, and you will know everything we know. We have to be ready for the islanders when they start moving north. There will be others to deal with. We need your skills to survive what's coming. Will you help us? Oliver, I think they were looking for you, not the family. Come talk with us. Tell them what we know and what we're planning on doing."

O'Brian spoke up. "First, how did you convince that other group that you could kill three to ten people with a single shot?"

William laughed. "We had a situation where we needed to kill three men all at the same time on our escape from Las Vegas. Maria and I were the only ones awake at that time. We sent two teams much like you did coming up the trail, one to each side. We used walkie-talkies to keep in touch with both teams. After they were in place, I linked with Ben and Jake, who gave the order. It sounded like one very loud shot, and all three men fell dead."

"That's not possible. Even three is so hard, but ten? Not possible."

"Well, if you are willing to stay, we will give you a demonstration of the one shot. Its sole purpose is to demoralize the opposing force with fear and doubt about the use of magic. So let's get down to why you came here."

"Well, the dreams showed us a place we could call home! A small part of our world we left behind still lives on this mountain, also because a young girl told me about you. Her name is Sonador and she is witting back at the campgrounds."

"Jake, I think it's time I met your surprise and see what she is capable of. Please ask her if she will join us for a short time."

While they waited, they talked about the others with them and the people at the coast. Soon she was walking up to the meeting room and over to their table.

"Hello, William. Please forgive me. I do not speak English yet."

"Sonador, you will learn it faster than you can believe. For now, just tell me in Spanish what you see in your dreams. I will understand."

So she told him of the first dream, the one from the morning of the event and just about every dream after that as well. John told of how she convinced him to look for the wizard and that they would all be safe.

"Excuse me, I have to talk with the others." O'Brian though he would leave to talk in private. Instead, he just closed his eyes for about thirty-five seconds. "Sorry it took so long. It was a lot to cover."

O'Brian was thinking that the wizard angle was a good tactic, and he made it look easy. Well, by any standard he held before the event, it was magic. Then William opened his eyes. He looked at each one of the SEALs, and it felt like he could see right through them.

"It is the opinion of the entire family that if you can show special skills and will teach them to us, you can stay. Like everyone else, you will need to accept parole and take the oath."

"I'm a bit confused. You said you were going to talk to some others. When is that going to happen?"

"John, you will get used to it very soon, but for now I will tell you the whole family saw you and your group's memories. And we all want you to stay and be part of our family. It took so long because of the large amount of information you all have brought with you. Now Lucy will take you all and go over the oath and make sure you all get all you want to eat and drink."

Lucy and Oliver took all twelve of them to the cabins set aside for new family members. They gave them food and drink as well as beds and a place to clean their bodies and clothing. The showers and restrooms were just at the end of the next building. After getting them settled, Oliver spoke to them all. He told them of his last mission to see the visitors and his meeting with William and the family, even the move to Indian Springs from Nellis Air Force Base.

Most of them had a hard time believing the visitors were real. O'Brian stopped them and asked why. "Can you find a better explanation for the state of the world?"

Lucy than gave them four copies of the oath and explained to them about being on parole. After asking if they had any questions or special needs, they prepared to leave. Oliver reminded John that William would be linking him into the silent council tonight.

"What time will they come for me?"

"It will be in about two hours or so. Depends on how long we spend on the feast and the cleanup after. You think we are coming to get you for an in-person meeting, don't you?"

"Well, yes, almost all these types of meeting are face-to-face for security reasons."

"Yes, that is what you are used to. John, the old world is gone, and here things are much different. When William comes for you, he will link with your mind. You do not have to leave this room. Relax and clean up. You'll all feel better." They left. As she was leaving, Lucy told them it was safe to go anywhere they wanted inside the tree wall but to not to go into the trees.

After they were alone and had all gone to the showers, they held their own meeting. "Does anyone want to leave?"

The Youngs said they were home and planned on staying. They would take the oath. The girls said this was their destination since the day of the event. They would stay with the wizard. The boys wanted to stay with the girls. They had bonded. They also wanted to become SEALs and go back home to avenge their families.

John looked at his team and said, "You are the best team in the service, and seems like the last. As of today, all your enlistments are up. You all have to make up your own minds on what your next move will be."

As one, they all said, "We want to stay here. This is where you're staying. So are we for the same reasons."

They had all just made their decisions when John got the call from William. He walked over and sat down in a chair and went blank as the meeting started.

"Just relax, and in time you will be able to sort it all out. And time is not the same here. This won't take too long. It's a regular meeting. It's called the silent meeting because only family members that are awake can join in."

"Why do you limit it like that?"

"We don't. Anyone who wants to can join. The only requirement is that they be awake. We have first-time family members almost every night now. More and more of us wake up every day."

The meeting started, and John though it took hours before William said, "Good night. Glad you're all going to stay. Get some rest.

"Jeff, ask him if he is all right."

"Why do you ask?"

"You've been staring off into the distance for the last minute or so and did not respond to my questions."

"A minute? It was only a minute! Get the team. We need to talk before bed!"

* * *

To help them adjust to the new home, William had the SEALs go to all the training stages being run, from archery then to hand-to-hand combat and zip line practice. Len had a question at the first stop.

"Why do you use bows and crossbows in battle? Are you low on ammo?"

"No, we use it to keep hidden when we flank our foes in battle."

"Len's point is good. How do you flank a foe that's driving you up the mountain?"

"If you wait, I will show you and explain it all at the last stop." They stayed just a short time at the hand-to-hand. Jeff and O'Brian started to talk at the same time. John kept going.

"You have the worst hand-to-hand we've ever seen."

"Well, you are the new instructors, so give me a new lesson plan as soon as you can."

They walked over to the training zip line along the tree line. They were running them as fast and as close together as they could.

"This is the answer to your question. John saw parts of our offensive plan last night. I could see his confusion when we kept retreating up the mountain. After we passed a certain point, the attacking forces passed our lowest zip line. Once this happens, our best scouts zip-lined to the last spot, hid, and let them all pass. Fully armed and with the extra bow or crossbow, whichever is there. They followed behind. At each stop after that, they get stronger and kept the force from being resupplied or warned us of reinforcements. Now do you understand why we have them?"

"Yes, it's genius, and it works from what that man told us on the road."

"We also use them for hunting. We never fire the guns if possible. Helps keep us hidden from people that come up the mountain."

"Is that all there is to it?"

"No, there is the one shot as well. So for you nonbelievers, here how it works! If you will look around, you will find twenty-five silhouette targets of men. Please check them for holes. Take your time go over or just look from here. When you find them all, let me know."

They worked well as a team. In less than three minutes, they found and verified they were all without holes.

"Okay, here we go."

William opened his mind and gave the order to shoot. Jake's and Peter's teams had been in place and were waiting for over twenty minutes. William started three counts, and just as he reached one, a single and very loud shot rang out over the hills.

"Damn, what kind of ammo are you using?"

"Just normal. How many shots did you hear?"

They all looked at each other and said one, and each of them agreed. They started looking at the targets, and they all had one hole in the heart or the head. All kill shots!

"How do you do it?"

"Scary, yes? All the shooters are awake or close enough to be linked in like John was last night. They all pick targets, and when they are ready or if the people are moving, they have set minimum target to shot at, they fire on the command of their team leader. Our one biggest advantage is we can talk to each other over great distances with no delay. We are not sure how far we can do this yet. We have not reached a place where we cannot be heard or hear the others. The one shot is known all over the state. After we defeat a foe, we give them a choice to stay and join us or go back where they came from with a special message. To never come back bearing arms against us. They all tell of the one-shot killing, three to ten people at the same time. Proof of our magic here on the mountain."

"Wow, you have instant coms during battle and magic powers. And you want us to train your troops SEAL tactics and hand-to-hand fighting?"

"Close. We want you to train us to be SEALs in every way we can. Everyone who has come to the mountain still thinks the world is the same. We know it is not. First, we need to survive the fighting that is going on now and be ready for what's to come later from above. That's enough for today. Let's go back. Oh, here are two more of your first students, Jake and Peter. They lead what we call RR or rapid response teams."

They all walked back to camp. Jeff and Vic went to the hand-to-hand combat training area to watch. Len and Angel went back to the archery area to take notes as well.

"They will have something for you in a day or two. I would like a tour of the zip lines if I could."

"It would be my pleasure, and I am going to have Jack come. He's really anxious to meet you in person."

"Why didn't he come meet us last night?"

"He had to get back to his post after following you to the camp."

"Oh, I would like to meet him as well. It's a rare gift to be able to follow SEALs and not be found by us. We all want to meet him."

They all went off in different dictions.

* * *

After dinner, the *Dream Wind* 12, as they were being called, assembled to take the oath. Maria took the three children under thirteen and explained that they would also have to take the oath. But before they could, they each had to explain it to her to show they understood what it was they were doing! She took Sonador first and was done in just over two minutes. The girl was advanced way beyond her years and knew just what it meant to take the oath. Next, she took Diego, and they spent fifteen minutes before she was satisfied with him. Martine was last, and as he had seen more and had been forced to grow up far too fast, he knew what it meant and was ready as well. By the time they reached the common house, the Youngs and Carlita had taken the oath. Sonador was just about to take the oath. They hurried up to watch and waited for their turn.

Soon they had all taken the oath and officially started their paroles. This was the start of a busy fall season. The SEALs took over all the military training, and the family responded to the higher level of training. They went from very good to deadly in just over six weeks. The family passed the halfway mark. More of the family were awake. After about two weeks, William went to the hand-to-hand combat training to give John a push. William was as good as John now but kept holding back. Today he needed John to move forward and become awake as the dreams showed many thing starting to move in their direction.

"John, today I want you to push me as hard as you can. And you need to guard yourself as I am going to beat you today. Winner is first two out of three falls, okay?"

"Admiral, are you sure that's what you want?"

"Yes, it's an order, if that makes it easier for you to try to beat me up."

John moved them out to the center of the practice field, and after the stretching, they squared off and started to spar. John attacked and pushed as hard as he could and William, much better than him, was just out of reach easily. So John changed tactics and came hard at him again. This was what William had waited for. He took John down and won the first point. They moved back to the center to start the second round.

"You've been getting extra time in with Jeff?"

"No, only you. We seem to have drawn a larger group than normal, so try to make it look good, okay?"

The next five minutes were a blur to John as William had him down faster each of the next two rounds.

"Okay, how did you do that? Some kind of new mind trick?"

"No, it's not a trick. It's the fact that I am awake and you're not."

"I don't understand. How is that not a mind trick?"

"Okay, look around. Of those here, who is the worst student in the group?"

"There, Larry. He thinks he knows this already so he does not put his full effort into it."

"Larry, would you come here please? I want you to spar with John, and I want you to not hold back, but do not hurt him please."

"You've got to be kidding. He's not good enough. I may hurt him if I fight like we did."

"You do your best and we will take care of any harm you manage to do to Larry."

In just five minutes, Larry had John down twice.

"John, do you want to know why you can't win now?"

"Yes, I do. How is this possible? I swear none of you had the skills I've seen today."

"No, we didn't, but we learn and remember everything faster than you do now. As soon as you're awake, we will not be able to do that to you ever again as your skills are much greater than ours."

"Okay, so how did this help me get closer to being awake?"

"You're embarrassed now, and only waking up will fix it. Come on. We have a meeting to go to right after dinner."

It was during this time of internal growth that the stories of the admiral started to grow and spread across the state, and as far as the islanders, Lone Pine had stop two raiding parties before they could reach the town. A number of ever more desperate groups in the valley had tried to take over the farms. In just a few day, after the training event, O'Brian woke up in just two nights. He had a dream about the people in the San Fernando Valley coming back. Within two weeks, all the SEALs were awake as well. Over 95 percent of the adult s were now awake. And all the members in the training were almost as good as the SEALs. O'Brian was the best again. Not even William was able to beat him in hand-to-hand combat as it should be. And after each raid, the family grew stronger as many of the defeated raiders wished to stay with them. Lone Pine had doubled in size. It now had almost one thousand people living there. They made the farms Aaron wanted and needed. They had to move people down to stay their full time. Most of the people who moved were awake, so they always knew what was going on in case they needed help of any kind.

The camp and its farms now held over five hundred souls above the age of thirteen as these were counted as adults, and all would fight as needed. Lone Pine was near one thousand now. Many more small groups of starving people came looking for the wizard to save them. All of them were taken in and given the choice of the oath or being sent on their way with three days of food and water and a block on where they had been. A few of the people who found their way there were sent by other groups with bad intentions. These never made it past the guards and were wiped and sent on their way, never knowing they had found them. A few tried to take the guards prisoners. They all died very quickly and never returned to report what they had found. This started to happen a lot more often as the fall came to its end.

Winter was fast approaching, and with the farms doubling in size, they were building defensive positions in the north and south ends of the trails leading to the farms and the main camp. William called for a full family meeting in the middle of the week due to the number of dreamers having the same dream. They had named these dreams telling dreams because they always came true. Even Sonador had this dream on her own. They all showed large groups of men moving up from the south. There was something different about them. They were much more disciplined in their actions, showing real military training. They were moving up the valley toward the southern farm. They were trying to avoid being seen as they came, moving only at night and staying down during the day. From the dreamers, they estimated the total number around two thousand men.

There was also a group forming in the bay area and had started moving south, slowly taking any ground and food sources they could and conscripting men into their army. They had good leadership and were getting stronger and moving into the central valley on the north. It looked like they were going to Sacramento first. The first real danger was in the south. This army was trained and disciplined. At the meeting, the whole family knew what was coming, and they started getting ready for more trouble.

Aaron was also planning for the spring as they would need to grow at least 25 percent more food to cover their needs and still have extra for the winter months next year.

It had been seven weeks since the SEALs had joined the family. Like everyone, they received a free day after taking the oath. After which they were assigned jobs. William, Lucy, and John sat down and assigned the military training jobs to team members best qualified for each task. And they added a few new ones. With more members waking up each week, the family learned very fast as John had learned from Larry.

They now had three fast reaction forces of twenty-five men each. John, Jeff, and Juan each led a team. These, along with Jake's and Peter's scout teams, gave them a much better force to make war in our fashion, not the invaders! We now counted over six hundred fighting souls, and forty-five of them came from the ones over thirteen years old. All of them were linked to at least three fully awake family members. Even with this, they would still be a three-to-one advantage for the invading force.

The teams of William, Lucy, and John with Chief Loggins linked in to decide on tactics to defend the camp.

"William, we have been clearing the road down to the pass at Tehachapi, and then we can get up the road to you much faster. We will be ready to leave at a minute's notice. We will be five hundred stronger. We should make it in eight to sixteen hours depending on what we find on the way. We have the two trucks. Each now has twin fifties mounted on the top. We will seal the back door for you. If you need them, we have another one hundred that can be over the mountain in two days."

"With the chief at their backs unknown and our three teams below waiting for them to pass, I think you fall back attacking is the right thing to do. I would change nothing. Keep your loses low and force them to lose large numbers in their advances. We will keep to the same plan. Only bows when there is no gunfire, and keep them from getting supplies and reinforcement up the mountain. Change nothing until someone figures it out."

"Well, Lucy, what do you have to add?"

"We only need one thing now to find out where they are and how soon they will get here! To that end, I have sent Steve and two others to make their way down the valley until they make contact with the force we are facing. They left at dawn yesterday. They took three bikes and handguns and bows. They are to recon only. They are offline until they find them."

"Maria, did you get all of that?"

"Yes, my love. I am making plans and moving food in case we need to go to the high hide."

"Okay, we will evacuate the farm as soon as we know they are getting near. As of right now, start moving all the food and equipment we can to safe places. When they arrive, we will repeat the first battle, making sure they see us run up the mountain but not the horses. And after the second stage, we will start falling out so the rear force keeps getting stronger as the extra men at each stage makes a longer stand at each stop."

Now they just made ready for the battle to come. They shored up the defenses and set their guns. Everyone not on the lines was loading all the guns and extra clips or making food for the fighters and filling water bottles. The fast runners and best fighters were left to man the farm. They moved there as soon as they had their gear ready.

It was the next morning when Steve's call came to everyone in the family who was able to hear him. "They are just entering Bakersfield this morning. They are marching as they have few trucks that are carrying their supplies. Their best time is one day's force march, but they'd be in poor shape to do anything at that point. I would say they will be ready to attack in two days. In the morning, their leader is named Blaine, but I can't get any more information than that!"

CHAPTER 30

Battle for Wizard Mountain

THE GROUP IN the north end of the San Fernando Valley was getting pushed by two larger factions from the city. One was living in the beach cities with fish as their main food source and small amounts of fruits and produce growing in small gardens. The others were the street gangs now in charge of most of the inner city. Both groups were looking for more room and food. These two groups had started trying to move north into the valley where Blaine was given the task of keeping them out. Blaine was thirty-eight years old, a major in the army with ten years of combat infantry training. He had been on leave in Los Angles when the event took place. He had a few friends working in the recruiting offices in the valley. Then he managed to find a few working vehicles and weapons and small amounts of food.

They came across a group of people trying to start a farm and grow some food. Others in the area kept coming and taking their food and women and anything else they wanted. Blaine and his friends happened to come across this group during one of the raids from the groups in the valley. Blaine and his group stepped in and killed two of the men and ran the others off. The others shared their food and made them an offer to shelter and feed them if they would keep them safe. This was just four days after the event. They quickly became the strongest group in the San Fernando Valley. Over the next few months, they grew bigger than all the rest of the bands in the valley. The only others in the valley were what was left of the street gangs whose only real skill was drive-by shooting. With no gas and fewer cars, they soon all fell to the better-trained army men with Blaine. They quickly stopped looking for trouble and came wanting to join them. By the end of June, Blaine's forces numbered close to two thousand men. The group they had become part of was now over six thousand souls, and they were just barely able to feed them all. Blaine was in charge of keeping the groups from the city out and was doing a great job of that. They had blocked the passes and had outposts.

They were called to a meeting with the leaders to talk about a small group in the central valley north of Bakersfield that had a large farm and was growing large quantities of foods. They were few just a small group, and they wanted Blaine to go and take over the farm and bring the people back to the valley. So Blaine sent a two-man team to find and check out the farm. They learned that it was not a small group but a very well-armed group, living near what was now known as Wizard Mountain. So it was decided to go in such a large force to make sure they did not fight. It took him about six weeks to arrange his forces and still keep the passes covered while he was gone. The next day, he started for the farm with a force of some two thousand men and support personnel. He would arrive at the farm the next morning!

The farm was at the base of the foothills just north of Porterville and less than an eight of a mile from the tree line. It was placed here to make it hard to find. It could not be seen from any road, and the trail up to it showed little usage from the valley side. Blaine and fifteen men came walking into the farm. They came around the bushes just in time to see the last few workers run up a trail at the far side of the corral. They disappeared into the trees.

Making the decision to follow them at once, he ordered a squad to stay and secure the farm and any foods they might find there. The rest of the force reached the trail, and they started up the mountain. The trail was easy to see with many footprints on it coming and going. They started up the trail, and in just one hundred feet, they were challenged from the thick trees.

"Stop and go back to your homes or face the wizards on the mountain at your great personal risk!"

The man leading the forward unit had orders to take no prisoners unless they'd surrender. He ordered the men to fire at the sound of the voice. They all shot up the trees around the speaker.

Alex and the five others with him moved to find and take up shooting positions and were waiting for them to cease fire. Once they stopped firing, the leader yelled his answer. They were ready to fire. As soon as he spoke, the family members, six in all, reported they had clean shots. Alex had the leader and linked. They all shot at the same time; six men died. Now the leader was dead and five others as well all with only one very loud shot. All of them at different places, none in a straight line. They had heard the rumors of wizards killing a lot of men with a single shot. Now they had seen it! Quickly, the second-in-command ordered the charge. They all rushed forward, firing at anything that moved. As they entered the trees, they found nothing at all. They kept moving up the trail. After a fifteen-minute hike, they found the edge of an even bigger clearing. Same as before, they saw the last three or four people move into the far tree line. They all started shooting and charged the tree line same as before.

The six mounted the horses again and raced to the next stop. There they joined Peter's group and took up positions on the line. The horses gave them a good lead on Blain and his men.

Blain was a better commander than the first group and slowed his charge and sent out scouts to clear or give warning of ambush. He was a bit bewildered that they had not caught them by surprise at the farm. They were already leaving before they arrived. It was just luck that they saw the last to enter the trail at the far side of the farm. The first clearing, six were dead with one shot. How had they pulled that off? Blain started a slow march up the trail, waiting for reports from the scouts. After a short time, they came to one of the scouts.

"Report."

"Sir, the others have not returned yet. I believe they are all dead, sir. In about fifty feet, there's another clearing. It's even bigger than the last one. If we try to cross it and it's defended from the concealment of the trees, we will lose many men!"

"How many do you think are over there?"

"From the sign I've found, it's hard to say for sure. However, I believe it cannot be more than ten to fifteen at most. What if we move around the edge, keeping out of the line of fire? It will be much slower but much safer."

Blain took some time to consider his options. Finally, he gave the order to split the force into three groups. His would stay just inside the clearing where they could be seen from the far side. The other two would move into the trees and move up the sides about halfway across in the cover of the trees, staying out of sight of the far side of the clearing. It took about forty-five minutes to get everyone in place. Blaine believed that he faced so few people he would overrun them in short order.

At the prearranged time, all three groups broke cover and charged into the clearing. As soon as all three groups were in the clear, a single and very loud shot was heard! Over twenty-five men fell dead all over the field. This time, the charge kept coming now, all firing at the tree line. Until Peter had the men return fire for the first time. They faced over thirty guns and one thirty-caliber machine gun right down the center that opened fire slightly after the others. The heavy fire coming back at them broke their charge due to the heavy fire. Blain had given orders to seek cover in the trees if the need arose. With yells and hand signals, they ran to the trees for cover. In just under ten minutes, the clearing went from raging battle to dead silent.

Blaine regrouped his men at the west side of the clearing out of sight of the center. He went over the attack and why it failed. First, there was a single shot, and this time over twenty men fell dead on the field. As ordered, the men kept the charge going and fired at the center as they ran. Then to his and everyone's surprise, over thirty guns opened up, giving return fire, followed up by a heavy machine gun opening up on the center of their lines. This started dropping men at a deadly rate, breaking the charge. As they had all ran to the same side, Blaine was able to keep control and send the remaining scout out to see what he could find on the positions of the defenders. They were taking single shots from time to time. However, whenever there was a shot, at least three men or more were killed. Magic or not, one shot was real and deadly. After twenty minutes, they started to wonder if the scout would make it back. Sitting there helped the wizards and hurt their morale. They could not be in the open after dark, and he had a timetable to keep. Just as they were ready to start moving around the east side of the clearing, the scout returned. He was a pale white.

"What's the matter with you? Are you all right?"

"They're all gone. No one was left in their gun positions. I looked over their placements. If we had not stopped, they would have killed or wounded over seventy-five percent of us before we could overrun them! Then as I was looking around, five of them just appeared all around me. Like one second, I am alone, then there are five men and women all armed all around me! Guns pointed at me. They told me the next time I go out to scout them, I will die! I was allowed to leave to give you the message. Blaine, this is your last chance. Turn around and go back to the San Fernando Valley or you will all be killed!"

Blaine looked at the scout, a friend of his and a brave man.

"Do you believe they can do what they say?"

"I was told you would ask that question first. They told me I could say whatever I wanted to. I do not know if they can kill us all. From everything I've seen today, I would say we have close to a ten to one advantage over them. They have a preplanned defense, which is causing us heavy losses. I did a check. In just three shots, they have killed thirty-six men, no wounded, in just three single shots! If you do not break through their defenses, they will win."

Blaine stood there for a full two minutes without saying a word. Finally, he asked a last question.

"Do you think they know of the second force sent to the north? And will it be enough to make a difference to carry the day?"

"I don't know, but every time I tried to hide something, they knew it! If any of the men who know of the plan are caught, the plan is compromised."

"Okay, you go back to the farm. I see you need the rest, and get some good food. Great job on not getting killed. We will talk more later."

Now knowing that the line was no longer being defended, they sent two squads to check and sweep it before moving on. Many of the advance groups reported KIA on the other side. However, the sweep found no bodies and very little blood anywhere. The only dead they found were theirs! No wounded on either side were found.

The second group should be close now. They would have heard the gunfire and corrected their path to get higher and behind the sounds they'd been hearing all day. They needed to be close so they could attack from the higher ground or at least even on the northern flank. With the surprise attack on their flank, it should break their line and give Blaine the upper hand at last! In just a few minutes of marching they came to a very wide and short clearing. Like the rest, they could not tell if there were defenses at this one or not. Blaine stopped his troops at the lower tree line, setting out his plan for the charge up this clearing. Just about this time, as his men were taking their places, a voice called out to him by name.

He moved close to the tree line. They asked him to come out in the open as they were. "Bring as many with you as you like."

Blaine asked if they would be safe.

The voice answered, "We make no promises of safety due to the fact that you and your men are the aggressors in the matter at hand."

So he took some time and then stepped out to the edge of the trees. Three bullets hit the two trees he was standing between.

"Come out and face us. If we just wanted you dead, any of those shots would have done that. To not come out will be your last act!"

Blaine fell to the ground when the bullets hit the trees. He went pale and did not move again until they told him to come out again. He then took three steps out in the edge of the clearing. He could see three men standing on the far side just outside of the tree line. One of the men spoke up again (William)and gave this message.

"This is your last chance to turn back. You have gained ground on our mountain at a much higher price than you planned on. I give you credit. However, your secret plan is also going to fail!"

At the mention of his secret plan, Blaine had a very short panicked thought of the northern force and if it would still be able to support his next charge. William felt and saw the truth on Blaine's face. His guess was right. This man was a very good solider. Opening to Jake and Peter, he sent them new orders.

"Both of you start searches for this force. Find and trail them. Report to all so we all know what they have in store for us."

They both acknowledged him. One was going to the south, and Peter was going to the north the way the SEALs came in! At the same time, he made his pitch.

"You are a large and formidable force. We are going to need men like you. Mankind needs to grow and come together to fight what's to come! Please go back to your homes. Take food from the farm. We will come to you soon!"

Blaine saw this and thought it was a bluff to save them.

"You are much weaker than us, and we will beat your defenses. If not on this attack then on the next. Surrender and we will let you live!"

"As you wish. The shame you bring to your people in the valley, you will have to pay for it if you return. We await your charge, and from this point on, the only quarter given will be to naked unarmed men." Then in a loud voice that carried all over the field, he added, "Let it be it known that Blaine should only be killed to save yourself or another family member. Just as William got ready to step down from the tree he had been standing on. He ordered for the one shot they had been setting up during this time. He was down behind the large sequoia tree when the shot rang out. Now with over sixty fighters, they all fired at once. Around the edge of the meadow, men fell dead. The five standing closest to Blaine also fell dead at his feet. Blaine sent new orders out at once to charge! At that very minute, Peter sent the news to all.

"I found them! It's a force of at least two hundred men. They are north of us and changed course as soon as the shooting started there. They are coming right through our positions here. We are hiding and hoping they pass us, and we can take up trailing positions. We managed to get into the trees, and they are running past us now."

"Okay, I am going to break this off now and start the fallback to the next position. Peter, link with Jake and get behind them. Use bows only on the rear of the column. Guns only when they are all firing. Chief, how long before you can reinforce them?"

"We just reached the farm and started up the mountain. We can send the bikes and get twenty men up there in fifteen minutes."

"Do it. Follow as fast as you can! We are sending the people in camp up to the high hide just at the tree line in back of the camp. That is our last line of defense."

Blaine ordered the charge just as the last one shot was ordered. He was shocked as five of his eight captains dropped dead at the same time. Blood and brains sprayed everywhere. Each of the one shots they fired seemed to take out his leaders. He was thinking, *If only we could do that.* In the meantime, the charge was met with even higher return fire, showing even more guns again. Blaine was at a loss on how their resistance kept getting stronger. For about two full minutes, the fire kept increasing from the tree line.

Then the new fire started to the north as Blaine's second column arrived and joined the battle. There was a large increase in their fire on the right flank from just slightly higher ground. It brought even bigger increase in fire from the tree line. Then it started to fall off, only increasing when solders showed themselves. Blaine gave the order for all sides to charge the center. This rush should finally overrun their position. They received very heavy fire but only from heavy machine guns, and they only covered the heavy or stronger position Blaine used. In short order, they overran the gun emplacements!

They found nothing. A small amount of blood here and there in some places, but no bodies and no weapons that were in working condition. Like the others, the blood was the only sign they had hit any of the defenders. He kept the troops moving to keep them from mounting another defense up ahead. The flank had failed as the man had said it would. How could he know that it was even there? As the first men moved into the trees, they found horse tracks. A lot of them. They saw no one fleeing. This time, the woods seemed empty. It was clear they were way ahead of them, waiting somewhere with another stand at a clearing. Blaine ordered the troops to keep moving slowly up the mountain and called his remaining commanders to a meeting in the center of the clearing.

"What's our count? How many have we lost?"

A man at the back answered, "I just came back from the aid station that's been right behind us. They tell me the WIA is about fourteen. The KIA is close to four hundred while MIA is near two hundred men, sir."

"How can we have MIAs?"

"We think a small number have been captured. The rest we believe just ran away."

"Okay, we broke their last stage, and they are running. We can follow them and break them again. We now know to just keep going. They are running out of mountain. Get all of the men moving up the trail now!"

* * *

Peter had been keeping the second force just in sight for about five minutes. With only bows, they started taking out the stragglers. All shots had to be clean kills, head or neck, so they could give no warning to the rest. Once they came to the north side of the clearing and this group opened fire, Peter and his team would be able to use their guns as well. Only one single fire so as to keep their presence a secret as long as possible. They had taken out fifteen men by the time they reached the battle at the clearing.

As soon as the second group opened fire on William's people in the clearing, Peter told his team to open fire on clear targets. As soon as their first volley was sent, a larger portion of men at the back realized they had people behind them. They turned and charged down the hill at them, firing as they came! It was clear at once that they had to escape. He sent orders to make it to the nearest zip line and escape, adding, "Make sure they do not see you go up or sliding down the hill!"

The plan worked just as William had hoped. It gave the defenders the small amount of time needed to pull back to the main camp where their defenses were the strongest of all.

When Peter arrived at the zip line stop, the rear guard was just coming into view, walking up the mountain with the force from Lone Pine. Peter thought if they had been at the battle, the last fall-back might not have been needed! Jake and his team were securing the zip lines and were waiting for the rest of the family members who would be joining them after Blaine and his men moved past the clearing. O'Brian had his team on overwatch with orders to kill anyone that might have seen anyone on the zip lines or found them. As soon as the main camp was ready to receive Blaine and the rest of the valley people, they zipped down to Jake, and they started to form the net set for the finale battle. Peter took half of the Lone Pine force and went back to cover the north side while Jake took the south, leaving Ben and the remaining part of the townspeople with Jeff and his team to hold the middle if they broke and tried to run. By Jake's count, they had killed over 275 men. They had taken another 125 prisoners as they tried to flee the wizard's magic. The family skills had grown so fast since the SEALs had taken over the training. The family was, in all intents and purposes, an army of SEALs, counting Lone Pine and the rest of the family close to three hundred strong and more about to be tested. The family now had close to 2,500 fighting members. From the young ones to the ladies, they were all fighting as one, linked and aware of everything happening on the field. They got instant updates. It has been this talent that had kept their losses down. Their total KIA and WIA was just over 120 souls. O'Brian was directing the battle and keeping everyone moving in the same direction. As he was awake, Lucy was helping him with his control in the link to the rest of the family. From the two thousand plus Blaine had started with, he still had one thousand or more still at his command. O'Brian gave the rear guard the task of keeping them from retreating down the mountain or to come up and break the attack if it was going badly at the camp. All the parts of the rear guard were clear now and in place.

The main camp had close to 450 fighters, more than Blaine had faced in any of the other sites. The line closed behind Blaine and his troops. He had sent men back down the hill many times now, and none of them returned. He had been worrying as none had returned.

The speed of the battles had kept him from seeing the obvious. He set his force all around the camp. The camp was very small from what they could see of it reinforcing the idea that it was a small force they faced. William and Ben had planned and built in the back clearing and the trees so the casual eye could miss it altogether.

Blaine stepped up and stood just out of the tree line and called out, "You in the trees. You do not need to die today. Give up. You have no place to run. We have you outnumbered and overmatched. You have five minutes to give your answer!

"Did everyone hear that they will attack in just over five minutes from now?"

He heard thousands say yes at almost the same time and laughed.

"I know I told him we would kill them all, but as I am sure you all know that's not the plan. Only kill to save yourself or another family member please. Good luck and stay safe if you can!"

The woods had all gone deathly silent. No bird or animal sounds could be heard from the camp. It had been a long day with only about forty minutes of full sunshine on this side of the mountain. So as soon as the five minutes passed, Blaine ordered his last charge. His men began firing at the tree line at whatever they believed to be a target. Then the first half of the men jumped up and ran up the middle of the clearing, firing as they ran. Then the rest reloaded and followed them up the middle. Now with Blaine in the middle, they had over seven hundred men charging the tree line. The rest of his force had taken up defensive positions in case they needed cover fire for any reason. They had learned that the safety of the trees was not true as most of his loses happened in the tree line full of pits and booby traps. So this charge was straight up the middle.

William and O'Brian had counted on this change from Blaine after the other battles. William had O'Brian take charge of this field. John had Len do this field. Len set the first line of charges right in the center of the clearing about halfway across. It had ten charges in it, made to kill and wound as many soldiers as possible. The next two lines started about the seventh charge in the first line. Each with ten charges, but these ran on an angle heading to the tree lines on each side of the center to get as many of the men as they could.

Blaine lined his forces up to run right into it.

The fire from the sides showed no slowing down. They had no waiting for reloads as a lot of the under thirteens stayed to keep loading the clips and reloading the guns. This increased the fire rate by some 25 percent! Blaine was right. This would have been the end of the family if not for the skills of the SEAL team.

Blaine's charge was chewing up the center of the clearing. They were just short of the middle when he got his first report of an attacking force from behind them. His last effort to get the rear guard to come up gave him the report.

"Sir, they have at least two hundred men closing on our back trail!"

As he listened, he heard the first explosion on the field. Then they started to come one right after the other!

"Okay, you go back. Get the reserve force and make a stand against the forces coming at our backs. You just have to slow them down. As soon as we take the camp, this will be over! *Go now*!"

Now turning his attention back to the charge, he ordered the force to split and head to the sides and keep moving forward! At that moment, three large caliber machine guns opened up, cutting his men down in large numbers. Then the two mortars O'Brian had set up, one facing each side of the field, started lobbing rounds at the sides of the field. There was one large building to the left center of the field. A large number of men took cover there. The others had broken and ran to the side and back the way they had come to avoid the shelling and machine guns! The charge had *failed*! His men had taken cover wherever they could! By now, Blaine knew that an even bigger force was moving up behind him. Blaine worked to get his troops safely in the tree line and regroup. Why had they changed their placement of the trap lines? As he was getting his men set to move up the side of the clearing, Blaine never knew how many men were in the back. He had a hard time believing it was the two hundred.

The sound of the firefight was getting louder and more intense. Taking a moment to move back and look, Blaine saw the reserve force being pushed out into the open to get away from the larger force. Now in the open, the fire was coming from all four sides, and his men were falling all around him now! Then a voice was heard as clear as if they were standing in a quiet room. William spoke to them all.

"All of you fighting or hiding, drop your guns and strip naked. Then sit on your uniforms. Hands on your heads."

Many of the men obeyed the order at once. Others turned to shoot the men stripping. They were shot at once! All over the fields, they heard William again.

"If anyone turns a gun on a sitting man, they will be shot at once!"

In just a few minutes, it was clear to all the battle was lost, and Blaine was at a loss as to how it happened. It was the end of the day, and his men had reached the camp of the wizards, and they should have won. Everything worked as he had planned, and still he lost it all in the last battle. He was brought before William again and told the terms for letting them live. While talking, other family members passed them, offering parole to any who wished it. In total, 278 members of the family were killed or wounded. At the same time, there were only some three hundred troops left unharmed. Some 185 took parole, and many of the others wished to but still had family in the valley.

"Blaine, as you can see, we are taking care of your men. They will be treated for any wounds and given the choice to stay with us or going back with you to the valley you came from. You will not be given the choice. You must go back and give your leaders my message."

"And what's your message?"

"Now do not be angry with us. Remember, it was you who came looking for a fight, not us. You know now you never had a chance from the very start. You played right into our plan!"

"What plan? Running away from us at every chance? Your horses gave you a small speed advantage. We should have won easily. I still can't understand how you did it."

"Later you will figure it out. And when you do, we will need you and your people to join us in the real fright that is coming. This is our message. Never come back with armed troops or they will be wiped out! You can send four men to us when your need is great, and we will help!"

"Why would you do that?"

"Like I said, we need you. And once you figure out how we beat you, then you will need us more than we need you. We are aware of your problems in the city and are willing to help if you make the right choices."

"I have questions. Will you answer them?"

"Ask your questions, but I make no promise to answer them."

"Okay, first, are you really wizards here on the mountain?"

O'Brian answered before William could. "No, we are not. We are the best trained army left on the West Coast. Thanks to the admiral here."

"You're an admiral?"

O'Brian sent, *Let me respond, sir*, at the same time telling Blaine, "Yes, a Coast Guard four star. We are the last operating part of the US government. We will be giving support and relief where needed where the people take the oath."

"Why would you do this?"

William spoke at last. "The event that struck us last March was an attack, and the people who did it are coming to take our planet. If we want to survive, we must be ready for them. That is why I will always give people the chance to join with us. You, Blaine, do not qualify at this time. You may in time, but not now. Go back. Tell them we will be coming, and we come to help, not harm or make slaves of anyone. We live by the constitution and the bill of rights here on the mountain. Tonight you and the others who did not take the oath will spend the night in the large horse corral with two guards."

In the morning, they all marched back to the farm, each one given their guns back and three days' food and water and sent on their way.

CHAPTER 31

Expansion

In the three weeks since the battle with Blaine and the San Fernando Valley people, the stories had spread far and wide of the defeat of the large force that attacked Wizard Mountain. They had heard the stories had even reached Lone Pine and the farms on the edge of the valley. People would come and ask for help and food. The numbers were growing very quickly. Aaron's new farms would soon be overtaxed again. He needed to open new farms, and Bull was asking to start new line shack. They needed to have stables and zip lines to the locations. All needed to meet the needs of the family as it was growing at an alarming rate as far as the food supply was concerned.

All the stories had counter stories coming out of the city. And from farther south, there was news of the islanders now moving north. They would soon be in Mexico and then into the West Coast, and they only had the winter to get ready for the new bigger threat coming.

In the weekly council meeting, they had a number of new projects to consider and get started during the winter months ahead. Some of the first things they needed to do was expand and get the new items they needed to feed and protect the growing numbers of people finding them and taking the oath and parole. They started arriving just weeks after the battle. William, Oliver, and O'Brian had been talking about the threat of the islanders and what it was going to take to even have a chance of surviving their coming north. It was a sure thing that they have heard of the wizard and of the admiral as well. The two items that kept coming up was ships and aircraft. O'Brien had information gained from the group they had taken out on their voyage up the West Coast. It was clear that they had massive sea power and some small air wing, mostly helicopters, one aircraft carrier used as a troop transport, and a variety of other ships from the naval base in their position. So after a longer than normal meeting, the family agreed on three new projects to undertake. Maria was placed in charge of the home front, getting the new farms up and running and organizing the new zip lines and stables that would be needed. She had set meeting for Ben, Bull, and Aaron to coordinate their efforts to make the work as quick and efficient as they could. Unlike at the start, they now had many more hands to do the needed work. Aaron and Bull took a small party to find tracks of land that they could farm and at the same time secure from raiders. They left the next morning, a party of eight with two pack mules.

They had two goals in these teams—air and sea power. They needed to find and bring back the assets needed to give them a chance against the forces moving toward them. They planned for the SEALs to undertake these missions. It was decided that Jeff was to keep the training programs going with Angel and Victor. The new people were out of shape and underfed. And they needed to get ready as the time they had was unknown. They left O'Brian, Juan, and Len to take the other jobs. Peter was also going as one of the strongest minds in the family. He and Juan had become friends and would go to Naval Air Station Lemoore to see what they could find. They were given sixty men to take and four trucks with enough gas for the round trip. Also the airmen from Las Vegas as well as the pilots were part of this group. Peter also asked for two of the bikes for fast scouts.

O'Brian was given his pick of any of the family with naval service or skills. He picked nine men, and Wayne asked to go as well. They would be going back to get the *Dream Wind* and sail north to find a navy for the family. Len was also going with just three men.

They were going to Avila Beach to make an alliance and ask if they wanted to become part of the family and take the oath and parole. The family members chosen were from the group that was willing to relocate to the coast. Make no mistake, if they were attacked with little warning, they would be all alone until any help could reach them. It would be this team's job to get them ready for what's coming.

The second team was led by Trent, and Steven was going as the second-in-command. Juan had served on carriers before becoming a SEAL. All three pilots and the airmen who came with Oliver were on the team, and any others with any experience in flight operations. They loaded the four-by-six with all the supplies they could spare. Trent's team was to go to Naval Air Station Lemoore and see if they could make use of any of the assets they would find there. They had a hundred-man security force to secure the area. By the end of the day, both teams were ready to travel and would leave as one, only splitting when Juan turned north to the air base.

The next morning at sunrise, they started down the mountain from Lodgepole heading west. Their plan was to be well away from the mountain before they were seen by anyone that might be around the areas they would be passing through. The distances they had to travel were not far; however, the conditions were unknown.

The other project William was starting was the ham radios they had taken that first night. They had four people in the family that had some small knowledge of them but not the skills needed to get them up and running. That all changed when the SEALs came. Victor was the radioman and had a vast wealth of knowledge of them.

In the first days, while wandering around the camp looking for weakness in their defenses and checking on assets, Vic had found the radios in the back of the armory.

"William, what are your plans for the radios you have stored here?"

"We planned to set them up and try to find out how many others are out there like us trying to get by."

"So why don't you do it?"

"None of us have the skills needed to get the job done. Do you have a reason for asking?"

"Yes, I would like to set one up and try to reach my family if I could."

"You can do that?"

"Oh, yes, I am the radioman on the team. This stuff is easy."

"Great. Hold on a second." William opened to the others with the interest in the radios, linking them with him. "Vic, I have all the people that are now your radio team linked, so tell me what you need to get this up and running."

Due to the fact that he was not awake, it took him over seven minutes to list what they needed, and the team all took part of the list, and they all would meet after lunch to put their plan together. So operational talk started. Now they were getting ready to search for good locations for the antennas to be placed. It had taken weeks to find all the needed parts and to rig solar power for the radios themselves. Vic and two other scouts took supplies and hiked into the mountains for radio sites. It had been decided to make three different sites, all at least ten miles apart and all on different peaks from the main camp and not on any path leading straight to one of the farms on the valley floor. They returned from their search a few days after the first antenna was built and the solar power checked and found to be in working order.

In conference with the family, it was decided to put the first setup at the overlook site at the peak between Lone Pine and the main camp. It already had a shelter built for the lookouts. It could be expanded easily. Because the signal could be traced, they would never use the same one twice. They would use a different site on broadcast days once they had the other sites up and working. They were working on getting the other two sites built on the two other peaks selected. The first site took Vic only two days to have up and working. Until the other sites were ready, it was only used as a listening station. It was used on two six-hour shifts. From the first day, it was on from 9:00 a.m. until 3:00 p.m., and then again from 9:00 p.m. to 3:00 a.m. If any traffic was heard, it was to be logged and sent to Maria at once. On the fifth day, they heard their first call from a small mountain town in the northern mid-west. They listened to the call for fifteen minutes, which received no response. It came back on random days and times. With Maria being linked to William at all times, he knew as well. They started a search for the sender. The highest awake member on Vic's team started a dream search for the sender.

It was about eleven days later when there was a second radio transmitting, and they followed the same plan with it. The next week saw the second radio up and working at last. William asked Maria to test the two working sets. She was asking William if Vic should be told to run the test.

"Are you talking about me?"

"Vic, are you awake at last?"

"Yes, Maria, I am. I think it was yesterday. I heard you talk to Wendell about the two different radios we found."

"Great, yes. Vic, run a test as secure as possible please. And let us know the range and quality we have please."

"Okay, you will have your answer later today."

Vic set up three different test times for the three radios, sending out four teams with recorders to check distance and strength of the different sets. It took the four teams a total of four and a haft hours to reach their different destinations. As soon as the last team reported ready, Vic ran the test broadcast on each set. All the radios worked well, and all had sold signals.

Vic reported that they should cover at least all the pacific and east as far as the Mississippi River. They set up a schedule for transmitting and regular listing. They also set up around-the-clock listing. One set would be on at all times with an operator listing any messages. The other thing they started was finding the location of the two radios transmitting as well. Using radio triangulation, they confirmed the first radio was in Wisconsin. The second was much closer. Now that he was awake, Vic was put in charge of finding all the places they received signals from. This would keep him busy for the next four months. After one week of listing, they started sending out their own messages, a different one from each set so as to look like three different groups. Each radio had a different message that was sent four times a day on their set transmitting days. If they received a response, they were to respond to them. They kept the response time to ninety minutes before shutting down transmission from that station.

Like all their other outposts and farms, they set up zip lines in the trees for quick escape as needed and had horses as well. Regular rotation shifts were set up, and the family now had a second source of information on the rest of the western part of North America.

The expansion project was up and running with the three teams already making their way to their objectives. They all left on the same morning from different points of the main camp and farms. O'Brian and Len shared the road back to Avila Beach, and the others moved into the mountains. And last, Juan and Peter were taking a scout team to Los Angeles and the San Fernando Valley to keep an eye on the larger amount of people that had stayed in the city and valley.

The three SEALs went back down the road to Visalia, where they split up. Juan and Peter turned south to the city while O'Brian and Len retraced their tracks back to the coast.

Juan's team turned and disappeared in the morning sunlight as the others kept straight back to the coast. They made much better time and arrived just outside of the five city's area just before noon. They started to drive slowly into the cities, calling on the PA system and announcing they were back and wanted to meet any and everyone willing to listen to their offer of help at the fishing pier in three hours. They made the pier in about one hour. Time. There was already a group of over one hundred people there waiting. Len went to talk with the people waiting for them.

"Who's in charge here?"

A tall man spoke up from the front of the group. "My name is Dallas, and I am now in control of seventy percent of the cities."

"Hello, Dallas, glad to meet you. Can you tell me what the situation is with the rest of the people still living here?"

"The others do not want to work and just raid our food and other supplies. We tried to get them to come in and work and share all we have, but they seem determined to fight and take what they want."

"Okay, I understand. I have only one more question for you all. Are any of you awake?"

There were a lot of strange looks and a few answers of "what do you mean?" and "of course we are awake. You are talking to us."

"Okay, I just need to ask. We are back, and if you all agree to what we have to offer, we are here to stay. There are dangers coming. You may have heard of some of them. The LA gangs and the islanders from the pacific are all coming this way. At this time, we do not know how much time we have to get ready for them. If you can get the leaders from the others to come, that would be great. Have them all here at noon tomorrow. Tell everyone we will be holding a feast to celebrate our return. Anyone who wishes can stay for dinner tonight as well."

Only about ten people stayed for the food, but they mostly asked questions. They told most of the truth to them, others were put off until the meeting at noon the next day.

While this was going on, John and his team had found a large schooner and were making it ready for the open sea all evening. They had it ready to sail at about 9:00 p.m. and loaded it and were ready to sail on the morning tide. Wayne would sail it to the *Dream Wind* where they would split the overloaded supplies, and then both boats would sail away to find the family a navy to face the islanders with. They all had a good meal that night as planned to show the people living in the area what the family had to offer! It was the best meal they had that year! One of them asked if they ate like this all the time.

John answered, "Truthfully, no, it is a show for you. Most nights we only have three courses—meat or fish, vegetables, and a soup. We have a great variety of fresh fruits as well. And on special days, we have a much larger feast."

The people asked a lot of questions after that answer. William told him at all times, "Tell them the truth if it's safe to do so. In any event, never lie to any of them. If it's the enemy, you can say anything you like." The truth now added to the help they received when the SEALs arrived. They had very good feelings for them. The last question brought the evening to an end. "So what did you find in the valley?"

"We found a group of men who tried to overrun the wizards on the mountain. They had lost badly. They could not tell us how to find them due to the wizard's blocking them from talking about them in any way other than they lost the battle with the larger force on their side. So we followed their trail and found an unmanned guard post and started up the mountain. They let us come and only stopped us at the edge of their camp. We had no idea that they had us covered on all sides almost at once, and we never had a chance for anything other than a peaceful meeting. Add to that, they knew we were coming weeks ago. Now before you ask, no, it's not magic, but to the average person it sure looks like it." With that, most got up and left with a lot to think about. There was a group living in the mountains with powers that looked like magic. Len set a guard, and the rest went to sleep till early morning.

* * *

John had his team up and ate an early fast meal. They went and got the zodiac. It was right where they had left it. They loaded it on the second boat and started to the *Dream Wind*. They put the raft back together and had it working in just two hours. The second boat the trip only took a little under three hours.

During this time, John linked with William, and they talked about the small groups he had sent to the farm. The total was around fifty in all. Most were looking for food and shelter after a cold winter of living without heat or clean water and food. Last, he showed William the three groups he had turned away. When asked, he said it was a cold turning in his gut. These people were looking and watching for something. They felt like a bad dream, and a dark cloud seemed to hang over them. "If we had not been a large party, I am sure we would have been attacked by them. We sent them north away from you and the coastal cities. We are about to shove off here with the two schooners in search of our new navy."

* * *

Len had a larger crowd than excepted for breakfast. And well before noon, thousands of people were coming to town. All of them were armed. Jake and Lucy took the feel of them all and decided they had no plans on violence, but they all stayed on alert all the way past the end of the meeting. There were no locals that showed signs of being or becoming awake at all. Still the family members all asked the question to all they met. As in the beginning, they received strange stares from the locals.

"It's okay. We believe you will soon learn why we ask. At any time you think you know, find one of us and we will show you what it means."

At noon, Len called them to order and addressed them all as one group, not many different ones, even as they all stood apart from the other by at least two feet. Then Len addressed them all.

"My name is Len. I want to thank you all for coming today and in peace. We all face a grave danger. There are forces all around us, and they are moving this way! A large part of this is because of us! Many of you know us as the Navy SEAL team that landed here some five months ago. I am a member of that team. I am also now what you have been calling a wizard from the mountain. All of us are. We came here to help you better your lives. Even more important, we come seeking your help.

"To the north is an army, and it is well trained and has many weapons it can bring here. They will try to take over or just kill everyone and then move in. It has done so in a number of towns in the north. As bad as they may seem, to the south is an even larger group coming out of the Pacific Islands. They have been raiding and taking over all of South America. They have a small naval force, and at our last information, they have an army of well over fifty thousand fighting men. And they are moving north now. Soon they will be at the southern border of Mexico. We believe we have eight to twelve months before they arrive at the boarder of San Diego and come north to us.

"We offer better food supply and weapons and training on how to use them. We will teach you the skills you need to survive in this new world. If anyone has doubts about this, you should stay after the meeting as we will hold a briefing on what we know, and then you can make up your minds. Now our head of security will explain your options and what they mean. Lucy, step up please!"

Lucy then told them a short history of the family and how it held together for so long. She had planned on their being about a thousand or so people to be here. The group had taken sections and counted as best they could. Had they been awake, the number would be known almost at once. They had a rough count of 4,500 souls at the meeting.

"I had not thought to find so many people living here. I am afraid I did not bring enough copies of the oath, so we made a large copy on the wall at the boathouse. We need you, and you are going to need us if you wish to live free. After the meeting, any of the people living here can take the oath and become members of the family. If you choose this path, you will have all the rights of a family member, with full rights as any other person in council meetings." A few people shouted questions at this point. Lucy waited until they fell quiet. "I or any other family member here will answer all questions, even if it takes all night, but we will not answer any questions until I am finished.

"Those of you who decide to take the oath will be on probation. Each person's time on probation is based on their actions as a member of the family. You all have questions on this. They will only be answered if you take the oath. For the ones who want to take the oath, we will give copies out that we have with us. If you don't get one, go to the boathouse and read the wall. All the people living here form a community, and we want to make a formal alliance for mutual defense of our homes. We have enough food to feed all of you for two years on the mountain. Even if you only decide to be allies, we will make sure you have food. Understand we will always take care of family first than our allies.

"Next, we will train you all on how to defend your homes and families. When you need us, we will be here, and will expect you to answer our call if we need you at the mountain. It is not bragging when we say we are the best fighting force on this continent, and we keep getting bigger and better. Our problem is, we are still smaller than the forces we have faced. That has not been a problem till now!

The two forces we are facing are well trained and much larger than us. At this minute, we can put over five thousand fighting members of the family on the field. If it is all or nothing, every member of the family can take the field. Everyone over the age of thirteen is trained in guns and bows and hand-to-hand fighting. All of you who will take the oath will start training in two days from taking the oath. You will all be some of the best fighters in the world, all SEAL-trained. Our allies will also be trained to fight alongside us.

"Now what you've all been expecting, the catch! Well, the catch is this. If you as a majority decide to not accept either offer, we will leave and move our naval base to another part of the coast. If more than half want us to stay and give them the things I talk about, we will stay. Any of the people here who refuse to join the family or the local collective will have to leave and never return. Any who try to return will be shot on sight. We only shoot to kill and have done so far too many times already. We want and need all of you to help us in the coming war! Now if you know what you want to do, this is how you do it. Take the oath, move to the boathouse, and you will be given a copy of the oath or allowed to read the wall. If you are in favor of making your own group, move to the piers, and there you can start building your own community, and we will make an alliance with the family. For the ones who have questions, stay here. Myself, Len, and my husband, Jake, will answer all of your questions. Please listen as someone is sure to ask the same question you want to ask. Just one more thing you all need to know!"

The talk started getting louder as they thought it was over, so to be heard, Lucy used her ability to amplify her voice over all the noise!

"*Quiet now! Everyone, listen to me!*"

They fell silent at once. Everyone was aware of the power of a wizard at the same time. She continued, "You all need to know that we cannot be lied to if you try. We will wonder why. Please, we only tell the truth and so cannot be lied to. Now it's your turn. We will start with the questions right after a short break for us all to get a drink or take care of other needs."

After a fifteen-minute break, the three different meetings started. The largest group was in the questions group. However, after about thirty minutes, it started getting smaller, with most of it going to the boathouse. A very few left outright, and the rest formed a new city and wanted to form the alliance with the family. The question that started the biggest movement was when an ex-army ranger asked who was in charge of the army they were building. Jake asked for quiet as he repeated the question and gave the answer.

"Our military leader is known as the admiral!"

At once, the ranger and over half of the remaining people got up and moved to one of the other groups. It was a two to one division, most moving to the boathouse. The meeting started after lunch at about 1:30 p.m., and the last of them left a bit after 2:00 a.m. to go to their beds. In a quick silent meeting, they all agreed to start the oaths after lunch as it was going to be over 2,800 people. And everyone who was to take the oath was told they all had to stay until the oaths were all given. At the end of that day, the family grew a third of its size The family linked for the day, and at the end, the new parolees were greeted by family members who were awake. They now knew why they were called wizards. They all had mental powers of unknown strength and abilities. After a long day, all were given the next day off. During this time, the team members set up classes and times three a day morning mid-day and evening classes. They also formed work details for clearing land or replanting it with crops for food. Others were set to make fortifications to keep the unwanted out. And one team was set to scour the local cities for cars and trucks and anything that could still be of use to them. Here they also had a team on the water looking for working boats that they could make use of. By the end of the week, work was well underway. At this point, some of the locals that had not taken the oath started to worry about the food as they could see it was running low. They came to Lucy and asked what they had planned to get food as they had far more people here than just a week ago.

She told them to send a representative to the east guard station to guide the supply truck for them to the desired unloading location and to have a team there ready to unload it. It should be there by noon today. With the first trucks, the whole coastal valley started to change. That night in the meeting, they reported that this new outpost would be ready with over two thousand fighting members to go where needed and still leave at least one thousand to guard the city.

The third team turned for the road south to the second largest city in the United States, Los Angeles. Juan and Peter had two scouts with them. They had six of the motorcycles for the trip, used for the ability of off-road travel if needed. They reached the top of the mountain and had lunch at the Gorman exit. They were not sure what they would find there. As it turned out, there was a guard post set up just before the top. It was manned by four armed men, and they seemed to be keeping a close watch on the road up the hill. Juan stopped well before they were in gun range. He and one other took their bows and walked off into the woods to flank their positions on the guards if they could. Even in the best shape of his life, it took Juan and one other just under two hours to get in place to cover the team as they drove up to the gates at the guard station.

"Stop at the red line. Do not pass it! What is your business?"

Peter gave answer agreed on. "We are soldiers looking for work. We heard we may find work in the valley below. Is that not true?"

"It is, but first you must surrender your guns and be taken to the counsel. They will decide if you're fit to join or not. How many men do you have?"

"I am sorry. That will not work for us. We will go back and find another way into the valley."

At that, six more men came out of the woods and with guns up now at the ready.

"Sorry, we are not to let you leave once you have found our gate!"

"How do you plan to stop us? Will you fire? We carry our weapons at rest by our sides."

"We will fire if needed. Please come forward now."

Juan told Peter to move forward but not to pass the F-150 Ford at that point. They would have angles on all the guards.

"Okay, you make a good point."

They all got off the bikes and started walking to the truck as told by Juan. He also passed on targets for each man if needed!

"Here we come."

With their targets, they all walked, spreading out so as to have the best line of fire if needed.

"That's good. Come ahead and please do not reach for your guns. Please stay together. Do not move so far apart."

"Sorry, we will not make it easy to shoot us all. If you mean no harm, you will not shoot us."

At his last word, they all stopped and were at their firing places.

"Do not stop there. Keep moving to the gate!"

"I am sorry. We cannot do that, and we cannot go to your leaders at this time."

"If you refuse, we have orders to shoot any that come to our gate."

"We have no plan to hurt or harm anyone in this place, but we are free men and will not be taken. Will you kill us if we try to leave? At the first sign of hostile action from any of your men, they will die!"

"How will you do that? We hold our guns. You do not. We have you outnumbered two to one."

"I wish not to kill any of you, but at the first shot, you and the man next to you will die. When you came to our mountain, we invite you in and gave you the chance to leave after each battle you lost. We are from Wizard Mountain! You are surrounded already. all of you who wish to live, holster your weapons."

"It's a bluff. It's just you four!"

In the link, Juan was asked to put one arrow in the wood post of the fence just to the speaker's right.

"Just move to your left a half step please."

Just as he was about to ask why, a single arrow made a loud thunk as the head bit deeply into the wood fence post!

"As you can see, we have you covered on all sides. Tell your men to lower their guns and move to the open area just behind your place by the fence please!"

"You are the wizards from the mountain. Men, lower your guns and move to the parking lot behind me at once."

As soon as they all dropped their weapons, Juan and Peter all came into the gate area. The leader, seeing how many men they had, just started laughing.

"Blaine told the truth. You are sneaky and smart."

Wasting no time, they got the bikes and all their supplies and made ready to get over the mountain. Juan linked with Peter and soon learned how to lock the information in their minds if they were asked about them. They could not take the memories from them. They could lock the information in their minds. They could remember it, but if they tried to pass the information in any way, it came out as gibberish in whatever form they tried. Juan was able to do it after only seeing it done twice. They soon had the entire group blocked and moved on down the valley to set up camps in the valley and in LA so they could find out what shape the people were in.

CHAPTER 32

We Can Fly Now

After the first reports from the beach teams, the family decided to go to Lemoore Naval Air Station. Jeff put a team together, putting Trent in charge of the R&R team with Sherman and the airmen from Nellis, and anyone with flying skills from ground teams to pilots was added to the team. With the news of the warlord in the north, the R&R team was made up of two platoons, fifty men each. Steven was his second-in command. After the training from the SEALs, they all had even better reaction times, and the one shot was even bigger as almost all the adults were awake now. So once linked, they had instant communications. It made it seem like one shot would seem to kill up to fifty people at the same time. As before, the family never tried to wound with the one shot. It was meant to scare or kill all the leaders they could at the first shot. Blain in the San Fernando Valley was the only one William had spared from this for reasons of his own. Trent and Steven talked about this. They would fire first and with maximum one-shot numbers to demoralize the enemy and hope for a truce from there. Trent took his half of the company strength R&R team to the front, and Steve had the rear of the formation. In all, they had over three hundred people in their group to keep track of. This meant that anyone scouting them would see two hundred and fifty people that would need to be protected by the troops.

Sherman was in charge of the airmen and all the support personnel. Their job would be to find all the working aircraft and other equipment they could use. He had them made up into four teams. First was the crew to set up a base camp for food and shelter, and others were for needs of the full team. Next was special supplies needed such as tools and fuel and support equipment. The third was to find all aircraft and try to find out how many were still able to fly. The last group was to decide which aircraft they could bring up to active flight status as soon as they could. The priority was on combat aircraft fix wing or rotter. It did not matter.

Their trip was in fact the shortest drive. It went north into a part of the valley they had not been to. They would need to take care to be ready for whatever they ran into as they were too big not to be seen. Everyone had weapons but kept them out of sight. They were not part of the R&R team. Everyone on the mission was fully trained to the SEALs standards, and all were deadly in any form of combat even, hand-to-hand.

They stayed on main roads to hide their final destination as long as they could. Trent had brought four of the motorbikes for his advanced scouts to find the fastest way to the base. After only two route changes, they were only ten miles from the gates. They had passed a few people along the way. These always ran and hid when they saw the size of the motorcade driving up the freeway. Now as they were getting closer to the base, the people all seemed to slip away into the orchards or houses, not to be seen at all. The people were so freaked out. It was the only way to describe their thoughts. They could feel over 1,500 people hiding from them. They were on all sides but so scared that they posed no threat at this time. Trent put three scouts out to keep eyes on them.

They covered the ninety or so miles in just under four hours, and as of the last turn around the orchard of what looked like olives, they were driving alongside the outer runways.

"Sherman, I served here about ten years ago before becoming a master sergeant. This is the emergency runway and should be our first one to clear as they usually keep it clear for anything. They may need to land in a hurry."

"This is Trent. For some of you, we are completely surrounded, and we all need to keep focus on safety first please."

After passing through the open gates and moving into the base roads, they had seen no one at all. After they passed the first buildings, they started to see people slowly coming out. This really did look like a scene out of an old zombie movie. They all looked half dead from lack of food. Yet they had been driving past fields after fields that had growing crops of all kinds, all left untouched and just waiting to be picked and then eaten. In one of the biggest growing valleys in the world, people were starving to death with food growing all around them. The team members all kept their guns up and ready. Even though none of them had any weapons on them at the mount, some had knives. One man came up to Trent, standing in the back of the yellow pickup truck with the twin thirties mounted on the top roll bar.

"That's close enough, friend. What can we do for you?"

"We are just a few left here, and as you can see, we need food badly. Can you spare us anything?"

"No, we can't, but less than one mile back the way we came, there are two orange groves running over with ripe fruit and a bit closer is a grove of some kind of nut trees that seemed to need picking as well. And just here across the road is a field full of some greens growing. Just walk over and take what you need."

"It's death to take food from the warlord. He has spies that see everything everywhere. By now, he knows you're here and coming to you!"

"I see. How much time do you think we have before he shows up?"

"He will not come for a group as small as yours. He will send the dog soldiers to kill you all, as well as anyone who takes his food from the fields!"

"Ah, he's going to try to kill us, is he? Well, again, how long will it take for these dog soldiers to get here?'

"Not less than one full day. Sometimes it's two days. If you leave now, you may get away!"

"So we have one to two days to get ready for his troops to get here. It may surprise you, but we came here hoping to find him."

"You're going to wait for them?"

"Yes, that's one of the reasons for our visit. We need to talk to him and his people."

"My name is Alberto. May I have your name?"

"Trent is my name. Nice to meet you, Alberto."

"I speak for the few of us left. We stayed too long and are now too weak to leave."

Trent reached out to William while Alberto was talking. It was decided that if they wished, they could come to the farm. Maria had already sent a bus to bring back any who wished to come. The bus should be at the base before sundown.

"Well, sir, it seems this is your lucky day. How many of you wish to leave and find shelter and food?"

"There are no places like that anymore!"

"There are, and more than just one, but for now you will be welcome at the northeast farm. It is still growing and needs more workers for the fields. It is part of a place you may have heard of it. Can you think of no place like that?"

"Yes, one, but it is not real. The Wizard Mountain with magic bullets and a ghost army that never loses a battle no matter how large the invading force is!"

"*Wow*, I never heard that story. When did you hear it?"

"The warlord's men told us. Said they were here to keep us safe. They took all our weapons and food, leaving us to die here. They have one or two men working for them. They always seem to eat better than the rest of us."

"Okay, well, I want you and all of you hiding nearby or just out of sight to listen as well! My name is Trent. My team and I have come here from what you call Wizard Mountain! We come in peace and have homes and work for all of you if you wish it. Right now, you are unfit for work, so we will feed you and let you regain your health.

Then when you're fit and have regained your health, you are free to leave or take the oath and become part of the family."

Slim came to the front where Trent gave him the orders. "Take them back to the camp. Get them food and water for the trip to the farm. The bus is already on the way. Should be here by sundown."

"You're not leaving with us?"

"No, I have a job to do here, and it's time I got started. Just one more thing. Before I go, a warning. Do not lie to any of us. We will know it at once! To prove it to you, I want Alberto to tell me three things about yourself and make one of them a lie." Alberto did so and Trent exposed the lie, and then he got ready to go.

"Senor Trent, may I stay with you here? I may be of some help."

"Are you one the men working for the warlord?"

"Dios, Senor Trent, no."

"Okay. You're my aid. Let's go."

Slim took some thirty people down to the main camp and took the next three hours getting them ready for the bus ride to the farm.

Trent put three more guards out, and then they started looking for the choppers William wanted. This had been an Apache base. It had three full wings of Apache attack choppers stationed there.

The three airmen, having a better idea of what to look for, found the hangar with the Apache in it. It had everything they needed to check and start the birds if they could. They opened and told Trent and William what they had found and started to check them over. The armory was located and opened, and they started unloading them with supplies that would be taken back to the mountain landing pads that were being built and hangars to keep them out of most of the harsh winter weather they had on the mountain. They had a great need of the armory as they used a great deal of the ammo in the last few months. The battle with Blaine had been much closer than they liked to think about. They gained six more fifties with close to three million rounds each, as well as cases of mortar rounds with three more tubes to fire them from. The armory was untouched before they got there. This was a great deal of luck for the family. By the end of the day, they had both of the trucks loaded. The equipment team found two tanker trucks, and they only needed minor work to have them running. They filled them one with gas, the other with diesel fuels. They also had two Hueys and four Apaches up and running.

Sherman had taken control of the air wings. His first priority was to get a fully armed Apache in the air on guard for the base. With the airmen who came in with Oliver and the rest of the pilots in the family, they made great strides forward. In an adjacent hangar, they found four fully armed Apaches which were ready to fly in just hours. When Trent asked for the status of the operational birds, Sherman told him they had the two Hueys and six Apaches and would have at least three jet fighters and two stealth boomers as well. That night, at family meeting, there were questions that needed answers.

"I would like to speak to the family, if you can open it to all for me, William. I am still not up to that level quite yet."

"I see your mind, Sherman. They are all listening. Speak your mind, my friend."

"I am not part of the first family. And as everyone in the family knows, that makes no difference in this council. Many have been asking what I am hiding and not sharing. Well, I did not want to say anything before I was sure what I meant and what I would need. Tonight I am ready to share my idea for a vote of the family. After only three days, we should have eight Apaches and four Hueys and a full wing of fighter jets and still only two bombers. All are ready to go. We also have four air tankers and four tanks of jet fuel and two more of diesel fuel and four of gasoline, all of them between half to three quarters full. For these and many other reasons, I have been planning on staying at the base. If we can hold it against the warlord, it will be a great asset in the coming wars. We know they are coming, and we know we need to be stronger than those we will face. They are all much larger forces than we have faced so far. We grow every day, and still we fall behind. We need this base and the weapons that it gives us. I will need another one thousand people to man and hold the base. The only other option is to take all we can and then destroy the base completely, leaving us with finding another supply base in months. With the base, we have at least one full year of worry-free airpower. In time, we will have three fighter wings and two full boomer wings, and we believe fifteen attack helicopters. Good thing we did this in silent council, as I talk too much even here." There was laughing all around the camp. It reached his ears as William voted first, which was not his normal timing as he never wanted to influence the others.

"I vote yes. Keep the base."

With that, the whole family said yes. Ben in Lone Pine was so close behind William, as well as all the others.

"Thank you, Sherman. We must get you the extra men as quickly as we can from Sonador and my dreams. The warlord himself is going to come in the end, and the long-awaited dog soldiers will be there in the next thirty-six hours with three thousand men."

It was decided to send men from Lone Pine and the camp and farms, but even with all the available members, they still came up short, about four hundred men. William and Maria were trying to find more men and still leave the farms and all the places the family had expanded into with men to defend them. They received a call from Len.

"Didn't think you'd forget me so fast. We are doing well here. Did you miss the numbers I sent you?"

"Sorry, Len, yes we kind of did as this place is so new. We did not include you in our planning. Did we miss something?"

"Yes, we stay here for about five days before coming to the mountain. We had a little trouble, as you all know. However, I made a few friends and gave them information to help them get stronger, and it is paying dividends now. They have all taken the oath, and they have grown from about seventy to three thousand with another two thousand. Jake and Lucy are helping to set up their own group. Both sides have decided to act as one in food and defenses. The area is very stable, and they told us of three different groups that came, trying to take over running from the south into the north. Two of them were sent packing after very short battles. The third group stayed and ask if they could join them. They took the small harbor it is stable and well-guarded now. In short, I can send you fifteen hundred men in about six hours straight to the air base. They will need to be armed and may need a bit of training, but they have all been in battles."

"Great, Trent. Did you get all of that?"

"Yes. How soon can they leave?"

"Well, as everyone's so busy, I started them about three hours ago. Jake is with them. They have about twelve men that are close to waking up, and they can be put in a link. Jake is working with them as they travel. They should be able to function with you once they get there."

"Len, William and I are happy to hear from you. Let us know if you need anything. You should be ready for anything there as well. Do you have enough men for your own defense?"

"Yes, we are building a wall that we can all pull back, giving us the high ground and clear line of sight with good cover. If any of the dog soldiers try to come here or use it for a back door, they will find it shut tight. We will let you know if we see any of them."

* * *

It was getting dark at the airfield, and they still had not seen the dog soldiers that Alberto talked about, but they have been seeing a lot of people moving south as fast as they could. After stopping a few, they knew the fight was getting closer. After the other discoveries, Sherman split his team, half to get all the birds ready to fly, and the rest had started loading them to capacity with ammo and fuel. Trent with Alberto helped find and close all the holes in the fences. He and Steve were working a plan to hold the base if the dog soldiers got there before the reinforcements arrived.

"Trent, we will have them ready to fly in three hours. The weapons loading will take at least one more hour. Until we get more men trained, that is going to be our weak spot. If not done right, the weapons may not fire, or worse. If someone rushes and drops one while loading, we could lose the craft and a lot of men. I have two crews that have done this work, and each team has another group watching as they work. As soon as they have all the working birds ready, they will go to two birds I set up for training and teach them to do the jobs. By tomorrow, we will have four teams that can do reloads. Oh, and one more thing. When we got the second bird up and running, we found that its GPS is working and sending us live information on things moving in the valley. From the last report, we have about three hours before they can be here. That will be about one hour after full dark."

* * *

Slim had taken two of the motorbikes taken in the battle with the San Fernando Valley people, and they were scouting to the north of the base, having gone up three different runs, looking for the dog soldiers of the warlord. It was just before full sundown when the second scout came back, pushing his bike and making the motion across his neck to hill the motor on his bike. This was one of the best scouts Slim had and one of the last not to be awake yet. Slim linked with him and took the report without words. At first, he could not get in as Willie had his mind blocked as he was trained to do. When he felt the pressure, he looked at Slim and, seeing it was him, dropped his shield and let him see the troops and what they were doing.

"Trent, they are stopping for the night, making fires and cooking. It looks like fifteen to two thousand men. I recommend we get about eight more scouts, all awake, to set a watch on them. Did you get our location?"

"Yes, Steve is getting them moving as we speak. Am I right? That's only about four miles from us on the northwest side?"

"You got it. They plan on coming in the far west end of the runways where that huge hole is in the fence."

"Good. We hope for them to try that. I need you two to move to that area and make sure they do not see what's going on here. From now until we engage them, no scouts are to be allowed to return. Kill them with bows only. Your relief will be their soon. Then you get back here. I need you to lead a section of the defenses here."

"Be right there, boss."

With the dog soldiers holding up for the night, it gave Trent the time to place the extra troops where he wanted them as they arrived. With each new group, he enlarged the engagement area, giving them a better position over the dog soldiers. In just over two hours, the largest group from Avila Beach arrived.

"Trent, where do you want us?"

"I am going to use you as shock troops. You will all be in the hangars, and if they get that far, you will come at them from three different sides. I am happy to have you and hope we won't need you."

Two hours before dawn, Trent had everyone in place. All were linked. Just as the sun was clearing the mountains in the east, the dog soldiers started to advance on the airfield at the west end of the runways.

"Sherman, what's the total count now?"

"We have five working fully armed birds ready to fly on your order."

"Okay, get them ready as they are moving to the end of the runway now. I am going to meet them. I have small hope we can avoid a fight, but we now have a force of almost equal size for the first time. Our numbers are smaller than the warlord's total force, and we may have to face them soon."

* * *

"Captain Barns, where are my scouting reports?"

"Sir, none of the scouts came back. I was just informed. No reply to any of the radio calls, and we intercepted no radio calls either!"

"I see. Well, we cannot wait longer. We march as planned to the west end and move on to the base in fifteen minutes! Get the men moving now."

"Yes, sir."

The soldiers move up to the end of the airfield, not trying to hide their approach in any way. In the last year, they had been in many fights and never lost a one. They had better weapons, and most had been in the army or other services. Well trained and solid discipline. As they reached the gaping hole torn into the end of the field, they lined up by section as planned. The major gave the order to move in. They started a slow walk, everyone looking for trouble as they went.

Trent, using normal attack patterns for the family, waited until they had the entire force pass the fence line. Then he challenged them!

"*Halt! Who goes there?*"

"I am Captain Barns, leader of the first company of the dog soldiers. You will lay down your arms and step out in the open or we will open fire!"

"*Who's your commanding officer? I do not deal with underlings!*"

"*I am in command here!*"

"*I see. This is going to have to be done the hard way!*"

In the link, he checked to make sure all fifteen of the men had a shot and told them to use one shot on his go.

"*It seems you do not know that we cannot be lied to. If you do so again, I will kill you and fourteen of your men. Who is your leader?*"

"*I told you I am—*" *Bang…*

The captain and fourteen men dropped dead at the sound of the shot!

"Now who's in charge?"

A voice from the back spoke up. "I am Major Morrison. Are you the wizard?"

"No, I am not. My name is Trent. Please step out where I can see. You have my word you will not be harmed."

A man a little over halfway back in the formation stepped out and came forward. Trent climbed on top of the small wall they had made here.

"Major, I carry a message from the admiral for you to take back to the warlord. Will you listen to it?"

"Why should I? According to my information, we have you outnumbered by at least twenty to one."

"Well, three days ago, you would have been correct. Not any longer. Just so you understand how this is going to work. If you refuse to listen to the message, you may not survive the fight we will have here. However, if you do listen and agree to give the message to the warlord, you will not be harmed and may be the only one to return to give the message. That is totally up to you."

"You're trying to tell me you're willing to engage us in battle, outnumbered as you are? As well as offering me safe passage just for taking a message for you."

"Yes, it's short, and we have a hard copy for you as well."

"Okay, I will listen, but first did you take out all our scouts last night?"

"Yes, we did. Now listen, the wizard and the admiral want you to stay north of San Jose. Come no closer. We wish to be allies in the war that's coming. If you do not, we will have to eliminate you and your army. If you agree, send this man back to discuss the agreement between us. That's it."

"First, I should tell you we don't believe in Wizard Mountain and this admiral who is good, but we are better. We will not leave any of you alive to tell him this. *Open fire*!"

Trent was off the wall, and the battle was on. They held the wall for all of three minutes, and then they ran back to the next wall. The dog soldiers were as good as they had been told. And they pushed on much faster than Blaine had. The difference here was the SEALs training they had. The family fell back in a much more disciplined order with good cover fire. They still lost two getting to the next wall. The last man across the short bridges hid the waiting hellhole they had waiting for the dog soldiers. As soon as they all reached the wall, everyone turned and open fire. The dog soldiers kept coming. That's when the rest of Trent's men rose up and started firing as well.

The major saw this and ordered a full charge as he knew he had half of the opposing force at his guns and they would fall.

Trent could see over two hundred men running right at them. He sent the image to the mortars site with the command to fire as soon as they were over halfway. The men on the wall kept the fire up, and the dog soldiers kept coming. As they passed the line, in Trent's mind the mortars went off. There were three loud pops at the same time, all aimed at the firepit, one on each end and one right in the middle followed by three blasts each, killing at least ten dog soldiers each. Men fell to the ground when they heard the mortars go up. Trent counted on training to have them all laying on the ground when the three to four hundred gallons of fuel went off a two hundred by thirty-yard trench of burning fuel oils. Less than twenty men got out of the trench alive. All had burns. The major ordered them to fall back, and they started up the road toward the gate. From the added light of the fire, they could see many defensive positions they would have to breach to achieve the goal.

"Report. How many did we lose, Sergeant?"

"Sir, Captain Barns and his whole team are gone. The few left alive are all burned and out of the fight, and I believe most of them won't live out the day."

"Okay, have all units switch to fire and move with cover. Let's go. Do not give them time to get ready for us again!"

"Major, you have cost me two men. I have taken a whole company from you. The stories about us do not give the full truth. If you keep this up, you will be the only one to live. Stand down now. Surrender and you and all your men can go home. And the next time we fight, it will be together against the real enemy we all have to face soon! Will you stand down?"

"You are insane. We will have your heads by noon!"

"Good luck!"

"I want three-man scout teams out now, all with radios. We are moving to the main gate now. Orders are shoot on sight anyone you see. Let's get going now."

"Sir, Captain Smith wants a word if he can."

"Send him in."

"Thank you, sir. Is it true we're fighting the soldiers of the admiral? They have good discipline, and all seem to be excellent shots. They do not spray the shots all over. They hit something every time they fire. We need to adjust our plan so as not to find another fire trap or something worse!"

"Yes, I agree, and that's why the three-man scout teams."

"I found our scouts we sent out last night. Everyone was killed by a single shot to the head or neck."

"And so they are good shots. So what? So are we."

"No, sir, you don't understand. They were all killed with arrows. They could have people behind us taking out the rear without making a sound. We cannot assume they will be like the others we have faced. Or we may win, but how high will the cost be?"

"Arrows? Are you sure?"

"Yes, I went and saw them. We are in danger here."

"Okay, have every unit put a drag out. Three men as well. Keep an eye on our six. Do it now."

* * *

Trent and all the men from the end of the runways were now in their positions for the fight for the gate. Like in all these attacks, they fell back to stronger and stronger positions while inflecting heavy losses on their opponents. Like all the others, the dog soldiers had not learned the cost of following them. At this position, they would have close to eight hundred men, and the motors had been set up here as well as their two fifties in a crossfire set. And they would be the cover for the fallback to the last position. The plan here was to keep the extra forces out of the first round of fighting. Then when they adjusted to flank the primary position, one of them would then open up, halting the move. In time, they would try the other side where the last group was waiting to give them more of the same.

"Maria, how are we doing?"

"You have lost forty men so far, killed or wounded. The major is so mad, we can feel it here. You have won, and he can't see it at this rate that only he will survive."

"I will try to save as many as I can. The chopper and the fifties are our last retreat now."

"Smith, how many men have we lost so far?"

"Sir, the count is not confirmed, but it stands at KIA four hundred and thirty-five. WIA is over seventy-five. The worst part is MIA is over two hundred!"

"What MIAs?"

"Sir, we caught one trying to run away. He was white with fear. He said a wizard spoke to him and told him if he moved one step forward, he would die like the man next to him. At that very moment, he said there was one shot, and eight men dropped dead!"

"What? They believe in the one-shot story as well?"

Steven was listening and asked how many men had shots to the major. He had eight men all confirmed. All were in sight of the major. "Okay, Trent, I am going to one shot eight men by him at your go!"

"Major, this is Trent. If you're wondering why you're having such a hard time getting to me, it's because you already lost. This is your last chance to save lives on both sides. Order your men to cease fire and lay down their guns. And just to prove it to you, I will kill the eight men with you now with one shot, even Captain Smith right next to you!"

Bang!

Smith and seven others all dropped dead at the same time!

"We have moved to our last station and are waiting for your answer. If you come in alone, we know you gave up the fight. If anyone other than you comes in, we will only show quarter to naked unarmed men sitting on their uniforms."

The major went white and ordered all his men to fall back to the road and await new orders.

"We are all going to go in once we see the last wall. We all will charge at once. I want smoke rounds fired at the next wall and a full charge. They are bluffing. That one-shot thing is a trick. Everyone check your weapons and make sure you have all the ammo you can carry. We leave in five minutes. Get ready." They were all ready and waiting when he came back in his full battle gear. He was going to lead the finale charge.

The lookout at the gate was the first to see them and sent the word they were moving out into the road to the first hangar where a small force was waiting for them. Being just out of sight, they were to escort the major and his escort to Trent or be the rabbit they were to chase.

"Trent, Steve, looks like we are the bunny with teeth."

"All right, men, we are doing the bunny hop. Steve, make sure everyone is running early. We lost too many today. All we want is for them to chase you, thinking they have won."

"War dogs, lets show them how hard we can bite. Charge!"

As soon as their yell went up, the escort came out firing and turned to run to the wall. They quickly slipped behind cover walls and ran to the main wall. Steve had already started the slowest runners back, and in the lane that the dog soldiers would see, the rest set the autofire system up on the heavy machine guns, three fifties and four thirties all with two thousand rounds loaded into them.

"Steve, Sherman, are you all ready?"

"I have started the slow runners to make sure they think we are trying to get away. The auto systems are all set up. We are ready."

"Trent, we have four Apaches ready. They can be up and at the field as soon as you call. We move to cover on both sides of the field. Less than half will face the auto system."

Trent opened to all the fighters on the field.

"This is the last wall. As soon as the autofire stops, get back to your positions and man the wall. Do not fire at them unless they aim at you. They will be beaten, and many of them are forced to join, so only shoot the ones that aim or fire at you. Here they come."

The dog soldiers were firing and running in three large groups, not a wild mad dash like so many before them. They were catching them when they just seemed to disappear as they went behind the walls. By now, the entire force was in the road and runways, making the target area as big as they could so the guns on the wall could not get as many in their line of fire. At this time, many of the dog soldiers saw the men running from the wall and sent up to yell their retreating charge.

They increased their rate of fire and held to their lines. The men on the wall would not be able to stop them. Just as they were reaching the halfway point, a loud rumbling was heard all over the field as soon as the four Apaches cleared the building. They had been waiting behind the rotter noises, all cleared up to the sound of helicopters. There were two on each sides of the field. The major saw this and tried to give the order to take cover, but it was already too late. The first two Apaches made their run on the front of the forces, stopping the advance as soon as they cleared and started their turn for a second pass. The other two took the rear of the formation and broke its run as well. In less than one minute, the major's force was less than four hundred able men with about eight hundred dead. As the front ran to the wall, the auto systems lit them up with the machine guns firing until the magazines were empty.

When they stopped firing, the major called for his men to gather behind the wall for cover and to regroup there.

Once they were all there, the major noticed that his force was much smaller than he was excepting to see. He had only seen part of what happened to the rest of the men. The major addressed the remaining men.

"We have few choices. We can fight. I believe we still have the larger force and better training, or we can go back and deliver their message, in which case I may be killed! I can't order you to go on. I believe that man is right. We have lost already. So what say you all?"

"Sir, we all will go back and give the warlord the wizard's message."

"Okay, everyone, stay here. I will go and see Trent and see what kind of terms he's willing to give us."

At that moment, five Apaches and two Hueys moved over the top of them all. They flashed their guns, firing to the distances. Then as they looked back down, they saw over 1,500 men all around them with guns pointed at them. A few started to reach for their weapons.

"*Stop! Do not reach for your weapons! My name is Trent. The offer I have for you is changed from the first one. Will you listen?*"

"We will."

Trent then laid out the terms for their surrender. First they had to unload their guns. Second, they had to make a choice—to stay and take parole or go back to face the warlord. If they chose to return, they would be given three days' food and water and allowed to keep their weapons, but just theirs. All the others would stay with the family here at the base. And last anyone, willing to learn about and willing to take the oath could stay and join the family.

"Why would you do this, Trent?"

"It's what William wants. You are not aware yet of the real enemy, but soon, if you live, you will be. We need all the men we can find, and you're really good fighters, the best we faced so far."

"Yes, we thought we were the best, but you outclassed me at every point. How?"

"I am from Wizard Mountain, and we do not use magic, but we do have other skills you may learn if you join us. Oh, and we are SEAL trained. Only an admiral could have a SEAL army, and we do. And you brought three thousand men. I had just under twenty-five hundred men and only used about fifteen hundreds of them. After you started the battle for the last stage, only men that stripped and sat down would have lived other than yourself. I am sorry to tell you this, but everyone here has the choice to stay, *but you must go back*! Here is the hard copy of the message. I hope he will see reason, and I hope to see you again as a friend, not from the other side of a gun. We have a car for you and enough gas and food. You will leave as soon as all of your men make their choices."

"Trent, can you answer any questions for me?"

"Ask. I will answer all that I can. However, some of what I tell you is not going to be repeated."

"You said it was a SEAL army. I do not understand."

"We have a full intact SEAL team, and they have been running our training for the last five months. Every man or women you faced here today has passed SEALs training before coming here. I have a smaller force than the warlord, but each one of ours is worth at least eight of yours. I am sorry. This is over. We have to get you sorted out and on your way. We have this base. It is ours, and will leave a thousand-man garrison here at all times."

Out of the three thousand men he started with, there was less than four hundred men left. And out of them, only twenty-six chose to return with him. They were that loyal to him. The rest wanted to take the oath and stay in the valley.

* * *

At the council meeting that night, it was decided that Sherman and Trent would manage the air base. The airmen, of course, stayed, and Alex sent farmers to take over care for the fields around the base. The family got the numbers a few weeks later. They could now feed twice the number of the current family size. The fields around the base were full of crops. They sent pickers out at once, and the large number of people Trent had seen came and joined them as well. The news from Lone Pine was of a different sort.

They had a large group of people mostly moving south down the highway from Utah. At this time, it was unknown if they were friendly or hostile. They might have to fight them, and they were outnumbered by at least three to one. So after the meeting, Sherman and Peter talked to their people, telling some they would be staying and giving the rest their choice of where to go. The new members formed the beach, and dog soldiers had a choice, but a bit more were limited in scope. They could work the new farm or, if they had experience, work on the air base. Or to go and help prepare Avila Beach to be the home for the navy O'Brian was putting together. The next day, the equipment was loaded with the other supplies needed on the mountain, as well as the fighters that would be going to the beach. And some would be going to Lone Pine to help if needed.

CHAPTER 33

The Battle for Lone Pine

Ben was waiting at the airport when the choppers came in. The first order of business was to fuel and service them. Standard SOP would be to unload and service the birds fuel and any reload of weapons if needed. They brought two Hueys and three black hawks filled with troops and weapons. Ben would give control over to Jeff when he arrived. He was still on the mountain. He would be on the last chopper coming over the mountain. He should be in Lone Pine by 9:30 p.m. or later. Scouts had the Mormons camping for the night just ten miles from the north gate. They would be at the gate before noon tomorrow.

Ben had the squads manning the roads. They used the snow barricades to block the gate and set up sandbag guard posts on each side of the road, north and south. There were few small trails or back roads into the city, and they had awake guards on them. A force of the size that was coming had little choice and had to come down the road to get into the city. Both gates had a squad of fighter stations on them ever since William had come back to help them with the soldiers. He was sending more men to man the gates.

Ben was surprised when William was with Jeff when he showed up. They set up a town meeting with the townspeople and with other key members of the family that would be helping in this encounter at Lone Pine. William's plan was to wait at the gate and give them the chance to return safely to their homes. If they chose to return, the family would help them with the gift of supplies to make the return trip. If they declined this offer and chose to fight, they would have a large force there to get by. It was clear they excepted to have an easy time taking this town, and that was about to change.

All the family members knew what was going to happen here, and more than 60 percent of the town had taken the oath and were now part of the family. The rest would be at the meeting and would march with the fighters to the north gate.

"For all of you that are not linked in, we believe that this group and the one we just dealt with on our side of the mountain have been sent by a third party to test us. They want to know how strong we are and what we can do. We are all being tested. This is just the beginning. Over the next year, we are going to be busy defending ourselves from forces from the north, south, and east. I cannot tell you much as you're not yet part of the family. This I can tell you. We will turn these people back, and we will only kill if they force us. We are going to need all the people when the real enemy shows their face. If it comes to fighting, only kill to save yourself or another of us towns or family. Now I want you to all to count off as one or two. All twos, get your guns and move to the north gate. Jeff and Chief Loggins will give you places. We all need to be in place before noon. I will answer all questions after this is over, so please go now. The ones need to stand ready as we will need you for backup as they will make it past the gate. You will receive orders later on where we want you to join us. Our hope is they will see a strong determined group and turn back."

William was sure now the warlord and Mormons in the east were being used to test the strength of the family. Now over one year later, the family covered the main camp on the mountain, the city of Lone Pine, and the two big additions of Avila Beach and the air base. Not counting the farms now controlled by the family as well. These now counted over ten since the air base was taken. They needed to turn back this invading force and still keep much of their strength hidden from the ones watching.

"Okay, for everyone who can hear me, we are going to make defensive positions, and just before they are able to overrun us, we will fall back to the next stage. At each stage, we hope to inflict more loses to them than we sustained. At each new position, we will start with the one shot killing as many of the leaders as we can. Then we will fight as long as we have the upper hand. We will keep this up until we reach the stockade where we will make our final stand. If they have not given up, we will bring more forces to bear on them from behind as we did before. Just so everyone knows, we are not in danger of losing. We are trying to hide how strong we truly are.

* * *

The next morning, the Mormon had started early and were approaching the gate as they were still working on it. William had gotten the reports from the scouts and had the others all working on the fallback positions so they would be ready as needed.

They approached the gate as the sun was rising behind them. They started to advance when the guard called for them to stop. They paid no heed to the order. Jeff, knowing they have come to take control of the town by force, had everyone in the one shot confirm they had a shot. They had planned for a twenty-shot first round. Jeff had twenty-three confirmed shots. He gave the order to shoot, and the twenty-three souls dropped dead in their tracks.

The leaders, recovering their wits, were about to charge when William, dressed in a full-length all-white duster, stepped up on a large tree stump at one side of the gate. He opened to everyone and, with his voice and mind, yelled for everyone to stop! The force of his mind was much stronger now than a year ago. All the Mormons froze, even their leaders. There were three minds that read differently than all the rest. Everyone in the link all felt it.

"You all felt it. Find them and take them alive if you can. However, do not let them get away. If you have to kill them and others to keep them from escaping, do it!"

Now turning back to the gate, he addressed them. "Who is in charge of this mob? Step forward so we can see you and resolve this with no further bloodshed."

No one moved, but many of the people thought the name Ezikle as their leader. Not waiting, William called for him.

"Ezikle, step forward so we may speak. If you insist on a fight, you will get one. The end will not be as you were told it would be. You will lose, and over half of your people will die! We never try to just wound. We kill our enemies. Look, after just one shot, twenty-three are dead already. Do we need to show that again? Come out. Talk with me. You will be safe. You have my word on it!"

After a short pause, William went on.

"We are not what you were led to believe. Lone Pine is under the protection and is part of Wizard Mountain! Ezikle, step forward. If you do not, thirty people will die with the next shot!"

Still there was no movement; however, due to weak minds, they found him. William had all the minds link for the next shot. "Take aim at one of the people standing near him." It took only a minute for the shooters to acquire their new targets.

"Ezikle, if you do not step forward now, the thirty people around you will die. You have thirty seconds from now!"

The time was counting in the shooters' minds, and if it ran out, they would all make another one shot. The time ran out with no one stepping up, and one loud shot was heard again across the town. Ezikle was standing about four rows back in a crowd of people, then the shot rang out, and he was standing all alone with nothing but dead bodies around him.

"I see how this is going. If you do not stop and change your plans for conquest of all other people, we will have to kill you all. It's your choice. Will you all die here today? We fought many better trained and armed and larger numbers than you have here today. They all failed, and lives were lost on both sides like today. People will die needlessly, and you will be defeated like all the rest. They could have shared, but none of them thought to ask if we would! They didn't ask for or offer to help if we needed it. Like you, they came to take!"

While he was talking to them, he sent for everyone to take cover and be ready as they had to defend the wall for at least twelve minutes before moving to the next position. Ezikle started to move. Six different shots rang out, hitting the ground all around his feet!

"I see you have no thoughts of stopping! Who is your second-in-command? Call him or her to stand with you."

Finally, Ezikle spoke. "Gaylyn, please join me. To whom am I speaking?"

"Do you not know or guessed? I am the chief wizard on the mountain. There are many of us. Many more than you were led to believe. You have all been fed lies. You have chosen to believe them, so you do not question them. The truth is there for you to see. You all have free will given to all by God. Use it. Does it sound good and right to force the smaller groups to join you and if not die? Is that what your Bible says? As you think on that, I want you to answer only one question for me. Ezikle, how many need to die before we can make peace between us? Think on that while Gaylyn and I have a talk.

"Now, Gaylyn, do you also want to go through with this ill-advised attack, or do you think we can talk and find a common ground to make peace and work for the common good of all? Now while I get Ezikle's answer, you think on yours. I will need your answer soon." Looking back and only at Ezikle, he said, "Remember, many lives on both side hang on your next words now. I need your answer!"

In silent speech, he asked if anyone had found the three people sending out the dark waves. The source of much of the current problem. If they did not find them, they would have to fight these people. He opened to Oliver.

"I need you to block me out and call the visitors and see if they can help us find the source of the darkness we all feel here."

Now as he focused on Ezikle again, he had fogged the minds of all the people around them. He then took the .357 pistol from the hostler at his back under the duster. Waiting now for the answer, he relaxed his whole body, not liking what he was about to do. This was a test made by the dark visitor or one of the many people under their influence. In the few seconds it took, Ezikle had given hand signals to his men.

"I don't know how many of you will need to die before you surrender and accept our rule of *God*!"

One shot rang out, and Ezikle dropped to the ground at Gaylyn's feet. He was dead before he hit the ground with a third eye all red appearing in the middle of his forehead.

"Now, Gaylyn, I need your answer to my question and also the one Ezikle just gave the wrong answer to as well. However, first I need the name of who's now your second-in-command now that you're the leader."

Gaylyn yelled, "Attack!" The whole force started shooting. They held the north gate for ten minutes from better firing positions until they tossed hand grenades, forcing them to fall back. They lost three men, and four others were wounded and needed help to get back to the next position. Many of the attacking force fell under the fire from the sixty fighters at the gate. Many more than they had been excepting to find there. The families always fell back as fast as the slowest member could go! Like the way the Navy would set course and speed for its convoys. They set the speed at the top speed of the slowest ship so they always had cover for the wounded with them.

The speed and numbers of the Mormons made this the most determined and deadly attack they had faced so far. The second wall was not too far, and the next was at the edge of the homes on the north side of the town. William ran straight to the third stage to wait for them there.

William checked in on his air forces coming to the aid of the Lone Pine branch of the family.

"Sherman, where is the best place for you to have at least two full runs at them?"

"With the placement of the ranch, the sports fields in the main city park is the only place to do what you want."

"Okay. Did everyone get that? Make the turns we need to get them to follow us across the park. I want the wall there to be safe but look like the weakest of them all. Sherman, how long before you can get here?"

"We lifted off, and due to the unknowns going over the mountains, we are flying the shortest way following the roads. We should be there in twenty to thirty minutes!"

"At the speed they are advancing, you may be late. If that happens, you have to find ways to hit them at the ranch. Understood?'

"Yes, I will do the best I can."

* * *

This was a large open space to cross, and the heavy guns and three motor tubs had been set up the night before. They were pre-aimed with four rounds each before they would fall back to the third line after firing. The four machine guns were set two in front of the tubes, the other two behind the tubes. They were all free to fire as soon as the last defender passed them. The front two were fifty-caliber air-cooled machine guns. With an effective range of two thousand meters, the two made a kill zone all the way back to the gate. The force had orders to stop at the guns until they started to fall back to the third line. The first half stopped at the fifties, the second at the tubes.

Then the thirties took over. They all stopped and gave support. Then all ran back to the third wall where the tubes were set up and fired two more rounds and fell back. Only the thirties were set up there as they were lighter than the fifties. These moved back two stages to hopefully work in concert with the air strike if Sherman made it on time! Even with all this firepower, they had only been able to hold the second line for eight to ten minutes. There had been heavy losses on each side. By the time they made the third wall, only twenty-eight of the defenders reached the third wall, able to fight. The force set against them was now known to be over 2,500 strong. And they had been right on their tails. It had not been easy on them as they were not set up for this hard of a defense and had little experience in this kind of fighting. Their losses were running ten to fifteen percent higher than the family. The ground between the third wall was littered with bodies even worse than right after the event. Jeff had offered a truce to help the wounded. They answered with a new charge at the wall. The machine guns and preset claymore mines stopped the first two charges against it. The machine guns had made three layers of dead zones. Just before the front of their charges cleared it, the six heavy guns would all open fire at the same time. Men were falling like fresh mowed grass. They held the third wall a full twenty minutes. Sherman announced his arrival would be in less than five minutes.

As soon as he reported, Jeff started the fall back, letting certain parts of the wall seem to get weaker as they moved the heavy guns out of the wall. Everyone was given a fallback time as the fire started to slow on one part of the wall. It drew heavier fire. The family losses started to go up within two minutes. Only the four light thirties were left on the wall. Jeff gave the order for all booby traps and motor rounds and the smoke canisters to be fired, and they all broke for the fourth wall. The massive number of explosives stalled the charge for almost two full minutes and gave the family at least a three-hundred-yard lead when the smoke cleared and the chase began.

Jeff had twenty horse' brought to the north end of the park where the first twenty members that were fully fit to ride and fight were given ammo and a drink and set to be the rear guard taking up guard positions. Their job was to wait for the Mormons to reach the park and open fire, moving around on the horses to make their number seem bigger and slow them for as long as they could then ride like hell to the next position. It worked for a good three to four minutes, and as the smoke started to clear, they all turned and made for the wall on the far side of the park.

Jeff had all the fighters set, and Sherman was waiting just one minute away. As the horses came into view, they all got set to hold as long as they could at this wall. It was made to be held for the longest time. It was also made to look the weakest to encourage the attacker to make a foolish rush. The first wave needed to be the biggest, and hopefully it would break the Mormons at last. Far too many have died here today. The horses made the halfway point when the full charge they had hoped for was coming across the field! After all the morning battles, they still hit the park with over three thousand men!

The fighters on the wall opened fire as soon as they had the range on the advancing forces.

At the back, the three men giving off the dark feeling had come together to whip the men in front of them to charge at the wall with no letup. William and Chief Loggins felt them and sent out calls if anyone was still near the north gate. There was one still there!

"I am here with two badly wounded men. We are hiding in the haze from the fires that started back here. I am also blurring all of us from their sleight."

"Ben, how are the wounded doing?"

"They are now stable. I have been blocked so as not to give my position away. I was just about to call for help getting out."

"Can you feel what we are feeling from here?"

"Yes, I can. It's the men we are looking for. They have all their focus on the fight. It looks like they are linked, but the feeling is so dark!"

"Yes, can you see them? Maria is sending a party to get your wounded. We need you to get eyes on them so we all can see them. They are not as strong as us, but they know how to block so we can see them without your eyes on them."

"Okay, I am sending the position to Maria, and I will go find them and get a look at them."

"Good, but do not put yourself at risk. We need to see them, but not at the cost of losing you."

"Why so worried?"

"Because you're in a dark place, and I cannot see you in my mind. I don't like it!"

"Okay, boss, I will take extra care!"

Ben had the two fighters take over the blurring as he made his way out of the thicket he had used as their hiding place when they rushed by them some three hours ago. He was keeping himself blurred as he came out, not knowing what he was going to find. He hoped to be at the back of them as the battle was clear at the large park in the middle of town.

As he came out, the full force of the darkness fell on him! It hit him hard, and he staggered under the weights of it. It came from three different directions. He started moving toward the closest one, and it was hard to move in that direction. There was a force that kept getting stronger as he moved toward the source of the effect.

Just past the north gate, the focus of Ben's search was one of the three men keeping the fighters moving to the front and kept the pressure on the townspeople. There were still more people coming up the road. There must have been five or six thousand fighting men in all. Ben passed this on at once and kept going to a place where he could see the face of the source of the dark force. He was at the same spot William had used that morning. Ben was about a thousand feet behind him, moving as fast as he dared while trying to be a living hole in the mass of fighters moving forward. The three dark friends had started to move to trap Ben. They believed him to be the one!

It took them a while to place him, being at back of them all. The back man was in danger of being killed, or worse, taken. They had a plan for this, and they all started to move to the places they needed to be in order to have the advantage they needed. William and many others felt the shift in focus of the three, just as the battle at the park was about to escalate to much more violence than all the other battles they had fought so far. It took them almost forty minutes to be in place and ready to take the one down! By this time, Ben had moved to the middle of the gate and just needed the man to turn so he could see the man's face. He had the strangest feeling that he was getting help. At first, Ben believed it to be William. Then William spoke to him to get out. They could not help him, and if he did not evade right now, he had no chance of escape!

"I know that, and I have been getting help so I can give you the information you need! I do not know how or even if I believe it, but Michael is with me and keeping me safe so I can get what we need."

"Michael? Which Michael are you talking about?"

"Michael who saved me for this day. Keep open to me. It's safe. They will not hear or see you in my mind. When this is over, tell the family we have a better place waiting for us if we stay true to ourselves. For the family, I am going to do this."

"How are you going to get him to look at you?"

I am going to shoot so much bright white light into his mind, he will turn and look straight at me. When he does, you will see all of them and the one that is controlling them as well. Michael says he cannot help me after that but will be with me from then on. Okay, be ready. Here I go!"

At that instant, every awake person on that side of the mountain saw the purest bright white light in their minds. Then far back at the gate, they heard a great many gunshots! He saw three men's faces and one dark hooded figure standing in deep shadows. They all screamed in pain, and Ben was shot and died at once with a peaceful sigh and thoughts of his children and wife. Every member of the family felt the great peace of Ben's passing, and all who knew Michael felt him as well! The man that Ben had targeted had died screaming. The other two fell to the ground out like a light. The will of the mighty charge they had been pushing was two-thirds of the way across the park with many stalling as if they just woke up most kept running. As soon as their minds cleared, they heard the new noise and knew it for the threat it was!

Back at the park, they realized that the numbers would over run the wall well before the last of them had even entered the park.

Jeff called for the air wing to strike!

"Sherman, you heard of the true size of this army? We need you now and will need you at least three more times just to get to the ranch."

"We will be there in forty-five seconds. They seem to have lost some of their will when Ben died. Do you know why?"

"No, but we have to use the time we have to survive this attack."

"Agreed. Here we come!"

The Blackhawks took up position on the north and south, firing at the front and back of the advancing force while the Apaches ran, strafing runs east to west until they had used the ammo and returned to the airport on the far southwest part of town.

Fighters paused when they heard the choppers, and as soon as they saw them start their runs, they dove for cover.

The Blackhawks opened up with their door guns and launched rockets back down the trail to the north gate, breaking up the inflow of fresh fighters. The other one hovered over the wall, taking out any that try for the wall for cover. These two birds alone killed over three hundred in just a few minutes. In the meantime, the Apaches had made four runs before they needed to go and reload for the next wave. There had been over 2,500 men in the field when the air wing came up out of the trees. There was less than six hundred men alive, and most of them were badly wounded! The charge had been broken. However, the attack was still coming as they were regrouping back at the north gate! They would not be surprised again and still had thousands waiting to come forward and attack the wall.

William took a place made for him in the wall, and he opened to all the attackers still able to listen to him.

"Hear me. Many men and women have died here today. This is senseless. Mankind needs to be unified to face the real threat that is coming! Once again, I ask you to stop this needless waste of our own kind. The real threat is coming, and we will need everyone we can get to face this real threat. We know you are being controlled by others. They have been subdued for a short time. They are under the control of the real enemies we are to face. You all have free will use it and go home. Live. We will need you as friends and family to stand with us, not against us. Just sling you weapons and turn around and go home."

A few turned and did as he asked. Others stopped and were just looking at each other. About that time, the two remaining dark friends came and started to use their minds to feed dark images of the horrors they had told them they inflected on others! Most of the fighters turned back to the park and were ready to charge the wall again. The birds still needed at least ten more minutes before they would be ready.

The second charge was started, and Jeff had the wall ready for it and started firing with one shot as soon as they could. When more weapons were in range, he gave the order to fire at will!

They ran at the wall with no care for their bodies. They fell by the hundreds that day. Just before sundown, they had all most breached the wall when the choppers came back for one more run at the raging hordes, and they fell back and took cover wherever they could. They could make only three to four runs and then had to fall back and reload and refuel. However, this time Trent had sent some special items to help hold the wall. Back at the air base, they had gotten three of the big CH-47 Chinooks in flying shape and had them haul three of the Abrams battle tanks and drop them behind the last wall in front of the ranch house. As the Apaches and other birds flew off to rearm and refuel, all the members on the wall retreated to the ranch house for the final stand. The question now was would they keep the attack up all night or wait until morning to come at the last stand.

The answer came shortly after full dark when the raids started all around the perimeter in different sizes from fifty to one hundred men. The plan was to keep them up all night and disrupt their sleep and rest, making them weaker when the real attack came in the morning. The first few attacks had the right effect, keeping Jeff guessing.

"Jeff, you need to use one shot on each of the attacks. This will demoralize the fighters, and if you have the family change their sleep patterns to sleep right after an attack, or as some of us can go up to three days without sleep, they will waste men, and we will be ready in the morning." The attacks kept coming with the guideline from William. They had the pattern and were waiting for the attacks and would kill 80 percent of them with one shot, breaking the attacks and then resting or going back to working on the defenses for the final battle tomorrow. There was one attack every fifteen to forty minutes. The last one came a half hour before dawn.

As the sun started to peak over the eastern mountains, the teams reacquired the dark friends that were leading the attacks. They reported that the numbers had grown to over five thousand and ready to charge the ranch, the first line of defense they had. It faced west in the back of a small box canyon, forcing anyone attacking to face the sunrise in a morning attack. The dark one would not like to charge into the sunlight. The last wall looked straight but in fact had a curve that would allow the fighters manning the wall to have the ability to shoot at the attackers that reached the base of the wall. They had the maximum numbers of fighters for the battle on the wall and were all fed and waiting after a well-rested night.

Jeff opened to everyone in the ranch to inform them of the coming plan for this battle.

"We are ready, and now I will tell everyone how we are going to beat this mass attack facing us. First, what we all know. Sherman has given us three battle tanks that will hold the breach. We are going to allow them to make in the wall. We have gained three more Apaches and will have air cover the entire brattle. We will make our move against them once they breach the wall and set off our defenses there. At that time, our scout teams will engage the dark friends, and we will open up with all of our defenses! This is by no means a sure victory. Remember, leave no one behind. Good luck, and remember that as this goes on, do not shoot or kill anyone that is not fighting. Ask them to sit and wait for one of us to reach them, no matter how long it takes."

The advance guards outside the wall reported that the attack was starting. The forces were massing behind the trees and houses, and once the units were complete, they moved down the road to the ranch and the last wall. Sherman and the others on the outside reported ready.

"Sections leaders, do not wait for them to fire on you. Open fire as soon as you can get a one shot or at least fifty or more. Then it's fire at will." As soon as the last group of attackers filled the sections, they all attacked at once. Firing started at different parts of the wall, and in just minutes all guns were firing as hundreds of attackers rushed the wall. As soon as they started to clear the trees and had to leave cover, the Apaches started for the field in front of the wall. Only two Apaches were on station at a time. In this way, there were always at least two of them on the field at any given time. They were killing the attackers in droves. And still the numbers kept coming! At first, they were holding the advance to just over a quarter of the way across the open field in front of the wall. As the numbers grew, they needed to reload and rest some of the guns, and they needed to get the wounded off the wall and the replacement on. This went on for about two hours. Sherman reported that he had to set four Apaches down, and so they had only one chopper at times. At these times they gained ground that brought them closer to the wall. At this rate, Jeff estimated they would lose the battle to hold the wall in another hour as their numbers seemed to be unending.

At the north gate, the two dark friends were sending more and more men to breach the wall. They were just berserkers with no training, just a mad unending rush to the wall. They had many more than any of them had seen.

"You have them. They will fall in a short time. Now keep the pressure on them."

The scouts at the north gate hearing this open to Jeff and William informing them of the dark ones present.

The two at the gate set up the men for the attack on the wall with satchel charges to blow a hole in it large enough to allow ten men at a time to pass into the ranch. Once they breached the wall, they would return the slaughter, killing every last one, moving to the wizards on the mountain. Once through, they would charge the ranch house and kill everything there. The scouts reported that the two dark friends had a power surge, and the fighters became more enraged and started running to the wall.

At the airfield on the far south end of town, Sherman had just received orders to hold all Apaches as the breach was imminent!

With the last chopper over the field and no replacement came the message. It was sent back, and they started the final push to the wall. By this time, they had killed or wounded over three thousand men, laying all over the field. The Mormons had identified the place in the wall with the smallest amount of return fire. And they redirected the attack to this point. They had amassed over two thousand more troops and sent them at once, and the special troop with the charges came up on motorcycles at a high speed. They faced a greatly decreased amount of return fire. No one saw this as part of their plan. They sent the rest right behind the bikes. They planned for maximum manpower to hit the breach before they could seal it. They now had three thousand men rushing the wall with no real heavy fire to speak of. They were two minutes out with the charges and facing almost no return fire as they let them see them running from the wall.

The bikes raced ahead. They had fifteen bikes rushing the wall. The remaining forces on the wall were tasked with letting no more than five of them reaching the wall. They started taking the front bikes out as fast as they could. The first wave of men had finally reached the wall, and the end sections not taking out the bikes started firing on the men there to give cover to the others at that place on the wall. Unknown to them, some of them had extra charges to lay at the base of the target section of the wall. They had some luck with the bikes as well. Seven made it to the wall. Once they were close, they pointed the bike to the section of wall and then just let the bikes go the last few yards as they ran for cover. Less than a minute later, a massive explosion rocked the town as a ten foot section of the wall went up in smoke and flames. Even before the normal smoke would have cleared, they rushed the breach, running into the smoke at full speed, never to be seen again!

* * *

"Sherman, now. Launch them all. The breach is bigger than we wanted, and the tanks and wagons may not be enough to allow us to hold them." At that time the, first men running into the breach found that their own efforts had set off the firepit behind the wall, a pit dug last night, three feet deep and twenty feet long filled with diesel fuel and fifteen gallons of gas to set it off. That had ignited two thirties, each mounted in the backs of blocking trucks they had placed in front of the breach. Just in the front edge were eighteen large truck tires, also set with gas to start them smoking and burning at the front edge of the breach. Adding to the second wall were two wagons that they rolled, one to each side of the breach. They each had two thirties mounted in the back with two squads each as support. Just behind this, the tanks rolled up and started firing over the wall as well as the mortars that had been moved to predetermined firing stations. At the same time, the fighters all returned to the wall and resumed their fire on the troops on the field. At about the same time, every chopper that could fly and had guns rose up from the south and started runs on the back of the field. Now all eleven choppers had a devastating effect on the rush, causing large gaps in the rushing men.

At the north gate, the blast was the signal for the scouts to attack the dark friends! The two teams would each attack one of the men. Each team made up of six would take turns blasting the minds of these men with blinding white light straight into their minds and eyes if they had line of sight to them. The other three teams were tasked with tracking the dark visitor if they could and attacking its mind in the same way. If that failed, they would try to get a location on them. To this end last night, William had Oliver close him out of his mind and called to the two visitors he had met with on the air base last year. They hoped they could help locate them.

Blasts of light hit their minds and eyes. The shock sent waves of pain all through them. The shock wave from this rocked the dark visitor far away to the north. The other teams followed the shock wave and sent their own blast of light down it like a phone line. They received a shock back as it reached the dark visitor. As soon as that happened, the other two teams sent their own blast down the line as well. The dark visitor was not ready for this, and all control of the attacking force was gone! As soon as the support was gone from the visitor, the two men at the gate fell dead on the spot. This all took less than two minutes, and many of the attackers seemed to wake up to what was going on and turned and ran. This was going on all over Lone Pine.

Back at the wall, the men there had little choice as they were in an open field attack. To stop meant death at once. The first effect was the charge slowed but did not break. The troops used for this were the best they had, and they kept coming, but any of the troops behind the tree line did not move forward anymore. Now they started to move to the edges and entered the field behind the wall to a mass of machine-gun fire and facing three tanks and the two wagons with the thirties on them. Now Sherman moved to block the gap in the wall from the sides as well as they could for as long as they could.

It had been almost ten minutes, and the fighting was still raging at the breach. William reached his place on the wall, and to the amazement of everyone on both sides, he stepped out in the open, drawing fire that seemed to stop just short of hitting him!

"Everyone, stop firing! The battle is over. You're free to choose again. We have broken their hold and you are free again!"

Still some men took shots at him. His guard killed them at once. Soon they stopped shooting at him and the fighting slowed, but many took cover and kept fighting. The family quickly encircled these groups and waited them out, only shooting to protect themselves. William had repeated the terms of surrender.

"Drop your weapons and strip naked and sit on your uniforms. Wait until one of the family reaches you!" Many of them had done this. Once the visitors had been hit, the force of will had been broken, and the last two dark friends had died. Without leaders, they fell apart with no clear direction. It took the rest of the day to quell all the holdouts. These holdouts were kept in separate areas from the others. The family members moved among them, telling them the truth about the family and the oath and parole. All the wounded were treated as equals. William was called to the medical center where he learned something one of the new doctors had discovered.

"Hello, William. It's nice to meet you at last! There is something I found out quite by accident. Last week, one of our scouts was wounded by a large IED. It split him in two. His body was hanging together by a narrow strip of flesh. In most cases, he would have been dead before he reached the center. I was with them on that patrol and was treating him. He was still awake and talking to me. He complained of a terrible itching at the wound site. I pulled the blanket back, and to my amazement, I could see his body repairing itself as we drove to the med center. It was a twenty-minute drive, and I started an IV drip and started to sew the edges together. If you would like to meet him, he is still here. His body is whole again, but the legs and lower parts are still reconnecting. I now know why you are called wizards. This is like magic."

"I was aware we were curing our bodies, but I never dreamed of this. So if we lose a limb and can retrieve, it you can restore it and our bodies will make them like new?"

"Yes, we can cut our losses and keep getting stronger."

"And you're not awake?"

"No, I have only been here about three weeks and still learning about it."

"May I link with you?"

"It would be my honor."

William opened to Dr. Jason Barr and found him wide open to the link. Next, he asked if Maria was in as well. As almost always, she was.

"First, Jason, you should not be so open when letting anyone link with you. And always remember, even you can stop anyone from being in your mind. As always, I want you to think or say. I want quiet now please."

Jason did as he was told, and he lost the link at once. He heard William say, "Good. Now, please open again, but not so wide."

"How is this possible to hear you and Maria? And where is she?"

"Hi, Jason. I am at the main camp. We have not found a limit as to how far we can still link with instant communications."

"Jason, please just remember what you told me about the healing you saw."

It took only seconds, and Maria was amazed by the new ability he saw. The next day, Jason was a very popular member of the Lone Pine branch of the family. The second thing to come from the battle was all the Lone Pine people taking the oath after the battle. As William was still there, they had meetings and decisions to make on the two groups of prisoners they held.

As was normal and regardless of the numbers, each person took the oath one at a time. Due to the large numbers of people they, started at the noon meal. The remaining townspeople took the oath first, and when they all took the oath, William stood up and made a private link with all the new members of the family, first in private and then open to all that could hear him.

"We are alone. The only other person that can hear me is my wife, Maria. You have all taken the oath today, but to the family that came here over a year ago, you have all been part of us. Taking in strangers and helping is what we are all about, and so we welcome you to the family."

The last part was different. They realized only the members of the family from a year ago were greeting them in the open link.

"Now before we go on, I have a statement to make to the new members of Lone Pine. Your parole started yesterday. It will be over when the sun rises tomorrow!" In their minds, they all heard the cheers from the family all across the state.

They took the oath and made 1,500 new parolees late into the night.

Some wanted to go home, and Ben had a few townspeople that had family there and asked if they could go as well. So it was decided to allow it, but they would need to keep a low profile as the safety of the family was unknown there. It was sure to be different than when they left to come here. The family would need a gate to the east as soon they might need to move that way or just to spread out as they were quickly becoming the largest organized settlement in North America. The family now numbered over 39,000 adults and many children under the age of thirteen. When it was all settled, over 1,400 were sent back to the southern border cities. At least 150 family members mixed in and went back with the others.

With the cleanup well underway, William and the rest of the family members started back over the mountain. They took the trucks, and the choppers made runs as needed due to a larger snow fall in the high passes over the mountain. William and the rest got the count from Maria. KIA was over three hundred. WIA was well over five hundred, all now going to fully recover due to Dr. Jason's find. The count for the attacking force was so very sad with high numbers. KIA was 3,356. WIA was 1,416. Only about one-third were expected to survive their wounds. All the wounded were kept in Lone Pine until they were well enough to decide if they wished to stay or return home. Gaylyn had made it through the battle and was in the wounded, healing. William went to him and they talked. William used his mind, and soon Gaylyn noticed this.

"We are talking, but your mouth is not moving!"

"Yes, you just discovered the secret we have here. You don't need to talk. Just think. It's much faster, and there are no lies in our talk. I want you to stay and see how we live. And when you're ready, you can choose to stay or return to your home. I have other business now, so I will leave you We will talk later in this way, so if you have a question, I will answer. Just think of me and I will get back to you. Get well and make up your mind."

* * *

O'Brian took the two schooners south to sit off the Long Beach harbor and one off Point Fermin. Each boat sent a three-man scout team to cities to check conditions there. "Look only. Do not be seen. Intelligence only." They stayed for two nights, and on the third day they sailed north to find the admiral a navy to fight the islanders and the warlord with. After getting all the information, O'Brian passed it along at the nightly meeting. The news was not good. There were at least four to five hundred thousand people still trying to survive in the LA area. At this time, there were three main groups. The gangs, now known as the Crip-Bloods in the inner city, were the most brutal of all with a darkness over everything they did. Their numbers seemed to be well over two hundred thousand. They shared only one common trait to the family. Everyone who could shoot a gun was a fighter. The only difference was that they had no age limit.

The next group called itself the South Bay Protection Society. It was started by the police working and living in the South Bay. They had over one hundred thousand trained police officers and their families and a lot of locals staying with them, working together. It was not perfect, but it was better than the gangs over the hill. The last group was the smallest, living in the north end of the San Fernando Valley.

"This is Blaine's group. We found him but did not make contact as he has been reduced to a section commander due to his loss at our hands. Things look bad for them as they don't have food and crops. They cannot protect with the people they have, and without Blaine's leadership, they won't last a day if they are attacked.

"William, if you do not send help in time, we will lose all the people in the LA area."

"I know. We are looking into it. I will need ships go get my navy."

CHAPTER 34

Saving Los Angeles

At the next silent council, they took up the matter of the three groups living in the greater Los Angeles area. With the limited information John had given them, they set about making plans to learn more.

"I have kept tabs on Blaine but have not pushed the link I made with him. Has anyone had dreams about anyone or thing from LA?"

There was no one. They had Jeff set up three teams of three members each, one for each of the groups they knew about. They had very special orders to watch and report only. They gave reports nightly on numbers of fighters, food, water, and ability of the troops to travel.

Team 1 was going to the San Fernando Valley group. He made sure that Blaine had not met or seen any of them. He gave the assignment to Slim, Nancy, and Phil, all top scores from John and Jeff in all their training with the SEALs. And none of them were near the battle with Blaine. Team 2 was Jake, Lucy, and Kevin. They were headed to the city to check on the South Bay beaches and what they were doing and what resources they had. Last was the team going to the LA inter city area. Juan picked Valerie and Berry to go with him. They all had special skills or connections that might help them in their task. Berry was a pilot. Valerie had family living in the area and would try to find them. She had dreams of them from time to time, so she knew they were still alive. The teams were all set.

The teams were all ready to go in two days. They had weapons and transportation and food for the first week. Then they would need to forage for food in the city. They were to leave at dark from the south farm. They had been given motorbikes and extra fuel to make the return trip. They would travel together as far as possible. Once close to their groups, they would establish a base camp to hide their extra supplies and the bikes. From there, they would walk. The long winter nights helped them reach the top of the mountain at the grapevine. Here they took side roads and dirt paths to avoid the guard stations that were there. They split up there as their different groups demanded. The teams would keep in touch on a private council each night with only William, John, and Oliver linked in.

In Los Angles, after the event, people were in shock. All their planes fell out of the sky all over the city from the two major airports and many smaller ones all over the map. The time of the morning, the roads were packed with the last of the morning rush hour, blocking all the freeways and roads. For the first two days, people just made their ways home when they could. Almost all of them believed that the civil authorities would start setting things right in the next day or so. On the fourth day, the fighting started taking place all over the city. Mostly over food at first then over shelter as places to take shelter were getting harder to find. The fires were still burning out of control all over the city. By the end of the next day, it was clear that no help was coming! It was every man for himself. A major city of some sixteen million people turned on itself. People were killing for the smallest of things, like a bottle of water or even a can of dog food. Millions died in the first six days alone.

After two weeks, it was clear that a few groups had some form of order. The gangs in the inner city were the biggest faction. The Bloods and the Crips had formed a new alliance, becoming the B-Cs (Blood-Crips). They had leaders and access to guns. This gave them power and a large area with lots of manpower to hold. They took over any place with food and guns and put up barricades all around.

There were other gangs, and they tried to move in. They were wiped out in vicious gun battles. Only the girls were left alive and put in pleasure houses. If they fought, they died quickly. If they let themselves be used, they had a chance. They got to eat and live for a while at least. The gang's plans were simple, to find and take what they needed. They kill anyone who got in the way. They had their own way everywhere they went in the city.

After about two months, things started to get harder to find as most of the food sources in the city had been cleaned out by now. The leaders desired to send groups to other parts of the city to look for needed food and water. They found little in the way of resistance and little food. One group went to the beach cities to find food. Normally they'd send ten-man teams and get what they wanted. The ten that went to the South Bay were gone for two days before a single member returned.

The lone survivor was helped back to the main house in the Englewood area. He was in bad shape, beaten and starved with severe dehydration. It was two full days before he was able to speak. Once he was talking, he told them of the sudden and deadly attack from the police running the beach cities. He told them of the warning of trying to come back in any form other than small parties for trade. Any others would be wipeout, and no one would return. They would be hunted down and killed.

In response, they put a hundred-man force and sent it to the beach cities. They never came back, and no word was sent. So they sent five hundred and got the same results. No return. After the second group failed to return, they decided this was who they needed to overcome. They sent four men armed only with sidearms. They had a fifth man follow them to report on what happened if they failed to return.

It was here where Jake, Lucy, and Kevin came to find how and why this part of the city was so secure and stable. They found a small cave on the hills behind the old Hollywood sign. They made their base camp and stored their extra supplies. This was a bit hard to reach, and you could see anyone that was coming up the hill long before they could see you. It had many different escape routes if needed.

Most of them led over the hill to the San Fernando Valley where they might find help if needed. That night, they made their plans to each find a different pair of eyes in the area. Once one of them found the right person, they would make contact while the other two would be on watch at a safe distance.

The next day, they made their way down to the strand at King Harbor. Here they found pick-up's and push carts in the large parking lot and down the strand a bit as well. With daily trading in progress. Also, food would be easier to obtain. It was fish for the most part. As they had plenty of meat, fish would not be a bad change, like ocean fish, not trout. As they moved toward the ocean, they saw that the homes in this part of the city had been abandoned, and many of them burned to the ground many months ago. They saw very few people as they passed by. Staying out of sight, they took note of the ones they saw. Most were barely alive. They looked like the pictures of the survivors from a World War II death camp, just skin and bones. The real walking dead. They wanted to stop and give aid, but that was not possible at this time. As they reached the access to the South Bay, things started to change as soon as they passed the airport to the south. The damage to this part of the city was very little, and they could see many more people moving about. All the parks they passed had been used to grow crops where possible. They saw almost no animals of any kind. Most had been trapped for food. Unlike most of the city, here only a few buildings showed signs of the horrors of the event. A few blocks would be burned out, but otherwise the area was in good order. They all got a sense of the marketplace from the stray thought of the people they could sense. They found a vacant house and spent the night there. Lucy was first to find a possible person to be their ears and eyes in the South Bay area. They met at the market in her dream that night. It was a young women who was dreaming of sailing away from the city. Chelsey was a young woman of twenty-six years. She had been living in the El Segundo area at the time of the event. She had just moved to LA from the Des Moines, Iowa. She was tired of the cool winters there. With few friends in the city, she had to take care of herself from day one after the event. Most of the people in the city did not know that they were on their own.

Chelsey had grown up on the family farm outside of the city. She had many skills. most in the city did not have. She found a hidden place in the hills near the beach road where she had started a small truck patch. She had about a half acre of crops—corn, tomatoes, strawberries, and grapes. She was eating better than most and had extra for trade at the marketplace for the things she needed. Her biggest fear was the rape gangs that roamed all over the city.

So Lucy made her way to the marketplace just south of Hermosa Beach at the strand in Redondo Beach. She hoped to find Chelsey there as she was looking for a compass. Chelsey was looking for the compass as a needed part for the sailboat she was repairing to escape the city.

The market was always held on the strand, giving a large open access to all. It made it safer for all as everyone could see everyone else as well. Lucy was in the market just after it started to fill with people looking to trade at the makeshift stalls for the things they needed. This was the most normal sight the three had seen since the event outside of Lone Pine. The walkway was about fifteen to twenty stalls of tables and covers from large umbrellas and tarps roofs. Many different items could be found here. The rare and helpful items were bought higher prices. Payments were made in trade goods or services, food, weapons, and some even traded their freedom away for food and a safe place to stay. Lucy was passing a rare food trader with some of the items they brought with them. That first morning, they entered an hour after the first traders opened their stalls. As they all entered from different sites, Lucy opened to Jake and Kevin, letting them see and hear all she did. All the stalls had their backs to the ocean and the open fronts at the parking lots. In most stalls, there was one seller and one or two armed guards in plain sight, making them wonder if there were some they didn't see. In just over one and a half hours, the market filled with people looking for the things they needed, mostly food. The most common was to see groups of three to five people moving around the stalls. At least one was openly armed. There were almost no single people in the marketplace. The team kept track of each other, and all looked for Chelsey as she would be a lone female After a few hours, Lucy left the marketplace, not wanting to be seen there all day doing little or no trading while there. She came back about two hours before sunset. The market would start to close as the light failed. It was too dangerous to stay longer without good light. With no luck on the first day, the team went to the second camp they made in a vacant house a few blocks from the strand. It was too far to travel to the base back in Griffith Park. They made a meal. And after they ate, they made the connection to Oliver.

As they all opened, they filled Oliver in and his small group, helping him keep track of the reports from the other two teams. They gave the history they had learned from the minds in the market. As most people in the city they worried about danger to their personal safety and none to their thoughts. This was where they learned most of the history of the last year up to the time they arrived.

The LA sheriffs working in the Redondo Beach area had taken control of the beach cities from the Palos Verdes perusal to the south end of the airport. They closed the area off, blocking any roads that had remained open, putting in defensive positions which they maned day and night. Only officers were allowed to stand in the early days.

They were one of the stronger groups as they had a system of command and control already in place. In the first few days, they were trying to keep things in order until help arrived. North of them, the gangs from the north beaches to the inner cities were fighting for control with each other and what was left of the department there. The gangs had larger numbers but were constantly fighting among themselves. This gave the South Bay time to get ready for the gangs. They closed off access streets and made defensive positions along main roads. They went back to all the stations they could reach and emptied the armories as well as all the gun and pawnshops, giving them some of the best weapons in the city. It had only been a few weeks since the gangs sent the negotiating team, and they came to an agreement. The gangs could come and trade like all the others, but never more than four members at a time and with sidearms only. They had to arrive in the morning after sunrise and must be out of the South Bay before dark. When they would arrive, they were given a guard to keep pace with them more for their safety than the people of the South Bay. They planned to return and do a couple of trades, trying to locate Chelsey by doing so. Lucy's plan was to start asking for the same things she was looking for, hoping to get a lead on her.

* * *

Slim, Nancy, and Phil had no problem finding the group that had sent Blaine to take over the farms in the valley. They had the shortest trip as they had set up their main base at the north end of the valley, giving them distance as their first line of defense against the groups over the hills living in the LA Basin. They hid their bikes on the small access road leading to the five freeways just outside of the city of San Fernando. They made this their safe camp and left most of their supplies hidden here. They spent the first night here when they woke. They walked into the valley.

They took the side roads and started to take note of all the security measures they had in place. As they came to a security post, they walked right up and asked to enter. It was here they learned much of what was going on there. Each was taken away to be questioned alone so as to find any reason for not letting them in. A very good system of getting to a lie that they might be telling as the stories would not match. This might well have worked on any other set of people trying to enter their group. As all of the team was awake, they all knew what was going, on and at every stop, there were questions. They learned more than the people asking the questions. Each of them would answer the question, and as they were all linked, they all gave similar answers. At the end of each answer, they would ask a simple question back. Most often it would be something like "Why is that important?" or "Is there some problem I need to know about?" If the person responded or not to the questions, they all thought of the things they were looking for or worried about. While the guards saw only people looking for work and food and a safe place to live, they gave up everything they had to the team. One thing that all of the guards held was that without Blaine leading their troops, they were sure to lose when they were attacked. So in this way, they worked their way past three rings of security. They had been directed to a large building. It had been a large high school. It came with tall chain link fencing all the way around it. At the weak points were large barricades of wrecked cars and whatever they could find to block these points. Behind this was the sports fields, giving them a large open killing field as they had been building a second wall much stronger than the fence.

They turned up the main road to the school and started walking the two blocks to the gym. It was now the headquarters for the group. It was not long before they were spotted by four armed men that approached them. They stopped and waited to let their weapons hang from the straps.

"Who are you and what do you want? And how did you get past the guard stations without an escort to guide you?"

Slim answered, "We are here looking for Blaine. We told him that we would be coming soon and may be able to help! Can we see him please?"

The lead man answered, "Blaine is no longer in favor and is working a post at the south end of the valley. You will need to be taken to the bosses."

"Okay, that's fine. May we ask why Blaine is out of favor?"

The man thought for a minute and then said it was not his place to say. They would have to take it up with the bosses.

All three read the man's thought on why: *He was our best commander and took our best men north on orders from the bosses. He and only a few of the men came back. Of the men, none of them could reveal anything of what happened to them. Blain had a crazy story of wizards and a magic sniper that could kill up to twenty men with one shot. So he was set down and sent to the southern line holding against the growing gang forces trying to enter the valley.*

"Now if you just tell me who you are, I will take you to the bosses."

Slim answered, "This is Nancy and Phillip, and I am Slim. We are the help Blaine talked of to your bosses. We are from Wizard Mountain. We come to offer aid and support in the coming days."

"What help can the three of you be? We don't believe in wizards!"

"Before we continue this talk, you will send two messengers. The first to bring Blaine to the meeting and the second to the bosses so we can start right now! Please. And let's get going as the valley is close to being overrun from the south."

The guards just stood there, looking unsure of what to do.

Nancy stepped up and spoke. "I see you're still not sure what's going on and what to do." She told the others what she was going to do so they would ready themselves. "Now I don't want any of you to tell us your names!"

The second she said it, they all thought their names, and all three of the team now knew the names as well.

Nancy spoke, naming them all. "Trent's the leader, Marty was second, Kent the unbeliever, and Willy the youngest. Now will you get over it? Wizard Mountain is real, and your only hope to survive what's coming is with our help!"

Trent spoke to Willy. "Your fastest go and get Blaine and bring him to the meeting rooms. Kent, they will take more notice if it's you that brings this news. Go find the bosses and get them to the meeting rooms ASAP please." He then started for the auditorium of the high school. "I will need your weapons as well please."

Slim spoke for them. "We will keep them, but we will holster them. That is all."

Trent just now noticed that they all had their sidearms in their hands.

"How long have you had your guns out?"

"Since we approached the first guard station over three hours ago. Do not worry about it. We have no thoughts of using them. It was for our protection. Now we know we are safe and will put them away. Now let's get going. Time is not our friend. We have a lot to get done before Blaine gets here." With a very small mental push, they walked on. This was going to be hard, but they had to accept that!

* * *

The council had three men sitting at the table in the center of the stage. They looked greatly surprised when the three people walked in, armed with a four-man escort at their sides.

"How dare you bring weapons into this room."

"Sit down. If we had come here to kill you, we would not have allowed your men to escort us to you in this manner. We are in a warzone and will not give up our guns to anyone."

Before they could address this, they were told that Blaine would be here in five minutes.

"Who sent for that man?"

"I did. My name is Slim. I am William's agent from Wizard Mountain. We need to secure your village for the sake of California and the human race in total. Before he gets here, I want to know what he reported when he returned here after our battle."

With a little prodding, they retold what had happened at the battle. When they finished, they all said he was lying to save his position in the village.

"Did it ever occur to any of you fools that he had told the truth to you?"

"How could any of that story be true?"

"Well, William will clear all of that up shortly after Blaine gets here. It was all the truth, every word of it! It is clear that there are a few agents working in the village. Once we have them all identified, we will take them. If they live or die is up to them. If they fight, we will kill them."

"What gives you the right to decide who will live and die?"

"When it comes to the dark ones and their agents, we will do what is needed and ask no one for the right to defend our planet. This battle is not really for who controls the city but which side will win. Light and dark are at war on this planet, our planet. We are hunting a dark visitor and his agents even now. You have traitors among you. How high it goes, we are not sure.

"We've come to help you as Blaine told you we would. He is your best chance of surviving the battles ahead. And as we understand it, you placed him in the most dangerous post you could find, hoping he will be killed! Of all the groups that have attacked us, his was the only one we feared might succeed in their quest."

"That may be so, but he still lost twenty-five hundred men that were not here when we needed them the most."

"He told you what happened. We gave him chances to stop and turn back. However, he followed your orders to take our farms and camps and bring our food back to your people. And what was it you said to him in private, first minister? Oh, yes, I remember. At any cost, you must win or don't bother coming back. Do you remember that conversation? He would have succeeded if not for the early warning systems we all have."

"We do not believe in wizards and magic, so don't try to scare us like kids."

Nancy spoke up. "I see you don't believe him. Your problem is he's too popular with the people, so you sent him away into danger, hoping he'd be killed in battle, making a martyr of him. You would kill the one man that has the best chance to win this battle for you. Slim, how long now?"

"It should be in the next two minutes from now."

Two of the members checked their watches. No one spoke, and in almost two minutes to the second, the door opened. The team never turned around as Blaine walked to the front of the auditorium in two minutes as told.

Nancy took control of the meeting at this point. She laid out what was about to happen. "First, we will not tell you how to govern your people. However, our first reasonability is to put this man in charge of your troops. If you refuse this, we will take him and any who wish to follow him, and they will become part of us. We will then pull back and await your fall."

"What in the hell are you talking about?"

"Well, what's it going to be? William is waiting on your answer!"

"You can go back and tell that son of a bitch he's not running us as his slaves. He won't even come here to face us!"

With these words, Blaine stepped forward with his eyes closed. He stood there for a full minute, not moving or saying anything. Then his eyes shot open.

"Of course you're not. Their secret is they have instant communication. They have ESP. They can talk with their minds. They have dreams showing them what is going to happen, and so they are prepared for whatever is coming. They can't force you to do anything against your will. Free will is the one thing they cannot change. They all know if you are not telling the truth at all times. That is how they beat me. They knew beforehand what I was going to do and counter it. At each stage of the battle, everything showed we had them on the run. It was what they wanted us to see. They kept giving me chances to stop and fall back to save my men. They said they would need us later. Now they are here. As he said, they would come when we needed help."

The three members started to talk among themselves. At that minute, Blaine heard William talk to him in his head.

"Very good, Blaine. You will be the first to awaken in the valley. You need to spend one hour each day in meditation. Nothing hard, just fine a happy memory and be happy. Sounds silly, but the results will astound you. Talk to the team there. They will tell you what you need to know."

The council spoke to the team again. "Why should we believe him now!"

Nancy answered, "We need time to take care of other threats, both larger than yours was! We sent the few back who wished to return to warn you and help you get ready to face the same danger! This was the reason you sent Blaine in the first place. We are aware far better than you of the dangers coming.as it's a threat to us as well."

"That all sounds good, but when it's over, you will take control and we will be your slaves!"

"Blaine, do you trust me?" William spoke in his mind.

"Yes, I do."

"I would like to talk to them through you if you will let me."

"How can you do that?"

William opened to the team and let them understand what he was about to do so they could be ready for whatever might happen next and explained it to the council members.

"Blaine, just open your mind to me. In other words, give me permission, and you must mean it. You will feel strange and may need help just to stand. When it's over, you will need food and rest."

"Okay, I am willing."

With the permission given, William entered his mind. In the few seconds this took, Nancy spoke to the members, telling them, "William has heard your concerns and is with us now, wishing to speak with you now. I will need two men to stand by Blaine as he may need help standing. After it's over, we will care for him."

As the two men took their places at his side, Blaine's body went limp. Only his head seemed to move on its own. Looking at the three men, he spoke.

"Well, gentlemen, Blaine was kind enough to lend me his body and this time to speak with you. So listen, for as soon as I am done, I will go back to my own body and will be as you see Blaine after this talk is over."

They all started to talk at once, yelling and making wild accusations and threats. William used his mental abilities to amplify his voice and yelled for silence.

It brought the three men and the entire village to dead silence.

William then started speaking to them.

"Sit and listen. I have a lot to say, and as I am forced to use this voice, it will take some time. Get paper and take time to write your questions as I do not have the time to answer them now. Once I am back in my own body, you can ask your questions. You will hear my answers.

"So far you have been fairly truthful, only holding back or lying on a few key issues. You were told that we cannot be lied to, and like all the others, you still tried. Now you need to know that when anyone asks a question of someone, they think of the answer and then decide if they wish to answer with the truth or a lie. We see and hear the truth when you think of it. So even if you lie, we already have the truth. Now like most, you do not believe me, so I am going to tell you a few of the things we learned from you so far. You have over eighteen hundred assault rifles and over four million rounds for them. Three small field pieces that you hope will turn back the attack you fear from LA groups. You also do not have nearly as much food as you say you have. We know the truth of all the questions we ask you in the same way. So here is my only question. Do you want to live free or die and the only survivors, women and children, become slaves? Now before you answer, you should know everyone in the camp has heard everything I have said. We keep no secrets on the mountain. We came to help, and if you choose to go at it alone, that's fine. We will take anyone back to the mountain with us that wishes to go."

As they started to answer William, Blaine stood up on his own and looked at the three team members and nodded to them. And still before the words escaped their mouths, everyone heard William in their heads.

He was back at the mountain now.

"Good. We are here to help. We will always help as long as you follow the people and their rights. Together, you will become stronger. Work with the team. Give them your trust, and they will give you theirs in return. If we all work as one, it will be okay in the end. I will be listening and will answer questions if needed.

CHAPTER 35

Battle of San Fernando Valley

THE WEST SIDE on the coast and the inner city from South Central to east LA had in the last year become the two major groups. The largest was the Blood-Crips. The two gangs that had been at war and hated enemies for years were now the largest armed force in Southern California. They could boast of twenty-nine thousands soldiers and over one hundred and fifty thousand living under their rule. No one entered their territory without permission. Any that did never return.

The other groups were two smaller groups that moved and formed one in the South Bay center in Redondo Beach. They were the remaining officers of the LA police department and a large number of military personnel in the area that stayed in the city like army, navy, marines, and coast guard. They had around 9,700 men and women trained in police or military forces with another sixty thousand family and friends that moved here right after the event and some locals, bringing their numbers to about sixty thousand living in the beach cities south of the airport. They had the best training and better weapons than any other group in Southern California. The city was mostly wasteland. Finding places to plant and grow food and be able to harvest was a major problem. Due to the common needs the two groups, both looked to the San Fernando Valley as their answer. After the gangs had lost so many men trying to take control of the beach area, they sent the four men and started talking. They started to come and trade. Finally the leader agreed to meet, and they started to talk about the valley as their only hope, and so the unholy alliance of police and gangs came to pass. These were the two groups the other two teams here scouting for the family.

It was a total wasteland as four or more airliners had crashed into the gas refineries located there. It had burned for over six weeks with thick black smoke filling the air. Once it was over, a few people went in and didn't even find bodies after going more than two blocks into the area. No one came here, so they had privacy to make their plans. They started meeting there as needed, and now they met once a week. And after months, they still did not trust each other completely. Together they had approximately 38,700 fighting men and women under arms. They were still working out the details, and this was the information the two teams were looking for. They planned to take the entire valley before spring and grow a lot of food. They met every Wednesday night just after dark. So far, they only made small attacks on the east and west passes, trying to make them believe it was one or both of these passes they would attack through.

The San Fernando Valley leaders had been debating over trying to get more soldiers to make these positions stronger against the attack they all knew was coming soon. Blaine was still trying to understand what had just happened. The team was with him, helping when they could. He remembered it all like seeing a movie. He was once again in charge of the troops. He was going over the reports of troop displacement and response time of reinforcement troops if needed. Attacks on the east and west passes could only be for one purpose, to weaken the middle of their defenses. He was looking at the numbers and knew he would need at least 450 men at all three passes to hold them at all. He sent the request to the council and waited for their answer. His next move was to get people that knew how to lead and motivate the troops. He sent runners to get the people he wanted. With them, the tale of the wizards coming and Blaine put back in charge was in most places, met with a new sense of hope they had not had in a long time. To others, they worried about how Blaine was going to treat them after the way they had treated him.

* * *

Slim was very impressed with what was going on and was just making a report to William about the changes they could already see when Oliver burst into the briefing.

"William, I am sorry, but we have a serious problem regarding the San Fernando Valley operations. The visitors just made direct live contact with me concerning your safety! The dark pair is setting a trap for you. Are you going to the valley? They have sent a team to kill you there! Why would they do that?"

"I talked to the ruling council earlier today. I did it from here. You remember Blaine that we sent back?"

"Yes."

"Well, I asked him if I could use him as my voice, and he agreed. So I sent my consciousness to his mind and took over for about fifteen minutes to address them."

"Wow, I did not know you could do that!"

"Neither did I. However, it was necessary. So they now think I am in the valley?"

"Yes, that is what they believe now!"

"Great. Slim, contact the other teams and put them on lookout for any signs of the dark visitor and dark friends like the ones at Lone Pine. I am going to get the members of those teams dropped at the school tonight. They hope to set a trap for me. I think we should let them, no, better yet, help them. I am also sending an R&R team to keep Blaine safe. He will be a target as well. Someone reported that it was him who addressed the council today. They are not to leave his side for any reason, okay? Oliver, stay in the link. You will need to know this as well as get information from our friends."

"Okay, I will go back and break that connection and rejoin in a minute." He was gone almost three minutes. He had been given a lot of information before they let him go.

"We cannot tell the council or even Blaine how we plan to help until the attack is underway. I will need the figures on how many men we will need to stage for the counterattack at the last second. We want the others to think that the wizards helping was just a lie. When they are sure they are going to win, we hit them hard from as many sides as it is safe to do so!"

"How many we send won't matter if they gain the upper passes!"

"Yes, it will because their supplies will not cross the passes. Okay, the R&R teams are in the air. We are getting the trucks loaded, and they will be moving to the valley in the next fifteen minutes."

Los Angeles

On the second day at the market, Lucy picked up a tail. Two men had been on the back side of one of the stalls she had been asking questions at. She had been trying to set a price on a compass she was using as bait to finf Chelsey with. When she moved down two stalls and started over again, the two men slowly moved to be across from her, where they could hear her talk with the stall's trader. They moved close enough to hear them talk about the compass.

Both Jake and Kevin were aware of the two men showing so much interest in Lucy and taking great pains on her not seeing them, staying just behind and out of sight when she stopped. They decided not to tell Lucy unless she became aware of them as well. For the next two hours, the five of them worked their way to the far end of the stalls. Just before the end, Jake went on ahead to get in front of Lucy as they would now have to tell her what they wanted to do if the men followed her out of the stalls.

Just as she was about to turn and leave the market, she saw a young girl, maybe in her early twenties, stop there. She was surprised when the girl addressed her.

"Hi. I've been trying to catch up to you for about forty minutes since you left the book stall."

She stood at about five-five, bright blond hair hanging in a long ponytail. She had the deepest sea green eyes, sharp and clear. Her entire appearance was almost like that of any family member.

She was overall healthy and full of energy. Lucy knew at once it was Chelsey, and she told the others.

"And why would you be after me?"

"I am looking for a working compass and was told a girl fitting your description was trying to trade or sell one. Is this true?"

"No, it's not. And yet at the same time yes, it is true."

"Well, I am sure I don't understand. Unless you bait for those two."

She looked at the two men that had been following her. As she had opened to the others, they brought her up-to-date at once.

"I have never seen them till just now. Who are they?"

"If that's true, you have trouble. They have been on you ever since I spotted you about ten minutes ago."

"Well, thank you for telling me."

"Well, if you know and are okay, maybe we can do some business?"

"I hope we can as well. I am Lucy from the north. I was wondering how you look so much better than the rest of the people living here."

"I eat better and more often than most of the people living here. Name is Chelsey, and I would like to hear your price for the compass."

"Fine by me because I know it was meant for you."

"We will want to take little time due to the men waiting for you. I will want to get away from them before leaving the market."

"Chelsey, I don't want to scare you off, but we are under a bit of a time problem. So here's the deal. If you will help us get information on the beach city involvement in the upcoming attack on the San Fernando Valley group, if you agree, the compass is only a fraction of the help we can supply you with. The information is the price we need."

"That is quite an offer. Well, while I decide, we will have to lose those two before we can talk about anything. They are very bad men. They will grab us and sell us to the sex traders in the town. Being a sex slave is not for me!"

Lucy looked right at the two men and said in a loud voice, "Don't worry about them. They pose no threat to us. Come with me. We have a camp nearby where we can talk."

"You can't leave the safety of the stalls until we lose them." She was getting visibly nervous about leaving the marketplace. "Things are not going to work out as you think."

Lucy started to laugh with a silly look on her face. When she stopped, she looked at Chelsey.

"I am not alone, and those two I can take alone if needed. I told my friends about them when you told me. They already knew and are keeping an eye on them.

Chelsey took a step back, and fear crossed her face.

"Oh, yes, I do. I want them to follow, and I want to take them and question them for all they know. And then we will send them back so they won't be missed. It's all right. If I am right, you have been having dreams that are leading you to the coastal towns, am I right?"

"Yes, but how could you know all of this? We never met before today."

"I've seen you in your dreams. That is how I know so much. The rest is from a friend of yours. Alex asked me to keep an eye open for you. We did not know we were both looking for the same person."

"You're talking about a man in my dreams, not a real person."

"Chelsey, you're about to wake up. When that happens, your whole world is going to change forever! Let's keep walking. We need to get out of sight of the marketplace."

No sooner did they drop behind the crest of the hill than the two men rushed at them. The two women were just standing there a short distance ahead. They looked to be waiting for them. They got to within twenty feet when the girl they had been stalking suddenly had a gun in her hand. They both heard her yell, "Stop or I'll shot!" They were not used to armed resistance. They turned to escape and found Jake and Kevin waiting for them. Just as this was happening, Jake warned Lucy of two men coming over the back side of the hill. With no time to explain, Lucy told Chelsey to step in front of her and stay as still as she could. Just then, she saw the two men running at them. Lucy stepped up and then ran at the two men. She leaped at the first man, landing a double leg lock around his neck and twisting him around and flipping him to the ground. Then she hit him in the belly, causing him to expel all of his air from the force of the blows. Jumping right up, she attacked the next man. He was waiting for her and came after her. Even with the lack of surprise, she took him down in just three punches. By now, the others had reached them as well.

"Chelsey, these two are the rest of my team. This one is Jake, my husband, and the other one is Kevin."

"Lucy, who are you people? And where do you come from? You have lied to me!"

"No, we never lie. I told you, we came from the north. That is true. Most people react badly if we tell them too much. We do come from the north, Wizard Mountain. The dreams you have been having are real. We have shared four different times and about five with Alex. I made myself look different in our shared dreams. We have a coastal town, and it is the same one you're looking for in your dreams. Okay, guys, let's get back to camp. After we get there, I will give you all the information I can. If you wish to leave us, you can safely return to the market now."

"I think I know you, and I even want to believe you, so I will come to camp and listen then decide, if that's okay."

They took the four men and Chelsey back to camp where the boys asked questions to the men as they woke up. As Chelsey watched, she seemed confused at the way it went quick and easy. They asked a question and got lied to and asked another. Lucy gave her the information she asked for and told her what they needed.

"So you want me to see what I can find out about the two groups' plans for attacking the other side of the hills in the San Fernando Valley? And how am I going to get the information to you and then get out? What makes you think the information I may find will be any good by the time I can get it to you?"

"Look at me, Chelsey, right in my eyes, and tell me if you can hear me."

"Of course I can hear you. I am sitting right next to you."

"Yes, but you're not looking."

Chelsey turned a bit and looked at Lucy's face.

"Ahhh, that's better. Can you hear me better now?"

"No, it's the same as before."

"Are you sure? Look closely at my face. What do you see? Am I talking to you?"

Chelsey's face went white as she saw that Lucy had her eyes closed, and her mouth was not moving.

"Why do you make that face? Is it because I am not talking to you but reading your mind and letting you read mine as well? Yes, this is how we know so much. Now listen, I cannot force my way into your mind if you so desire. I want you to say aloud or just in your mind *I want quiet now*. Do it."

She said the words aloud, and at once she could not hear Lucy anymore.

Speaking again, Lucy asked her for permission to speak to her mind again and received it. "Whenever you need to talk to me or Alex, just think of us and ask to be heard. We will listen and answer as needed. You will only be alone when you wish it. Would you like to talk to Alex now?"

"Is this possible? Is he here?"

Lucy told her to call for him in her mind and then listen.

She did so, and in the next instant, Alex was talking to Chelsey as Lucy had done. He told her about being a dreamer, and they talked for what seemed like hours. Then Lucy, who had joined them early in the talk, said it was time to send the four men on their way and get some food and sleep.

"And we talked for so long. I am sorry to have kept you so long, Lucy. You must be very tired."

"Chelsey, how long do you think we've been talking here tonight?"

"Oh my, it must have been three hours at least. Yes."

She laughed again. "No, although that was a much longer talk than normal, it was not a record. We have to talked for a bit over ten minutes to break the record! We only talked for six minutes and thirteen and a half seconds. Speaking mind to mind is so much faster, but we still speak normally most of the time."

Chelsey agreed to go back and get the information they wanted from the Redondo Beach group. "Look at everything you can. If you see it, we can look at it as well once you make reports. This is our biggest advantage. We can talk instantly, and distance has never been a problem if the person is linked or awake. Do not be surprised if others join and ask questions. Only family members can join. It is totally safe. Last, when you see pass it in your dreams. However, if it is something that can't wait, just yell my name in your head and I will be there to help however I can. Last, do not ask questions. Just listen. We can replay what you hear from your memory. Now get some food and sleep. You leave first thing in the morning."

Chelsey woke to the smell of eggs and bacon cooking along with hot coffee. Jake brought her a plate and cup of coffee. She started eating at once. After a few bites and sips from her hot coffee, she asked how they made the coffee and eggs just as she liked them.

"Lucy looked at you yesterday and now can recall what you like, so we did our best. Sorry, no pancakes here, but if you get to the mountain, you can order them any day you like. Now eat. We all leave soon."

"Okay, I will be ready in five minutes. What will happen to the others?"

"They will sleep for at least three more hours and wake up with very bad hangovers and no memory of all of yesterday. And should they run into someone that can see they had their minds wiped of all events, that is all they would learn, so you could walk up to them and ask a question and they'd have no memory of yesterday."

Jake and Phil had each linked with two of the men and would hear and see everything they did until they broke the links. They all left the camp. The team returned to the park to refill their supplies while Chelsey went down to the pier where she had a few connections and would start looking for information there.

* * *

Juan and his team had circled far around to the south of the city to enter from the south closer to where his cousins lived in Compton. Valerie also had family living in the southern part of LA, and they would try to locate them first. After talking to a friendly known person, they would set about getting as much intel as they could.

It had taken them two days to get safely to the southern part of the LA Basin. Once there, they compared notes and decided to track Valerie's family first. Their last known address was in the city of Lynwood, a mixed community of Latin, Whites, and Blacks. The address they had from her dreams was a small street just off of Firestone Boulevard. Juan liked the address as it was what they needed to bring to the city, 2608 Hope Street.

Having moved across the eastern hills of Pasadena, they then moved west along the riverbeds and freeways to reach their destination. Having arrived early in the morning, they took watches, not wanting to just walk in. That would cause too many questions. They opened to the area they had set their watch on, hoping to get a stray through or two. Getting names and other information would be helpful.

Valerie's family was there living with another family in a small three-bedroom home. The plumbing no longer worked, and they had to go five blocks to get water. And they had to take a guard and all carried guns. It was unclear if the house belonged to either party. As the day wore on, it was clear they had moved in at the same time as there was safety in numbers. The bigger your numbers, the safer you were. They each kept to their own bedrooms and only mixed in the common rooms, kitchen, and living room. The house was never left empty, and at least one member from each group was left to keep watch at all times. This was a very unstable group. The feelings were mostly fear and hunger from all of them.

Valerie had at last seen one of her nephews, Tae-Tae. He was seventeen. She believed he had come home late just before dark, and so they planned to contact him in his dream tonight and approach him when he leaves the house the next morning. Valerie had found his thoughts and focused on him, waiting for him to sleep. After about forty-five minutes, he lay down and was quickly in a deep sleep. Valerie slowly entered his dreams. They were scary and dark nightmares. She slowly took control of his thoughts. Luckily, they were clear and not dark as it first seemed. She moved him to a dream he had of the family getting out of the city and finding food and a good place to live. When his mind became calm, she entered his dream.

"Tae-Tae, there you are. I've been looking for you for the longest time. Come on, we need to get home. The family's ready to go. Did you forget it's moving day?"

"Auntie Valerie, where did you come from? We missed you."

"I was looking for a new home, remember? The good news is it's just to the north. I found it, good food and clean water. Come on, it's moving day. You need to get packed. We are leaving soon."

She then pulled out, leaving him with his own good dreams.

"Juan, there is a darkness all over this city, and it's growing. They are still clean as far as I can tell, but as my family, you two will need to check them as I may be biased in this matter."

"Well, as we have all been opened since coming into the city, we saw what you saw and you're right. We need to get them up and out as soon as we can. You will be waiting just out of sight of the house when he leaves tomorrow."

The next morning, the team was up. Juan stood the last watch, and when Tae-Tae woke, Juan got the rest of the team up. Valerie was down the street, a few minutes before Tae-Tae left the house. She was standing just out of sight of the house so she would not be seen by the others as she waited.

Tae-Tae started his walk to the center where they gave out work assignments. He hated the jobs they gave out at this center, but no work, no food. The problem was the work. It was growing larger, and the food payment less each week and now by the day. There were signs: "Join the B-C and eat all you want." Some of his friends had joined, and for a while they were the hottest thing on the block. Then they got sent to the beach to get them to pay protection with food for the BCs. They were given a mission and happily went off to get some beach booty. None of them came back. The story was that they were now running the beach cities and things would be better soon. More men were needed to help settle and organize the work there. So another group, much bigger this time, left at night. so no one knew how many really went. None of them came back. Tae-Tae knew they had all been killed by the police living there. Thinking some things never change, he turned at the corner and was brought up short by his auntie Valerie standing there, big as life.

"Hey, Tae, surprised to see me?"

"Auntie, how did you get here? Where have you been? We all thought you were dead!"

"Not yet, but with the war that's about to start here, we all may be soon. Come on, let's walk. Where are you going?"

"To the center for work. Work and they give us food. No work, no food."

"Sounds a lot like home, but I think it's a bit different here than home from the little I've seen."

"Home? Where's your home now?"

"I am living north of the city now."

"In the other valley?"

"No, don't ask questions now. I need information on what's going on here. Can you help me? And before you ask, once we have the information, you and everyone in the family is coming with us if they want to."

"What kind of information do you need?"

"This is the bad part. We need to know how strong they are, men, guns, and plans they are making. Here's the easy part. You just have to listen and look at as many maps, and later we will look at it all together. Remember, never ask questions about what you see. That will keep you safe. To get what we need, you will have to join their army."

"Auntie, you can't be serious. All my friends who joined are dead at the hands of the police in South Bay."

"Yes, we know, but the B-Cs are planning an attack with them against the group living in the San Fernando Valley, and it's going to happen soon. When we have enough information, we will leave that day. I can't promise you it will be safe or easy, but we will stay near you at all times and get the family out if needed. It's time to make a choice. Sorry, but in this world, we all need to make hard choices."

"How can you alone hope to do all of this?"

"I am not alone. We have three teams and backup if needed. You just need to make a choice, and we will have your back and do all in our power to get you out if needed. Now if you're in, we need to start making plans to get you all out when the time comes. So what will it be?"

"There are eight of us back at the house. How are we going to get so many out?"

"No questions now. If you choose not to do this, we will still get you out if you want to come with us. Go now. Decide what you're going to do. When you get home, tell the family and the other group that family is coming over and will bring food for all. We will arrive a half hour after you do. It's good to see you."

She turned and walked away without looking back and turned the corner and was gone from sight.

Juan and Berry joined her, and they went back to the edge of the city riverbed and got the food they would need to make dinner for the large group of people they would need to feed later today. They knew that giving food would be the best coin they could have in dealing with the people having to live under the B-Cs and their feudal systems of keeping their people under control. They got home and worked long hard days for food. No work, no food. And they would run you out of the city or just kill them. Life had no value here. Fear and terror was the way of life.

Juan sent that they were on their way home and would be there in fifteen or twenty minutes. Valerie and Berry got the food ready and were ready to go. As soon as Juan arrived to carry his share, they would start to the house. At this point, Valerie opened the link she had made with Tae-Tae that morning. He had signed up as she had asked, so he made the hard choice of his own free will.

They started toward the house with enough food to feed them for a week compared to their normal rations. They had forgotten one thing. The smell would bring others that needed food. She sent word to Tae-Tae that they were coming. This would be his first real understanding of who and what his auntie and friends were!

"Tae, can you hear me?"

He was sitting alone after telling his mom and sister of what he had done today. They had taken the food and were about to cook when he told them to put it away and keep it, that a full meal was on its way as they were having company tonight and to tell the others they were invited as well. Just as they left and she knew he was alone, she spoke to him.

"*What*? Where are you?"

"Quiet, please. I am just leaving the park down the street. We will be there soon. You are hearing my thoughts."

"How can that be?"

"*Tae-Tae, quit speaking out loud*! You talk to yourself just in your head. Do it now please."

"What do you mean? Like repeating things silently in your head to help remember them?"

"Yes, that's it. We have far more food than we will be able to eat, and it's attracting a small group of people, so we may be a bit late."

"How is this even possible?"

"Tae, we are from Wizard Mountain in the north. We know you decided to join for us, and after we decide about the others in the house, we will start making plans to get you all out of town safely."

"So my auntie is a wizard?"

"Yes, all three teams are awake. Now get them all ready to eat. We are just lost family, and we have food is all you need to say. See you soon!"

They had to deal with thirty some odd people, giving them food and a mental push away and no memory of where they got the food. After that, they put a null field around them. If they had not, people would keep coming to the smell of the food. They reached the corner and could see the house. The curtains were pulled, and some light was slipping out around the edges.

They reached out and got the count of people waiting inside. Her cousins and the four strangers put in the house together. Her family was free of the darkness that was spreading all over the inner city. However, the others were a different story. The three girls were terrified of Antwan and hated him for putting them on the street, hooking for food. They had a lot of anger and hate in them. Antwan was able to run his girls without problems from the leaders of the B-Cs by passing information to them on the people living in his four-block area. He had a black soul and carried a darkness with him wherever he went. Antwan's girls were Sadie (eighteen), Sheila (eighteen), and Bree (sixteen). None of them were part of his family, just his string of girls.

"Well, Antwan will need to be dealt with in some way. Ideas on what we will do with him? The girls are free to make up their own minds after they understand they are free to do so."

"Yes, Tae and the rest of the family are ready to leave before we arrive but had no way out."

So Juan led them the rest of the way to the house, and they entered with all the food.

They entered, and everyone was introduced. They sat down to eat. They had normal family talk as they ate. What happened to the rest of the people on each side? For Gloria, it was a sad tale of death and hunger over the last year. At least now the B-Cs had food and they were living. Then Tae-Tae told them how he joined the army today. At that, Antwan's head came up. Something new. All three of the team took note of his reactions. The meal was coming to an end. Antwan said he was going out for a smoke. Juan asked if he would like some company as he liked to smoke as well. They went out together.

The backyard was dark and cool as they opened the door and stepped out into the darkness. Juan was quick to light Antwan's and his cigarettes. It was easy to get permission to enter the unsuspecting minds of the sleeping people.

"Will you be open and truthful with me, Antwan, if I ask you about living here under the B-Cs?"

"Sure. Are you thinking of staying?"

"If we can find the right setup, yes."

With that one word to state agreement, Juan and the others linked. It had opened the door to all his thoughts. Nasty and dirty and cruel. It was like swimming naked in a cesspool of human waste. Juan started at once to read the history of his time there in the city. The history of the girls was passed to Valerie to use to get them free, and Juan learned of the informant to the leaders of the B-Cs as well. They decided it was not good for him to just disappear, so they started to place blocks on him to keep him from talking about this night. They could not take his memories. But like others, they could make it so they cannot talk about them and everything they have seen. From this place in time, anything that had to do with the team and family was sealed. They could try to say things, but it would come out as nonsense. They could now talk more freely to the others if they wished to.

"Tae, do not respond. I have a few things to tell you and the rest of the family. I am going to speak in their minds as well." Valerie then asked the others if they would allow her to speak to them openly. They all said yes. She opened to each of them, slowly staring at Gloria then the girls.

"Gloria, can you hear me?"

"Yes, dear, I am not that hard of hearing yet."

"I know that, but it's not hearing that I meant. Please do not speak. Look at me. What do you see? But don't say anything, please!"

"What?"

"Do not speak. Just think and look again. Think what you see!"

"This is silly."

"Just think what you see!"

She was looking at Valerie the whole time.

"It's not when you understand. I have not spoken one word to you since you agreed to be open with me. Do you see me talking now?"

"Oh my god, I can hear your thoughts and you mine!"

"Yes, and now I want you to just listen or talk with Tae-Tae while I bring the girls in the link as well."

In just a minute, she had the girls linked in as well.

"Okay, now you know our secret. We are from Wizard Mountain, and we defeated Blaine when he came north. We promised to come help him when it was needed, so we are here now. I have known you're all here and alive because I visit you all in your dreams. Do you remember the times you see me in your dreams?"

With words and nods, they all remember them.

Tae said, "That is how you found us?"

Juan came up and spoke to them about what was going to happen next. He told them not to worry about Antwan as he would remember everything, and no matter how hard he tried, he would not be able to tell anyone no matter how he attempted it!

Valerie moved over to talk to the girls and needed them to want to come with them. They had trust and fear problems that had to be overcome quickly if this was to work out well. The team hated the thought that they might have to leave them.

"Girls, there are a lot of things I'd like to tell you. First, we need to trust each other, and you ate our food and are wondering what the cost is going to be. Okay, so here it is the price of our food and as much more as you can eat is your silence on how and what we are doing here. That's it. Nothing more. However, if you will give a little more, we will give you something with even greater value! Are you willing to hear what we offer?"

Sheila was the hard one of the group and spoke for them all by the others' consent.

"We know that nothing is free, so why should we trust you complete strangers?"

"Okay, here goes. First, we will take you off the streets tonight, and you will never have to do anything of that sort again unless you wish to. Bree has had it the worst, and we want to give her back the feeling that it is her body and not Antwan's toy to pass around! Selling yourselves for food for him is over as of right now. We are from Wizard Mountain, and if you will trust us, we will take you away with us when we leave."

Bree started crying, and the other two yelled, "How do you know these things?"

"*All of you look at me.*"

With that mental yell, they all looked at her. Then with just her mind, she told them the family history in just over ten seconds. Bree spoke first.

"You're not talking, but I heard every word!"

"Yes, how long did I speak?"

Sadie answered for the first time and knew to just think. "I am not sure, but it seemed like forty-five minutes or more."

"Had I used words and my voice, yes, but at the speed of thought, it was just a bit over ten seconds!"

Bree again asked, "What's it going to cost us? Really, what do we have to do?"

"Bree, please do not talk. Just think of what you want to know. I can hear it. And in some ways, it will sound the same, but truly it is not. Each day, all members of the family are required to meditate for one hour. The choice is yours, morning or after dinner. Everyone has a job to do each day. Twice a year, everyone is required to help plant and later harvest our crops. The only other requirement is combat training and learning how to use bows and arrows. Last is hand-to-hand combat. Everyone over the age of thirteen is required to do these things. However, after we get you out of here, it will be your choice if you want to join the family or go your own way."

"How can we all hear you as I can hear everyone but Antwan now?"

"Really, that's amazing. You should not be able to hear them yet."

"Bree, Valerie and Berry and myself are awake, and it seems that you are as well. I think it's the shock of this meeting and your past that has awoken you so fast. Will you do something for me please?"

"What do you want?"

"Ask Antwan a question that you won't know if he's lying to you! Then ask one you know he will lie to you about!"

She asked him the questions, and he lied on each try. Frustrated, she asked one more. "Antwan, you say you love all three of us. Which one do you love the most?"

Antwan, like everyone when hearing the question, thought of the truth and then decided to tell the truth or a lie. All three girls saw in his mind that he had been looking for four new girls so he could put them all out as they all looked used up and ugly to him now. They were only good for sucking his member now.

"Bree, you know it's you as I like my girls young!"

All of them said to the team, "What do you want us to do so we can go with you when you leave?"

Juan turned and told Antwan to go sit in the chair in the corner and sleep. Antwan walked over, sat down, and was asleep at once.

Juan then took over the discussion, and for what seemed like hours, he told everyone what was needed. When it was over, the coffee they had been drinking was still hot. They made plans for gathering information and having dinner each night. Juan would stay near Tae-Tae, keeping him safe. Danny was watching the girls, and Valerie was with her family, getting them all ready to leave. She was looking for others who would be able and willing to leave with them. There was not much going on this far from the front in the hills. A few people, mostly loners, came by, wanting to know who the extra people were that had been seen yesterday and again this morning. After about three hours, Val had these few going and getting the others like them living under the very nose of the B-Cs. They were what they had come to find the ones wanting and needing help to get out. By the end of the second day, there were over fifteen of them, all loners.

* * *

Tae-Tae reported to his training unit, and Juan blurred himself so no one ever looked his way. He stayed in the sidelines, never in groups, just keeping a lookout for danger to Tae-Tae. They kept a link open, and so Juan saw and heard everything Tae did. Nothing special happened at first. Once Tae was evaluated and sent to his training officer, Juan took special notice. Due to the poor food he had been getting, Tae-Tae was sent to a starter unit with light work and three meals a day, plus the food taken home each day as pay. They assigned you to your unit by the training officer name. Juan heard one name he had heard some four years ago at Coronado Beach at BUD/S training. Jamal, master sergeant, had been his training officer. In the link, he instructed Tae to ask one of the other recruits about Jamal. The answer confirmed it was his old training officer. The other recruit told Tae of Jamal's SEAL training, and only the best fit and strongest got sent to his group for advance training. The rest of the day was routine. They did learn that Jamal would take Thursdays off and go away for a full day. As it happened, this was Wednesday, and Jamal was leaving at the end of the day. They had learned that the B-Cs tried to follow him and failed every time, losing him in the same place every time, at Sunset and Vine just in sight of the Hollywood sign.

"Tae-Tae, you need to go find Jamal and give him this message for me, and then you will be alone for the rest of the day. Berry is going to link with you if you need anything or help."

"Sure, I am okay. Berry is already in the link. What is it you need me to do?"

"You need to talk with Jamal and tell him Juan from eighteen will join him tonight at the meeting place. Just that, nothing more. Do not wait for an answer. Just go back to your duties and then go straight home."

"All right. What do I tell the others?"

"Nothing. They already know. Be safe. See you tomorrow before you leave for home."

Juan then turned and left the training camp. He headed to the city and was gone from sight in no time.

CHAPTER 36

Extra SEALs

Bryce and Jamal had been meeting in the park ever since they had split up to check out the city. They had been on thirty-day leave after their last deployment in the Middle East. The mission had been a success. The victory had come with heavy losses to the team with three members gone, two dead and one wounded so badly that his return to the team or active duty was unknown at the time they left on their leave.

They would be going to San Diego after their leave to rebuild the team. They would pick new members and start training protocols so the team would be ready when needed. Once they had this done, they'd be put back in the rotation with the other teams. There were two other team members that had taken their leave and gone to Wisconsin, the other to Brownsville, Texas. They tried to reach them after the event. They had no success in doing so. As the city tore itself apart in the days after the event, they kept hidden and gathered supplies they would need. After a few weeks, it was clear that the gangs would be in control of the intercity area while the police in the South Bay had already taken control and set up a strong group in that area. They had a great food source of fish fresh every day. Seeing how things were going, they decided to split up and check out the two groups that seemed to be taking over the city. It was in the early days when the Bloods and the Crips joined together and started to attack any other groups that showed any resistance to their rule. This included the police. Soon the remaining officers fled the city, many going to the South Bay and taken in with open arms. It was at this time that they decided to meet once a week in the park. They both knew of the trouble in the San Fernando Valley. They were getting stronger as they had access to both food they grew and the fish from the sea. Blaine, the leader, was a combat specialist from the Bid Red *One*, a major with over ten years' experience. He had earned his rank at a very early age by winning many battles in the fields of war all over the world. Well-liked by his men, they kept a watch as he closed the three main passes into his valley. They had the strongest force in the city until something happened to the north and they lost a lot of men about six months ago. They had heard the story of them fighting the wizards in the central valley and the one about the admiral with the highly trained force of men and women who had defeated Blaine and his troops. They tended to believe the story of the admiral. They both felt it was time to make a choice and leave the city or take a side. They were ready to get out before the battle began. They needed a place to go.

* * *

Jamal was first to arrive at the sign at this trip. Bryce was about three hours late. They shared a meal Jamal had ready and a drink. Neither drank when in the cities.as they never let their guards down unless they were together. It was on the second drink when Bryce saw the lone man walking right toward them. They took cover and started to watch the man walk straight toward them. It was clear he was coming right to the camp at the sign. Bryce took out his sidearm and placed the silencer on the barrel and ready his shot.

"Wait, don't shoot."

"What the hell? He knows we are here. We can't let him leave."

"I didn't think much of it at the time, but just before I left the training camp, a new recruit came up to me. Said he had a message for me. He said Juan from eighteen will join him tonight at the meeting place. Then he turned and walk away."

Coming up the hill, Juan was waiting to hear his name as he slowly came up the hill. He had seen the other put the silencer on the pistol as they took cover. He now knew that Bryce was his companion.

He yelled up to the camp, "Jamal, it's me, Juan from eighteen. Is that Bryce with you? Please don't let him shoot me!"

The two just looked at him and said, "Do you know a Juan from eighteen?"

I trained a Juan years ago. Not sure if it's him or not. The man I trained did go to—"

"I went to O'Brian's team. I can hear everything you two are saying as well as thinking! I come to you for help and to give it as well."

They were both at a loss as they kept a very close watch on their back trails when coming to meet at the park. So this man claiming to be a member of eighteen was odd at best. They went to using hand signals so he could not hear them. They would wait to see who he was before taking any action. They got set and were waiting for him to get closer.

"It's nice that you will wait to see who I really am. I told you, I could hear you and also your thoughts. If I were you, I would not have believed that as well. It is true, however. Jamal, the recruit was telling you the truth. I was above the back street where you always lost the tail they put on you. I do not have time. You will need to believe me, so I am just going to sneak up behind you and not kill you, okay?"

Bryce was still not sure of the man they were watching walk up the hill.

"Why should we let you do that? We can see you in an open field about two hundred yards in front of us right now!"

As they both took aim on the man down the hill thinking he was a real threat, just waiting for some sign, they heard him speak again from right behind them.

"Look again. Am I there or sitting right behind you?"

They spun around and tried to lift their guns but found them too heavy to move.

Juan was sitting there with a big smile on his face, looking at Jamal.

"Jamal, you taught me to never be where the enemy thought you were. My time on the mountain has given me new skills as you have just had to deal with. Now if you will both put your weapons away, we can talk."

They were so unnerved, they put their guns away and listened to Juan. Jamal knew him at once, seeing him up close. Bryce did as well once they got a good look at him. They also put their guns away without a problem.

"Juan, how did you get behind us when we had you under our guns the whole time?"

"As I told you, I could hear your words and thoughts the whole time. I put the man on the hill for you to keep an eye on. I was behind you all the time, coming down from the small cave on the hill."

"So, Juan, Jamal and I want to know which side you're on."

"We are here to save the group in the valley. We need growers more than soldiers. And Blaine would have been able to defend this valley for years if they had stayed here and not came north to our mountain! William stopped the killing once he saw us saving them from what's about to happen. First time he ever gave quarter before it was asked for."

"Who's William?"

"Why, the wizard, of course."

The two started talking about the bet they had. Bryce was saying how magic could be more real than the admiral was. To the side. Juan started to laugh at them. What's so funny, Sergeant?"

"Well, if I have this right, you're trying to settle a bet on which of the two scary figures to the north is real. Is that right?"

As one, they said yes. Juan laughed all the more.

"Well, I think I can help. Back in the valley, depending on what the subject is, they take turns being in charge."

"So there are two and they share a power."

"No, they are the same person. He is called by both names because there has never been in a fair fight. We are always outnumbered, and we have never lost. In all this time, this is the first time we have come to aid another group that is not part of the family."

So Juan told them the story of the fight back to the coast of California and at Avila Beach. Then the trek to the mountains where they found the team in the same spot they had just been in with Juan. He told them about the people they brought with them and about the islanders that were coming as well.

"So why did you want to meet us?"

"We are hoping you can give us information, and we hope you will come back with us and, if you like what we offer, join the family."

"So who's in charge?"

"There are lead people in all area there because they are the best for the jobs and they want it. The council is in charge of the overall running of the family. They meet once a week and can meet at any time it is needed."

"How many sit on this counscil, and how are they chosen?"

"It's hard to explain, but everyone over the age of thirteen is allowed a voice in the meeting, and the whole body of the people make up the council. No new orders are given unless the people all agree on it. We use the constitution and the bill of rights as our base. It's a new world out here, and we aim to make it better than the old one.

"When John got us to the camp, William had been waiting for us. He had seen us in his dreams, and now he is the admiral we follow. We need information, and we need to get to our positions for the battle. It is coming very soon, we believe."

"Positions?"

"Yes, we have three teams working in the city already. More units are moving in as we speak, and when the battle starts, our job will be to disrupt their supplies lines. And once we have enough troops, we will attack their rear areas, causing even more confusion in their ranks."

Jamal spoke up. "I think we'd like to stay for that if we can."

They heard a new voice at that time.

"John has told me that we can trust them, and I believe them as well. You send Valerie and Berry back. You take over all command of the rear. Use them as you see best, and they are willing to take it on. Thank you. You men will make a great addition to the family!"

"Do we want to know who that was?"

"It was the admiral. Today, after the battle, we will give you the oath if you wish to stay in the family. Well, I can talk to you at any time I want now unless you block me out. No matter how strong a person is, they cannot force their way into your mind. And if you feel like someone or thing is trying to get in, just say 'I want quiet now!' In your head or out loud. And it will close you minds from intruders. Try it one at a time please."

Soon Juan was on his way back to Tae-Tae's house. Everyone there knew what he had done. They had started planning to leave. Tae-Tae had seen a lot of things, and it was time to leave. They had given him a full day off. By the time they knew he was gone, they were far up in the hills east of Pasadena. The group was now almost one hundred people trying to escape the city. They would be leaving one hour after curfew tonight!

* * *

Chelsey had been poking around the market in her normal fashion. The seller who told her about Lucy asked if she had found her.

"Yes, thank you. We are working out a deal. She has access to a few other items I may trade for. You were a great help to me, so if you need anything I can help with, I will make you a great deal!"

They talked a bit when the police patrol walked by. She excused herself and turned to walk the same way the police were going. She would stop behind them or go just past them, always staying close so she could hear them talking. Just before they reached the end of the stalls, they stopped at a food vendor to inquire of special food items. The vendor saw her and called her over. She turned and went over to the three men.

"Yes?"

"Chelsey, these men are looking for specials foods for a formal dinner they are having soon."

"Well, I still have a few items that I may be willing to trade for. Do you know what they want or need?"

The lead officer answered, "Well, not really. They asked to find someone and bring them to the office if they'd be willing. Would you be willing?"

"Yes. As you know, food has a limited shelf life, so we need to do this soon. When did they want to see me?"

"Is now okay? The only reason we came down today was to find a source of food items."

She called Lucy. "They are looking for special food items. I am going to the station to trade my food items to them now."

"That is great. Just be a trader. Only ask about the trade. Listen to everything and glance at as many maps and papers as you can. Do not stare at anything or person unless they are talking to you, understand?"

"Yes, I do."

"Okay, we will be linked from this point on. Be a good trader just like normal. Good luck."

The time it took still amazed her. That entire talk was only seconds without any delay. She agreed, and they started back to the life guard station which had the best view of the area. They walked in just before noon that day. After about ten minutes, a large man of about six-foot three inches came in with a woman in tow.

"Are you the vendor with the specials food items?"

"Yes, I am, but I'm not a vendor. I sell to them as well. My name is Chelsey. And I have access to a few hard to find foods."

"Sorry, Chelsey. My name is Chester. I am third in command, and it fell to me to get this dinner ready on short notice. This woman is the head cook. If you and Freida will make a list of the things you can get and we want, I will see that you get paid for the goods when delivered. Is that acceptable to you?"

"Why, yes, Chester. It sounds very good. How soon will you need the items we agree on?"

"The dinner will be held within the next two weeks as soon as we get the things we need. After that, it would be too late."

With that, he took a long look at Chelsey, making her feel a bit afraid that he knew what she came for.

"Settle down. You're safe. He likes what he sees and is looking forward to your next meeting. He is a man, and you are one of the best-looking women he has seen in a year. And he is single."

Hearing Lucy laughing in her head, she turned to Freida. They started going over what they had for a menu and what they needed. As it turned out, this would take most of her stores as she was likely not going to be staying after this deal. She made good but not unreasonable request for payment. Chelsey was given a low-level password so she could come and go in the main compound. Chester had gotten it for her. He came back, and the three went over the items needed. Chelsey said it would be at least three days together to bring the items into town. They offered her protection, but she declined for safety reasons of her own. Before Chester let her leave, they had dinner together. He was interested in her. They would spend a lot of time together in the next week.

"Told you he has the hots for you. If you want some private time, you know how to get it."

"Yes, he is one of the nicest males I've ever met before or after the event, as you call it."

* * *

In the three days since Blaine took control of the defenses, the morale of the troops had gone back up. Most still believed they would lose, but now at least they had a chance. The three new captains were tough. One of the old commanders took an issue with Joy's orders one day to completely change his station. She told him to do it or face the consequents of his choice. That was his last mistake.

"I am willing to face anything you can do to me, bitch!"

"Okay, except watch post, everyone gather round. Your ex-commander is going to demonstrate what happens to soldiers that do not obey orders from me. Asshole, step into the ring. If you can pin me to the ground, you win!"

"This will be fast and fun!"

For the next ten minutes, Joy beat him silly. He finally fell over after trying to get up one more time.

"Medics! The rest of you get back to work, or do you need a seconded lesson?"

The men got back to work, and the talk started to spread to the guards and the other who had duties in other parts of the valley.

"What's your name, solider?"

"Hardy, sir. Sid Hardy."

"Well, Sid, I want you to know you are very important to Blaine and the soldiers in this valley. You have a heart. You knew after the second attempt that you would lose, but you did not stop! *Why*?"

"Sir, we are facing a losing battle already, so knowing I was going to lose made me mad and determined not to stop!"

"That's what I read as well. If you learn to control your anger and channel it, none of the enemies will defeat you, Major!"

"I think you missed my rank. After what I did, it should go down, not up, Captain."

"From this moment on, you are Major Sid Hardy. When I am not here, you are in charge. Is that understood?"

"Yes, sir. You have to convince Blaine of this promotion first."

"He already knows and has always had a better opinion of you than you know. Now I have real work to do at the other sections down the hill."

Trent was at the base camp building its new defenses and showing the soldiers how it would work. It was like nothing any of them had seen. So they were sure the attackers would be bewildered by them as well. The more they learned, they knew it was not going to be a one-day battle that the family liked. William called for a full meeting to discuss the changes they would need to implement to make the battle come out the way they wanted.

William had Peter, O'Brian, Jake, Lucy, Joy, Oliver, and all the valley officers and council members. He had family members with them to link them all into the family.

"Can everyone hear me?"

The amazing thing about the link was that it was always static-free so things went quickly.

"First, I want everyone to know that our response will be hidden right up to the time we engage the invaders. They must not lose faith in us. We will be there just as things look the worst for them. Blaine knows what this will do to the invaders. We have many advantages they have no answer for. The one thing they have is many more soldiers than you have here. We will know the time of the first attack! The day before I will arrive in the valley with our troops to give you all the support you will need. I have already started them on their way. Your jobs are to find a way to make them pay for the passes for at least two days. They will need to take another full day to reach the main camp where we have our most powerful assets to bring to bear on them. What we need to know is what you need to make this happen. We will make sure you have it! And last, I will be flying in the day before as well. There is a special reason for this, and if you need to know, you will remember they are coming for your food and women. We are coming to stop them at all cost. Now the family members there will take over. See you soon. We are going to win!"

It was later that the council learned that the very last was heard by everyone in the valley, including the enemy scouts they knew were there. The talk started at once, and the whole valley was spreading the story that the wizards were coming. The story kept getting bigger with each retelling. The story was in the two camps by the end of the day.

"Oliver, did we get the reaction we wanted?"

"Oh, yes. The visitors got the reaction from the dark one at once. They have a large force in Blaine's camp, and they have ordered them to kill you when you arrive. They also passed the word to attack as soon as possible."

"Great. Things are looking good. Tell our friends thank you. Then get ready. We leave in the morning."

Things were coming together as the three teams had all started to draw back to their positions and prepare for the attack. The only person not getting out of danger was Chelsey. In her dream last night, she had a message for Lucy.

"Lucy, I know you told me to get away and return to the market so we can leave. Sorry, I can't. Chester has asked me to go with him up the coast. It seems that they do not trust the B-Cs and are sending a third force up the coast. I hope to learn the purpose of this move and will let you know as I know it myself."

Then she was gone. She even broke the link as Lucy had taught her.

That night, after consulting with all the different missions they had running, William had them move to the San Fernando Valley or their assigned positions to await the attack. The others he set to making plans to be in position to lend any and all support they might need.

With few noted exceptions, every team joined Blaine in making the fallback positions stronger than the one before it.

This stage had been so deceptive to every group that has faced it. All of them had superior numbers anywhere from three to one, or as in Lone Pine, the number there was finally set at fifty to one at the best count of the dead there. All of them kept rushing to the next wall where a great many of them would die. And the defenders kept getting stronger at each stage. Going over all of this, Blaine learned that his plan was a sound and effective one. Just not against wizards! He saw the strength in it and how it gave them a force multiplier as well. At the three passes, they had made very strong defensive positions. And then they started making the five lines below them. All of which the enemy would have to get past to reach the main camp. Between each wall, the kill zones kept getting bigger after each planned fallback.

At first, Blaine was resistant to the constant retreats as it made them look even weaker than they were. He believed this would encourage the attackers to advance as fast as possible, allowing them to overrun them long before they reached the next defensive wall. At this point, he was no longer going along with the plan and advice of the teams.

"Blaine, please take a break and speak with me."

Blaine was shocked to have William speak to him at this time and in this fashion. They were set to have a council meeting later tonight. This was also the first time he had spoken to Blaine in this way. It was just about suppertime. He excused himself and got a water and some food and walked off a distance to be alone.

"As you get closer to being awake, this will be easier for you and the rest of us. This will make the distance between us seem as nothing."

"I understand, but why not wait for the meeting after dinner tonight as always?"

"Because you are fighting the battle plan we are going to use. It is not going to be the same as the one you faced, but it is the same basic plan, and if fully supported, it will carry the day just as you lost. So will they. Tell me why you do not feel this way."

"Well, we are not wizards. And if we do not make them pay more than you did to us, we will not make it to the third stage and the first really big open field. I do not have the men to hold that long. The information I have is that they will open the battle on the three main passes with at least fifty thousand men. How can we hold that many men back with your quick retreat plans?"

"I want you to remember the entire battle from the farm to the last wall at the main camp if you would, please."

William took the block from Blaine's mind and looked to see the strange look on his face as the full memory returned.

"Why did you do this to me? My memories are back, and we are not trained to fight in this manner. How can we do it like you did it to me?"

"When this is over, many of the people here on both sides will take the oath and become part of family. Right now, we all think of you as the first. I cannot tell you details, but we have been moving support troops into the hills for the last two weeks. In the morning, I am sending five thousands troops to the main camp. And as you know, I will be there in person the day before the attack begins."

"Yes. Is that wise? We believe there are spies and agents in our main camp. It will be very dangerous for you."

"Yes it will be, and it won't be the last time. It is being done to get them to show themselves, and we hope to uncover the real threat to us. By getting them to move the day before they can launch their true assault, we have the advantage. So their third column in our ranks is exposed."

"How is that going to work? They have been here, and we have not found a one, and the men I have looking are the best."

"Yes, but are they awake?"

"How will that help them?"

"Do you remember when near the end, you wondered how we always had an answer for your changes in plans? Over half of us were awake at that time. Now we are over eighty percent awake, and all are linked. Anyone who has a thought of anything like a violent action will be pinpointed at once, and there are other safeties we can't talk about. Do not worry. I will be safe. Now you need to get all of your people behind this defense. You can tell them that we will be there when we are needed most! And our troops will be the rear guard on all of the planed fallbacks. Just like the one you faced. The only difference is you must hold the passes for at least thirty-six hours. And then hold the third position until dawn of the third day. They will know by that time all of our support except the last ones. Just as they think they have you, we will unleash all our secret support and in the open for all to see. With our help, if you can hold to this timeline, they will have lost on the first day just like you did."

"So you don't plan to do this in one day, and we will need to hold as I thought, but you already knew this."

"Yes, we all know this. Can I have your support or not?"

"Yes, you do."

"Fine. This was a very good three-minute talk."

"Three minutes?"

"Yes, you need to eat and get back to work. It's going to be the same as your battle with us, just longer. We need the battle to last four days or longer, and we win. This is our biggest advantage over our foes, and soon you will be awake and many others. And when that happens, the council is done, for the way it is working now is old world, and it's time its past."

From that time forward, the lines went up faster, and the training for the battle began with only seven or eight days left. The troops responded to Blaine, and the team members and things started to come together. The battle of Los Angeles was about to start!

CHAPTER 37

Battle of Los Angeles

THE TWO BIGGEST gangs in LA and the remnants of the LA police departments almost equaled to the gang's numbers of some twenty thousand soldiers while the South Bay police numbers were just about fifteen thousand police officers and military men. And after their few conflicts, they joined together to move on the San Fernando Valley settlement for their farms and food stores. In the last few months, both of these groups had become aware that the large well-trained force they had in the San Fernando Valley had suffered a great defeat and was no longer a threat to them. So they started making plans to go over and get the farms and other resources. The people in the valley had built a farm system second only to the farms of Wizard Mountain.

* * *

Chelsey was now in Malibu and had reported that the troops would soon start up Kanan Dume Road and come into the valley from behind. She had spent two days getting this information. At the same time, the South Bay troops had been filling up the east and west passes with troops. The only purpose was to make them believe that the main attacks would be at these points as they were the weakest points. They moved over five thousand men into each pass. They had more than enough men to overrun the defenses they had there. The plan was to get men moved away from the main pass along the five freeways. The one thing that helped the valley secure the San Fernando Valley was the event happened while the freeway system was still full of cars and trucks. And they have not been moved as there was no good or easy way to do so. As a result, all the freeways were of no use for traveling. Blaine had seen this as his first line of defense. He had set good cover fire positions on the ramps and larger positions on the side roads that crossed the passes. These were the places where the true attack would hit them, trying to drive a wedge down the middle of the valley. They knew Blaine had around ten thousand men. He had sent five to the middle pass and twenty-five to the east and west sides unknown to the B-Cs and the South Bay forces. Trent had an extra two thousand men which he split in the same percentages as Blaine had. The difference was they were not in the defensive positions. They were on the outside. They had taken hiding places on the LA side of the hills. They would attack from behind only if the position they had was in grave danger of being overran before they were ready. Then when it was time for Blaine's people to fall back, the wizards would fill their places long enough for them to make it safely to the next wall. They had been told that they needed to hold the first days of attack for at least thirty-six hours before they would fall back.

After all the supplies had been dropped off and only the men posted there were left, Blaine called them all to a meeting, even the guards. They thought this dangerous as there had been exchanges of fire already. He made them all come anyhow. They didn't know that Juan and Jamal and Bryce had taken over their watches for this small time. During this time, they had killed every scout and sniper in the area. By the time the B-Cs replaced their eyes, the thousand men Juan had would be well hidden and waiting for the counterattack.

At the meeting, Blaine told his men of the wizards waiting out in the woods and their job at this post. They were to make sure they held for the proper amount of time. Then they would filter in and cover their retreat to the next wall. Blaine moved to the other two posts and had similar meetings there as well. With everything in place, he moved back to the main camp to get ready for William's arrival the next day.

* * *

It was a warm clear day as the two Blackhawks and one Apache helicopter took off for the Van Nuys Airport. The two rapid response teams were in place and waiting for the arrival of his aircraft and the weapons he had brought for the main camp defenses.

Many people made their way to the airport to see the wizard that was coming to save them after his declaration to come and save them all. The time and place had been leaked by the team members to make sure as many people in the valley knew when and where he was going to enter the city. The fact that it was an airport gave rise to many stories, and more people moved to the airport if they had no work duties to keep them from it. Trent had the count at just over eight thousand people waiting to see if wizards coming to save them all were real!

It was just before 7:00 a.m. as the sun was just clearing the eastern most ridges of the mountains. The sun's orange rays filled the valleys to the west, filling them with the bright light of the day. The crowds could hear choppers coming out of the east, washed in the sun's rays, making them almost invisible. The real reason was to hide him from the dark one said to be working in the valley. The light hid him from them for a bit longer. The dark visitor knew him to be coming, but where and when was not clear.

The two Blackhawks landed with no problems and started unloading them at once. There was extra food and eight heavy machine guns (six fifty cals and two thirty cals) and ammo for them as well. More were in the trucks that arrived yesterday with the two thousand soldiers.

William was off to the side, talking with Blaine and the council members face-to-face for the first time. They moved toward the stage they had made on the edge of the landing field so they could be seen while trying to rally the people to the cause. The guns and food were on trucks, getting moved to their needed positions. The one member of the council had a request.

"William, the people are waiting to hear you speak today. We would like it if you waited and addressed them after this is over."

"No, let's go address them now and get them ready to fight if needed. You now have the guns and all the other items that were needed here."

They started to walk to the stage at the nearest hangar. The people started to move with them.

It was then that every awake person felt the dark visitor move as well!

William sent to all in the link, "We knew they would send agents and posed men in as well. If you feel threatened, blast your mind with the brightest light you can find in your memory." They all started looking at the crowd.

"Stop. Only the ones already on security should keep looking at the people. The rest of us should not use our eyes. However, we will keep looking. This is the same type of attack they used in Lone Pine. Come on, get it together. If you were not in Lone Pine, check the memories of others so you know what you'rr fleeing for!"

The snipers were in place as well as the inner ring of security he had sent in the last week for this very reason. They had an outer ring as well. They had been flying three flights a night with supplies and weapons for the last two weeks, as well as a total of 3,600 fighters kept out of sight, and many of them were moved to the far side of the hill where Juan assigned them to a post. They had nearly five thousand men that no one knew of. Their mission was to hide and let the attack force pass them and then stop all supplies from reaching the troops. Then at the critical moment, they would attack the rear of the B-C forces, causing chaos at their rear. So today the camp saw the choppers for the first time. It was meant to be a sign of hope! Its main goal was to break the fleeing that they could not win. Add to this later in the day the troop convoy with the reinforcements. They would reach the camp, swelling their ranks. It was just five hundred men, but they were all wizards to the San Fernando Valley. They reached the stage and were climbing up to address the people. His two teams were covering him. One was working the inner circle, the other on the outside.

William wondered how anything ever got done before people started waking up. Since the day of the event, his mental powers and its range kept getting stronger. The reach seemed to have no limits. If William knew you, he could reach you with his mind. The dreams now came at his bidding as well as on their own. These were generally dreams that others were having about him, both good and bad. He had set this up, making sure they had everyone here to trap the dark visitor and his agents.

* * *

The dark visitor had moved from the camps in Los Angeles to the valley as soon as he had arranged for the truce and combined assault on the valley. Since moving here, his work had been to weaken the resolve of the people living in the valley. It just happened to be Blaine's group. They had farms and a small herd of cattle and a few milk cows, hens, and goats, even a few sheep. They had much better food and more of it than most. So the visitor started to weaken the resolve of the weaker members, and it started to spread on its own!

He found a young man walking on the edge of the main camp one night in the dark, looking at the cooking pots. Probing his mind was not hard as hunger and cold had weakened him over the last few weeks. His plan was to get him to go into the camp and learn all he could and report back. As the dark visitor looked into his mind deeper, he could see that Ruben was not strong enough to do the job. The dark visitor reached out to its mate to inform her that he was going to replace Ruben and move into the village as one of them. He moved back to Ruben, and in just a few seconds, it was done. Ruben's body fell dead. He left the body where it fell. They made a link so she could see and hear everything he did while in his human form. He did not really change forms. They had the ability to change themselves so they looked like whatever they wished you to see. He walked out as Ruben. Ruben had been in the camp for three months by the time William came to the valley. As soon as they knew the time of his coming, the plan to kill him was set in motion!

After leaving the cell at Nellis, the visitor had been busy causing men to turn on any one they came across. He was the cause for much of the blood and killing from the first night. When he had gotten far enough away from the other two visitors, he was able to contact his mate. She informed him that the *one* was in the Las Vegas area, and he needed to find and kill him. They only knew that the one lived in the city and was aware of the attack before it happened. They also knew he was planning to leave the city that very day. The best hope was to find him and kill him as soon as they could! He searched all over the city, looking at any organize group. When he found one, he would move among them, causing fighting and disorder if he could. After five different groups, all came up empty. The last group he heard about was small and was not killing people on the far side of the valley in the southwest side. They just had a standoff with police and then took the police into their camp as a gang attacked them. In a short battle, they killed half of the gang. The visitor moved to the gang and flipped them to serve him. They took off after the five SUVs headed for Death Valley not too long ago. It was this group under his control that was racing to the gas station at the end of Blue Diamond Highway. They arrived just as Ben blew the station up. He was in the last truck and barely survived the blast. The one slipped away into the darkness of Death Valley, only to reappear in LA in opposition to plans to crush the best of the settlements in the area.

Getting the forty followers together was easy as there were many lost souls in the Los Angeles area since the event. Taking control over them and training them to kill for him was quick and easy. The plan was simple. Once they took the stage, they would all open fire from all directions.

All the pieces were in motion now. The four attack groups were on the march and would be in the valley the next day, and the attacks started the next morning or near dawn. On the next morning, the fourth group would enter from behind, unopposed from the north. And today he would complete his primary mission: find and eliminate the *one*!

He had to endure years of that bright prison cell to reach this point.

* * *

The council members and the *one* walked to the stage on the edge of the landing strip. The PA system was working, so everyone could hear the words of the councilmen and William. They walked slowly as William stopped to talk with anyone who talked to him.

The second assault team was on its way and should prove more than enough to get the job done. He had been waiting for this day since the *one* disappeared into Death Valley the night of the attack.

CHAPTER 38

The One Is Revealed

The party of men walking to the stage were halfway there, and the dark one still did not know which of them was the *one*! There were three councilmen and guards and four other men all walking to the raised stage. He wanted to identify the *one* so everyone would shoot at him. With the assailants all over the field, he would have no chance of missing him. The walk to the stage was taking too long. The plan was for them to move quickly to the stage and there raised above the rest as easy targets. Just then, the second wave came in. Cars were crashing the gates, firing from the windows. At the sound of gunfire, the people all started running for cover. Others pulled guns and started looking for a target to shoot at. With the attack on at the gates, the dark one gave the order to kill all the men headed to the stage. At that time, the forty men he had around the stage all started to fire at the stage and the men walking toward it. They started the run to the stage to kill everyone they found there.

William and the others all started to run at the first warning he received from the outer circle. They were running right at the gunmen appearing in front of them. Just as they got the order from the dark one to open fire on them, they dropped from sight! They ran and jumped into the defensive ditches William had dug last night on both sides of the stage. Once it was seen where they were, the site drew almost all of their fire. The snipers were taking out anyone who stuck their head up to high.

Back on the field, the dark one had his men all take cover because there were far more guns than they had expected to face. His information was there would be ten to fifteen men with guns here. It seemed that every adult had a gun. Most were poorly trained, but they were all around them. They would wait for the motorize group to break into the field and then let them clear a path to the stage and the *one*. As the battle raged, the noise from the outside grew more intense.

A great deal of the people that had come to see the wizard were in total panic and running all over the place. They drew fire from the attackers who shot at anything that ran their way. They were waiting to rush the stage and kill the councilmen and the *one*. Many people fell during the first few minutes of the fighting. This gave encouragement to the attackers.

Although many ran, more took the path into the trenches and the blinds set up last night. They all had weapons and started to return fire. The second force was finally starting to make entry at the north end of the field.

Daniel and the second rapid response team had a loose outer circle and were on watch for the second wave to come from the north. Having all the defensive sites all facing south gave them easy access to the airfield and the stage from the north. The defensive plan was to simply give them a token fight then fall away, letting them push forward into the airfield perimeter. Then they would hit the outer lines from behind hard and fast, trying to break through to the stage. They made it past their next wall in less than a minute. They pushed on past the next three as well. Not as fast as the first one, the leader of this group just checked the slower time to the loss of surprise and kept moving forward as fast as they could. And it took more time at each emplacement. When they took over each wall, they were expecting the soldiers to flee back to the airfield. They all ran out to the sides, disappearing into the burned homes there. Not back to the airfield as he thought they would do. By this time, there was just one more wall to breach to reach the landing strip and the stage. They had been losing cars at each wall and were down to the last one. It was needed to slam the stage. They had taken a few loses but were ready to strike the wall shortly.

* * *

Daniel now had twice the number of fighters and had started to follow, taking out the ones at the back with bows and arrows so as not to give themselves away. At every chance, they took them out and moved on. Up at the front, as soon as they started for the main wall, Daniel ordered guns when the shooting started. Now about to breach the last wall, they set the attack. The leader was still not aware he only had half of the men he started with. The situation at the stage was going bad, and the dark visitor forced his men in both positions to launch the final attack on the stage. With the mind of the dark one pushing them, they all started at the same time. They all became consumed with the thought of overrunning the valley and killing the *one*. William, with this, pushed all the remaining attackers. All charged the stage, breaking the wall and rising up in the airport. Some thirty people charged from many different places on the field, all heading right at the stage.

At the moment, the dark one opened his mind. William was aware of him. He then gave his orders as well. First was for all awake members to open fully and let their minds be seen by the dark one. That was over eighty people in the airfield alone. But there were over five thousand awake family members in the valley who also opened their minds. And back at all their base and camps, there were close to one hundred thousand open as well.

Ruben felt the surge in mental power but could not focus on it as it was coming from everywhere at once. William now had everyone shut down at the same time. The dark one went from massive overload to just one small mind behind him on the stage. He turned to find a single man standing there. Many of his men kept rising up to shoot him and fell dead as soon as they tried to shoot him. Some from farther out managed to get a few shots at him. These bullets either moved around him or just stopped and fell at his feet. The power he could sense was so low, and it felt deep. Then he realized the man was looking straight at him! Then he knew that this was the *one*. He opened his mind to send a shock to his brain. As soon as he started to open, the man hit him with something he never felt before. It was a blinding flash of light that looked to be a bolt of lightning, as that was William's inspiration. Ruben fell in a heap on the ground. Then for all to see was a ball of light from around his head. He fell back to the ground, screaming. A shock was sent through the link he shared with his mate. She at once sent supporting powers to him. The surge of power would have broken William's hold had the other two not been there and took part of the jolt. They could now feel the second one, and like planes used to do, they followed the line of power back to her position. She was still in the north above the San Francisco Bay.

"Oliver, did you feel that?"

"Yes."

"Okay. Did you get the people you need, the only ones and twos? If so, attack that one at once. I will contact you later!"

"We are doing it now."

"Daniel, take over the cleanup here. I am going to be busy for a while, I think."

"Already on it, boss."

Now his sole focus was the being standing at the far eastern side of the landing field. Daniel was quickly ending the battle, and the gunfire started to die down. William and six of the family's strongest members moved to stand around the man encased in the light. Three of them kept the light solidly around him, and the others supported William with all the power he needed to hold the head. The dark one had not tried to move since he managed to get back on his feet.

William talked out loud so as not to break their mental hold on the dark one. They could still feel the link between the other one in the north. Oliver and the others were pushing hard. They stopped her, and she would move and start sending power as soon as she moved. It would only take them a few seconds to find and push on her again. On the last move, she managed to get some kind of a shield that allowed her to send a steady but much weaker power to her mate.

After ten more minutes of fire, the attack was over only. Six of the attackers were still alive, and the valley had heavy losses as well.

William said, "We need a way to expose what he really is!"

Jan, one of the strongest family members, spoke up. "How can he keep this up? We can see the strain on his face. He's completely encased in light. He's not able to move!"

At that remark, William had another take his place in the ring.

"Is that really true? We have him, and it's a good cage we made. However, they are still connected, and he is still drawing power from the other one. If the light is as complete as we think, they should not be able to still have the link. We hit him with everything we have, and still he just stands there, not moving."

"Well, what's the key we're missing?"

"First, I think he can move, but for some reason, he won't even try. We need to know why."

"What was that you said, Jan?"

"He has no physical injuries, but he never moved since your first strike. He just stood up."

"Thomas Covenant. It's like Thomas Covenant, the Unbeliever. A book I read many years ago. A man is somehow shifted to another world where he is the promised savior. The enemy tracks him by his shoes on the ground."

"I don't understand. How is that relevant to us?"

"It's the ground. They are connected by the ground."

William then opened again to the family in the valley.

"Can any of you lift?"

"I can lift. I just started about a month ago."

"Hector, how much can you lift?"

"It's not much. It's still new to me."

"That's okay. You will have help. You will lift, and we will give you all the strength you need. I will need three to link and support Hector now."

The plan was to lift the dark one off the ground, allowing the light to truly encompass him, breaking his contact with the ground and hopefully the other one.

It took a little time, and then Hector signaled he was ready for the lift. By this time, there were ten of the strongest family members standing by to give whatever help was needed.

Time passed, and after three minutes, Hector spoke.

"I can feel him get lighter, but the weight is greater than it looks."

"Okay, Hector, we are going to have you lead a high lift. You will be the focal point and lead us, okay?"

"All right, sir. When you're ready, I am open."

So William got the family members there to form a link with Hector. Lifting was a new skill, and few even knew about it. The link was formed, and they were ready to try again as there was still a small amount of the large gun battle going on back near the stage.

Again Hector signaled, and they prepared for the lift. This time, the dark visitor started to rise up! His eyes popped open at the first upward movement. Fear and amazement flashed on his face and through his thoughts. Even more astonished was his mate. She reacted to this and gave away her position, and Oliver's team attacked her again with better results. In just under five seconds, both feet cleared the ground. Instantly, the light cage made a complete case around the dark one, and Hector dropped the lift.

He started screaming and fell to the ground. He was now totally alone and cut off from his mate and she from him. William could read this thoughts, as could every other family member. It was fear and panic. He also started to shimmer. William had everyone back away for safety. Then as it became clear, he opened to everyone he could reach.

"This is William, or as most know me, the wizard. If you're in the airfield, come and see the real enemy. This is one of the beings that caused the collapse of our world. Come look. It's safe. See who and what we are fighting."

The dark one shimmered for a full two minutes, and slowly he grew bigger and darker and totally not of the earth. His true form was revealed to everyone on the field and to everyone linked. The screaming was a mental blast as a real scream. With only a few hard-core fighters left, the attack failed, and order was restored.

They moved the dark one to the school and placed him in the assembly hall where anyone could go and look at him. The cage of light was to keep the dark one cut off in bright light at all times. After they cut him off from his mate, he lost his hold on his disguise. He was so weak that it only took one person to hold the entire cage now and could do so for up to six hours. William set the watches at two hours and alway in three-person groups.

Blaine was busy making final preparations for the coming battle. He was about to try to hold back an overwhelming force. At best, they had a six to one underdog. Even with all the extra help, they still would need a miracle. He was thinking what they needed were real wizards to win this battle.

CHAPTER 39

Battle for Southern California

THE NEXT MORNING, the line to see the alien was still over two hours long! An alien was there and most likely responsible for the destruction of the world's governments and the current state of affairs. The people of the San Fernando Valley got mad, and that was a good thing. It was going to give them the extra strength to fight the coming battle. This was something Blaine needed and could give him the edge he was looking for. Tomorrow or the next day, they would face the attack from the army coming over the passes from Los Angeles.

* * *

During the night, Lucy received a dream from Chelsey. She finally had the mission of the fourth column. It was to start moving up Kanan Dume Road to Calabasas at first light and should reach the top by the end of the first day of battle. From there, it was clear they would attack from the rear. Same plan that Blaine tried. This would have worked if they had not discovered it in time. Lucy passed the information onto the family.

"Lucy, we are working on ways to counter this move and will pass the information to you as soon as we can. We need you to get

Chelsey out of there. Have her move north up the coast road. We are sending an RR team to pick her up. She will be safe with them. I had a dream about her, and she is going to be very important to us in the coming months. They will be looking for her. Keep her safe. She will know them by the code word *compus*!

* * *

In Los Angeles, the B-Cs were massed at the main pass into the valley with over twenty-five thousand men waiting to push straight down to the school at the far end of the valley. While at the east and west end, the police from the South Bay had over eight thousand men, waiting to launch the opening assault on the valley. Blaine had been able to increase his force to nearly twenty thousand men after they saw the attack at the airfield and the capture of the dark one who was still on display in the meeting room. Now their only hope was William's plan. He knew the plan to be sound, and he had lost to it in the mountains. He had to trust it. He took stock in the fact in how it had defeated him. That and the knowledge that he was better than the forces he would soon face. Whatever help William had in mind was still unknown. So as the battle would start in the morning, he and his men would be on their own.

For William and the family, it was a crisis point as well. This would be the true coming out party for them. They would be fighting a battle far from home against a larger force with mostly unknown abilities on their home ground. Would the plan work? And even if it did, would it be enough? Added to this was the fourth force moving up the canyon behind them that had to be stopped or they would all lose. How many lives would it cost? And could they afford to lose them? William knew he needed as many of the people on both sides as he could get for the real battles to come later.

After a quick link with all the SEALs and others, they devised a plan and sent Lucy the details and gave her the instruction for Chelsey. They already started on getting the manpower together, and it would need great timing to pull it off on such short notice. Their plan was simple but on such short notice, and so little assets were left to counter this other threat on the coast road. It had to be timed just right to work.

As the dawn was approaching over the mountains to the east, Blaine was worried as the light was spilling over the tops and down the hills. As he was going over the plan, more and more troubling thoughts were crawling in his mind. Trent spoke to him.

"Don't worry, Blaine. I have the times and will tell you if and when you need help. Just remember, you had a five to one advantage over us when we used this very same battle plan when we defeated you. The plan works. Trust your memory of your loss to us."

In the three days since he was back in control, he had them changing the position and personnel in the passes to men he knew would follow orders and held them as long as he needed. He had sent squads over the top and cleared the enemy troops off the top of the passes and moved his gun placements so they were shooting downhill. If he managed to hold the first day as they needed him to, as soon as it was dark, they would move back to the other positions down the hills for the next day's attack. They only had to hold about six hours the next day. Then they would fall back to the first real wall they hoped to finish before they started back to them.

On the other side of the pass, the three different groups had been moving all day to get into the positions before the dawn attacks. The South Bay forces made a lot of noise in their passing. They had gotten reports of the defenses at the tops and the much stronger walls about a mile lower than the pass. They saw no evidence of the changes Blaine had made, and none of the family hiding there were found at any of the locations. So the family part in the coming battle was still a secret. The dark visitor was still in a near coma, just standing and not moving. While encased, he was unable to communicate to his agents. As a result, they moved forward with their plans, unaware of what they faced in the coming battle. Their plan was to overwhelm the passes and then rush the walls. Here they wished to overrun the walls and scatter the defenders. They hoped to take the valley by dinnertime. Had Blaine not made the changes and the family not come to their aid, their attract would have succeeded. All reports confirmed the rumor that the forward positions had been abandoned right after dark.

At first light, the east and west passes came under heavy fire from the the pass. The response was limited to only a quarter of the men there, showing the pass to be guarded by far fewer men than expected. Encouraged, they started to press their attracts. Both sides sent word that resistance was lighter than expected. They told of their intention to press their advantage.

As the light grew and the word was passed, they started to move up to the top of the pass. They knew that the defense just over the top of the pass was empty and so made ready for a full charge to be covered by a large smoke screen. The men in the front all had smoke grenades and were to throw them from the top of the pass. They started up the hill with over twenty thousand men moving as one. They reached the center of the killing circle of the hidden positions. Here they stopped as the men in front were ready to toss some grenades.

As soon as they pulled the, pins Juan gave the silent order to fire. As the guns roared, the front two rows of men fell dead. The B-Cs charged, and the fight was on. It was a mess as they did not know where the fire was coming from. Ash and smoke was so thick, they could not see where to return the fire. After about twenty minutes, the fire slowed, and the smoke started to clear. There were over four hundred dead, and they found no enemy dead. They started to move to the top again at that point.

That was when Juan called out, "Stop! If you continue your advance, we will open fire again. This is your only warning!"

"So you slipped back into your positions, hoping to keep us out after all."

"No, you think we are Blaine's men. We are not. We come from the mountain!"

"What you saying, man? Like you want us to believe you're a wizard, man! That's shit!"

"Believe what you want. Listen to what I have to say first, then you can try to kill us if you can!"

"Why, man! What's it get me?"

"You will get to live a little longer at the very least."

"Are you making threats, man?"

"*No*. It's you who's marching here to take that which is not yours! Here's the deal. There's a bigger threat coming, and we are going to need all the fighters we can get to win! They are the ones that attacked us last year. So if you surrender now and take the oath and accept parole, we can all share in the bounty of the land. No more food shortages, and you'll have a safe warm place to live. What do you say?"

"Man, I think we are getting that anyway after you're all dead! You're no wizard!"

"Well, in that case, let me prove it!"

As he said his last statement, he knew through the link they had twenty targets confirmed by his team. Once he finished talking, a single shot rang out, overly loud, and twenty men dropped dead where they stood.

"Dude, you suck. Such a bad shot. You missed at this range!"

"Did I miss? Look around. How many died by that single shot? I think you'll find twenty dead from that one shot!"

It took less than forty seconds for him to order the charge. Juan shot him dead and retreated back to the trees and over the pass to the original positions. The battle was now going, and only a plea for mercy was going to save anyone.

The two positions they had just over the top of the pass opened up on the men they could see, forcing them back even more. The men here called for reinforcements and waited for them to show up. The family members started taking shots whenever they got one. Juan started to give orders to fade out and sent that they were leaving the pass open. They would be coming over in the next attack. By now, the defenses were fully manned and ready for the next charge. It was getting past noon now, and they had not met the full charge in the valley. The east and west passes were still exchanging fire, and they still held their first position on the top of the pass. But the pressure was growing, and soon they would have to fall back to their original positions at all three locations. William's plan to move the first engagement to the far side of the hill had slowed them down a lot. Now the family was moving back to their hiding holes. And in the center, Blaine was about to face them and needed to hold them to the second wall by day's end. He had been promised help if needed.

The second wave was starting up to the top well before they could hit anything. They started firing and tossing grenades at the places they believed to be the gun positions. It took them ten minutes to discover there was nothing there. After a short rest and reloading, they formed up and started to march over the hill. It was here that their lack of training showed. They still believed the positions over the hill to be empty. They started to clear the top of the pass and came under the guns now guarding the pass. They just marched down the middle of the road. The troops manning these positions had orders not to fire until Blaine shot first. Blaine had the place marked so all could see the range to hit the men in front and just keep firing up the hill once the shooting started.

The gangs were keeping their eyes open and kept moving forward when the hills and houses all around them started firing, and the old placements were firing and were fully manned. They all scattered and took cover and started to return fire. Without their smoke and surprise, they had only one advantage—numbers. They had them outnumbered at least five to one. They had been surprised at the top of the hill and then came over the top to a second one as the defenses were still intact and waiting for them. They dug in and found cover and started to lay down heavy fire of their own. After about three hours, they had a large reduction of return fire. They sent a runner back to have a third group ready and come up and charge the positions as originally planned with smoke and grenades. They kept the fire up on the positions. A runner came back with the word. The third wavr was moving up the hill and would give a signal so the men on the front would keep their heads down. They ran over them and took the gun positions. It was now near 2:00 p.m. when the grenades and smoke went off, and they ran down the hill to the gun positions. For a full two minutes, they ran firing at any movement they saw. As soon as they cleared the others on the line, they jumped up and ran after them. In just a minute or so behind the third group, they found them in the gun hides, and there was nothing there. Once again, no bodies, and nothing but some blood here and there. They had pulled back to the wall, and still they could not point to a single body of their foes. The talk had already started. Where were the dead? They had all heard about the man at the first site claiming to be a wizard from the mountain in the north! The leaders now reasoned that they should move down the sides and flank the next wall from the sides.

Juan sent to Blaine that he was sending twelve fighters to help them hold the wall at least until full dark.

"Blaine, you will need to put together a high-powered squad to fill gaps, and be ready for anything. You will have to hold till dark. If you know you're going to be pushed off, call for me. We will have some special help. It's only three to four more hours, okay?"

"Yes. And how do I call you again?"

"Just yell my name as loud as you can. I will hear you!"

The gangs made three attempts to break past the wall, and the coast was high on both sides. The fights on the sides were not going as they had hoped as well. On each side, it had taken over four and five hours to reach the second defensive walls. As full dark was rapidly approaching, the B-Cs pulled back and started to reform their lines. The leaders had called for more men to fill the lines. They also made a third line that was more than 50 percent bigger than the one at the sides.

Their plan was to start at the sides, and when the battle was fully engaged, they planned a full rush at the middle of the wall with explosives at the lead to blast a hole. With only thirty minutes of real sunlight left, they started the attack. Same as the other times, they threw hand grenades and heavy fire from the edges as the men began their move to the walls. No sooner than the shift of fire did the real attack began. There were many men. They all tossed smoke bombs and filled the field with a thick clinging smoke. Then they ran at full speed, making no other noise. The third group rushed the middle of the wall. Blaine had warning from Juan and had moved all the men from that part of the wall. They took up new positions to fire on the soon-to-be breach.

"Blaine, hold as long as you can. I have called for help, and it will be here in time to save you. Have some men start making a second wall behind the main one as I am sure the breach will be made. This was part of William's plan. Then start moving the wounded and dead back to the next wall. After the firing stops tonight, start sending half of your men back to the next wall. You will not need them. Only keep the fit and fastest to stay behind. Understood?"

"Okay. I understand and will do as you say. However, I will talk with William later."

Blaine started at once, getting things in order as he was told. He sent runners to the sides and had them send a quarter of their men back to the middle. He had the healers start to remove the wounded and dead back to the rear.

Just as the adjustments were set in motion, the center of the wall exploded inward and up into the air, over fifty feet. And they could see a very large force rushing the breach! They opened fire and killed many of them, but they just kept coming. They saw an opening and ran for it. Just as they were within thirty feet, a large truck was rolled into the breach, and it was loaded with heavy weapons and fully loaded with men as well. They still kept coming as victory was assured if they got behind the wall. They were getting closer, and Blaine could see over four thousand men rushing the wall.

"*Juan*!"

"I am here, and we know your need. And if you will look out, you will see why we needed this to happen. Keep to what I told you!"

Blaine turned to look at the ruin of his wall and the death coming for them. All he heard was a strange noise that he had not heard for a long time. Choppers, more than one. He yelled orders to his men. "Hold and keep your heads down!"

In the last glow of the sun, five Apache attack choppers came roaring over the open field, unleashing thousands of rounds on the men in the open field. This went on for five minutes. Finally, they broke and ran for cover. The ones who tried for the wall all died. The men at the wall all cheered. The choppers all disappeared as fast as they had come.

Juan sent to Blaine, "Get moving. They will not be back tonight. We are coming in to take up the guard positions. Pass the word not to shoot at us, please."

"My god, man, why didn't you tell us you had those?"

"Because we wanted it to be a surprise for them. They had you at the wall and knew it, and that last group would have had you for sure. It was the extra men they keep finding that we needed in the field before we let the Apaches lose on them."

"Okay, you're safe to come in. They are all waiting to cheer you."

"No, they are to remain quiet and start back to the next position now!"

Blaine got his men moving, and as always, dead and wounded went first, and they all moved back to the third wall and were given their new places on the wall.

The east pass was never going to fall. The positions were too strong and the number too even. Both sides had taken losses. The men from the South Bay were taking the worst of it and unable to move forward. Trent, seeing this, started working out a plan that would allow them to fall back and make the attackers believe they had broken their line. For the plan to work, all the attackers needed to reach the final wall at about the same time, giving them the belief that it was almost over and they were going to win at last. Blaine had lost over 340 men in this pass. The attackers were close to six hundred and needed to move forward soon.

Trent made a small hole in the base of the wall and filled it with gasoline. And as this was an area they kept hitting, it would go up in a big explosion and fireball, breaking the wall and giving them the belief they had won this engagement. In truth, that part of the wall's men were already carrying the dead and wounded back to the next wall. The rest were waiting for the attack, and as soon as the diversion went off, they would all break and run for the safety of the next wall. It was a good bet. It would be soon, and if they kept to their habits, they would toss grenades at the wall, setting off the gas.

* * *

Donnie was having a harder time holding the wall at the west end. Here they had better supplies and could get replacement for their attack, so the pressure was greater here and losses higher. They had lost close to six hundred here. The RR team had to attack the rear five times to hold the line. And as they were leaving, he had the Apaches strafe the lines to push the attack back. He passed on that there was a darkness here, and it was driving the attacker to take much greater risks, and it was paying off. He had his plan ready. They had filled the small moat with gas. And as soon as the attack started in the morning, they would light it and run for their next wall. All the wounded and dead he started back at once, and then started to send the ones that needed the rest back as well. When the next attack came, he would have about a quarter of the men left, and all of them in the best shape for the run.

* * *

In the center, they had taken the highest losses and were short on supplies. Only a small amount of food and ammo was getting to them. They sent back runners, and only a few of them made it there and back. They still had not figured out that there was a sizeable force working behind their lines. Juan had over three hundred men now, and their main job was to keep them short on needed food and ammo and also to keep their information limited to just what they wanted them to know. They stopped all of the big supply trains from getting past and only let a few smaller ones go by. They didn't destroy them. They took them and hid them in the woods and some in burnt homes. The food and ammo would be needed later.

After the choppers left, they had orders to let them send messages back and forth and let more trains get by as if they didn't have the means to attack. The plan would fall apart very quickly. So Juan had his men go to cover and wait for orders.

Trent had Blaine start moving the rest of his troops back to the next wall while he and thirty of the family moved in and set up six heavy machine guns with interlocking fire. He had half of the team set to digging a large pit right behind the center section of the wall. Then it was filled with gas and lined with old tires also soaked with diesel fuel for the heavy black smoke when they burned. They took up positions along the center of the wall and waited for the morning attack.

The two passes had orders to stage fallbacks when the center was attacked and the explosions went off. The plan called for all three forces to reach the center at approximately the same time for the plan to work.

On the eastern pass, Lucy was in charge with the new major, and she was getting ready for the first charge. The major was already moving his troops back to the next wall where all their troops would be together at their strongest position yet. She stepped on a large tree stump and called over to the men hiding in the rocks and sparse trees.

She enhanced her voice so all would hear it and she would not have to yell.

"All of you men waiting for the center to launch its final assault on the wall, listen to me. This is your last chance to stop this. You all know that the people in this valley are much more like you than the B-Cs will ever be. You need to join with them and make a better life for all in this valley."

Someone yelled back, "Why should we? We are winning this battle, and soon we will have all that you say, but on our terms!"

"You think so?"

"Yes, I do. We have beaten your great valley forces at every wall you hid behind. You have lived over here and kept us from sharing in the wealth of food and shelter here."

"So you're the leader here. You are working from the assumption that you're winning and I am from the valley. What is your name, sir? I am Lucy."

"Well, Lucy, I am Sidney. And yes, I'm leading this force of men, and we have taken each of your positions as we see it. You have only one more before we have you all in one place and can than get your surrender or wipe you out. What do you say to that?"

Laughter filled the air for all the men in the pass to hear.

"Sid, time is getting short. The center is about to go off, so I want to clear some things up for you. First, yes, we are from the valley, but not this valley. Second, you have not taken any of the walls by force. You believe you are the attacking force and driving events toward the end you want. None of that is true!"

"What are you talking about? Our scouts tell me you are far fewer holding the wall now than yesterday."

"That is true, but one of my soldiers is worth at least twenty of yours, and we are used to fighting larger groups. Now all of you listen to me. We are not from this valley. We came to help Blaine as we promised him after we defeated his men on the mountain. We came from the central valley to save him and you. Did you not hear the Apaches break the charge that would have won this battle for you last night? Have you not wondered how a force as small as Blaine's could cover so much space and hold with so few men?"

"Did you hear that they are wizards? It's true." Many men started talking all at once until Sidney yelled for quiet.

"So now you want us to believe in wizards?"

"That's a name given to us by others. It's not what we call ourselves. However, all the stories you hear of us are based on some fact. It's just that the stories get bigger with each telling. All of Blaine's troops have returned to help their friends and family, all twelve hundreds of them. We currently have ten thousand fighters in the valley. And, Sid, Chester will not be coming in our back door anytime soon. And if he does, it will be as a prisoner or fighting for us if needed! Your end run has failed."

At first a few then a lot of them were talking about how the plan to come over the pass was real. Again, Sidney yelled for quiet.

"I do not know what you're talking about, lady. I think it's time we took this wall."

"All of you listen to me. If you feel this has been wrong and wish to quit, you are free to do so. Just put your guns on the ground and step back. Then strip naked and sit on your uniforms. We will not hurt you or allow anyone to harm you. For those who still wish to fight, go ahead. We will give no quarter to anyone holding a weapon!"

"Stop. If any of you do this, you will be shot at once!"

"Sid, any of your men so much as point a gun at anyone that is sitting will be shot at once!"

"And how can you do that?"

While talking to Lucy, he gave hand signals to a man standing behind him. He in turn signaled two others, and they turned and walked back to find a large group of men stripping or already sitting on the ground. They started toward the closest men.

"Sid, you still do not believe me, I see. If you value the lives of the men, you just order to go and stop this. You will call them back now!"

"I am sure you cannot see or shoot my men. As soon as we quell this problem, we are taking this wall."

"Sid, there are only thirty of us holding this wall in front of you. One full charge would normally take it in minutes. What you still do not understand is you are cut off, and you're low on everything. Just small amounts of food and ammo are getting to you. Only a few of the messages you sent have been answered. We have over two thousand fighters behind you, and it is they that are covering the men sitting." *Bang*. Sorry, it's too late. The three men are dead."

"What, you're nuts. One of the sitters was shot, not my men!"

"All of you look. It's safe. We will let no harm come to you. Sid, who is your second-in-command here? Not Jeff. He's dead now, following your orders!"

Sid turned and saw her words to be true and gave the order to attack.

They started the escape plan to the next wall at once. Lucy saw a large number of men moving slower than the rest. She knew they would not pass the wall here, and she smiled as she ran to the woods and houses behind the wall, the family disappearing again.

* * *

Trent made ready for the counterattack and had the team and get set and find targets for one shot. He planned to do it twice and then open fire with everything they had. In the first rays of sunlight that started to creep over the hill, they started into the clearing. They were learning and crawled on their bellies to use the high grasses as cover to get closer to the wall before their charge. The team started to report they had targets. It took over ten minutes for all of them to find targets. Once they all reported ready, Trent ordered the one shot.

One overly loud shot rang out over the valley, and thirty men stopped moving, dead where they lay in the grass. In just over a minute, the team all had a second shot ready, and Trent gave the order again and another shot rang out over the valley. At this, they all jumped up and charged the wall, firing wildly as they ran. The team opened fired with all they had. It was clear to the B-Cs that the rate of fire was much lower that it had been. This gave them false hope that they had just about beat them at this position. They charged the center of the wall with seven hundred men. At just over halfway, a small group of men stopped and fired eight RPGs at the center of the wall. Another group off to the left had stopped and threw grenades at the center as well. The blast made the desired hole in the wall, and they saw it and, with wild yells, charged the hole which was filled with a dense black smoke.

Trent started the automatic fire machine guns and ordered the fallback. The fire from the heavy guns started to fail, and the B-Cs came running into the pit. Many of the frontrunners ran right in and started screaming and died in the fire there as they learned of the danger. They tried to stop, but the rush from behind pushed many more into the pit and a horrible death. They finally got the charged stop, and as the guns on the wall stopped firing, they started to work around the pit fire. The smoke was now the worse of it, and the fire would burn for at least two days if they timed it right. Both of the other two passes had broken and ran at the explosion and were all safely to the next wall. The South Bay forces followed closely behind, thinking this was the break they had been working toward.

After they made the hole in the wall, Blaine waited a safe two hundred yards behind the wall hidden by the smoke. He was getting reports from Lucy and the others when they were less than one hundred feet away from the breach still covered in smoke. Blaine set off the firepit with a flair gun. It had taken three nights of working in the dark to dig, fill, and cover the two pits. The first pit ran just a foot or two behind the wall filled with gas and diesel fuels. This pit was lined on the front side by as many old tires as they could find. These had also been covered in a tar-like paste to make them burn quickly and smoke a lot. They should make smoke for days. Just beyond this was the second pit. This one was covered completely and filled with punji sticks like they used in Vietnam. Just the sticks there was nothing on them. These were mainly to wound, not kill. They were forced by the charge to jump the fire, and as the first ones jumped, they fell into the second, and the screaming started. Many of them fell into the fire as others kept pushing from behind. Others were still being forced to jump to the second pit.

It took them over two hours to get all the men around the wall and reformed to march on the next wall. As they moved forward, they came around a large stand of trees as the retreat went into a large golf course. It was then that they saw the other two columns coming in from the sides. Just a bit farther on, they saw the next wall! It was lower than the other had been, and they could see the soldiers manning the wall. They were excepting to face around one thousand men at this point and soon be done with this fight. Looking out at the wall, they saw a lone man standing on a rinsed section of the wall. It was William standing there!

CHAPTER 40

Malibu Canyon

CHELSEY HAD GONE as far as Cross Creek where Chester told her she had to stay. He started up the road at first light. The troops had made the tunnel entrance after a five-hour forced march. They moved into the tunnel to get out of the hot sun. There they took a rest break. The heat was growing with each step they took. At the start, the temperature was a cool fifty-four degrees just before sunrise. As they moved up the road climbing the hill, it started to get hotter. Once they reached the lower end of the tunnel, it was a very warm seventy-eight degrees and getting warmer. After a thirty-minute rest, they continued up the road again. It took a few minutes to get everyone up and ready to move. Depending on traffic, the drive through the tunnel could be anywhere from two minutes to fifteen if there was traffic on the road. This, like many other popular places, always had traffic, and the tunnel was not completely full but had many cars and trucks left inside that they would have to move or go around if they could. They had moved four cars out of the end of it so they could get out of the sun. It was going to take a while to move past them and out the other side.

Joy moved over to the tunnel to take charge of this operation. She had a few problems to overcome as well. Her first was if the tunnel would hold all of them as even now a small part of them had not made it into the shade. It looked like once they started and cleared a path, the column would spread out, and the front would be in the open before the rest had cleared the lower end.

She had one of the drones searching the upper end, and it was clear that once they cleared a path and started to exit the top end, the troops would be too spread out and not all in the tunnel at the same time. She was working on a plan to counter this with as little fighting as possible. She had planned on sealing them in the tunnel as it seemed now that plan was not workable. When the column entered and moved the cars out of the way to make a rest area for the rest stop and close ranks, she got the break she needed.

As the last of the column entered the area at the lower end, she set her plan in motion. She had the coast troops move up as fast as they could. Their job was to block any retreat down the hill until they could block this end of the tunnel. As they started to move again, she got the rear guard ready to hold the lower end.

The tunnel gave them great cover, but it also had them trapped. Only a limited number of troops could be in a position to return fire. In effect, it was to be a standoff, a smaller force holding a much larger one at bay. The rear guards' job was to hold them until Joy had the upper end of the tunnel blocked. The last part of the third force was still not moving very fast as they could not really go far up the tunnel yet. If they could not stop them things, would be far worse in the valley by the end of the day! As in all battles, it was the small things that would turn the battle one way or the other.

Now everything was in motion, and timing was going to be the deciding factor. Theirs, not Joy's. As soon as she had gotten the outline of the plan and the equipment they had sent, Joy had the east end of the tunnel set to blow once they were all inside.

Back at the lower end, they started to snipe a soldier here and there, wounding them if they could. This was to make then rush into the tunnel so the top could be sealed, and then they would do the same at this end. They put as many guns in the opening as they could and rushed to get the rest of the supplies inside. They had been put in the rear to keep them safe. Word was finally brought back to leave a strong rear guard and get to the top as fast as they could. Chester had sent that they were just about to exit the tunnel, and they needed to hurry if they planned to be at the back door before sundown.

Joy was looking at a video display from the drone when they started out in force and on guard from the action at the other end. Most of her surprise was gone! In the ready position, they quickly marched and then ran for cover at the upper end. The bottom would soon all be in the tunnel, but how many would be out of this end by then?

"All ground troops open for now. Remember, try not to kill if you can help it!" She had a hundred and fifty troops at this end, and they all opened fire at the same time. Chester and his men went to cover at once. They were trained well. This stopped the advance at once. However, another large group of soldiers came rushing out to give supporting fire and cover needed. Too many were coming out.

"Okay, change of plan. Rear guard, as soon as you can, rig the back to blow, and inform me when you're ready! Second, we need to drive these men back into the tunnel as well. I want to form a half circle to hold them, and once we have that set up, bring the Apache in to force them back to the tunnel."

In the middle of the battle, at the upper end of the tunnel, the family moved to make the circle and put more intense fire on the troops trying to move up the road and break their positions. In just over ten minutes, they had them holding as they covered all the high ground. They could fight from where they had taken cover but had no opening to move forward. Like the bottom, it was a stalemate situation, they believed.

From the north, they all could hear a low noise coming toward them getting louder by the minute. Joy had told Berry what she needed and showed him the positions of the men outside the tunnel and gave him the go signal.

"Chester, can you hear me? My name is Joy, and I am in command of the forces you are facing. I need you to surrender now or we will be forced to destroy you all!"

"How do you know me? And how did you find us here?"

"Really, you already know we have eyes and ears in your camp. You have three minutes to decide. After that, it will be all-out battle until you or we are all dead. I should tell you, we have never lost a battle, and we have always been outnumbered just like now. Time's running. Ninety seconds. Your decision, please."

"Fuck off, bitch. We are going to put a flag on your dead ass ending your never lost a battle claim. How, do you think you are the fucking wizards from some mountain in the next valley?"

"Why, yes, we are. How did you know? Are you awake? Oh, well, I hope you survive. I like you better than the others in your ruling council."

Just as Chester was about to speak, the Apache roared over the top of the tunnel and started to put extremely accurate fire on all the positions they held, causing the men to flee for their lives. In a matter of seconds, they all started running for the safety of the tunnel. Berry flew up and over the top of the tunnel, hovering there so they dare not go out. Then Joy had the ground forces open fire into the darkness and forced them back even deeper.

"Okay, everyone take cover. Berry, we lost the connection. Would you please do the honors for us?"

At that, Berry sent three rockets to the sides and top of the tunnel, setting of the C-4 that had been rigged there. Its sound deafened the men inside, some for weeks and were slow to react. But in short order, they started to send men to see if they could get through to the road. They got reports from the snipers covering the few holes that looked as if a man might find a way out there.

"Chester, can you hear me? Are you there?"

"Who's that talking? Yes, I can hear you!"

"Good. Listen close. Your men are trying to find a way out the upper end of the tunnel still. If any of them shows the tops of their heads, it will be shot off!"

"Who is this again?"

"It's Joy. You are trapped in the tunnel and are going to stay there until you surrender. Then we will get you out not before!"

"Where are you? I can't see very good, but you're not in the tunnel with us, are you?"

"No, I am still just outside. You may want to cover your ears as we are about to seal the lower end of the tunnel!" Another series of explosions sent smoke rolling up the tunnel with the noise and shock wave. The men were knocked down at the lower end, and some died as small parts of the roof fell in on them. There was almost no light, and the air was bad!

Coughing, Chester tried to speak to Joy again and could not talk without gagging and heavy coughing.

"Don't try to speak out loud! Just talk in your head to me! Before we go on, you need to get your men sorted out. When you're ready, call my name."

At the back, there were two gaps that would allow people to squeeze by. They were covered, and their people trying to crawl out there were given the same information. Show your head and be shot. The soldiers were relaying request for orders from all points in the tunnel.

"Okay, soldier, get help and tell everyone to work back to the closest opening and stay there. Do not try to leave the tunnel. Get the wounded to a place where they can get clean air, and get water and food to everyone ASAP. Send another runner to get all officers to meet me here at the upper exit." When all the officer were there, he told them what had happened. Many did not believe him. "Joy, can we talk?"

Then from one of the openings, a small female voice came back.

"Yes, I am going to give you the only terms we accept for surrender. They are the same for all of you. So tell me now. Can you all hear me?"

Quite a few answered her.

"Okay, now I want only people at the lower end to answer. Can you hear me?"

Again, a lot of yeses were heard, but very faintly.

"Good. You can surrender and take the oath of parole and become part of the family. If you choose this, you will have an equal voice in all family decisions as well as same rights. The only thing you're not allowed is to ask questions that are not related to your job outside of family meetings, where you can ask anything you like. Each person's parole is based on their conduct while on parole. You will be watched at all times until your parole is lifted and you're member of the family.

"If you choose to go back to South Bay, we will give you a handgun and food and water for three days. And after the battle is complete, you will be released to go back or move on. It is your choice. *What say you, one and all?*"

"Joy, they asked to think about it, so I told them to take their time. I have a question or two if you will answer for me."

"If I can, as you're still not a parolee yet."

"You sound as if you already know I will choose to join you!"

"The one thing no one can ever take from us is free will, so I don't know for sure, but I believe you will."

"How did you get the upper hand on us? We have great discipline, and no one talked that I know of. The B-Cs, as you said, do not know of this."

"We are called wizards for a reason. We do have powers and abilities you do not. We know a lot of things happening all over the Western Pacific."

"Okay, good. Are the stories true about the islanders? Are they coming here?"

"Yes, they will be coming. That's why we need you and hoped not to have killed you in senseless fights."

"I still don't believe in wizards, but are the stories about the admiral real?"

"Hmmm, so why do you want to know that, I wonder. Oh, never mind. Yes, he's real. Would you like to talk to him?"

"Oh, yes, that would be great. I can wait!"

"Good. Here, Chester, I would like you to meet the admiral, William. He has been listening to all our talks and is glad you have seen the better way."

"Chester, you are a fine man. I am glad to speak with you, and we will talk later tonight when you reach the base. Oh, and one more thing. I am also the wizard you heard of. What is it you wish to ask me?"

"If I get my people to surrender, will they be treated fairly?"

"Yes, no member of the family lies to parolees or other family members. And all accepted into the family are forevermore part of the family. But Joy is my real daughter from before the event. Trust in her and me. Save as many of the people in the South Bay as you can. Sorry, I have to go now. We will talk later. Did you get what you wanted?"

"Yes, you're right. I will take the oath. Now I have to talk with my people."

"That is good. Call when they decide."

* * *

Both passes on the sides were blocked with cars. They were still the best way to get to the passes, and Blaine had them watched and made the necessary adjustments to hold them at the top of the passes. These two positions on the sides were too easy to see the attacker, and so at each of them, they had to fall back to keep the plan whole as they could have held each pass for days if they had wanted.

The two columns at the east and west passes fought well but were only able to move forward when the B-Cs broke the middle, and then all three position would fall back to the next set defense as one. At the next wall, the South Bay forces got the surrender pitch, and they just charged the next line. However, many of them from the South Bay were not as sure as they were just a few days ago. Their views of the greater good they had been fighting for was changing. Without the influence of the dark visitor, their natural feelings and thoughts were coming back to them. Many on both sides, east and west, wanted to surrender.

However, the inner-city gangs had been living in slums and in a dark and deadly lifestyle for so long. It was their way to use violence to get what they wanted with little thought of tomorrow's needs. It was easy for the dark one to get them to do his work and think it was theirs. Once the government broke down after the event, they quickly took over the poorest parts of the city. So their aim here was to kill or make slaves of the people in the valley and the police in South Bay. All were to be killed as well.

The action at the tunnel was just about over. They would be coming out soon. After William talked to Chester, it was clear they would march into the back of the school from the north. The ones still fighting at that point would believe they had now gained their victory. Then the third force from the South Bay took up positions, faced the gangs, and started to fire at them. They would be confused and scared of what other tricks the wizards had to play. By now, all parties knew that it was Blaine running the defenses again and that the wizards had come from their mountain to help them. They somehow made the Apaches fly again.

In the valley at the center, the B-Cs set up at the tree line and houses on the golf course. They had a clear view of the last wall and made no move toward it. This one was much taller. It had a strange midsection that was a good four feet lower than the rest of the wall. It was built with a slight curve, so the ends extended out farther into the large open space they would need to cross. They could still see the man standing on the lower part of the wall. They believed it to be Blaine. Knowing he was in charge had slowed them from rushing in, and they started to think before charging. They had sent six scout teams of four men each about an hour ago and were waiting on their reports before moving on the wall. They had been told of the third group sent to get around behind them as well. When they saw that they would be there, they would attack the wall and hit them from behind as well. This time, they would breach in different places in the wall, hoping to avoid the same type of booby traps as the last wall. After a day and a half of fighting, they had seen less than twenty dead in the march down the valley while the gangs had lost eight to ten thousand KIA and at least four thousand WIA. The South Bay forces suffered losses. Theirs were equal to 25 percent of the force in whole.

It was very clear that the gangs decided to wait on the other columns to arrive. The one from the north and their last secret, another thirty thousand men move up the south side of the pass. It was clear that everything depended on the gang's defeat and total wreck of their fighters here at the north side of the valley. The gangs could still see the man just standing on the wall.

Joy was speaking with Chester about his men and how many would be taking the oath and moving on to the school and the final battle for the valley. Joy then spoke mind to mind with Chester.

"Sir, as I'm sure you know, you have a few men that have a darkness about them. These men will need to be dealt with before we can start giving the oath to the rest. I believe you know the ones I mean. Would you like us to deal with them or take care of it yourself?"

He had not realized at first that she was not using her voice. At her question, he heard her again!

"Chester, you thought of three people in quick succession. Was it hard to pick which one was the leader?"

"How if not magic?"

"It's easy for a wizard! We have mental powers, and they are getting stronger all the time. Earlier when we talked, I asked you to be open and honest and not try to hide anything from me."

"Yes, and I have been."

"Yes, you have. That's not my point. I have had accesses to your mind ever since then. Even William was able to read your thoughts. You and almost all the men here will become family members as soon as today for some. However, first these three men need to be dealt with. So again, do you want to deal with them?"

"Yes, I had a plan in mind for days about them and a few others. I will go take care of it so we can get moving again."

"Thank you. William, we will be there about one hour before full dark if I have the timing right."

"I am sorry this took so much time. We will not make it to the valley today."

"Chester, please open your eyes. How long do you think we've been talking?"

"At least forty-five minutes."

"We've been talking only about two minutes and all in our minds. As you can see, it's so much faster, and there can be no lies."

His eyes popped open. He didn't remember closing them.

"How?"

"That is one of our gifts. The good thing is we have only found five people that could not wake up and receive their gifts. Blaine is waking up quickly under the pressure of running this battle. Chelsey was another. She was waking slowly when we found her. As a matter of fact, your parole is due to her actions in this affair. I already knew of your decision to do something about the darkness in your ranks."

In just over an hour, they had taken care of the dark ones. They tried to escape out the west end but were stopped, and after a short gun battle, the three leaders were dead, and the two Chester had with him were tied and under guard.

"I will take care of them now if you don't mind, Chester. We have a questioning system that never fails. In fifteen minutes, we will know everything they do and more."

She had the two put on a chopper and sent to Oliver, who was waiting for them. The rest would soon be coming in the back door to the surprise of many waiting at the old high school. Now the South Bay force was marching up the road again, and as soon as they reached the top of the hill on the freeway, they made their call. It took them four tries to finally get the message sent to the walkie-talkies they had. The attack was about to begin.

* * *

Back at the wall, William and the all the rest got the word at the same time well before the gangs. They readied themselves. William, still standing on the wall, turned on the PA system they had set up. He was making ready to make his last plea to the B-Cs and the men from the beach cities. Everyone got to their last stations for the final push.

"Oliver, I need you to make a call to your general friend and tell him we need more air cover. I need to know how much support he can give us and how long it will take to get here."

Oliver went to make the call. Since the dark ones' capture, many of the South Bay and gang members no longer under the influence started to just hang back and, when safe, turned and started back to their homes. None of these made it past Juan and Jake's rear guards. They were rounded up and put in a safe place to await the outcome of the battle.

Oliver went to the school and retrieved the sat phone and dialed the general. The phone rang twice and was answered by the general.

"Custer speaking."

"General, it's Oliver. We have a lot to talk about, but first you need to talk with the *one*!"

"Oliver, your timing is amazing. We have been wondering how to reach you as your phone is off most of the time. We have problems here."

"We know and will get to that soon. Now I need you to talk with William. He is the *one* the visitors told you about!"

"Great. How soon will this happen?"

"Hello, General. Is now fast enough for you?"

"Oh, yes, it is. We have problems here, and I think we need your help!"

"First, General, I believe we need your help and very soon. However, I need you to just listen and be open and truthful with me. Hide nothing. Are you willing to do so?"

"Yes, of course, if you will do the same with me. And answer just one question first."

"That is fair. Ask your question."

"We have been getting warning that the wizards will be coming here to attack us. Will you help us if that happens?"

"I am not sure how to tell you this, but the wizards will be at your gates in two days' time, and you have four days to leave that base as it will be destroyed at that time. The force that is giving you this information is your true foe, not the wizards. You see, General, I am the wizard, and I am also the admiral as well, and the force I have sent is there to help you get out and over to the coast, not attack you."

"What, you're both of the men we hear so much about?"

"General, that's two questions!"

"Oh, sorry, but you're already sending help. How could you know?"

William laughed. "That's three now. Please, we need to be fast. Time for both of us is getting short. I want you to hang up the phone and listen to me please."

"What? I can't hear you if I hang up!"

"You're talking to a wizard now. We don't need it any longer. Please open your eyes and put the phone down. I am going to talk with you like the visitors did, all right?"

"You can do that?"

"Yes, and now listen. I need more air power that I currently have. This is what I am facing, and I want to know what help you can give us and how fast it can be here."

"Okay, tell me what your needs are. No, wait, I know your needs. Let me get on that and will call you back as soon as I know what we can have for you. Now how do I call you back?"

"Just call my name and I will answer. If, for some reason, I can't, Oliver will. I will hear everything you tell him."

* * *

"To all the men attacking this wall, listen! This is your last chance to give up! We have the upper hand and always have. You have us outnumbered, yes. We have many forces that you have not even seem yet. For any man who wishes to leave, you may do so now. After the battle begins, we will not offer surrender. At that point, you must drop your weapon and strip naked and sit on your uniforms with hands on your head."

At that point, Joy came into view at the back of the school. To all appearances, she looked like a prisoner with her troops being led in by the fourth column from the South Bay. As soon as they were in full view, the B-Cs ordered the full attack on the wall. Many thousands of men charged the wall from at least five different places. For a full fifteen seconds, there was no return fire from the wall, and the lone man just stood there. It looked like a surreal moment in time where no one was shooting at him. He turned and left the wall, and then every gun they had on the wall opened fire. Added to this, the charging men were well into the killing zone, and on came the Apaches. This time, the two Blackhawks came as well. They all started at the back of the field, driving them forward into the heavier fire zone. After ten minutes of this, they broke and returned to cover.

William had given orders through Blaine that once they retreated past the halfway point to let them regrouped. They could see that they were in a bit of shock as the men from the South Bay at the back of the school were still just walking slowly forward. They were inside the fence now and still not attacking. Having refilled his ranks, they launched rockets at the wall and smoke to give them more cover as they charged again. They had been tracking the choppers and knew they would need at least another ten minutes to rearm and return. It was their belief that with the fourth group now in the school, they would take the wall before the Apaches could return! Once again, at the halfway point, Blaine opened fire. As the attack kept getting closer, Blaine asked how they would stop this charge.

"It's now time to show you what I've been hiding in the woods, just to the east and west of the school. Trent, now, if you please!"

At that moment, six battle tanks opened fire from the cover of the trees on each side of the school. All had been targeted days before for the maximum effect of the attackers. By the fourth round of fire, they broke for cover again, leaving many more dead or dying on the field. Blaine called to them to cease fighting for the night and they could see to their wounded men on the field. The B-Cs declined while the men from the beach went out and got all the wounded they could find. Most of them were confused as during the last attack, the fourth column all finally took action. They all ran to the weak places on the wall and started firing, but only at the B-Cs in the middle. So the second day of fighting came to an end with Blaine still holding them out of the school. And they now had to take this time to plan on how to deal with the artillery they faced. Having not seen them, they didn't know it was tanks they faced.

* * *

William held a meeting with all the commanders, introducing General Custer that he had linked in. "We have the night to organize our defense for tomorrow as well as our attack plans. They are trying to find our tanks, and they are now calling up whatever they've hidden from us. Whatever it is, General Custer is going to handle it for us. We will hold the wall as long as we can with just the men on the walls. When the pressure is too great, the Apaches and Blackhawks will attack. When they have to withdraw, we will allow them to make their breaches in the wall. We have the secondary plugs ready?" Serval voices responded yes. "We know they will not try the center again, so that is going to be the strongest fire positions. Oliver, how far out are you?"

"Three minutes. The rest in ten."

"Okay. When the B-Cs launch their surprise, we will answer well before they get near the school. Oh, Oliver, tell Blaine how many men you'll bring him, please."

"Blaine, I have fifteen thousand men just three miles behind the school."

"How is it I don't know this?"

"You forget you gave us the back door to watch, and we have it closed to everyone but us."

William took back the dialog at that point. "All of you will have to tell the troops that are not linked or awake what to expect tomorrow. It will be the last day of battle. It will come down to whose surprise is the best and how willing we are to stand our ground. Maria has given me the grim numbers. So far, the San Fernando Valley has lost close to a third of its troops at just under twenty-two hundred with seven hundred wounded. All of them will recover. We have lost close to four hundred men, mostly on the walls covering the withdrawals. For most of you are still thinking, we are running. We are not. This is how we attack. Always make them come to you when and where you want. Look at the numbers. they tell the tale. Right, Blaine?"

"Yes, William. At each wall, I saw why I lost and can clearly see them losing in the same fashion. Now we can win. And unless they leave now and go back to LA, they will lose."

"Okay, everyone, get some food and sleep. It will be a hard day, and how long we just do not know!"

William then reached out to Custer.

"General, I believe the final attack will begin thirty minutes to one hour after daybreak. They will bring everything they have.

We will need all of you got to turn their last charge. As soon as they reach the halfway point, we will send in the choppers and fly them all at once, forcing them to send the massive last wave. We now know it's around fifty to sixty thousand men, and they've been amassing just over the pass for the last thirty-six hours. If you fail to stop this charge, we will lose here!

"Since we talked, I went out and got some special aircrafts ready for this operation with the right bomb loads for the job. With my tanker, we will able to be on station for up to ten hours if needed. The problem will be if a second load is needed, the flight time may be a problem."

"Not to worry. We have taken Point Mugu and have two runways open and are using it all ready. And we have two tankers on station as well."

"In that case, we got your back, William!"

* * *

The B-Cs had put their plan into operation at full dark. They had some of their best fighters fully loaded with ammo and food and water. They started across the field, crawling to the farthest point they could reach where they were to lay in wait for the full charge at dawn. First light came over the hills. This would put the light right in the eyes of the men on the walls looking out on the field. So when they started to fire on the charge, they would give away their positions, and the three hundred men lying in the field would open fire, giving cover for the charge. They took hours to crawl to the wall and the positions they wanted. They were crawling over the dead, and some were still dying. Now they just had to wait for the sun to rise in the east.

* * *

"Trent, do your scouts see what I am seeing in the field?"

"Yes, it's a good tactic if they could get them there without our knowing about it. How do you want us to handle it?"

"Use only personnel that are awake, and try to read them. Some may be there under duress. Spare them if you can. The others, take out with bows My count is over two hundred and growing. Take the ones nearest the wall."

"Okay, we are on it."

Trent gathered the best bowmen he had, and each was given fifty arrows and a section of the wall to cover. As soon as they were all in place, Trent gave them the go order. They started reaching out to their targets and tried to read them. Surface thoughts were easy to read in undisciplined minds. Unlike the SEALs, most of these men were scared, and it was easy to hear their thoughts. Any that where closed and unreadable were shot at once. All shots were to the back of the neck, just below the base of their skulls. Even if the shot did not kill them, it kept them from making any noise. As the men moved across the field and came to a stop, the scout in their section would read them and kill the ones that showed a willingness to do this. A small amount of them were scared to death, sure they were going to die. When one of these were found, the scout would reach out to the man and talk to them. The first one they found was in Donny's area.

"Sid. Your name is Sid, am I right?"

The man started to answer, startled by the voice so nearby, thinking it was another of the snipers sent out.

"Do not speak. I am from the mountain, and speech is not needed. Just think your answers to my questions, please. Are you here against your will, forced to fight for the B-Cs?"

"Yes, many of us are. If we do not fight, our families will be killed back in the city."

"Okay, listen, and do not try to lie to me. I will know if you do. We know of your mission, and it is going to fail. If you wish to live when the attack starts, just stay down and play dead. We are killing all the others that do not agree to these terms."

"If I do not fight, they will kill my family!"

"Many of your fellows are dead already. When this group is to start its attack, only a few will be left alive. So if you stay down, no one will shoot you. There will be one of us watching you, so do not try to get up unless we tell you to. Do you understand?"

"Yes, but who are you?"

"My name is Donny, and I am from what is called Wizard Mountain by most of you."

"Wizards? You're real? Most of us have heard rumors."

This and similar conversations were taking place all across the field. Over fifty of the snipers agreed to stay down when the attack began. When the time came, less than fifty of the three hundred would be left, and if they fired on the wall, they would be killed at once.

So with that order, William stepped back on to the raised portion of the wall and waited for the sun to rise in the east. In just a few minutes, the sun would crest the eastern mountains. William opened his mind and used it to make his voice heard all over the valley.

"Blaine and I, William, who you call the wizard, make this last offer. You surrender. Or if not that, simply return to your homes in the city. Any who stay will face almost certain death at our hands. Your leaders hide back on the hillside, ruling by fear and intimidation, forcing many of you to fight. Yes, I know you can hear me. I have been listening to the two of you talk all day. You think you're winning still. You should know that you have no more secrets from us! Do you wish to surrender now? I can read your thoughts, or you can just say it out loud, and we will go from there. Also, you cannot lie to me or any of my people. Try if you like. It makes no difference. Would you like to spare your people by giving up now?" Like any good salesman, William waited for the others to speak first. It took a full minute and a half to respond.

"You stupid honky. We have more numbers and are far better off than you think. We won't stop until you have all been killed or are begging for mercy, which we will not give you. Just painful death. Only your women will be kept as sex toys."

"You should know that I have let everyone hear your words as they hear mine. Do you not want to tell them the rest? As soon as you finish with us, you plan to attack the forces from the South Bay area as well. Do the same to them as you wish to do to us. Go ahead. Deny it if you can!"

They both laughed, and the Crips leader spoke up. "When this is done, we get first pick of the bitches."

"Yes, the perks of being in charge. Why do you keep your men charging into the machine guns? Do you have any compassion for your troops you send to their deaths in this fashion?"

There was more laughing.

"Do you play chess? The pawns are for sacrifice and have no real value other than to occupy space!"

"So you do not care anymore for your own troops than ours, as long as you get what you want! Well, I can see you're ready to make your next move. I wonder, will the members that take your place feel the same way?" They both thought of the next in line for leadership. "Thanks for their names. Oh, and one last thing. Our talk was heard by everyone in the valley and in LA as well. I am just guessing that a lot of them won't be happy at what they heard. Also, the three snipers you sent to kill me will be dead before they see if they hit me or not! One last thing. Your plan to surprise us with some thirty thousand men just over the crest of the pass. They may get lucky and win their way to the fence line, but no more."

During the last bit of his talk, William had given the order to turn on the massive lights they had been installing all around the field as well as the regular field lights. It had taken three full nights to get them ready. They had tested them just before dark fell.

The order was given to attack as the first ray of sunlight fell on the valley. The troops were staged in large groups that had been slowly moving on to the open space between them and the final fence. Close to three thousand men were just waiting on the sun to lift above the hills on the east, putting the sun in the eyes of the men manning the fence line.

"Juan, how many are exposed now?"

"Close to three thousand are in range of the lights and forward gun placements all ready. The sun is just six minutes from cresting the hills."

At that monument, William gave the order to attack. The lights all flared to life, washing across the sports field and out into the open spaces of the golf course, clear back to the far houses and tree line.

The forward positions opened fire on the startled men standing in the open as the bullets ripped into them from three different directions. The tanks, now hidden behind blinds, also opened up on the tree line and houses, hiding the rest of the forward force.

Quickly, the commanders gave the order. They regrouped the men and started for the wall where the hidden troops were waiting to take out the men on the wall, focusing on the heavy guns there. They charged again at the wall. Now their numbers were half of what they started with just ten minutes ago. The sun was now just peeking over the hills, and the rest of them attacked now. Another three thousand came roaring out of the far side of the golf course. All were running to different places on the last wall. The forward men had not gotten halfway to the wall when the ground in front of them exploded into walls of fire, shooting at least ten feet into the air. The advance men at the wall had never opened fire, it seemed. Only later would it be learned that most of them had been killed as soon as they took up their places on the line outside the fence.

The leaders in their hidden blind saw that their attack was falling apart and sent orders for the last wave to go. Opening the bunker, they had one of their personal guards take the order to the last group to attack now. Meanwhile, back at open the field, their numbers were going to win the wall. They had made the three breaches, and they were staging just on the back side of it, waiting for enough men to start the last rush to the walls. Seeing this, they gave the order for the last group to wait for the Apaches and Blackhawks to make their run. As soon as they withdrew, they were to charge over the top and not stop until they were in the school.

The B-Cs that had come from all over the southern parts of the state had now massed at the top of the passes and started moving closer to the front. They were all back in the first big battlefield where the first firepit was dug. It was still smoking, and they were using this for cover. They had all massed and formed into groups, four in all. And they were just waiting for the choppers to attack and withdraw. As soon as they received word that they had started to withdraw, they would charge, leaving them no time to rearm and get back before they had taken the school. It was the perfect plan and was sure to win the day!

* * *

Juan and his rearguard force was trailing these men, and he had Jake with his R&R team ready to take out the leaders at their bunker. As soon as the message was sent to put the last group in motion, Jake's team had taken the guards out and taken their place outside of the bunker, waiting for the men inside to come out or open the doors.

Juan and the rest of his force, now numbering close to five thousand men, were to only fire when the group had opened fire so as to keep their secret and keep them safe. Everything was working out as planned. The extra men were still a problem if the general did not have a good answer for them.

"General Custer, can you hear me?"

"Yes, Sergeant, we are on station just two minutes out, waiting on targets."

"Okay, this is going to happen fast. Please have all your pilots give their call signs so we can hear them."

"This is still strange to me. How do I do that?"

"If you can hear them, we will hear them as well. Quickly, please."

The order was given for all pilots to give their call signs in order to start with attack wings first.

The general had managed to get three full wings up for this attack. The first was old B-52 loaded with napalm and explosive bombs. There were ten of them. Next was a wing of Warthogs loaded for ground support. The last flight was what they called dragonflies in the old days. They were planes armed with six large caliber mini guns, and each gun was loaded with fifty thousand rounds of ammo to be put wherever it was needed. After their attack, they would go to Point Mugu for reloading for a second attack if needed.

"William, the general is here, and he has what we need. Everything is ready. Send in the choppers. We are already working with the pilots, and it is going to be devastating to the B-Cs."

* * *

Back at the wall, William was still standing on the stage in the middle as the lights flared to life, showing how many men they had rushing the last wall. At that point, three shots rang out from three different sides of the school field. They were answered by a single shot. This was the signal for the men already in the field to make for the fence, so they all started running, firing as they ran. At this point, all hell broke loose on the battlefield. The Apaches had been waiting for this to start their runs, which they would make very quickly, clearing the way for the Air Force planes to do their jobs as well. They came in and this time started at the front edge, working backward from all previous attacks. They quickly ran out of ammo and started to pull away.

The final wave was given the signal (a flair shot in the air) to make their run. They all started to jog across the clearing, heading to the last wall. They had just reached two-thirds of the way when a strange whistling could be heard, and it kept getting louder. They kept moving, unaware of the danger they had ran into. The first bombs fell just feet in front of them, blowing up on impact. Men flew backward hundreds of feet. Even before the information registered on the other men, the rest of the booms started going off all over the field. Ten bombers each carried thirty bombs, a mix of HE and napalm. As quickly as it started, it was over. The leaders regrouped and now started at a dead run. They had been found. Only speed would save them and win the day. They had another two hundred yards to go before they have cover again. Just as they had all gotten up and ran, another noise filled their ears. Jets were coming from behind them. Those who looked back saw death from above as the five Warthogs started their runs from behind, forcing them to keep going forward. In the open, the men fell by the hundreds on each pass. The Warthogs made five runs in all till their guns went silent. And they pulled up and away.

The force had made it to the cover of the houses and trees on the golf course and started for the last field before the school sports field and chain-link fence with gun post stations at different points. They could see the first wave moving toward the fence. They had also lost a lot of men. They all started to run to reach the first wave and overpower the base before the choppers could return. So after a very short break to catch their breaths, they started their the last run to the school. As soon as the entire force cleared the line of cover, they heard more planes. Looking up, they saw the dragonflies flying on the sides of the field. Yells to run fast carried over the field. The men already on the field saw the last group as they entered. It was very large, but they knew it was to be much bigger. Then they saw the planes for the first time, and the five of them rained death on the men in the fields. They went up the west side, turned, and came back down the east side with guns firing. They made three passes before the guns went silent, and what was left were eight thousand men. They had all gone back to the wall as it was the only good cover in the field. Now altogether, their numbers were about fourteen thousand men strong. From all the information they had, like Blaine before them, they knew they could still win if they just got past the last fence. They started their charge!

* * *

After William stepped down from the wall after the snipers all took their shots at him, he went over to the four captured South Bay soldiers. He gave two of them one bullet each that had been shot at him.

"Did you all see what just happened?"

Billy, one of the original members, said, "I saw. Still not sure if I believe it."

"This is what I want you four to do. I want you to go back to the men you were with and tell them what you saw. Tell them we are going to win, and there is nothing that will change that now.

Go home. You all saw your fourth detachment come in just as you planned and then take places on our walls, defending us as it should have been from the start. Tell them what you saw. Then just start home. I hope most will go with you. Any that stay will not come to a happy end, alive or dead. They will not be the same ever again. I have two scouts here to get you behind them and safely on your way. Will you do this for me please?"

They all agreed and were off at once, still talking about how William stood there as three shots were fired at him and they just stopped. He picked them out of the air as they just stopped in midair about a foot from hitting him. It took them a good three hours to get the men where they told their stories. The men in each camp had all heard the conversation William had with the two leaders. The Apaches and the ever-increasing fire that Blaine was able to bring to bear was enough for them to decide to pull back. Both groups started to slowly fall back. And as soon as they had the opening, most of them turned and started back to the beach cities. The story about the bullets was still being discussed when the fighting started. They heard the jets as the bombs started falling. As the first shock wave hit them, they knew that Willian was right. The battle was over for the B-Cs and any that stayed with them. They picked up their pace ant went back to the South Bay. Not all the members left the field, and all that stayed suffered great pain by the end of the day.

At the wall, the two forces joined and were ready to make the charge to the last fence line. The choppers had never returned in less than two hours, and the other aircrafts had left as well. They figured they had ninety minutes at the least. And the next fence was poorly defended. They had three groups and themselves for the last charge. It was full daylight now, so waiting served no real point. They all reloaded, and as soon as all the leaders checked in. they charged the fence.

Blaine was at the center of the camp, getting the last wall ready. This wall was a rolling one. All the trucks that William had sent were made into sections of wall. When they were lined up end to end, they made a wall of one hundred and fifty feet long. These were to wait to pull in front of any breaches they made in the walls. Each truck had two heavy machine guns mounted on them as well as fifteen men, all armed with machine guns as well. As soon as the trucks were deployed, the tanks would take up covering positions. As soon as they were in place, Oliver would send his group to reinforce the fences as well. The last pieces of the defense was just arriving. On station were the Apaches and the Blackhawks, fully armed and ready.

* * *

They deployed smoke grenades. And as soon as the smoke covered the fence, they charged three different places on the fence line. The full charge was coming fast, firing at places they received fire from. Blaine's defense was strong but had little cover. In the short time it took them to cover the distance, they blew three large holes in the fence where Blaine had the weakest points set. As soon as the holes appeared, the full charge began. The three groups ran to the breach they had made. The end was in sight. They were just a about fifty feet from the first breach when they heard the truck come rolling up the field from behind the gym building, filled with men and their two heavy guns blasting away. Two trucks pulled in front of the breach, blocking it completely and putting out a heavy rate of fire. The same thing was happening at the other breaches on the far east. It was now their best hope as it had only one truck blocking the breach, and it was not a complete cover. So they redirected their remaining troops to that section of the fence. Men started to get around the truck. Blaine saw this and ordered Oliver to move to that point at once.

William, seeing that their berserker charge was coming faster than anticipated, called on the Apaches to come in now. The B-Cs just kept coming, and when they heard the choppers, they ran all the harder for the fence. Mixing in was the only way to counter the air attack coming. They here just starting to reach the back side of the truck when a large force of men charged them from the east side of the building. They had to take cover and counter this attack before going forward. The other breaches were gaining ground as well. They only needed to clear about one hundred more feet to get behind the trucks blocking the breaches. Just as the tide of the battle was shifting in their favor, the tanks rolled forward and started firing with all guns in support of the trucks. At the fence itself, the Apaches were now making runs parallel to the fence line. The Blackhawks took up positions behind the tanks, giving them cover as well as the trucks. The five thousand men charging from the east was overrunning the east end, closing the breach completely. The few B-C leaders left on the field started yelling to retreat and run for their lives. The attack was falling apart.

* * *

Juan, with his squad, had taken out the guards and were waiting for the door to be open again so they could take the leaders. Their wait was just about over as the two leaders had a clear view of the last battle taking place below them. It became quite clear that they had made a great mistake, and that the wizards and Blaine had beaten them from the first day. Every advantage they thought they had was as nothing to the smaller force they faced. And now with the fourth South Bay forces taking sides against them, they knew that they needed to leave. They had both been talking about where the tanks and planes kept coming from.

They called to their guards and got no answers. They called again, and still no answer. They believed that they had already ran off after seeing the same things they could see. Getting out now before they were found was the only thing to do. They opened the door, pushing it all the way open and started out.

Juan waited for them to come completely out of the bunker before saying anything. They had them with no place to go. By this time, all they could hear were the Apaches and their guns with the tank fire. The noise was much greater outside. They almost missed the orders to stop and raise their hands. They turned to see the SEALs with their guns at the ready. They bound them and started for the school. Juan led the way.

"Well, you were right. You will be spending this night in the school. Look over there. That's your army running for home."

Bryce, seeing this, got mad and started talking about how they could not let them get away. Juan informed him that was the plan all along. "Later, we can use them. We are going to need everyone we can get to win the battle that's coming."

Not able to leave all the horrors he'd seen, he and about five men went with him, charging off toward the pass.

"Juan, what was that? Something very dark is about to happen!"

"William, it's Bryce. He seems to have lost his mind in a rage over your plan to let them all just go back to the city. I am leaving Donny to come take over here. I'm going after them."

"I want you to be careful as I have never seen this before."

Juan was already running as he talked with William already. Just ahead, he could hear gunfire coming from the defensive position. Their problem was they did not give good cover from this side. He reached the pass and called out so no one would shoot at him. As he entered, he saw about eight dead gang members and two wounded team members.

"Bryce, you have to stop this at once. We have a plan, and it must go forward."

"It's your plan, not mine. I spent a year watching these people kill and use the people, and they are going to pay and not get to just go back and start over."

"They are going back to receive the justice they deserve from the very people you are claiming the right to kill them for. There is much more going on than this small battle. You're not thinking like a SEAL. You're working from a rage that would have kept you from making the teams stop. Look at what you're doing!"

"Juan, get out of here or fight with us. More are coming, and they are not going back to LA."

Juan left and quickly circled around to try to warn the members to turn aside. They just ran past him. This was a much bigger group than the last. A gunfight started just up the road, and screams and yells started coming back to him. He felt the deaths of three of the men as he had been linked to them all during the battle. He could tell it was going badly for Bryce and his men. He started back up the hill to see if he could be of help to the ones still alive. He came up on them and saw that Bryce was about to be shot in the back! He yelled and rushed the shooter. At that moment, both he and Bryce were shot many times by the larger number of men rushing to get over the top of the pass. All over the state, everyone in the link with Juan felt the pain of his passing. John was first to react to the senseless act of killing on both sides. The entire family of awake or linked members all felt every loss in the last three days. All of them in the name of peace and hope for our race. This one was different due to the fact it should never have happened! Now with the small force broken, the retreat of the forces was all but over.

Jack's team had picked up the leaders as they came out of their blind and had started back down the valley to the main camp. The battle at the fence was still going on. It was over, and Blaine and the rest of the valley people knew that they had won. Blaine spoke to William at this point.

"This is just like my attack on you at the mountain. It looks like they're winning, and they keep rushing to the next wall to claim the victory that is just there in front of them. Then at the last and weakest position, they charge your strongest position, and you have the upper hand!"

"Yes, this is how we always win. By the time they realize that they no longer have the numbers and we have the upper hand, it's too late. Now it's about saving as many men on both sides as we can. Tell your people to only fire on people still firing on them. Now if you will excuse me, I have to be the wizard now."

Now as he did in Lone Pine, he went to full open. William shouted mentally to everyone on the field and all over the greater Los Angeles area.

"*Hold your fire*! Look to the south. You will see all your leaders are dead or running. If you wish to live, stop shooting, drop your weapons, strip naked, and sit on your uniform with your hands on your head."

People on both sides wanted to know how they could hear William, and no matter where they were, they all heard his voice and could see what he sent to everyone's mind. William had lifted the two leaders and all the dead bodies of the leaders that had fallen in battle.

He brought them to the to the fence line for all to see. He held them all six feet above the ground and facing the B-Cs still on the field, still hoping to win! This brought the fighting to an end. Everyone on the field looked on in awe of what William was able to do. The shooting had not stopped everywhere, and Willian told Blaine that some of his men needed to be brought in line at once.

"Maria, what's the count?"

"My love, it is not as bad as we feared. It is still high. The valley and ours is KIA one thousand five hundred and thirty-six. WIA is two thousand eight hundred and forty-six. About one third of them may not make it as all thought they are all family. Now almost all of them are not awake yet, so we cannot help as much as we could. I know you're busy. See you later, my love."

It was going to take weeks to find out what was left of the South Bay and the people in the inner-city areas. William set up food deliveries at once to feed the people in the LA Basin. The city was far from safe, but it was now open for a new start.

CHAPTER 41

Union of Western States

The battle had lasted three full days, a lot longer than they planned on. It was to be a surprise attack and wash over the defenders like a tidal wave. Blaine and William talked all the time about how to prolong the battle. Each day they prolonged, it brought them one day closer to victory. The three days gave them time to adjust and keep the attackers off balance. The battle of LA set the stage for uniting the southern half of California.

In two days, Blaine with Travis and his scouts went back to the South Bay, accompanied by the South Bay troops that came up the back way with Chester to unify the beach cities and make them a part of the new city that was born from the battle. Like all conflict in the new world order, food was the driving need for so many. William had the three trucks loaded with food for the relief of the people in the city.

"We will need to get farms set up as soon as we can manage it. I need to get Aaron on it ASAP."

"Darling I met with Aaron four days ago, and he is coming over the grapevine pass now. He will be there by sundown and has eight farm kits on the trucks. We should have four farms in the inner city and south beach areas ready for the next planting season. He has breeding stock as well."

Blaine now had well over twenty-five thousand in his army, well trained and blooded in the battle for LA. The members of the South Bay had also pledged to support him in all his actions as needed. Jack was sending Travis and nine of the scouts into the inner city. As soon as they settled the few holdouts and established the city, the state of California would be well on its way to being one unified group from LA to San Luis Obispo to Lone Pine, and there had been a group from Utah that wanted the wizards to take them in and protect them. The loose count was 750,000 people living in the western area.

The council decided it was time to quit hiding and to announce to all the other groups that the wizard and the admiral were here to unify their country. At least what's left of it. It was now time to reach out to the rest of the world. It was time to broadcast on a global scale.

"Oliver, get the visitors to the mountain. It's time we met and take the next step to save our world and theirs!"

* * *

"O'Brian, report."

O'Brian sent an "aye, aye" to the admiral then started going over all that he had acquired and learned since he left the mountain. After getting Avila Beach settled, they left for the sea in the *Dream Wind* and a second schooner named the *Sea Voyager*. With sixteen men and women, eight on each boat. They sailed north to the San Francisco Bay. They needed to find a navy for the family. They hoped to find working naval vessels ships of the line and needed support vessels as well. They also would need men to man them.

His report was a mixed bag. They had found four ships, one oiler and three destroyers. He also sent a private message about the warlord. They had found a larger population than excepted to be in the city. They came with the warlord or had been forced to come. It was his labor force. They were under guard at all times and fed just enough to keep them strong enough to work. He was a cruel and deadly man. As soon as he found that O'Brian and the others were in the area, he sent death squads to find and kill them after they answered a few questions. They were poorly trained and, in most cases, easy to avoid. They did find out a lot about the warlord during this time. His name was Frank Sorenson, age forty-five. He had been a buck sergeant in the California National Guard. He came to power due to the luck of his duty the day of the event. He was the sergeant put in charge of the armory. He had three men under his command. After it was clear that they were on their own, he had the men with him get their things, and they moved into the armory, making it their base. With a number of other guards, they were in the strongest and safest place to be. It was in the early days when Frank was making thing safe for many of the people left in the city. It was soon after that the dark visitor started to work on them, turning many of them to the darker thoughts, and soon the fear started. Frank was one that craved power, especially over others.

O'Brian was trying to find as many seamen as he could that were not under the dark one's influence. In the few weeks, they worked the bay area, looking for anyone not under the influence of the dark one. They were able to enlist some four hundred seamen and five hundred marines, all still operating as military units. They soon had them under oath and well supplied. They hoped to greatly increase the number and type of ships and personnel. They had learned from one officer, a commander, that there might be many ships in the San Diego shipyard and hopefully many more trained men as well. So they pulled out with all the men and ships. They had Sherman arrange for food and other needed supplies they needed. So the small fleet sailed south. Two schooners and three destroyers and the oiler headed to San Diego. They were passing to the south when the battle was raging in LA. O'Brian asked if he could help. He was given a very strange reply.

"John, you're to keep going south. It will not be long before we have to face the islanders. Your task is vital to our very survival in the coming encounter. I was told by a young girl that you've had some troubling dreams about that. Is this true?"

"So the dreamer is keeping track of me? Yes, she is right. I am not sure what to make of it. But one thing is clear. I am not the best man for this job."

"I agree. So instead of you coming to help us. I am sending you help. Her name is Chelsey, and she is on a Blackhawk on her way to you now. She is newly awake and is a naval historian by choice. Her last name is different from her ancestor. She is a third-generation niece of Chester Nimitz. She has knowledge and skills that you need. She will need your knowledge and nerve to become my naval master. Treat her as your equal. Help each other."

"Is she the one who gave us the fourth column from the beach cities?"

"Yes, she is, and still young. Take good care of her, and she will save you from the dream. Good luck."

The Islanders Are Coming

Since the merger of the general and empress, their forces have not been defeated. All of their endeavors had been easy victories due to their much larger forces and superior training. And with each victory, they forced the people to work and fight as needed. The remnants of the drug cartels quickly joined their army and secured safety for themselves and families. All the places O'Brian had fought or passed by on their return to California were now part of the islanders' holding. They had fuel and ammo and were now in command of an army well over 250,000 men.

Of the scouts they had sent to California, only one was allowed to return carrying a message to the empress! "Stay in the old southern worlds. We hold the borders, and we will defend them! The wizards you heard of are real." He told them of the battle losses and the skill of the wizards. "Always outnumbered two to one or ten to one, they never lose. No matter the odds, the wizards never lose.

"While on search, we found a greater number of people living in the city than we had excepted. So keeping a low profile, we started checking local bars for information. We didn't push, just asked about stories and news, as we said we were fleeing north, away from the fighting in the south. As ordered, we always left half of the men at the boat. So me and five others were in a small waterfront bar called Barnes's Place. These three guys came in. They were asking about us and if anyone knew where we could be found. We all stood up and circled them. The leader's name was O'Brian and did all the talking. He just started asking questions like he was the big dog in the yard. We either did not answer or just outright lied to him. They never pushed the point on anything we said. It was strange. By this time, we had a great number of questions to ask them, and I was quite sure it would require some form of force to get the answers we wanted. At this time, we told them they would have to come with us and answer questions for the queen.

"They all laughed, and O'Brian told me that he was going to let me live if we told him where our boat was moored. I did not answer, and he never asked again. I did tell him that he and his men would go with us to the boat. I still can't believe what happened next. I had my best men with me, four of them behind them and me and Lopez facing O'Brian. Before I could do anything, the two men with him attacked the men at their backs. In less than two minutes, all four of my men were on the floor. When I looked at him, he attacked Lopez, and he was down on the floor, unconscious. Then I was down on the floor and in such great pain. I could not even move. Again, he told me that he was going to let me live. He said it was to deliver a message to you. He told me that I would have to walk back as the rest of my men were already dead thanks to my telling them where the boat was. This is his message. He made me repeat it many times to make sure it was given to you word for word.

"We hold the borders and we will defend them. Stay south of them. We know you have heard of us and believe it's just stories. The stories are real, and so are the wizards. If you come north of the border, we will kill everyone who comes bearing arms. Peaceful delegation would be allowed. Just four people with only sidearms. Any other group or size will be lost to you and never return."

At this point, the key William had set all those weeks ago when John told him of what they had found went off!

"General, what's wrong with him? He seems to have passed out yet he still looks at us."

William allowed him to speak through their scout just as he had with Blaine a few weeks ago.

"Do not touch your man. He is under my control for a short time. I have done this so we can speak openly and in real time. My name is William. You may know me by other names. Your scout here called me the wizard. It seems the best for this talk. Maybe we will talk again, and I will use my other name. However, that time is still not clear to me."

"What the hell is this this? I don't believe in magic!"

"Smart man, but that's not what I have to talk about! Your blind use of force against the people of South America has to stop!"

William paused to listen to their thoughts. He could read them easily they had no knowledge of what he was doing. The general was clear that he was not going to ever stop. The queen was not buying it either but had trouble fleeing at some of the things done in her name. William went on after a two-second pause to see their thoughts.

"I see you both plan to keep coming and rely on your firm belief that you are the strongest force in the world. You plan to keep subjugating the people you conquer in battle and make slaves of the rest that will not join your army. I was hoping to meet and come to a mutual arrangement for the good of all mankind, but that is not going happen at this time! So here's what going to happen now! You will turn your fleet around and stop all movement toward the US borders. Just to make this easy for you. I am giving you a valid reason to turn back. The fuel ship with you is about to be sunk. We know that you may need to tow more than one of your ships before getting back to Pearl Harbor. Please tell everyone on it to abandon ship. They have less than three minutes before I sink it!"

The general shouted to kill the scout, saying he can't do anything if he's dead.

"Kill your man if you like. He served you with honor, never saying a word about you or your plans. It will not stop the sinking. Nothing can now. I see you're not going to send the warning. Okay, I will!"

William opened to all the ships so everyone would know they had been attacked by the wizards.

"To all the sailors on the oiler, you have less than two minutes to abandon ship. It will be hit by a Hellfire missile and be blown in half. To all the rest, this is your only warning. So do not come to the California coast or you will all die. Your leaders were told all of this over ten minutes ago and chose not to tell you! I wish for as many of you to live. Get safely away from the ship go now!"

With the last word, he gave the order to fire in thirty seconds. A few men stared jumping overboard. Then they stopped as others started shooting the ones jumping in the water. By this time, the predator had fired its two Hellfires and was on its way back to O'Brian's ship. The two missiles could be seen by almost all the sailors on the east side of the ships. Two flaming trails was all they could see at first. The shooting stopped as everyone was trying to jump ship at this time.

"William, I think that very few will survive the attack."

"I know. I tried to change this outcome, but it was a true dream and had to happen. If that is so, the rest will be true as well. Do we know which ship they will use?"

"Hello, William, I believe it will be that *Arleigh Burke* class that they will send."

"Hello, Chelsey. So did you find a place you like, or is this just for as long as we need you there?"

"I have been asked to stay. Still not made up my mind yet. Sorry, I have to go."

They all turned back to the Hellfires just as they struck the side of the oiler, piercing the ship's hull right at the water line and exploding. At a split second's delay, the full tanks went off. They blossomed in two a giant red and orange fireballs, reaching over three hundred feet into the air. The shock wave rocked even the carrier as it spread burning oil and fuel for over two hundred yards across the sea, burning most of the men that had made it to the water. The escorts near it had to go to flank speed to get out of the burning fire quickly spreading even farther out. That was all that was left now. The ship was gone. Only things that would float were left, and they burned like everything in the water for over three hundred yards.

Back in the cabin, the general had the scout shot.

"So I sink your ship and you kill the one person who tries to help you! You've been warned. If your ships do not turn back, they will suffer the same fate as the oiler did."

"Wizards are a fake. Hellfires did this, not your magic. Give the order!"

At that mount, the *Arleigh Burke* went to flank speed and shot out ahead of the others and brought it seawiz online. It was already too late! At his thought to go forward, Chelsey launched the next drones of Hellfires. Just as the ship settled from the acceleration to flank speed, the seawiz came online just as the two Hellfires hit the hull at the water line. The second ship went down. It took a lot longer to sink as it had set condition zebra. The islanders were in complete disarray after the second sinking.

"As you have learned, wizards do not lie! Turn back or suffer the same fate as the oiler and the *Burke* did. We will talk again!"

The End

Coming Soon
Unionification WARS

ABOUT THE AUTHOR

Mr. Walker is a first-time author who has found his voice. After many attempts to put his stories down on paper, he has found his voice. It comes out of a pen. He wrote this book while driving for Uber. While waiting for his next ride, he would write the story in notebooks. Not working regular jobs most of his life, he gained a different view of the world than most. He is also very interested in history, which you found in the book. He went on a tour of duty in the United States Coast Guard, leaving with an honorable discharge. He tried getting work as a merchant seaman. Without a lot of jobs at the time, he started working as a drive-in theater manager in Southern California. He would work nights and spend his free time at the beach. After this job ended, he bounced around a lot, taking whatever came up. He has always wanted to see different places, so whenever the opportunity arose, he would move to new places. He has lived in six different states before finding his home in Nevada. Here he worked in the gaming industry for twenty years. He still lives in Nevada with his wife, with two daughters, two grandsons, and one great-grandson also living nearby.